ONE SCHEME OF HAPPINESS

Ali Thurm

Retreat West Books
retreatwestbooks.com

About the Author

Ali Thurm was born and brought up in the north of England but has lived in west London since she left university. After balancing a career in primary teaching with bringing up three children and writing part time, she was taken on by the literary agent Emily Sweet Associates in 2016. Under a previous title, *One Scheme of Happiness* was shortlisted for the First Novel Award (Daniel Goldsmiths) in 2017 and the Cinnamon Press Debut Novel award in 2018. It is her first novel.

Ali reviews fiction and writes about books and writing on her blog: alithurm.com.

For my mum, Margaret

'There will be little rubs and disappointments everywhere, and we are all apt to expect too much; but then, if one scheme of happiness fails, human nature turns to another; if the first calculation is wrong, we make a second better; we find comfort somewhere – '
Austen, *Mansfield Park*

'What exciting lives we lead, don't we?'
from *Brief Encounter*

We stand at the point of greatest change –
the distal point, a shingle spit
at the end of the longshore drift.
Fiona Moore, *The Distal Point*

PART I

ONE

ALL I HAVE is a handbag and a small suitcase. I'm out of breath, my hair dripping onto my shoulders.

'Made it just in time,' I say as the train begins to pull out of York station. The woman sitting opposite looks up and smiles. Older than me, silver-grey hair, a novel with a bookmark in it.

'Going away for a few days?' she asks.

'I really don't know at the moment,' I say, trying to slow my breathing. 'A few days. Maybe longer. It was a last minute decision.' I look out of the window as the backs of redbrick terraced houses begin to blur then, as the woman picks up her book, I shut my eyes.

When I look up again, there's a bridge, a field, a glimpse of trees standing in water. Everything reflects the light. Everything is dazzling. My hair has started to dry but I'm shivering and my cheeks are wet. I've been crying in my sleep.

'Is there anything…? Here.' The woman offers me a tissue to wipe my face but I can't hold back the tears.

'Look, the buffet must be open by now. I'll get you a

hot drink.'

She has a kind smile.

'Tea. Thank you.'

When she comes back and puts the tea and biscuits on the table in front of me, I rifle in my bag for my glasses.

'I usually wear contacts, but I was in such a hurry. I didn't have time to…' Then I break down again and have to take them off. 'You see,' I say, sniffling, 'my mother died.'

'I'm so sorry.'

'Then everything changed.' I try to warm my hands on the cardboard cup. 'It was all different after that.'

Outside a skein of geese is reflected over a flooded field. The woman opens the paper tube of sugar, stirs it into her tea with the wooden stick. As she sits back I lean forward, elbows on the table.

'You don't mind if I tell you something, do you?'

The woman smiles, shaking her head as she pushes her book into her bag.

'I'm Helen, by the way,' I say.

***

NO, IT DIDN'T take long. Yes, I took good care of her as long as I could. Plumped up the pillows, helped her to eat and changed the flowers – all those beautiful yellow roses like little suns in the fusty air of the sick room. They all died too. In the end she unravelled into an assortment of pain, petty aches and demands. But I did my duty. I took pride in the last role reversal. I did what I could.

It was the twenty-third of November. I went back into the room and there was an odd quiet, as if all the air had suddenly been sucked out. She was like a shrunken bird, curled under the hospital blanket.

'But I only went for a few minutes,' I said to Sylvia, who'd been sitting with her. Sylvia who's always been there for Mum. 'I needed some fresh air.' Sylvia put her arms round me. She smelled of Imperial Leather soap and the heat from her body warmed me. As the sun smoothed out the lines on Mum's face, it flattened her even more against the bed.

I was like a child building a sandcastle, not noticing the tide coming in. After twenty years of looking after Mum, I'd woken up cut off from the shore.

AT THE FUNERAL I almost giggled at the portrait of a stranger masquerading as my mother. 'She found it hard to say no… a ready smile…' The standard issue crematorium eulogy. I didn't know whether to laugh or sob. Julia from choir squeezed my arm. 'It's okay, Helen. You're allowed to cry.' Her own face was red and shiny, and she hardly knew Mum.

Afterwards, we went to the Royal Hotel. Sylvia organised it – I didn't hesitate when she offered – ham sandwiches, cake a neighbour had baked, cups of tea and a bottle of warm white wine from Ed. How like him not to think of chilling it. I didn't invite him. It must have been Sylvia; she thought of everyone. As he handed me the bottle his hair gleamed gold and his hand grazed mine. Those chewed down fingernails. The familiar smell of fried food. 'Thanks for coming, Ed,' I said. But when he moved to hug me, I turned away and took refuge in Sylvia's ample bosom, shedding tears of confusion more than grief, and summoning up clichés like a daytime TV star.

'I just wish I'd been with her at the end!'

'Och, Helen, you've been wonderful staying here all this time.' Sylvia held out a tissue. 'She was my best friend, but your mother was never an easy person. Not every daughter would give up so much. I can't imagine my Vicky…' She dabbed at her own eyes.

'I'm sure she…' I started, but it was true. I couldn't imagine Vicky sitting through all those evenings in front of the TV while Mum knitted; the nightly ritual of Horlicks and hot water bottles. The annual trip to the Lake District to the same B&B, which didn't quite have a view of Lake Windermere. All those Christmases on our own, with a small glass of icy sherry, kept at the back of the larder for special occasions.

But I didn't mind; Mum needed me. And you get used to things, don't you? Like the lighthouse. I was eleven when they turned it off for good and it wasn't until a few hours after the sun had gone down that we missed the rhythm of light then dark sweeping over the town. At school the next day, someone said, 'The lighthouse keeper killed himself!' It was probably Vicky. That's just the sort of thing she'd say. But we got used to it. What started off as strange became normal. If you can't change things you adapt. When we took the bus back to the East Riding after every short trip away, every holiday, the lighthouse beckoned me like a slim, white finger: this is where you belong, Helen. And I obeyed. I've always done what I thought was right, what I was told. Even as a small child I wanted to be good. It's just how I am. I like helping.

BUT IT'S FUNNY, after the funeral I was standing in the kitchen when I realised something: all along I'd been expecting some kind of denouement, like the end of a novel, everything tied up and resolved. Or a last minute revelation. I'm not sure what. But not that silent space – the empty house with the same view from the kitchen window, the tap dripping like a heartbeat into the washing up bowl of cold water.

The mugs of tea I'd made for the undertakers – milk plus two sugars – were drained down leaving a tawny streak circling the bottom of each mug. They were on the wrong side of the sink, so I moved them over to the 'dirty' side and made sure their handles were at right-angles to the white splashback then I emptied out the cold water. As I ran the hot tap, steam clouded my glasses so I had to take them off and wipe them on a tea towel. The garden was a disaster – bindweed had pulled the rose bushes down at wild angles and the wind from the sea whipped fallen leaves in obsessive circles. The path was covered by layers of moss and debris. When the weather was warmer I'd have to get out and do something. Mum had never let me near the garden. *No, Helen! I don't want you pulling all the flowers out.*

NOW SHE WAS dead my friends all wanted to jump into her shoes. I suppose they were trying to be kind but the phone never stopped ringing. I couldn't believe it. Living with your mother when you're forty-two might be odd to some people, but they weren't me. Julia offered to go through everything with me. But, would you want your friends looking at your mother's clothes and underwear? I would do it myself thank you very much when I was ready; it was a perfect opportunity to get rid of the rubbish. I was more than capable.

Even Mum's best friend, Sylvia, who'd known me since I was a child, wanted to organise my life. We met one morning, when I was queuing in the butchers to buy stewing steak. I planned to put it in the slow cooker then it would be ready once I'd cleaned out the loft. Even if I didn't feel like it, I had to eat. I could make a big batch then freeze some for another day.

'Once everything's sorted out you'll be wanting to travel a bit, now you've got some money.' Sylvia patted the shiny leather of her handbag. 'You could go abroad, visit your Michael in Australia.' She leant towards me confidentially. 'It's a difficult time, but you have to look on the bright side, dear.'

'I'm not planning to go anywhere.' Why would I give up the comforts of home to wait around in airports and be ruled by timetables? Why put up with strangers and foreign food? I went abroad once and I didn't plan to do it again in a hurry. 'I don't want anything to change. This is where I want to be. I'm going to do some clearing out. I've hired a skip.'

I turned away quickly to place my order.

Sylvia leaned towards me. 'You know I'm happy to help. Come up to me for your tea whenever you like,' she said, once I'd paid for my meat. 'You need to make sure you're eating properly, love. I know how you get. Just like poor Elizabeth.' She sighed. 'Och and before I forget ...Vicky sends her love. She's *so* sorry she couldn't get back for the funeral. Travelling around France in a camper van with the children. Not my idea of relaxation . . . but you young people! So many opportunities!'

Her voice rung in my ears as I closed the shop door

behind me and stepped out into the cold and rain of the high street. *So many opportunities!*

But it was always Vicky and Sam who'd had the opportunities, even when we were at school. The good old days, apparently, but I've never understood why people say they're the best days of our lives.

TWO

FOR A LONG time Vicky was my best friend. Together we were the best at everything. I was clever and good at reading. Vicky was good at dancing and acting. But then Mum took me to the optician's because I was squinting.

In the darkened room the optician said, 'Let's begin with the lion in the cage.'

I stared blindly into the machine, the cold plastic cupping my chin, waiting for the lion.

'Now, there's the lion and there's the cage. He's a bad lion. Sometimes he escapes, so you have to put him back in. Move the lever until he's safely in the cage.'

But no matter how hard I tried the lion wouldn't stay in the cage; he always escaped and the optician said I had a lazy eye. I had to wear an ugly patch of pink sticking plaster over my good eye. Otherwise my bad eye would stop working and I'd have a squint like Smelly-Ann who had crooked eyes and no friends. So, in the end I became a *speccy four eyes* like Edward who could only read words like 'cat' and 'dog'. Now I would never be perfect like Vicky who always looked pretty with her shiny blonde hair and shiny shoes, and her perfect eyes. Even at school she was allowed to wear black, patent leather shoes. Mine were brown lace-ups because they didn't get scratched and you could clean them properly. Every Sunday I polished them until they looked like conkers just out of their shells, but they never looked like Vicky's. She once told me she had chocolate pudding every day; we had milk pudding or yoghurt because it was better for our teeth. And her teeth were the whitest and brightest in the whole class.

I never felt very shiny, so I tried to be good: when Miss shouted at Edward, who had nits as well as glasses, it made my tummy hurt so I sat still and held my breath so she couldn't see me. I tried to be good. I did. But on the day of the school photograph I put my glasses in their case and shut the lid with a sharp snapping noise, then pushed them into the secret space under the chest of drawers.

At the front door Mum said, 'Helen, put your glasses on.'

'Michael was playing with them. Maybe he's lost them,' I said. 'I can't find them.'

Mum's face went pink. She'd already told Michael he was in her Bad Books, and we were going to be late so we left home without them. I'd never seen her Bad Book, or her Good one. I imagined it was something like the Page-a-Day diary Dad gave me for my seventh birthday. She only talked about the Bad one, but I was sure I was in the Good one.

At school we got into height order and walked to the playground in single file. Vicky had been practising her smile in the mirror at home but it was so cold even she had goose pimples on her arms as she beamed; mine were blotchy and grey like the chicken we had on Sundays. Luckily Smelly-Ann was off because she was the same height as me. No one wanted to be next to her; no one could stand the smell.

Big boys stood on benches at the back, small children at the front and we all looked at the photographer with his camera stuck on top of three skinny legs. Without my glasses my eyes were aching and the photographer kept splitting into two. I couldn't tell which one was the real one, so I hid my face behind Vicky. Then we were ready and had to say *cheese*. I tried to smile but everything was fuzzy.

The photographer came out from behind his camera and walked right up to me. 'You're so squashed in there, pet, no one can see you. Let's try again then everyone can see your pretty face.'

I had to squat on the dirty tarmac right at the front with the smallest children, where everyone could look at me. I concentrated so hard to make my eyes see only one photographer, that I couldn't smile as well. When the flash came even though I shut my eyes all I could see were big yellowy-red blobs floating around. My head hurt even more. I couldn't stop crying and all the girls were nice to me. Apart from Vicky. I could see her bottom lip getting wobbly; she was cross because everyone was ignoring her, but Miss told her to get me a tissue so she didn't have time to make her tears come. The other girls hugged me and someone slipped an orange sweet into my hand. As we walked home together I put it in my mouth and let it dissolve slowly while Vicky sniffed and said, 'Well, they're bad for your teeth you know.'

When Mum found the glasses in the secret place, she shouted at Michael and gave him a big smack. He cried so much he wet his trousers. But I could still taste the orange on my tongue for a long time. And Vicky couldn't. For once I didn't have to share it with her, and even better, everyone liked me and all the grownups said what a good girl I was.

THAT PHOTO WAS there when I cleared out the loft – Vicky was smiling in that special way she had, with her head tilted a little to the right, but I know her teeth are full of fillings. There were a few other pictures of me too but only one of Michael, in the sixth form glowering at the camera. Mum used to laugh over each one and tell us stories, but when Michael left home she never took the album out again. Then, a few days after Dad died I found her ripping all the photos up, tears streaming down her face. When she saw me she stopped and shouted at me: *I don't need reminders. I'm not about to forget what they looked like.* All the photos went in the bin. Apart from their wedding photo – it was in a frame and too good to throw out, she said; it was always on the dresser. Widowed at forty-two. Poor Mum. To be honest I thought she'd thrown this album out too.

It was unnerving that so much of my childhood was still there in the loft, preserved and hidden from the light. *Waste not want not* her voice whispered as I opened bags of old clothes and toys no child would ever play with again in this house. *Neither use nor ornament*, Dad would have said. The air was laden with soot from decades of coal fires; it was caught in the wooden joists and beams and settled on every surface. My red university gown, hanging from a nail, was grizzled with dust that drifted in the thin sun coming through the skylight. A sad ghost. A bitter reminder of a past that had been cut short. When I went back down, I had to scrub my hands with the brush to get the dirt out from under my nails and my feet left black prints on the carpet, but for once it could wait. I had so much time on my hands.

For Mum, cleaning was as essential as breathing. From when I was very young, Saturday was the day I tidied my bedroom. I put my ornaments in a row: a china rabbit, a teacup, a brass lady wearing a bonnet and a crinoline. She was a bell so didn't have any legs. There was a box for buttons and one for my pocket money. I had to dust everything and make sure my books were in alphabetical order, all my clothes put away.

Then Mum said, 'It's inspection time.'

Like being a soldier: if anything wasn't straight or there was a speck of dust she'd say, 'It's not good enough, Helen. You know how to tidy your room. You're a big girl now.' And I had to start all over again. That was just how things were in our house; if you wanted to get anywhere in life, you had to work hard. I always worked hard at pleasing everyone.

Dad always went to his allotment on Saturdays. When he came home, bringing the scent of earth and outdoors, he said, 'Good girl, Helen,' patted my head and gave me my pocket money. After lunch he took me to the library, just the two of us, and helped me choose books. Not childish ones with pictures – ones by writers who lived a long time ago. Then, for the rest of the weekend I took every opportunity to read. If I wasn't reading, I told myself stories. I made them up in bed at night and on car journeys, imagined elaborate scenarios where I had a clean house that nobody was allowed to make a mess in and there were so many books it was like living in a library. My favourite book was *Mansfield Park* and Fanny Price was my heroine. She never complained. She wasn't stupid like her cousins. She was patient and good at waiting. And in the end, she married the man she loved.

That became my plan. I would marry a man like Edmund, Fanny's cousin – he would be kind and he would never go away.

Not like my brother, Michael. He left after Dad died. Only eighteen. First to London then to Australia. After he'd gone Mum kept his room just as it was. The walls were covered in maps and he had a globe he liked to spin with his eyes shut then stop with one finger: 'This is where I'm going first.' He was going to be an explorer.

It was all still there frozen in time and I was allowed in once a week to dust and polish, to make everything *shipshape*; then Mum sprayed Brut around, as if she could evoke his adolescent presence.

For a while he remembered our birthdays, Christmas. Occasionally he'd phone – the line crackling in the middle of the night from the other side of the world. Then he said he was getting married. I pictured the Australia I knew from TV – Skippy, didgeridoos, doctors in helicopters and all kinds of questionable wildlife. For a whole week I imagined going for a long holiday, or even staying and being a different person, with loose vowels, my body hard and brown.

'After the wedding we could stay for a few weeks. Get some sun. You and me.'

'I can't go on an aeroplane all that way,' Mum said. 'All that way over the sea. You go, love. I'll be fine here.'

At the time I didn't think twice. She was so fragile, likely to break into tiny pieces if she had no one there. I couldn't leave her on her own, could I?

After a few years, he was busy with his own life and so were we. I didn't bother any more. Michael became the past. He didn't even come back for Mum's funeral. I can't forgive him for that. 'Sorry we can't be with you big sis.' Not that I'd expected him – he left all the responsibility to me.

THREE

I COULDN'T GET Mum's voice out of my head. *Have you been to see Sylvia yet, Helen? Don't forget she's expecting you.* To be good all the time you have to work hard and, over the years, I think perhaps something about you gets lost in the process. You get tired. But I hauled on Mum's old blue coat, headed for the promenade and down to the beach. Funnily enough, I was surprised it fitted me; it had been so much part of her that I still expected it to be too big. At forty-two, that might suggest I hadn't grown up, but I never had time to dwell on that kind of therapy nonsense. W*aste not want not.* You have to be practical about these things, don't you?

If Michael came back now he'd see a few changes, mainly shops along the sea front boarded up and scrawled with flaking graffiti, but most things stayed the same in Holdersea. As I walked along the beach in the winter twilight, the sea still pummelled the wooden groynes, still dragged the shore down the coast: two metres a year they said in the local paper. I looked back to where the lighthouse towered above the houses, built inland to stop the sea washing it away. It was like a steady point around which the hands of the clock slowly moved. Like the centre of the roundabout in the park where I used to sit without ever getting dizzy, watching Vicky hanging on to the bars at the edge, shrieking and spinning.

Smelly-Ann, Smelly-Ann
Greasy like a frying pan!

Now I could do what I liked, I walked back from the beach through the town the long way, re-visiting old places. In the fading light I was sometimes as insubstantial as a ghost; other times I sensed I was the only real character here, trawling through the past. Like someone in a film.

The amusement arcade where Vicky and I used to go looked small and tawdry; there were the usual kids messing about outside – smoking and drinking, whispering then shouting and laughing. The atmosphere I once found so exciting was sealed like a ship in a bottle. Even their cigarette smoke reached me like the memory of a smell.

Vicky and I used to walk along the promenade, as far as the slipway, then back to the boating pond, with one of us blind-folded – we called it the Helen Keller game.

It was my idea to ask Smelly-Ann to play.

I can still see her now sitting at the bottom of the

empty pond, her coat soaked from puddles of rain, her face shiny with tears. Vicky grabbed my hand and we ran, as fast as we could. After that time, we didn't play it again.

Now the boating pond is surrounded by a fence painted in luminous primary colours. With a warning sign: *Accompanied children only. Children to be supervised at all times.*

When I looked, the slick of water reflected the glow of the streetlights as they changed from deep red to greyish orange.

Smelly-Ann wet her pants.
Fell down all the way to France!

Of my school friends, apart from Julia of course as we sing in the same choir, Ann's the only one who stayed in touch; her long letters from Oxford evolved over the years into emails about her research at the university, her boyfriends, and invitations for me to come and stay with her, which, of course I always turned down. She'd sent her condolences, promised she would visit soon, but personally I think it's best just to email, keep it all nice and tidy. As I walked past her old house on the estate of grey ex-council houses, each with a white satellite dish like an Imperial Mint from the sweet shop, a girl on her mobile came out pushing a baby in a buggy, plugged in to its dummy. She walked past me in a waft of sound and perfume as if I wasn't there. It could have been Ann's youngest sister, or even a niece, but she was far too young. Too much time had passed. I don't know what I was thinking.

Ann says she'll never marry or start a family; life's too good. She managed to escape to the libraries and quads of Oxford from pebbledash and jacked up cars, but I was still here. Smelly-Ann.

BY THE TIME I reached Sylvia's it was dark. Her curtains were open and in the flickering blue light from the TV, she was ironing. Sylvia helped me the first time Mum was ill, when Dad died, as well as the last. I was doing my duty.

As I rang the doorbell my stomach jolted at a memory I couldn't quite grasp until I looked down at the letter box: the weight of a brown package in my hands; running back down the path to Ann. The heady, sick excitement of adolescence. I'd not been back there since Vicky and I stopped being friends, after I had a bout of gastric flu. *Please stop bothering me. I'm not your friend.* At the time it had been important but, now I was alone, it was insignificant. I fell out with Vicky at secondary school; and Ann had taken her place. Ann was always kind. I've seen it happen so often in my job as school administrator. A shift in allegiances. Girls are like that, aren't they?

'Helen! Come in, sweetheart. I'm so glad to see you.' Sylvia hugged me and patted down my hair, dampened by the night air. 'How're you feeling? You've lost weight. I'll get you something to eat with your tea.'

That's how it was in their family. Constant physical contact. Sylvia hugged people all the time. Perhaps it was normal for some families. I've always found it cloying. *How are you feeling? Are you alright?* In our house everyone said: 'What do you think?' 'That makes sense.' 'Did you know?' None of this need to constantly check on everyone's emotions and feelings. Something was tight in my chest – as if something was being crushed.

'I'll put the kettle on. Go and sit in the lounge...then I'll tell you the news.'

Mixed with the comforting smell of ironed laundry was a lingering smell of mince and tatties. I sat on one of the leather sofas placed at right angles to the fireplace. The TV was burbling away to itself in one alcove; in the other the old Singer was set up, ready to whirr into action. Apart from the ironing board which, now that I was there, would be hustled away like an unwanted guest, the room was perfect; everything coordinated in shades of claret and cream, matching lamp stands and floral cushions edged in a gold-tasselled fringe, and a gilt faux Louis XVI mirror above the fireplace. When Vicky and Sam got married, Sylvia had the whole house redecorated, as well as making the wedding dress and four pink bridesmaids' dresses spotted with scarlet roses. Mum told me all about it. Sylvia came round with swatches of fabric, photographs and dress patterns. I was always in the kitchen making cups of tea. I'm really not interested in that sort of thing.

On the mantelpiece was a photo of a young Vicky and Sam, in a shower of confetti, echoing that famous Charles and Di kiss; only Sam was the one straining down to meet Vicky's lips, closed in a smile like a tight, pink rosebud. In a second photo the bridesmaids nestled at Vicky's feet, gazing up at her, just like Sam.

I didn't go to their wedding – to be honest I can't stand weddings – and at the time I still had Mum as a reason not to go. For the first few years after Dad died she took a lot of looking after; she couldn't be left on her own for a minute. To tell you the truth she wouldn't have coped without me being there. Sometimes there were days when she was scared of nothing in particular, and everything. Scared of her own shadow. On the worst days, even if she'd had one of her little blue pills, I could spend all morning just trying to get out of the house to go shopping; we could go over the same conversation for hours.

'It won't be for long, Mum.'

'But we've got plenty of food in the larder. You don't need to go.'

'We've run out of bread and milk.'

'Can't we just make do, Helen?'

'Corner shop's still open.'

'You don't really need to go, do you?'

'We need to eat, Mum!'

'I'll stand by the window and wait. You won't be long, pet, will you?'

'I'll be as quick as I can, Mum. Come on. Let's put the radio on. And here's your knitting.'

Then I had to help her into her armchair by the fire and hold her hand until she stopped trembling. As I clicked the door shut behind me, I knew she would be up again standing behind the door, willing me to come back in. Poor Mum.

But what else could I do? We had to eat.

The day Vicky and Sam got married was one of those days, I couldn't have left her, just to sit around at a wedding. Who would have looked after her? Anything could have happened. Anyway, Mum was Sylvia's friend and Vicky and I were hardly what you'd call close anymore. I sent a set of expensive white cotton sheets and pillowcases edged with lace and roses from the wedding list. Very Vicky. How Sam could live with all that pink? But there were compensations – a honeymoon in Tenerife then, once the children came along, villas in France or Italy, and Sylvia to help out with her grandchildren. Mum told me all about it every time Sylvia came round for tea.

A third black and white portrait photo shows an older Vicky and Sam frolicking in a white room with a dark-haired toddler and a baby. Sam's hair, starting to recede, cut close to his head, curls all gone. Vicky laughing and showing off her boyish short hair that made her look younger, elfin, hardly old enough to be a mother, as if she'd walked into the room and been handed these two children.

Sylvia loved being a grandma and spent as much time as she could visiting them in Manchester. So lucky to have all that *quality time* with the family, Mum told me. A pity they're too busy to come back to Holdersea. And what a shame Michael had moved so far away. *I never get to see my grandchildren.*

'You'd hardly recognise them now. Holly's ten and Tom's nearly seven. They grow up so quickly, don't they? I don't know where all the time goes!' Sylvia was laughing as she came into the room with a mug of tea.

'You'll have some cake, won't you? It's a fruit loaf. Of course you will. You've got to try and eat, dear.'

Before I had time to refuse, she scuttled off to the kitchen again.

It was a long time since I'd had a meal with anyone and, after the walk in the cold air I was empty.

Sylvia put a plate down on a side table pulled out from a nest of three tucked away in a corner of the room.

'Now I can tell you the news!' she chirruped as I bit

into the slice of cake. 'Sam's got a new job – Head of English. They're coming home, back here at Easter. Vicky's going to look for a wee part-time job. Maybe start her own pottery classes.'

'You must be pleased.' I put my plate on the side table. I could hardly speak and started to cough, so gulped down my tea to release the sensation of closing up inside. I couldn't swallow the cake.

'Thrilled! You two together again. Och, just like old times.' Sylvia's voice was shrill and suddenly very Scottish. She ignored my struggle to catch my breath.

'But why now?' I sat back in my chair. The room was overheated, airless.

'Manchester's too much. They want space and fresh air.' She wiped her mouth to remove a few crumbs. 'Sometimes I don't see the children for so long I almost have to get to know them again. And now I can see them every day. I'm over the moon!'

Her voice trailed off and she leaned over and patted my hand. 'Och, but I'm forgetting myself. I'm so sorry, dear. Your mum loved to hear what Vicky and Sam...' A tear had begun to make its way down to the corner of her mouth. She licked it away. 'Poor Elizabeth. You must miss her. She thought the world of you, you know.'

The cake clung to my palette. 'Thank you.' I cleared my throat. 'It's great news about Vicky. It will be good to see them both. We lost touch after school.'

Sylvia nodded, then with a serene look on her face nibbled a few raisins that had dropped out of the cake. I took a mouthful of tea and forced the cake down. My ears buzzed with the silence. But Sylvia soon started prattling on again. She never knew why Vicky and I stopped being best friends. If she'd even been aware of it. Over the years Vicky called in to see Mum, but funnily enough her visits always coincided with the sick headaches I used to get. Just because she was coming back to live in Holdersea didn't commit me to anything, did it?

As I LAY in bed trying to digest the fruit loaf, I mulled it all over.

Vicky and Sam, the conquering heroes returning. At school they were the golden couple, the ones we all measured ourselves against, Vicky taking the best roles in the school play; Sam acting and directing, in control. I could see him, as the curtain closed, taking a deep balletic bow, his tight curls reflecting the stage lighting, a pair of wings on his shoulders. Acknowledging the applause with *brittle brilliance* as I recorded in the notebook where I wrote my poems.

I kept away from all that showing off and self-promotion. Not everyone's an extrovert, are they? I stayed in the audience – watching, silent. Then, at some point Ann and I started publishing poetry in the school magazine. We wrote our poems together – gloomy, teenage stuff. That was the fashion then; I expect it still is.

When school finished, people moved away and most didn't come back. And I got on with real life – Mum, work, choir. Our falling out became a blur. If I ever thought about Vicky and Sam at all, it was of Sam showing off: cartwheels and handstands, or taking his bow against the dusty red curtain in the school hall. And Vicky ... well something pink, probably a tutu or ballet tights. And her voice in my ear as she always liked giving me her advice, *'I know let's . . .'* or *'Why don't we . . . ?'*

If I'm really honest, there was more – like a tiny picture in a locket around my neck. The image of the "Ideal Couple".

As I eventually started to fall asleep, in my mind's eye two dots appeared in the distance next to the cliff, the new black and white Sam from Sylvia's photo executing handstands and cartwheels along the tide line, then running, hand in hand with the crop-haired, grown-up Vicky. Running along the beach towards me, coming closer and closer. If I could have looked through the binoculars on the promenade I would have seen them clearly. But it was as if I'd taken off my glasses – their faces were just a blur.

FOUR

'DON'T SING IF you start feeling upset, Helen. Stand at the end of the line. You can slip out if it all gets too much,' Julia said.

The first practice I'd been to since the funeral. We were rehearsing Mozart's *Requiem*. Apt I suppose for how I was feeling. Or ironic. *Dies irae. Dies illa. The day of wrath.* In the break she made sure I had two chocolate biscuits, but I still had no appetite. Especially when she said, 'Guess who I saw? Vicky and Sam Taylor. They're back. Can you believe it?'

Julia's a gossip. She had a bit of a soft spot for Sam at school, like most people. But her face was like the back end of a bus. Poor Julia.

'So I heard. Sylvia mentioned it,' I said flatly. 'She's excited to see her grandchildren.'

'You used to be good friends with them, didn't you?'

I sighed. 'I've more important things to think about. Mum's room to sort out for one.'

Julia's smile dropped. 'Sorry, Helen. I was just trying to cheer you up.' She hugged me then tried to persuade me to eat another biscuit, before rushing off to find someone more willing to listen to her gossip.

I had no time to fret about people whose lives didn't concern me.

I YANKED OPEN the green velvet curtains, which always set my teeth on edge, unlatched the window and pushed up the sash. There it was – the familiar street I'd looked at all my life, from a new angle, the way Mum had seen it. In the distance the ice cream van tinkled. On days when she was having a rest, when everything got too much for her, Dad used to let us run down with a handful of change when we heard the old tune, *Greensleeves*, then Michael and I had to keep our voices to a whisper sitting on the back step in the sun, trying not to drip everywhere.

In the corner, the commode was still sitting there. It was an eyesore. I would have to get it taken away. The sun was streaming in but I shivered. As I sat down on the bed, something moved under me with a flaccid, liquid movement. I put my hand in and pulled it out. I almost laughed – her hot water bottle, flattened and cold. Even when there was frost she'd never let me turn the radiator on. I held it to my cheek and breathed in its dank, rubber smell. Then I pulled out a wad of tissues from the box on the bedside table and crushed them into a ball. For a few hard minutes I let the tears come at last.

But I didn't make a sound. *No use crying over spilled milk.* I pulled myself together and started to strip the bed.

Tucked under the mattress were bottles and packets of sleeping pills and tranquillisers. As he was signing the death certificate *heart failure, advanced metastases,* the doctor offered me the same to help me through the first few weeks. If Mum was having one of her days, those little blue pills sometimes worked a treat, meaning I could leave her on her own for an hour and escape from the house. On winter afternoons when the light was going and the mist was beginning to pour in from the sea, I found the occasional small glass of sherry beneficial. But, no thank you to pills. I was going to face this new life head on, eyes open.

'Nowadays we'd never prescribe this amount, but for someone of your mother's generation that's all there was,' the doctor said, as he packed away his equipment. 'At least it kept her mood steady, when she needed it.'

I let him write out the prescription, just in case I had one of my bad days. That's when it really struck me. I was alone. There was no one to call me, to tell me what to do, to ask me to make a cup of tea, as I'd been doing for over twenty years. No, I'm deluding myself: forty-two years and three months. My whole life with four brief weeks away at university. Mum and me.

As I folded the blankets and sheets, I tried to remember those four weeks. They were like a hazy dream. I hadn't wanted to go but it was what everyone expected. Mum, Dad, friends, teachers. With my new haircut, and all the French novels from the reading list in my suitcase, I was prepared to stay at university. I'd slowly grown accustomed to the new smells, the noise of other girls chatting and laughing.

But in one quick phone call everything changed: *It's not good news, Helen. It's your dad.*

If I met any of those girls now, would they remember me? I can't remember any of them. What I remember is the view from the train as I travelled back down the coast to Yorkshire, gulls suspended over the sea like a holiday postcard. It was November. Bright sun. Not pouring down like this. The woman sitting opposite offered me her *Woman's Own* and told me to keep the pack of tissues. 'You look like you need them. Boyfriend trouble? Plenty more fish in the sea, love.'

Why do certain details last? She fell asleep just south of Newcastle. Her skin was matte with face powder; there were deep creases on either side of her mouth, as if someone had sliced through her foundation then tried to fill it in again; occasionally, at an uneven section of track, flecks of tanned dust flaked off and were blown away by the air conditioning. Her eyeshadow was like sand, after the tide's gone out leaving darker lines where seaweed and pebbles collect.

MUM'S WARDROBE WAS the hardest. It wasn't easy to touch shirts and jumpers that were so familiar they were a part of her. But I had to do it by myself. Her perfume was caught in the fibres of old dresses, some I'd never seen before. I pictured her all those years ago, slim and dark-haired, getting ready to go out to dances with Dad. Vicky and I used to play dressing up with some of her cast-offs, but she'd kept these hidden away. Why did she hold onto them? I couldn't imagine I'd ever have a life where there would be things that were so important to me I'd want to wrap them up and bundle them away.

Parcelled up in browning tissue paper, was a 1960s emerald cocktail dress. I pulled off the layers and a dusty smell of Tweed engulfed me – the only scent I remember Dad buying for her. She must have packed this away when she had children thinking she might wear it again one day. The silk slipped through my fingers with a delicious coolness. I threw off my clothes and tried it on. It fitted me perfectly. I rifled through the boxes at the bottom of the wardrobe to find some shoes. Wrapped in an old Yorkshire Post (March 16th 1964 – Elizabeth Taylor marries Richard Burton *"Her hair was adorned with hyacinth and lily of the valley")* was a pair of high heeled slingbacks. I couldn't imagine the woman who became my mother ever wearing them.

On the inside of the wardrobe door was a narrow mirror. The dark green set off my hair. At school the art teacher once embarrassed me by calling me a pre-Raphaelite muse; now I saw what he meant. Here I was in my forties still slim enough to fit into a dress Mum had worn in her twenties. Suddenly I was Cinderella. You *shall* go to the ball. I spun in the middle of the room laughing at myself. I was grimy and exhausted but behaving like Vicky and I used to, dancing to music on the radio.

I teetered around in the heels until four black bags for the charity shop and half a dozen for the skip were stacked on the landing; then, still wearing the dress, I sat down panting on the bed. Outside a robin started singing in the apple tree – clear and penetrating. A fresh, clean sound. If I gave the room a coat of paint it could be mine. It was bigger and brighter. The bed could go. I would buy myself a brand new one, with a soft mattress. My first double bed. And a big bookcase. I could read without interruption. I wouldn't have to buy my books second-hand, or borrow them from the library. Mum wouldn't call me away to watch *Midsomer Murders* or to ask for her Horlicks. *Always got your nose in a book, Helen. No good for your eyes, you know.* I could walk on the beach without guilt or the need to go back. I could take a trip to Hull or York to look round the shops and buy something new to wear.

The smell of the casserole I'd put in the slow cooker drifted up the stairs and, for the first time in weeks I felt hungry. *Close that kitchen door, Helen. I can smell onions all over the house.* Well, now it didn't matter. I hung the dress up and shut the door of Mum's room. I might even have time for a relationship. A boyfriend.

WELL, THERE WAS a boyfriend of sorts before. Ed. He'd answered many needs. It lasted for a few months, at least through *Messiah* and Brahms *German Requiem*. We stayed friends of a sort; he said he'd always be there if I needed him.

It was Sylvia who came to my rescue the first time Mum was ill; she offered to sit with Mum one evening a week. She always looked out for me. Nowadays you'd call it respite care.

'I don't like to see you stuck here, Helen.'

'I'm looking for a job. I've got an interview at the school next week.'

'You need more than a job. You want be out enjoying yourself. You're young. And so pretty and clever.'

At first I didn't recognise Ed. Most people look comical when they sing, especially tenors because they have to bounce up and down to be noticed; the women in the choir never take them as seriously as they do the basses. At school he'd gone from glasses and nits straight to spots – one of those nerdy boys who only ever speak to their own kind – so I was startled when he caught me up after the rehearsal.

'I know you'll think it were odd, but for me, you were the most beautiful girl in the whole school.' A secret crush.

I took Sylvia's advice and the following week went for a drink with him. By that time Julia was involved with one of the basses. 'His voice, Helen. When he talks to me on the phone you won't believe how it makes me feel.' The thing was I could. Julia was always like that. And reader she married him, more fool her. I knew it wouldn't last.

I didn't tell her about Ed; she would only ask questions and it was none of her business.

It was nearly Christmas so we were practising *Messiah*. It snowed all evening. We joked about his nickname.

'They reckon everyone has nits, at some point, don't they?'

'I never did.'

He didn't need to know about the time Mum dragged me up to the bathroom and anointed me with a stinking chemical to *get rid of the little visitors,* then wrote a note to say I had to stay at home with a head cold for three days.

Ed's hair was now a luscious golden blond and too long – an optimist would compare him to Robert Redford. After an engineering degree, he'd come home to work in his father's business. Something to do with computers. He didn't want to waste any more time studying. He wanted to get on with life.

He paid for the first round and I paid for the second, and then we must have had another couple. Then there's a hazy part before we went back to his flat for a coffee. We did it. I let him. I got it over with. I was nearly thirty after all.

When I woke, the room was eerily bright with light reflected from the snow. My mouth was dry, as if I'd been eating sand and I was shivering. Ed's face was smooth with a sprinkling of fine hair along his jaw line; he turned over in his sleep and his back was covered in angry looking acne. He mumbled something that sounded like 'Helen' or perhaps he was saying, 'Oh, hell . . .' and when he reached out towards me, his fingernails were bitten down so far the skin curved over the tops of each one.

Sex hadn't been as wonderful as I'd been led to expect; but I wanted that feeling again. I once saw Vicky in the dunes, eyes shut but smiling like the Mona Lisa. That was the feeling I wanted.

The second time was better. I relaxed more. We both did. The third time I started to feel bored. With the snow, the room was a white box, like being inside a fridge. We exchanged numbers. If I could forget his stubby fingernails, his hand had been warm on my hip. I liked that.

Every Monday Sylvia stayed with Mum so I could go for a drink after choir. What a relief to have a whole evening to myself.

'A boyfriend?' Sylvia said, smiling.

'Possibly.'

Ed was a useful distraction but he wasn't the love of my life. It was only a rehearsal for when I'd meet someone I could really care about. Like Fanny Price, I wasn't going to rush off with a fly by night like Mr Crawford. I could wait for that kind of pleasure. I could wait for the Edmund in my life, whoever he turned out to be.

Mum used to say, '*It's better to save your pocket money for something good rather than spending it on tat made in China.*' I was never going to leave the comfort of home for a one bedroom flat over the chip shop.

I didn't need a man now either.

Once the house was to my satisfaction I might glance through a holiday brochure, but I wasn't going abroad just yet. I've never been the sort of person to leap without looking. I didn't even have a passport. Vicky always called me a scaredy cat but I call it cautious, circumspect. We can't all be prima donnas, can we?

FIVE

'HELEN! IT *IS* you! Mum said you were working here!'

I jumped. No, I'd not forgotten she was coming back to Holdersea, more put it to the back of my mind.

'Weren't you expecting me?' Vicky laughed and showed her teeth in a way that was shocking in its familiarity.

'It's a surprise, that's all.'

'Have I changed that much? You're exactly the same. Still so seductive!'

And she hadn't changed either. Still so embarrassing.

I'd glanced at the admissions paperwork, but the surname had thrown me. At school it had been: Sam Taylor and Vicky Ross. *Victoria Taylor.* To me she'd always be Vicky Ross.

Victoria Taylor was golden and glowing. Her blue eyes, still the darkest indigo I'd ever seen, were highlighted by blue crystal earrings that pulled down on her earlobes and tinkled every time she moved. Apart from short hair and the growing web of laughter lines, the main change was her size. She was never skinny like me; even as a child she was taller and more substantial. Not fat. Now she was womanly, matriarchal. She was turning into her mother.

'Don't be tactful, love. I know I've put on a few pounds.' She looked down at her waistline. 'You know what it's like when you have children…the little darlings.'

As she unpeeled Tom's arms from her not insubstantial waist her earrings jingled. 'Say hello to Helen.'

Holly, the older of the two, smiled but Tom clung to his mother.

'But in school you have to call her Miss Farrish,' she whispered. 'She's *very* important. She's the school secretary.'

There was a striking resemblance between Tom and Vicky. It looked good on a boy: dark blond hair, the same rosebud mouth. *A heartbreaker*, Mum would have called him. Holly was dark like her father, Sam.

'Let's go and see your new classes,' I said, stepping into my role.

'And the voice, Helen.' Vicky said in a stage whisper. 'I'd forgotten your sexy voice!'

I laughed. Typical Vicky. Her talent for embarrassing me hadn't changed. People often comment on my 'speaking voice' and how I've lost my accent. Well Mum saw to that. Two years of *electrocution* lessons, as Dad called them. Vicky could always turn her accent on or off at will, depending on the role, but she still had a trace of her Yorkshire twang.

As they walked in front of us along the corridor, Holly's stride was like her father's, long and purposeful. It's strange how you don't forget. Precise images came back to me: Vicky leaving for university in a cloud of Miss Dior, hair in a chignon like a Hitchcock blonde. Sam, here, in this same building, stretching up in assembly to turn the old-fashioned hymn sheets with a wooden pole.

I was acutely aware of how small and run down it must look; but in her jeans and perma-tan, Vicky seemed oblivious. The same smell of pencil sharpenings and dusty lino as there had been on our first day as five-year olds. As if I'd never left.

'Nothing's changed,' she said and peered into one of the classrooms. 'Which was ours, Helen? Any of the old teachers still here? I couldn't wait to get away. And once I got the part in *Emmerdale* I thought I'd never come back! You were one of the cleverest, all set to go to university. What *on earth* made you stay here?' she said quietly, so the children couldn't hear.

I almost dropped the file I was holding. Surely it was obvious.

'I had to leave university when Dad died.' I heard myself, like a child making excuses. 'Mum needed me here.' Outside there were shouts from the school field. 'Once she was settled, I could work and not be too far away if she needed me.'

To be honest, it wasn't exactly true. Two years after Dad died, Mum was getting better, so I applied again. My A levels were good. I had unconditional offers. But when I came home from my new job, she was waiting with the offer letter from Manchester University in her hand.

'You've just started work, Helen! And now you want to run off to university. Jobs aren't two a penny, you know. You don't need to go love, do you?'

Her eyes were full of tears and she made it sound so reasonable that I put the letter away in a drawer in my bedroom and hardly thought about it again.

A whistle blew and a seagull flew up startled, white against the green of the field where we used to spend so much time practising handstands.

'I'm sorry about your Mum, Helen. Only in her sixties.' Vicky squeezed my arm, then hugged me. I could smell coconut sun cream. 'I wanted to come back for the funeral, but we'd paid so much for the holiday and Sam said we needed a break.'

I let her embrace me even though she didn't need to treat me like an invalid. 'Thanks, Vicky.'

'Now I'm back I mean to be a better friend.' She laughed. 'We can pick up where we left off, can't we?'

How patronising; I already had plenty of friends. I made my voice as bright as possible and moved so she had to let go of me. 'How's Sam? Enjoying teaching?'

'He's trying to get everything finished off in Manches-

43

ter still. And it's the end of term.' She made a mock dramatic sigh and laughed. 'Missing me. Living off take-aways. You know what men are like!'

That grated. For all she knew I might have had hundreds of boyfriends. 'Oh I know!' I laughed. Then I switched quickly into my professional role.

Once we'd left Holly and Tom in their new classes there wasn't much to say: she was staying at her mother's until they found somewhere to rent, and I didn't have time to stand around and chat.

'Let's have a coffee.' She kissed me on each cheek, leaving a trace of her perfume. 'I'll ring you. We'll have a proper catch-up before Sam gets here.'

As if she'd forgotten we'd ever fallen out. Forgotten everything she did.

ALL AFTERNOON I was irritable and easily distracted. It was one of those days when the phone never stops ringing and I had a pile of paperwork, as well as emails. So many parents coming to the window of the office to ask inane questions that if they bothered to read the newsletters they wouldn't have to bother me with. Irene, the girl who dealt with finance, brought me a cup of tea. She'd been quiet since Vicky's visit, but I knew she was desperate to speak to me about it.

She sat on the edge of my desk with her coffee in one

hand and her mobile in the other. 'So you know the Taylors? She seemed to know a lot about you.'

'We were at school together. Her husband too.' I didn't want to discuss my life with someone who wasn't even born at the time.

'She's off TV, right?' Irene glanced at her mobile for confirmation. Looks like she's done OK for herself.'

'A minor part in one of the soaps. Ages ago. A few TV ads. Theatre work.'

'Did you see that jewellery? Swarovski crystal.'

'I didn't notice.'

'She'd be pretty if she wasn't so . . . but she carries it well. Not as pretty as you though. You're lucky to still have your figure at your age.'

'Thank you, Irene.' She wanted a compliment in return but when she realised I wasn't going to chat, Irene slid off my desk and went back to her side of the room. She finished her coffee and scuffled in her drawer for her biscuit supply.

'Bugger! I must've eaten them all.'

'Here. I've got a few left.'

Irene was a regular at Weightwatchers and told me how many calories were in every piece of food.

'Helen?'

Finishing off the packet of Rich Tea fingers, she brushed crumbs onto the floor and aimed the wrapping at the bin. 'You're frowning. Is it one of your migraines?'

'I'm fine. Just so much to do.'

'When my nan died, my mum went part-time. Have you–'

'Look, thanks, Irene. I'll think about it.' I didn't look up, but I could hear her nails tapping on her phone. The ping of texts punctuated the next half hour.

IRENE WAS RIGHT though. I left early with a headache and went down to the beach. The waves rolled in quietly, frothing over the flat sand where the tide was going out, gradually exposing the long lines of groynes. The air was fresh and spray blew in, wetting my shoes. It didn't matter that they were coming back. I didn't have to be Vicky's friend again. *What on earth made you stay here? You know how men are.* For an hour I walked briskly, as if I had somewhere important to go, something I had to do. Until her voice stopped echoing and my head was clear. I couldn't face my usual treat: a chocolate digestive with my cup of tea. But at the weekend I would finally take the bus to Hull to look for new clothes. Vicky and I used to spend hours playing dressing up in her bedroom. All those games that started with *Let's pretend.* I always loved the smell of new clothes, the fabrics slithering through my fingers and around my body.

Mum and I had been happy in our own way. A simple, quiet life. What more did anyone need? It would have been nice to go to university and have a proper career. A husband and family. But look at all the unhappy marriages there are in the world. I could equally ask Vicky 'What made *you* come back?'

SIX

I'D ALWAYS BEEN Sam's friend from the first day he moved to our school when we were ten. Sam and I had never fallen out. He was tall and skinny, all elbows and knees until he was at high school, but what I remembered was his dark, curly hair and his jokes.

'Why is Edward's head like a nest?' he asked.

'I don't know.'

'Because it's full of eggs!'

We all giggled, even Edward who had nits, until he realised what Sam meant, then he tried to jab his pencil into Sam's leg. But Sam was too quick and Edward ended up in trouble, standing in the corner.

Sam was clever, and I think he was probably spoiled. He did what he wanted and got away with it. He proved to be good at games and gymnastics too. When I asked Vicky what she thought of him, she said he was too skinny, then she linked arms and pulled me away to play. 'He's a boring boy,' she said.

In assembly there were no hymn books. Instead, three large sheets of paper hung along the side of the hall and the oldest boys had to turn the pages over with a wooden pole so we could read the words. As I sat cross-legged on the cold floor, I watched Sam stretching to lift up the white sheets. If I didn't wear glasses, I'd be the sort of girl that boys liked. I slipped my glasses into my skirt pocket. Everything blurred so I had to listen hard to the words. We were learning a new hymn about a shepherd. Afterwards Vicky said, 'That boy Sam was looking at you when we were singing. He likes you.'

I ignored her and waited in line to speak to the teacher.

'Miss,' I asked, 'When me and Vicky play at spies we follow people. Why was that hymn about a quiet water spy and not about being good or going to heaven?'

Luckily I'd not asked her in front of the whole class.

'Helen, you silly goose. There aren't any spies, just 'the quiet waters by'.

I had to turn away because my cheeks were burning but as I ran out to play, Sam winked at me. 'The quiet water spy. Your secret's safe with me.'

When I asked Mum about contact lenses she said 'Don't be daft, Helen. Far too expensive. Glasses are much more practical.'

And Sam never forgot – I was always his *friend, the quiet water spy.*

He liked making fun of me almost as much as Vicky did. But he always did it with a smile.

I DIDN'T REALLY expect her to get in touch, and all I could imagine was the old days when we were teenagers – mugs of Nescafe with hot milk and a plate of custard creams. But she did, and although I was reluctant to break my Saturday routine of cleaning the house then having a swim, I met her in the Driftwood Café, on the seafront. It was curiosity more than anything else. Why had they decided to come back?

'You've really not changed a bit, Helen.' When she smiled, the lines radiating from each eye deepened. Her voice had acquired the larger than life quality of the trained actress but I could still hear her northern vowels. 'Still so mysterious – the dark lady!'

Vicky held me at arm's length then pulled me close and wrapped me in a hug. Her physical presence, coupled with smell of leather from her Italian jacket and her perfume, was overpowering. Like being buried in the ground floor of a department store. 'It's only now I see you again I realise how much I've missed you.'

I could only stammer. 'You smell lovely. Very posh for the Driftwood!'

She looked at me more closely. 'Is that a genuine tank top? How retro. You look like an extra from the seventies.'

I was wearing one of Mum's hand-knitted jumpers. It was a cold day.

'Let's sit by the window,' Vicky pointed to where a

pair of regulars were getting up to put their coats on. Eileen was one of Mum's school friends. I'd not seen her to talk to since the funeral. As they made their way to the door, she smiled at me.

'You're a bit brighter today, Helen. I hope you're looking after yourself. Time's a great healer I always say.' She looked out of the window. 'At least the weather's getting warmer.'

She was quick to turn her attention to Vicky.

'And here's little Victoria. Sylvia's girl. Goodness you're the spit of your mother. I was just saying to Margery "You don't get clothes like that in Holdersea!" And here you are. Back to stay. We used to watch you on telly, didn't we, Margery? When you were in that soap.'

Vicky smiled, but I could tell she didn't recognise her. 'That old thing. I've been mostly doing stage work since then. But now we're back for fresh air and fun!'

'Ooh, and you speak so nicely now. It's a wonder what all that training does for you, isn't it, Margery? It's lovely to see you doing so well for yourself...and you won't be so lonely without your poor mum, Helen. Isn't that marvellous! Sometimes things just work out so well.'

Margery nodded and adjusted her scarf.

'I'll tell Mum we bumped into you.' Vicky smiled graciously then, as we made our way to the table, she said, 'Who was that? One of the *locals*?' She was so loud. Far too loud for the Driftwood.

'It's like being in a time warp. This place. Even the wallpaper…'

'I think it was refurbished…and they changed the name from–'

'Is that the same waitress? She was ancient twenty years ago!' Vicky said under her breath, then smiled brightly. 'Two cappuccinos, please.'

'Will two coffees with hot milk do you, love? Machine's broken.'

Vicky raised an eyebrow at me, looked at the menu then ordered coffee for me and a hot chocolate for herself. And muffins.

Outside it was grey and windy – the grey of a familiar childhood photograph. Two girls messing about on the promenade could have been us all those years ago: laughing, and eating ice cream in spite of the cold. We used to spend hours on the sea front.

When our order arrived, Vicky attacked her muffin as if she'd not eaten for days. I cut a slice off mine and ate it slowly then let the rest sit on my plate. I'd already had my bowl of porridge. I could wrap it up and take it home for later. It's hard to eat when your mouth's dry and you've no appetite.

'You need the extra calories here…it's so bloody cold. No wonder people put on weight!' She stroked her stomach comfortably. 'But you've never had that problem. Lucky you!'

'But you've had two children,' I countered.

'I had to hold my tummy in every time I went for a part. Look!'

She pulled her stomach in with a pained expression on her face. 'I even bought one of those old lady corsets. Acting wears you out.'

'You always loved it at school.' I pictured her as Titania in *Midsummer Night's Dream*, drifting across the stage in a confection of gauze and sequins.

'Once you have kids it's not the same. They hated it when I was touring. And it didn't do much for Sam and me. You don't see each other for weeks on end and there are so many distractions, if you know what I mean. Out of sight, out of mind.' Her long crystal earrings tinkled as she laughed. 'My friend, Nancy always says we should play by tour rules. What happens on tour stays on tour. But it doesn't always work like that...'

'Nancy?'

'Another actress. We're best friends,' she said firmly.

Vicky put what was left of her muffin down on the plate, frowned and stared out of the window. In profile her face was heavier – the taut line of her jaw starting to slacken. Since Mum died I'd often caught my own reflection in the mirror and seen the changes that come with aging. But she was right. I wasn't going to allow myself to get fat. I asked what her plans were now they were back.

'When I was out of work I took a ceramics course at university. I loved it.'

'Very creative. Like your mother.'

'Holdersea used to have its own pottery – kitsch for the tourist trade.' She smoothed her fingers around her mug. 'I've taken a studio in the old fire station. I'm going to make stuff, and run classes for kids.'

'You're giving up acting?'

'You can't play Cinderella for ever, Helen! And I love working with my hands.' She laughed. 'I could've taught ballet or drama, but one teacher in the family's enough. I didn't want to turn into a weird dance and drama teacher with hennaed hair and an inch of slap. Remember Miss Wyatt? She used to hit us with the cane if we got it wrong. The old cow.'

'I never did ballet,' I reminded her.

'But we spent ages practising. I had a barre in my bedroom. We were both so into it. Little Billy Elliots going to hit the big time!'

Hit. There was a smudge of memory, something I couldn't see clearly. Pain and pleasure mixed oddly. *You'll never learn if you don't try harder.*

'I remember you wearing a leotard. You were so much smaller than me you always got my cast-offs, didn't you?' Vicky leaned forward.

'No, I never did ballet. You were the one with ballet lessons, not me. We used to play dressing up sometimes.'

I remembered the whirr of the sewing machine from downstairs. How slippery the dresses were over our slim bodies.

'Oh yes, when we were little. Any excuse to take our clothes off!' Then she laughed. 'It's weird what you remember. We used to have handstand competitions? You could always stay up the longest. Showing the boys your knickers! You were *so* precocious.'

SEVEN

BUT THAT WASN'T how I remembered it. At lunch in the summer we went to the end of the field and practised handstands until the bell went. It was a girls' area. The boys had the football pitch and the dark corner behind the kitchen where they played fighting. They never played with us.

But Sam was new. When he saw us he didn't even wait for us to say, 'Okay, you can play.' He flipped into a handstand and stayed up for more than two minutes, then just as he was about to wobble, he said, 'See you later, girls!' and walked off on his hands like someone in the circus.

Vicky's voice in my ear was insistent. 'Go on, Helen! Show him.'

Without thinking I was up on my hands and suddenly everyone was counting and I'd been up for over three and a half minutes before I remembered: I was wearing my summer dress. They all saw my underwear.

Someone told our teacher.

'It was an accident, Miss.'

'You're not in the infants now, Helen.'

Everyone else was playing outside but the windows were shut. Like watching a silent film. My hands were hot and clammy and I needed the toilet.

'You've got to learn what's appropriate.'

A fly was buzzing against the glass. Miss opened the window to let it out. There was a burst of voices then she shut the window and told me I could go. 'But no going on the field for the rest of the week.'

Sam was waiting. 'Helen! Are you coming to play?' He was bouncing on his feet. 'What did she say?'

I walked straight past him to the girls' toilets where I let the tears come but bit my hand to stop any sound. I was a good girl, wasn't I? I washed my hands under the cold tap until they were aching and red, and splashed water on my face. Then I went out into the sun.

'Amazing! You stayed up for nearly one whole minute!' Vicky was saying to Smelly-Ann. 'A good thing you're wearing trousers. Not like *some* people! She wants all the boys to see her pants.'

Sam was standing in the centre of a sprawling knot of boys, waving his arms and pointing, organising a game with rules only he could remember. He looked towards me and smiled. When I didn't respond he shrugged and carried on instructing the group.

Around the side of one of the outside classrooms was where the little kids played. Two boys were sitting in the shade with some trading cards. They didn't hear me until I was right behind them.

'Hand them over,' I whispered. 'You're not allowed them in school. You should know that.'

The boy with spiky ginger hair flushed but was about to protest when the other, smaller boy gave me his pack of cards without hesitating. I pinched him hard then put the cards in my pocket, keeping my eyes fixed on both of them.

'No cards in school. That's the rule. Okay?'

They both nodded. The one I pinched was crying.

At the end of the lunch break, I took the cards to the head teacher.

'Well done, Helen. What a sensible girl.'

A good girl.

***

VICKY WAS SITTING back smiling, muffin crumbs lodged between her teeth. I could still see the fly trapped against the glass and the look on those boy's faces. But as I watched Vicky laughing, I remembered my pleasure at inflicting pain.

'I remember getting into trouble once,' I said.

'You were *never* in trouble, Helen. Always the good one. Being nice to all the stupid smelly kids. You're such an angel.'

I tried to deny it but she changed the subject with the

question I dreaded.

'Anyway, are you seeing anyone?'

I always felt I was expected to apologise for being on my own. As if I'd failed an exam. I tried to make the relationship with Ed more significant than the few months it really had been.

'It couldn't last. We were too different.'

'I could've told you that, Helen! What were you thinking?'

'We're friends... And he's useful. If you ever need someone to sort out your computer. Anything electrical...'

'That's one way of looking at it!'

'Being on your own is okay. I'm starting to enjoy it.' I affected an ironic tone. 'I'm still waiting for the man of my dreams!'

Vicky leaned her head slightly to one side and put on her best sympathetic voice. Against the grey of the sky her hair was like honey, 'Helen, you've been a darling looking after your mother. You didn't have time to find a proper relationship ... But when are you going to lose the glasses? Take them off. Let me see ... You're still *so* pretty. So gorgeous. You should get contacts . . .'

Even though I'd thought I wanted them when I was younger, when it came to it the thought of anything touching my eyes turned my stomach. I shook my head.

'And your hair used to be so wavy.' She frowned and

59

assessed me with a practised eye then leaned over and pulled out a few wisps of my hair. 'So soft.'

'Easier it it's straight. I like to keep it out of my eyes. At work I–'

'If I were you I'd go natural. Much more flattering.'

When I didn't respond, she was soon back to herself – her plans, her children, and her husband.

Middle age had crept up on Sam. He'd slowed down. He could hardly jog, let alone run. In Holdersea he could walk to work and, away from the city, there'd be less stress so he could give up smoking. So many good reasons for coming back home.

I couldn't imagine a Sam who had slowed down so much he was easing his way into middle age. He used to run everywhere, as if he had to make the most of life, to be in the thick of it.

Vicky caught up the last few crumbs of her muffin by licking her middle finger, then stopped talking and looked out at the sea. There was a thin line of sugar dusting her lower lip. I ran a finger over my own, as if to brush it off. I almost wanted to… but I couldn't quite relax with her even now, after all this time.

'Are you going to eat the other half of that muffin?'

'You have it. I'm not hungry.'

She smiled and swapped our plates. Then the conversation went on – an exchange of memories and anecdotes. Childhood repackaged and unfamiliar.

Outside, the two girls on the promenade were joined by a third, but they turned their backs on her and carried on talking.

Vicky was studying them. 'Whatever happened to that girl? The one with BO. From the estate.'

'You mean Ann?' I considered Ann my best friend, Julia a distant second.

'Smelly-Ann!'

'We still keep in touch.'

'I'd forgotten all about her... Smelly-Ann. We used to let her into our gang sometimes, do you remember?'

'She's down south. Oxford.'

'Mother of six, milking the state for benefits?'

'Teaching.'

'No! I remember she passed the eleven plus, but I thought she'd end up like the rest of her family ...' Vicky pushed the plate aside. 'We liked having her in our gang, didn't we? Well you wouldn't want to be her enemy! She was tough. I remember that.'

EIGHT

ON OUR WAY home from primary school I walked with Vicky. You mustn't talk to strangers or accept sweets from them, even if they were your favourite. You mustn't get into a stranger's car ever, our mums said. Even if your leg was falling off.

But Smelly-Ann was allowed to go home on her own, on the bus, because she hadn't got a dad and her mum had too many children. Sometimes we tried to be nice to her like the Good Samaritan in RE, but Smelly-Ann had scabs and her hair was dull brown and greasy. Her teeth were brown too, like pieces of pointy fudge because she could eat sweets whenever she liked and never brushed them.

One day we were bored so stopped to talk to her. It was drizzling, but Smelly-Ann wasn't wearing a coat. She was so thin you could see her bones. They were knobbly, especially her elbows and knees.

'Are your teeth cold?' asked Vicky.

'No. What do you mean?' said Smelly-Ann.

'Then why are they wearing little brown jackets?'

We both laughed and got very close to her.

'You look like a drowned cat,' said Vicky.

'More like a rat!' I giggled.

'Why don't you ever have a bath?'

'Have you got any water in your house?'

'What's wrong with your hair?'

'It's like rats' tails.' I giggled.

'That's what you are …a skinny little rat!'

'I bet you've got a tail tucked under your dress.'

'Disgusting. Go on show us your tail.'

She backed away. 'You can't hurt me . . .' Her voice was small, monotone.

In the rain, her skin was clammy like uncooked pastry, and so white I grabbed her arm and pinched her to make a mark. She drew away but didn't cry. She stared ahead and bit her lip.

'Go on, Vicky. She likes it.'

'I'll give her two!'

Vicky pinched her on the other arm. A pinky-blue bruise was already coming up where I'd pinched her. There was no one around, and Smelly-Ann wasn't squealing like other girls would. I wanted to pull her hair, to make her cry properly, like Michael did when I did it to him, but it looked stringy and not like hair at all. I didn't want to touch it.

'Let's do it again, Helen!'

Smelly-Ann dived sideways, pushing Vicky with both

hands, and tried to run out of the bus shelter.

But Vicky was stronger. 'Don't touch me with your dirty hands. I don't want your germs.' She kicked her on the back of the knee with her shiny black sandal. Smelly-Ann's leg buckled and she stumbled onto the pavement, hitting her head on the edge of the bus shelter.

'Drunk like her smelly mum!' shouted Vicky.

'Smelly-Ann! Smelly-Ann! Greasy like a frying pan!'

Smelly-Ann's nose was running so she wiped her face with the back of her hand. It was covered in mud and dead leaves. Then she tried to pull herself up onto the bench inside the shelter.

But the bus was coming and we had to stop our game.

'Next time we'll really make you cry, you big blubber baby,' whispered Vicky.

I picked up Smelly-Ann's book bag which had landed in the gutter and threw it at her.

'Let's go to my house,' I said. 'We've got ice lollies in the freezer.'

We linked arms and walked off swinging our school bags.

***

'OVERSENSITIVE AS USUAL, Helen. Kids *are* horrible. It's part of growing up. You should see my two! Smelly-Ann was always pinching me and pulling *my* hair!' Vicky patted her own short hair, then stood up, zipped her leather jacket and looked at her mobile. 'I need to rescue Mum!'

'I'll get it this time.' I pulled out my purse. On some level I wanted to see her again even if it was only curiosity.

Outside the three girls had gone. A drinks can rolled around in the wind with discarded chip papers and cigarette butts. The lighthouse towered above us.

'I'm sorry about your mum, Helen. Must've been hard looking after her, then suddenly being on your own after all this time.'

'You would've done the same.'

She looked surprised then shook her head. 'No I wouldn't. I definitely couldn't have done what you did. I would've gone completely insane looking after my mum. Bless her. It's amazing what you've done, Helen. But did you never feel resentful?'

I shook my head. 'Of course not.'

'I know *I* would!' She smiled. 'But it means you're still here, Helen, after all this time. So we can be friends again.'

As I WALKED home everything looked different, unstable. Like a bubble when the colours become thin and faded, just before it bursts. Like taking my glasses off and looking through my lazy eye. Everything changing and going out of focus.

For some of us, doing our duty is the right thing to do and I had been happy looking after Mum. Well, most of the time. Vicky was trying to make me feel like a put-upon daughter, *oversensitive*. What was it she called me? *An extra from the seventies.* For her I was only ever an extra, not a real character. For her it was always The Vicky Show. Worst of all though was that she was right. Of course I resented it. Not every minute. Not every hour. But there were days when it gnawed at my insides until I had to have my sherry straight after lunch. When I wanted it all to stop. When I wanted *her* to stop. But I kept going. I did what was expected of me... little Fanny Price was my role model.

But that still begged the question: why had she come back to Holdersea? It wasn't just for Sam's health. Or for the children. Vicky liked shops and living in the city. She loved acting. I couldn't see her running her own business even if Sylvia was there to help look after the children. When Vicky had money she liked to spend it, unless she'd changed dramatically. She'd never balance the books.

There was more. Something else had made them come home. But I would have to wait and see. That claustrophobic feeling she gave me, like a seaside mirror that reflects your image and distorts you, was creeping up. Until Vicky came back I was starting to have fun. For the first time in years I was enjoying myself. I hadn't asked for her advice or her opinions. Mum was right as usual.

Glasses were more practical. And cheaper.

AT THE END of the promenade the wind had dropped. The horizon was a band of dull metal pressing down on the sea, like a grey lid on a pan of simmering water about to come to the boil. On the surface it was still but underneath the sea was doing its work, battering away, dragging the land, relentlessly eroding and changing.

When we were children, we sometimes had family days out further down the coast at Spurn Point where the land dribbled out in a slender, three mile long spit into the North Sea. Dad told us it was never the same, constantly growing as it stretched out and dipped round into the Humber estuary, like a long-handled spoon. We sat in the car eating fish paste sandwiches then Mum stayed in the car with a magazine and we walked as far as we could until the land dropped away. Michael ran around with a football, but I stood and imagined the sand moving under us growing and spreading. Perhaps sand that we'd played with on our own beach in Holdersea. There was a thrill about being at the end of everything.

At high tide it was disconnected from the mainland.

'One day they reckon it will be cut off completely. An island,' Dad told us. 'There's nothing anyone can do.'

I used to dream of turning round to find I was stranded there alone with only sea birds for company. As I ran back to find my parents, I'd wade through sand and stumble over the marram grass which would cut my hands and bare feet. When I looked up they'd be there on the mainland waving and waving, smiling as if everything was fine, then they'd recede into the distance, and I'd be on my own, out in the middle of nowhere. And there would only be silence and the sea.

NINE

JULIA FOUND ME by the tea urn during the break at choir practice – I was an alto, she was one of the sopranos. She took in a deep breath as if she was about to start *The Hallelujah Chorus*.

'She's moved into our road! One of the big houses on the hill.' Julia still called it 'our' house although her husband (the bass) moved out a couple of years ago leaving her with two children. 'I took some flowers round. And we were sat there…' Her voice was getting higher and higher, 'having a glass of wine when guess what … Sam walked in.'

I knew she was waiting for me to sound enthusiastic, but all I could think was, you shouldn't laugh so much with such horsey teeth.

I bit into my biscuit. 'And what was that like?'

'Aren't you curious, Helen? I thought you had a thing about Sam Taylor!'

'After twenty years. Don't be daft.'

'Well you should see him now. There'll be a few girls at the high school with crushes on *Mr.* Taylor.'

'You included by the sound of it!' I said tartly.

'Oh honestly, Helen… Your sense of humour!'

Since her husband left, Julia had gone through the tearful tragic phase and was now like a teenager chatting about 'lads' and preening herself in the mirror in the toilets. Every time she designed a garden for a new client she put in extra hours for single men.

'But it's nice to have them as neighbours.'

'I've been invited round for a meal,' I said. 'Vicky and I were close when we were younger.'

Julia's face fell, but she was quick to add, 'Well, *he's* not changed. Watch out for Sam's wandering hands.'

'Julia, you're *so* common sometimes,' I said, laughing.

'Honestly! Always trying it on.'

'He was friendly with everyone.'

She raised an eyebrow. 'I don't know how Vicky puts up with him.'

'Well I'm sure you'll be safe. You're very experienced at pushing men away, Julia.'

She hesitated, then punched me on the arm playfully as we were called in for the second part of the rehearsal.

Afterwards I left quickly so we didn't have to pursue the conversation. Julia was busy making eyes at Ed. Good luck to her. Beggars can't be choosers.

I HAD MIXED feelings about becoming more involved with

Vicky, but every time I ran to check the door mat or opened my email, I felt a pang of disappointment. Like a lover waiting for a letter. Which was ridiculous, wasn't it?

After a fortnight an invitation arrived. A card with a child's drawing of the lighthouse, addressed to *Aunty Helen*. In their Christmas cards (usually a bare-chested Santa surfing with koalas and kangaroos) Michael's children never called me anything but Helen; *Aunty* Helen had the ring of spinsterhood. At forty-two I was hardly an old maid.

BY SEVEN O'CLOCK on the Sunday morning when I had arranged meet them, the whole house had the aroma of bleach. The bathroom and kitchen were shining, everywhere was dusted and hoovered and my bed changed. I must've been five when Mum taught me how to tuck the sheets into proper hospital corners. Crisp and clean cut. You might call it obsessive and I know it's fashionable to stick labels on tidiness, but I reckon you'll soon find the ones with messy houses have messy lives.

I showered and exfoliated, washed my hair and shaved my legs. By eight I was ready for breakfast: orange juice, fruit and plain yoghurt. I was going out for Sunday lunch with old school friends and I needed to look my best. Vicky and I had met up twice now, but today I was going to see Sam for the first time in years. Who would he be?

The Sam directing the school play or inventing the rules for an imaginary game? The Sam who cared about injured birds and was like a big brother? Or the one who teased me, taking my glasses on the school field to set fire to piles of dried grass. My new dress, ordered from the internet, was dark grey and fitted, with a lace collar. I was hoping for Dorothea in *Middlemarch* but when I caught my reflection in the hall mirror I wasn't sure I had the spiritual intensity to carry it off. The navy suede shoes, bought for the funeral, had a heel so I'd have to keep off the beach or any grassy areas otherwise I'd ruin them. At the last minute I left my hair down.

AFTER A WEEK of rain, everything gleamed in the sun. The crocuses had withered and every flowerbed and front garden had a patch of bright yellow daffodils. But it was cold – it was only April after all – and when I reached the seafront, the wind whipped my hair into my eyes and stung my cheeks.

Vicky and Sam were renting one of the Victorian grey, stone villas at the top of the town with a view of the sea and the lighthouse. Until they found somewhere to buy in Holdersea, they'd let their terraced house in Manchester to a doctor.

'They can buy a *mansion* in Holdersea for the price of their two up two down,' Sylvia had told me.

No one came to live in Holdersea anymore. Or on holiday. There were *For Sale* signs everywhere. The beach used to be crowded with *diggers*, and all the shops and kiosks hung with buckets and spades, fishing nets, rubber rings and inflatable beach balls. Now people had holidays abroad, the old smell of candy floss and fish and chips had almost gone, usurped by burgers and kebabs, the air hazy with burnt meat fat.

As I walked up the hill, passing Julia's thirties semi where a board in her front garden advertised her design company, *Seaside Landscapes*, a blister started coming up on my heel and the wine in my bag weighed it down so much, the strap cut in to my shoulder. I'd chosen rosé and pink roses too. Yellow would have been warm and friendly but yellow roses always made me feel queasy, linked as they were with recovering from gastric flu when I was a child. And pink was always Vicky's colour: ribbons, dresses, the leotard and tights she wore for ballet, and of course her bedroom.

I fought my way up the gravel drive to The Laurels and rang the bell, but after five minutes there was no response so I used the heavy door knocker. It echoed in the house then after a long silence, the door was flung open.

'Helen! How lovely!' Vicky hugged me like a long lost friend. She'd clipped an artificial flower in her hair and was wearing jeans with something loose and floral. I'd describe it as comfortable but Mum would have said it was hiding a multitude of sins.

'Sam's gone for supplies. Kids are outside.'

'I'm sorry, I think I'm early.'

'Gorgeous dress. Almost puritanical.'

The house was just as I'd imagined. Tasteful but shabby. At first I thought Vicky had moved on from pink into some kind of Vanessa Bell phase with the flowery smock, but I was wrong.

'All this will have to go.' She gestured to the wallpaper and carpets. Every surface swirled and flowed with colour and pattern. 'Vile isn't it? Mum's going to help make it more civilised.' I noticed her looking at my shoes; I'd scraped them on the horrible gravel path and they were streaked with mud.

I blushed. 'I'm sorry I–'

'Don't worry. The cleaner will be here tomorrow. Two kids, a dog and cat, as well as a husband ... it's impossible to keep this place clean! Let's do the tour.'

Up the stairs were photos of the children, and on the landing some of Vicky in her various roles – Titania, Nora, Cinderella. It wasn't until she opened a door into a study at the top of the house, that there was any evidence of Sam. No photos but wall to ceiling plain, wooden shelves full of books, and even more books stacked all over the floor. Functional, minimalist – a metal angle poise lamp and a plain black office chair. Next to a laptop, on the desk in front of the window, was a neat pile of blue exercise books ready to be marked. A guitar was propped on a worn leather armchair near a fireplace.

'Holly helped him put all his books in alphabetical order!'

I smiled. 'It's so peaceful.'

From the window I caught a glimpse of the distant silvery blue sea.

'Always up here marking. Or playing his guitar. Or smoking. Anything to avoid childcare. He's been out for hours.' She banged the door shut. 'Come and see the bedroom.'

An almost life-size photo of Vicky en pointe, from her ballet days, dominated the room. As a child I coveted Vicky's bedroom: flowers stencilled on the walls, framed pictures she'd drawn at art classes, photos and paintings of ballerinas in tutus. This room was more restrained, but every surface was covered in jewellery, makeup or clothes; and along the mantelpiece Swarovski crystal animals caught the light. A nightmare to dust. And she'd not bothered to tidy the bed. I averted my eyes, heat rushing to my face.

'Sam's a pain as usual. Always nagging at me. Says I've got to be organised. But you know what I'm like! Life's too short for obsessive tidying!'

I was allowed a quick glance into the children's room – pink on one side, blue on the other, toys and books everywhere – then she slammed the door.

'Kids! Bet you're used to a tidy house. . . Come on let's go in the garden. Why don't you go and chat to them while I sort out lunch?'

Down a few steps from the kitchen, a patio led to a strip of muddy grass with a rusty climbing frame and swing; there was a border of shrubs overrun with nettles along one side and at the far end, a tree covered in buds. Dad would have known its name. A garden full of places where children could make dens and play hide and seek. Even a tree house. But I was disappointed: not a garden for sitting in and discussing art and literature. Which is what I'd hoped for. It made me almost homesick. Well that was the nearest label I could give the feeling; at home our garden was practical. A patch of grass where Mum put out the washing, and the rest for Dad's fruit and vegetables. Once we were old enough to play with a ball or ride our bikes, we were told, 'There's a park and a beach for playing. Not the garden.'

Mum's only concession to beauty or colour was a half-barrel next to the back door filled with spring bulbs and orange wallflowers, alternating with red geraniums in the summer. Like a council flowerbed.

Holly had made her own garden: flowers, a plastic windmill and a bucket of snails; she was trying to feed them with dandelion leaves. Tom was involved in a game with American-accented dialogue which involved noisy shooting and dramatic dying.

'Aunty Helen, are you going to look after us like Aunty Nancy?'

'I don't think so.'

'Daddy didn't like Nancy.'

'Oh?'

'We aren't allowed to say "Shut up" or "Go to hell" or hit each other.'

There was the sound of tyres on gravel and the slamming of a car door. Holly jumped up and ran towards the house.

'Daddy! Aunty Helen's here.'

TEN

SOMEHOW I NEEDED to prepare myself. I tried to merge the two images I had of Sam together to form a new one – my memory of the last time I'd seen him, taking a curtain call at the end of the school play, and the photo on Sylvia's mantelpiece, his curls cut to blend in with his receding hairline. Forcing two pictures together to make one. Like putting the lion into the cage at the opticians.

Here he was – neither of those images, and both. But I'd forgotten the third element – movement and sound; in memory and in a photograph everything is still and silent.

This new Sam dropped the carrier bags he was holding and laughed. 'Little Helen! The quiet water spy. You've not changed an iota.' He clasped me in a brotherly bear hug, not that Michael ever indulged in anything so brotherly. 'Well, only for the better. A few wisps of silver amongst the gold, but just as sweet and lovely.'

'Hello Sam,' I said, and wriggled away from the smell of cigarettes.

'And the voice of an angel. How could I forget your seductive voice?'

'Stop it, Samuel. You're embarrassing her.' Vicky came into the hallway with an armful of toys. 'He's getting worse with age … But it's true, you do have a very sexy voice,' she added in a whisper. 'You must know that, don't you?'

Sam took off his gloves and dropped them onto a side table. As he hung up his coat I saw how dark hair grew thick on his forearms; he'd been only eighteen when I last saw him properly, a skinny, smooth-skinned boy, about to set off for university.

I pressed down my dress where he had rumpled it. Teachers always praised my 'speaking voice' and I was often asked to read in class. Ann once told me I spoke like a lady, whatever that meant. At school mine and Sam's friendship had been built on jokes and harmless teasing, but now it was heavy-handed. He was making fun of me.

Vicky looked pointedly at him and Sam frowned. 'Helen. I'm sorry about your mother.' His voice was serious and he hugged me again. 'So young. How are you coping?'

'Everyone's been very kind. It's getting easier. At least I have work to go to. Routine.'

He took a step back still looking at me. 'Vic says you're working at the primary school? We always thought you'd have a career down in London, or Paris, didn't we, Vic? You studied French, didn't you?'

'I didn't go to university in the end. Mum needed me

here.'

He looked at Vicky for confirmation and she mumbled something I didn't catch. 'Well, it's great to see you. To see a familiar face. It's disconcerting coming back here. Especially now my parents are in France. No childhood home to come back to. Bizarre.'

Sam took a bunch of lilies from one of the shopping bags. 'For my beautiful wife and God bless all who sail in her.' Then he bent to kiss her on the lips. Some people would call it sweet, but it went on far too long for comfort, and might have developed into something more, as Sam's hand was beginning to slide under Vicky's blouse, had they not been interrupted by Holly jumping onto his back.

'And how are all my pretty ones?'

'Come on, Daddy!'

Sam was dragged off to the garden, and I followed Vicky back into the large kitchen-dining room that overlooked it.

She breathed in the scent of the lilies before she dropped them into a vase. 'Gorgeous . . . but yours are the best, Helen. I *love* roses.' Then she slid my rosé into a wine fridge and poured three glasses of red from a bottle standing open on the dresser. 'Let's save your wine for a hot day in the summer. If we get summer this far north!'

'Holdersea's only marginally further north than Manchester,' She was always one for exaggeration. The wine was heavy and rich. 'Last year was warm.'

'Where did you go?'

'Just here. At home.'

'So lucky! We had to spend the *whole* summer in France. Sam insisted on the full six weeks. I was dying of boredom by the time I got back. One week with his parents nearly killed me. They never stop talking!' She tipped pasta into a pan on the stove, took a mouthful of wine then poured salad leaves into a bowl. 'Going to the US in the camper van was much more fun!'

'Can I help?'

'No, love. All sorted. But you could put these on the table.' She handed me a jug of cutlery and a basket of bread.

'Smells delicious.'

'A recipe I picked up from a girlfriend. We were in *Emmerdale* together.'

I set the knives and forks out as Mum and I used to every week for Sunday lunch and at Christmas. How many years had it been since I'd set the table for more than two?

'Have you been to Italy, Helen?'

'I've not been abroad very often.'

'You must. France is OK, but Italy. *Bellisima!* Guaranteed sun. And the food of course.'

Vicky started a long story about travelling around Europe with the children. Once I'd finished the table I stood with my wine listening while she talked. To be honest, all she needed were a few nods in the right places. Speaking came as easily to her as silence did to me. I found my attention wandering. Beyond another display of crystal animals on a low window, Sam was in the garden chasing the children. What had Vicky been saying about him slowing down, getting middle aged? He was paunchy around the middle but still looked athletic and for a heavy smoker he could run. After a few minutes Holly was in tears, so he found a ball and started a frenetic game of football which culminated in Tom falling into a patch of nettles. How did people with children cope with so much noise and movement? It was exhausting watching them.

'So after that we could hardly go back, could we?' Vicky was waiting for a response. She misinterpreted my silence as disapproval. 'But we never did it again, Helen. We wouldn't risk it, not with the children.' She drained the pasta. 'This year I've persuaded Sam that Italy's the place to go.' She dived over to a brass dinner gong hanging on the wall and everyone was summoned for lunch. It was nearly two o'clock. I was starving.

SOON WE WERE sitting at the dining table eating pasta with a spicy, tomato sauce. The salad was all kinds of leaves I didn't recognise, but a few looked suspiciously like the dandelion leaves in the back garden. I didn't allow myself to think about the bucket of snails.

'Spaghetti *alla puttanesca.*' Sam made to grope at Vicky as she bent to cut up Tom's food. 'It means whore's pasta. My wife's favourite.'

'For God's sake, Sam! Tom. Eat your lunch. Nettles don't hurt that much.'

Sam laughed, but there was a slight pause, a hair's breadth of awkwardness. This was something domestic and private that I didn't understand. Tom continued to grumble to his sister, and when she ignored him he turned to me and whispered, 'I fell in the nettles. It's really sore.'

'Nettles sting a lot, don't they?' I said quietly.

'Helen's been looking after the kids while I cooked. While you were doing all your manly hunting and gathering. Before you decided to injure everyone ... It's only a little sting, Tom. You're fine.'

'It's hurting, Mummy.'

'You must be used to it, Helen. Working in a school.' Sam filled my wine glass. 'Okay Tom I'll find the Calamine for you.' He left the table and searched in a drawer.

'I'm more an admin person. Paper not people. I avoid the children!' I meant this as a joke but Vicky took me seriously.

'But you're obviously a natural with kids. Holly was all over you, Helen. You'd make a great mum.'

Sam smoothed cream over the bumpy white spots on Tom's knees. 'They always go for the pretty ones,' he added and winked.

It was a long time since a man had paid me a compliment. I blushed like a teenager.

'Can I grow my hair like Aunty Helen, Mum?' Holly whispered, but Vicky shushed her.

'He's right, Helen. You were always gorgeous but now there's something else.'

'Putting on weight I think it's called!' I said, trying to laugh it off.

'No, you used to be too skinny.' She smiled and leaned over to stroke my arm.

'I agree. A touch more womanly but to me entirely beautiful.'

'Samuel, you always go too far! It's boring. Helen didn't come here to be leered at.'

After such a dearth of male company, apart from ectomorphic primary teachers and hairy overweight men at the pool, I wasn't used to being the focus of attention. If this went on much longer I'd have to leave.

'Don't worry, Helen. I've always gone for the Rubenesque,' Sam said, and pinched Vicky's bottom as she stood to clear the plates.

She gave him one of those married looks she was so good at and stacked the plates then brought in the pudding. After all the salt and spice of the first course I was relieved to see it was a fruit salad.

'I hope there are going to be strawberries, my sweet,' Sam looked up at Vicky.

Vicky kissed the top of his head. 'Perhaps later, mon amour.' Then she rolled her eyes at me.

'What, no figs, darling?' Sam poked his spoon into his dish of fruit.

'Wrong season, love.'

'And I was going to quote what D.H. Lawrence said about–'

'You're always going to quote *someone*!'

Then they laughed and both looked at me, eyebrows raised. I was still expected to sit in the audience and applaud. I smiled. It didn't warrant a laugh.

'My knee's hurting, Daddy.' Tom held his knee up.

'Poor old Tom. Why don't you go off and play...' Sam said. 'Nettles are worse when you're a kid. I remember–'

'Remember our den, Helen?' Vicky said. 'Our gang? The smell of nettles always reminds me.'

'Sort of.'

'Course you do! With Smelly-Ann. We used to sting her with nettles if she didn't buy us sweets.'

'That's ridiculous!' I protested. 'I'd never ...'

'It's true. We both did. Our spying game. You re-member!'

'Helen Farrish. Miss Goody Two Shoes! I don't believe it. And poor Smelly-Ann. God I'd forgotten all about her!'

Why do people like raking up the past? All that stuff is part of childhood and should stay there. It wasn't that funny the first time round. But I made an attempt to join in with the laughter. 'I think she's forgiven us! We're still good friends. Keep in touch by email.'

'Well I suppose that avoids any unfortunate odours!' Sam finished off another glass of wine. Vicky nudged him. 'Sorry. Going too far again.'

ONCE THE MEAL was over and the children ran away to play, Sam pushed his chair back and yawned. 'I need to get some air.'

Time to escape to the comfort of my own house, and a few hours to think it all over. I sensed I was being dismissed too. Was this my cue to go?

'Coffee, Helen?' Vicky smiled at me.

'Perhaps she's a tea drinker. *The cup that cheers but. . .* 'Another of his quotations.

'Coffee would be lovely,' I said.

'Go and make a pot of each, Sam. You know you hate coffee after a meal.'

'And a quick ciggie while the kettle's boiling.'

Vicky tutted then, while Sam clanked about in the kitchen, she led me to another small sitting room overlooking the garden so she could keep an eye on the children.

'He can't help showing off. Once he gets used to you he'll calm down.'

She yawned and kicked off her shoes then dragged her legs up onto the sofa as if they were weighing her down, 'That's why I love him, I suppose.'

Sam brought in two espressos and a large cabbage-shaped teapot – one of Vicky's ceramic creations I presumed.

She put her feet on Sam's lap.

He added two spoons of sugar and stirred his tea noisily. 'She doesn't think I'm sweet enough,' he said to me, then started to massage her feet.

After half an hour Vicky said she'd sort out the kitchen if I didn't mind and Sam claimed he had marking to do. This was my cue to go. As I left I heard the sound of a guitar. It sounded like the twenty-third psalm. *The quiet waters by . . .*

ELEVEN

In bed, after a pleasantly solitary scrambled egg on toast, I thought how lucky I was: rain beating against the window and here I was tucked, snug as a bug in my bed. We were all adults now, childhood and the past put aside. We *could* start again from where we'd left off all those years ago. We could all be friends again. In my next email to Ann I'd let her know I was in touch with Vicky again.

I pictured Sam smoothing lotion onto Tom's knees. Vicky was right: to extract confessions from our enemies, our gang did use nettles. They were our most important weapon of torture. We met by the muddy stream, in a dip where the path had fallen away and nettles had grown up to hide it. On hot afternoons their scent was pungent.

It was the day we found the old mattress that we let Smelly-Ann play, but only after she borrowed money from her mum's purse to buy sweets for us.

'Let's use it to interrogate prisoners,' Vicky said. 'But, until we catch any, Smelly-Ann has to be the enemy.'

She always had bruises you could only see when she took off her clothes. She was used to getting hurt. Well she didn't say no.

First we shone the torch in her eyes so she couldn't see properly. Then, if you forgot your gloves, you had to hold the nettles tight so they didn't sting your own hand and say, 'Tell me everything you know, or else we'll have to make you talk.'

Smelly-Ann was good at being a prisoner. We only had to sting her for a few minutes until she confessed; she told us all sorts of things in her whispery voice.

'Before Dad had to go away, I threw up in the middle of the night and went to tell Mum and guess what … I saw them *doing it*.' Her voice was hardly louder than the stream in the background. 'Dad was grunting like an animal and Mum was moaning. It was horrible.'

She thought her Dad was trying to kill her Mum so she started crying and then they stopped and her Mum came to wipe up the sick.

'That's disgusting. Mum gets me a bucket or I run to the bathroom.' I said. 'I've never thrown up in my bed.'

'I've never even been sick,' said Vicky.

'I don't believe you,' I said.

'It's someone else's turn,' murmured Smelly-Ann.

'Give Ann your gloves.'

'I don't want to,' I said.

'But it's not fair if Smelly-Ann always has to be the prisoner. And she brought the sweets,' said Vicky. 'It's *your* turn.'

I didn't have any stories like Smelly-Ann. So they had to torture me. It hurt my arms and legs and I nearly cried.

Vicky said, 'Let's take her pants off. There's no boys here... Stop fussing, Helen. You're supposed to be fearless.'

They stung me all over my bottom and it really hurt. But then there was a nice tingly tickly feeling just between my legs. So I was brave. I didn't tell them a single thing.

At home, Mum said, 'What's that on your arms? And it's on your legs too.'

I was about to say 'I fell in some nettles.' But I was crying so much the words that came out were: 'Smelly-Ann pushed me and she stole money from her mum's purse to buy sweets. And she says bad things. And she makes me do things I don't want to.'

I cried so much Mum hugged me and stroked my back until I stopped, then she went to the bathroom for the Calamine lotion I had for chicken pox. I remember it so well because it wasn't like her to hug me; we weren't that sort of family. Mum took cotton wool and dipped it into the pink lotion then dabbed it on my arms and legs. She even made me hot chocolate and I was allowed to have it in bed. When some spilled on my carpet all she did was smile and say, 'Never mind, love,' before she got a bucket of soapy water then soaked it so much there was a patch of carpet that was always lighter than the rest because it was so clean. Later, when she kissed me goodnight and switched the light off, I put more Calamine lotion on my bottom and between my legs because it was still stinging; I had to pat it on until I got that tingly feeling again. After that, whenever we played spies I said I didn't mind being the prisoner. I had to take my pants off and let Vicky sting me down there. I was the bravest spy of all of us. They couldn't make me confess.

It's funny what you remember about childhood games.

TWELVE

WHEN I INVITED them back, Vicky took one look at Mum's collection of Royal Doulton figurines and laughed. 'It would be easier at our place, Helen! I'll ring you when the decorators have gone.' To be honest she was right. After decades of keeping the figurines clean and undamaged, I didn't want to spend the morning slaving away in the kitchen, then all afternoon on tenterhooks waiting for the crash of china. So for the next few weeks, while their house was being painted, I didn't see much of the Taylors.

At choir, Julia made sure Vicky and Sam were the focus of our conversation. As a neighbour, albeit one twenty houses away and on the other side of the street, she felt she had precedence. But I was the one who'd known Vicky all my life. Julia had mixed with the God squad, Ann and I called them Charlie's Angels, whose pleasures lay in Girl Guides, jumble sales and Sunday school. Singing in the church choir had been the height of Julia's ambition. That and seducing the married Sunday school teacher. Before sixth form she went away for a few weeks and came back pale and hesitant. There were rumours of a baby but it was never confirmed. And that was after we'd been forced to watch a graphic childbirth film – didn't she learn anything? It certainly put me off the whole business. After that she went straight into working a series of clerical jobs and spent her free time arranging the church flowers or embroidering hassocks. *The wages of sin* etc.

'At one point I thought I might become a nun,' she told me when she joined the Choral Society and we got friendly. 'Then I met James and realised life's too short to spend it developing housemaid's knee!'

VICKY FINALLY CALLED me. 'We're still in a mess. But you've got to come … a few friends and neighbours. Julia's coming. Don't get dressed up.'

An invitation to lunch and now a party.

Julia's daughter, Amy, was already there keeping Holly entertained so on my way I called for Julia. I didn't want to go on my own again.

'They had a team working round the clock!' Julia said as we walked in. 'When Vicky invited me round last week you couldn't move for men!'

'Well that must have suited you,' I said, smiling.

'Oh, Helen!'

ALL THE FLOCK wallpaper and chintz had been ditched in favour of bland colours and striped blinds. Behind the scented candles and flowers was a lingering smell of new paint.

'But there's pink in our bedroom.' Vicky laughed. 'I'm not giving in completely to his tedious minimalism. Mum's going to help me sort out some curtains, aren't you?'

'I know a nice little shop in Hull. He's done me some lovely pelmets,' Sylvia said.

Sam was pouring wine, surrounded by a crowd of women. Julia pushed her way through and put her arm through his.

'Julia! I was just thinking about you.'

'Something nice I hope?'

'What will you have?'

'Whatever you'd like to get me, Sam.'

'Well how about . . .' he whispered in her ear.

Julia really shouldn't smile so broadly. Those teeth. She raised an eyebrow and extricated herself; as she walked past me she said loudly, 'Where's Ed? I must ask him about my computer. I'm sure it's dying.'

'And here's my little water spy, quietly observing us all! Looking stunning as usual.'

'Jeans really suit you, Helen.' Vicky appeared in a fuchsia-pink dress and heels, her hair pulled into a close-fitting blond bob. 'I'm so glad you didn't bother getting smart.' She adjusted a strap on her dress. 'It's the weekend. We all need to relax.' She picked up a bowl of crisps and left us.

'Refill, Helen?'

I'd drunk my wine quickly, nervously.

'Thanks, Sam. The house looks ...'

But he was only half listening so I walked to the buffet table where Ed was chomping on a limp celery stalk. He raised the celery in greeting. In the dimmed lights and candles he didn't honestly look too bad. Almost hand-some.

'Eddie! You've got to come to my rescue!' Julia broke between us. 'Something's happened to my laptop. I've been faffing around with it all day but I've no idea. Do you think you could . . .?'

'Aye, right, Julia. Tell me what's up and I'll see what I can do?'

He stuffed the rest of the celery in his mouth and grabbed a fistful of salted nuts; as I moved over to speak to Sylvia, he was beginning to drone on about memory and gigabytes in a way that took me back to his room over the chip shop. The smell of roll ups and unwashed socks, long stories about computers. I used to feel I was being tangled up in leads and wires, in a web of incomprehen-sion. I knew he would be spraying nuts all over Julia in his enthusiasm. His bed always seemed to be full of crumbs. She was welcome to him.

Sylvia rambled on for half an hour at least while, over her shoulder, I could see Sam pouring lemonade for the children.

'Aunty Helen, you're here! … Aunty Julia said you were coming!' Holly hugged me. 'Come and see my bedroom. Do you like my dress? It's real silk. Amy's come for a sleepover.'

Her hair smelled of shampoo and was in two fat, shiny plaits parted down the middle by a clear white line. I thought of Mum, how her hair eventually became so thin her scalp showed through pink and tight all over her head.

Tom edged towards me. 'They're being mean to me.'

The two girls laughed. 'Stop being a baby, Tom. Come and see our new bedroom, Aunty Helen.'

'If you don't mind, Helen?' Vicky smiled encouragingly. 'I know how good you are with kids.'

As I followed the children upstairs, the sound of the party gradually faded until Tom slammed the bedroom door shut, and it was gone.

'This is my bed. That's hers.' Tom said, jumping on his bed. 'I. Don't. Like. Pink. But. She. Does.'

There was something of Vicky in the predominance of pink on Holly's side of the room, but the background smell of paint made it less stifling. I was expected to admire every item in Tom's collection of toy trains and books, but to be honest it was a relief: conversations with children are so much easier than having to make small talk to adults.

From downstairs I thought I recognised Julia's horsey bray. But it was distant. Outside the wind had got up and between the branches of the trees there were glimpses of the moon through scudding clouds. Away from all the chattering adults, it was peaceful.

'How about a story?' I said, and sat on the bed.

'A baby one first, then one for me and Amy.'

'I'm not a baby. I'm six.'

'Okay then. A little kid.' Holly was in a conciliatory mood.

Tom started yawning and soon fell asleep. I turned out his light and lay on the bed with the two girls and began to read. I heard laughter and voices and the front door closing. After about half an hour, the girls were both asleep too and I felt my own eyes closing; I let the book drop to the floor and gave in. No one would miss me. I wasn't planning to sleep, just rest for a while before going back down to face the party.

Then I heard the door open.

'Here she is.'

'Sleeping Beauty! Perhaps I should wake her with a kiss, Vic.'

'Don't be daft!'

'But she looks as if she's lying there waiting.'

They were whispering loudly. Drunk. I tried to regulate my breathing, pretending to be asleep.

'Control yourself, Sam Taylor… Mind you she does look gorgeous. I think I'll…'

Vicky planted a kiss sticky with Bacardi and coke on my forehead then I could hear them moving around putting toys away and tidying up. There was no sound from downstairs.

'Did you say she was seeing someone?'

'Yes, I told you.'

'Someone we were at school with?'

'Were you even listening? Ed. The one that Julia–'

'Not the anorak?'

'He's okay. Useful if you need help with your laptop!'

'Julia's fucking desperate. But Helen could do better than that.'

'Anyone in mind, Mr Taylor?'

'I have a few ideas.'

'Oh yes? … Come over here and tell me then.'

I recognised that tone. I knew exactly what it meant. I decided to make an entry so moved a little and sighed.

Someone sat on the bed. 'Helen, are you awake? You fell asleep, love! Everyone's gone.'

I yawned and opened my eyes. Vicky was looking at me with an odd smile on her face. As I sat up and tidied my clothes, Sam busied himself making sure the children were covered up.

'I'm sorry …I didn't mean to–'

'No need to apologise. Thank you! I knew you were good with kids.' Vicky yawned too then kissed my cheek. 'I think it's bed time. Julia said to tell you Ed was going to walk her home. I'll ring you a cab. I'm shattered.'

THEY OCCASIONALLY ASKED me to babysit. When I considered all the times Sylvia had looked after Mum so I could go to choir or to see Ed, it only seemed fair. And to tell you the truth I started to enjoy it.

One Saturday we did some baking for Tom's birthday. It wasn't difficult. I suppose Vicky was right, in a sense I was used to children. And I was certainly used to baking. I enjoyed passing on my skills. While we rolled out dough and cut it into shapes, Tom asked me questions about life and death, and Holly told me interesting snippets about her family that her parents probably never intended me to hear.

'Aunty Nancy tried once, but she was no good at cooking. Then Dad got cross and spoiled everything.'

'Oh dear. I'm sure Aunty Nancy did her best. She was one of your Mum's friends, wasn't she?'

'Sort of… Look, Mum! Aunty Helen showed us how to make biscuits.'

'Lovely, darling.' Vicky kissed Holly's floury cheek. 'Thank you, Helen. I never get round to baking. You have so much more patience.'

'I enjoy it. Mum and I used to bake every week. On a Friday afternoon.'

'You're such a Little Miss Tidy, Helen. And a delicious plate of biscuits! Even Tom is clean.'

'What are we going to make next time, Aunty Helen?' Holly put her slim arms around my waist and hugged me tight.

'Oh yes, that would be so sweet of you, Helen,' Vicky said and put her arms around me too.

I WAS INVITED for lunch again; Julia feigned a lack of interest and looked down her long nose at me when I mentioned it. By now she was busy with Ed. 'He's sorted out my computer and everything,' she said. 'It's a shame about his flat, but at least he doesn't have to pay for his chips!'

In fact Sunday lunch at the The Laurels became a habit. After a month I was almost one of the family. I really had become Aunty Helen.

So, it came as no surprise when they asked me.

THIRTEEN

'SO MUCH FOR quitting. Look at him. Thinks he's some kind of French intellectual, sitting there in his black polo neck. While we wash the greasy dishes.'

We'd finished lunch and were clearing up. Sam was at the far end of the garden on his favourite bench, cigarette dangling in one hand, stroking the family cat with the other. As if on cue he inhaled, shutting his eyes.

'Sartre?'

'The other one. Camus.'

'Yes. But– '

'The kids hate it when he kisses them. Daddy, you smell like an ashtray. Daddy my teacher says smoking can seriously damage your health? Daddy we don't want you to *die*!'

'Didn't his mother have surgery for . . .?'

Vicky turned from the window to look at me, her face pink.

'He's got the usual replies. Stressful job, nagging wife, useless quotation, artistic licence, blah-di-blah. . . .When I was in *Emmerdale* I never thought I'd be . . .'

I carried on drying the glasses, careful not to press too hard.

'Thinks he's a fucking matinee idol.' She laughed to herself. 'Mum says he's more bone idle.'

'He helps—'

'Oh, when *you're* here he's a superhero!' She banged a pan down on the draining rack. 'I hate the way he always wants to do things *his* way, he always has to be right about everything. I don't mind giving in to him to keep the peace but I wish he wouldn't smoke!'

Sam stubbed his cigarette out in a plant pot and stood up. He gave a mock bow then walked towards the house. For some reason he reminded me of a candle flame. A ridiculous, adolescent idea. The deliberately languorous way he moved, conscious that we were watching him.

'Sometimes I think we should've stayed in Manchester.' Vicky wiped her hands on a towel and sighed. 'I didn't realise how much of a change it was going to be. Nancy told me it wouldn't be straightforward.' She gave me a quick hug then looked directly at me. 'But I'm so glad you're here, Helen. It makes everything better.'

It was good to feel needed, but why did she have tears in her eyes? What did she have to be upset about? She had everything. Other people's relationships are a mystery, aren't they?

'Is something wrong, Vicky?'

She wiped her eyes but didn't answer.

'It takes time to settle in. You know where I am if you …' I started, but Sam flung open the kitchen door.

'Vic, have you asked her yet?'

'I thought we hadn't quite …' She gave him one of her looks then, with the timing of a professional actress, made a quick decision. 'We wondered if you'd like to come on holiday with us, Helen. To Italy. In the summer.'

Foreign food, mosquito bites and plane crashes flashed before me like a carousel of awkward luggage. Not that I'd ever been on a plane.

'I'm not sure what my plans are.'

'Please, love!' Vicky put on a spoiled child voice. 'We'd love you to. Mum's already booked her holiday – I think she's had enough of looking after these two!'

'And you're practically one of the family now,' Sam added.

'Is Aunty Helen coming with us?' Tom was sitting in a corner playing with Lego. 'Then Mummy won't get so cross with Daddy.'

Everyone laughed.

'I'll have to think about it. I'd love to of course. Thank you. It's a long time since I went abroad but–'

Holly jumped up and put her arms around my waist.

'–You have to come, then we can go up the Leaning Tower. Mum won't go because she's scared of heights.'

'Think of all those rich Italian men waiting for a little

English rose,' Sam put on an Italian accent. 'Sun, sea and–'

'Sam!' Vicky hissed. 'There'll be other families there, Helen. It's a working farm but they've converted some of the buildings. A private pool for each property.'

'Lying around the pool reading. What more would you want?' Sam said. 'Perhaps a single man in possession of a fortune…'

Vicky groaned. 'Do you have to, Sam?'

'Sorry, Helen. It would be great if you could come.

'Think about it, Helen. Please. We'd love you to… but we can't make you.' said Vicky.

NO, THEY CERTAINLY couldn't make me. And I had no intention of going. Being friends was one thing but going abroad was a step too far. Then there were Vicky's comments to consider. Sam liked being the one in charge: directing the school play, organising games or now, as a teacher controlling a class of kids. But he was so charming, so willing to please, I reckoned it was Vicky who liked getting her own way. It's usually stubborn people who complain most about that same quality in others.

***

MY ONLY HOLIDAY abroad had been a horror story of homesickness. Sylvia persuaded Mum to let me go on the school trip to France. All my protestations were taken as an unwillingness to waste money, rather than what it really was – dread. I was so wound up I vomited. I wanted to be adventurous like Vicky, but how could I be when my body let me down, when new things literally made me sick. How could I be like Fanny Price's extrovert cousins, falling in love and being dramatic? It wasn't my fault. Dad saw how anxious I was, but decisions to do with Michael and me were Mum's domain. I had to go. It would improve my French. I was pushed out into the cold. The unfamiliar.

The coach journey from Yorkshire was endless. I sat with a brown paper sick bag on my lap waiting for it all to be over while, across the aisle, I glimpsed Sam with his hand down the front of Vicky's shirt like a ferret. When we finally arrived in Paris it was nothing like I'd imagined. The Seine and the sky were grey and greasy, and the first evening we were served a thin, brown stew Vicky said was horsemeat as she wolfed it down. I hardly ate. Our room, a hot, dingy garret at the top of a hotel, smelled of foreign drains and vegetable soup. It was noisy so I couldn't sleep. The boys discussed French film stars and tried to smoke Gauloises; the girls spent their time using dry shampoo and discussing the boys. To make it worse, my GCSE French was like a mouthful of alphabet bricks. I was terrified of getting it wrong, so I didn't speak. I put my head down and read a translation of *Madame Bovary*.

But, in spite of the bleakness, I remember two small flashes of pleasure which lifted my mood. As we trailed round Notre Dame the sun must have penetrated the heavy layer of cloud at last: for a few seconds light shone through the ancient stained glass creating a vivid patch of red and blue on the grey stone floor.

Later, and more memorably I remember the taste of smoke on my lips.

Exhausted from the heat and dust we were in the Luxembourg Gardens, watching children sail boats on the round pond. Suddenly my eyes were covered and someone – someone who had been smoking – kissed me full on the mouth, twice. When they took their hands away, I was blinded by the sun and all I could see, as the boats were lifted out of the water, was a slow trail of gold drops. It was unexpected, the kiss itself, my first real kiss, but strangely unthreatening. Like the childhood comfort of the lighthouse beam at night searching out dark corners. That evening we sat eating another plateful of stringy meat and I looked around the table trying to work out who it could be. Most of the boys smoked, and so did some of the girls; it could have been anyone. I wanted it to be Sam, I can admit that now, but I suspected it was Vicky. It was just the kind of trick she'd play. As long as they were at other people's expense Vicky loved practical jokes. In the end I decided it must have been both of them. He enjoyed teasing me and they were all over each other. Inseparable and unpredictable.

WHY WOULD I spend a fortnight of my well-earned leave with people who were so impulsive? Summer holidays were for relaxing and enjoying yourself. Now I could do whatever I wanted, that's exactly what I intended to do.

When Dad was still alive, long before our annual trip to the B&B in the Lake District became set in stone, we had family holidays every summer, each one planned and researched and looked forward to. Dad's role was to borrow guidebooks from the library. He loved maps. While Mum watched soaps and Michael played some-where, he would take a map from the bookshelf and spread it out on the kitchen table. I loved the way the brown contour lines tucked inside each other; the tighter the better because that meant they were steep and exciting. We spent hours following tracks and roads, looking for places to visit and laughing at the strangeness of the names – Ecclefechan or Twice Brewed. I loved planning our long hikes without Mum and Michael. At the end of the evening Dad would sigh and close up the map, folding it along the creases, then put it back on the shelf.

'Not long now, pet.' He patted my hand. 'We'll have a good time.'

A small pink-covered rectangle could offer such a

promise of pleasure. The comparison to my own life – spread out, pored over then folded away – was one I tried not to think about over the years with varying degrees of success. All those summers with Mum at the Lakes, drying off in tea shops and hoping for a long enough gap between the showers so we could hurry back to our room.

'Let's go back now, Helen. Please, love. I need to go back… it's not safe here. I don't feel comfortable. Come on, love. Take me back to the room. We can get tea there. We can have a nice sit in the lounge if you really want…'

Those long afternoons when she didn't even want to leave the one room we had to share.

All the time I looked after Mum, my life had remained closed up. Perhaps, as Michael had done all those years ago, it was time to start exploring. I browsed holiday sites online. Beaches, lakes and mountains all full of smiling families and friends. There were very few pictures of people on their own, people looking solitary but happy. If I didn't go to Italy with Vicky and Sam, what would I do? There was no one else I could spend a weekend with, let alone a fortnight. When Vicky phoned I turned down Sunday lunch. I told her I was busy but I would drop round for a glass of wine later in the afternoon. I needed more time to think.

SUNDAY WAS COLD and blustery with driving rain and so

dull I had to put the lights on in the sitting room. The house was silent. They would be tucking in to their roast; I made do with a bowl of reheated soup and bread. But I wasn't hungry.

At six o'clock I was glad to get out. I'd made my mind up. Even if I had to stay in Holdersea for the whole of August I didn't want to go with them. There were so many other things I could do. I was considering driving lessons. I would tell them I was going to take an intensive course over the summer. Then I could travel wherever I wanted.

It was so windy my umbrella was useless and by the time I arrived at The Laurels I was soaked. Now, if I learned to drive and bought myself a little car...

'You're coming with us on holiday, aren't you, Aunty Helen?' Holly said, as soon as she opened the door.

'Oh, Helen you're soaked! . . . Let Aunty Helen take her wet coat off first,' Vicky said. 'Why don't you go and dry off upstairs?'

'But you will, won't you?' Holly said, smiling at me.

As I walked up to the bathroom, I noticed how the photos of Holly and Tom grew younger with each step until, at the top of the stairs there was a photo of only Holly, her body compacted and shrunk, her face puffed out and rounded back into a baby. It was counter intuitive. Surely you'd start with the youngest photos at the foot of the stairs; and as the children grew older, place each new photo higher and higher until you reached the landing? I had the wild idea that if I ran up and down I could make time go forwards and backwards at will.

Outside the bathroom, pairs of shoes were lined up to be cleaned: small red lace-ups scuffed and heavily grass-stained; a pair of well-worn black school shoes with an undulating surface that reflected the owner's feet, and finally Vicky's practically new brown boots.

I lifted up one of the black lace-ups, slotted my hand in and breathed a faint smell of Cherry Blossom shoe polish. It was Sam's job every Sunday, part of their Sunday routine preparing for the week ahead. I'd watched him once while Vicky was bathing Tom. He put his hand just here, rubbed the polish in gently at first with a small brush, then more vigorously with a larger brush and finally brought it to a shine with a duster. 'Good as new!' He smiled then picked up the next pair. 'Yours next, Vic.' My own shoes were at the front door, battered and covered in mud.

SUNDAY EVENINGS. MUM would be ironing, Dad finishing the crossword and half-watching TV in front of the fire.

'Make sure you clean them properly … and put plenty of newspaper down, Helen.'

I had to leave the warmth of steamed shirts and go out

into the lean-to. Even in the summer it was draughty, and there was a mouldy smell from water getting under the lino and lifting it up from the concrete floor. In the winter my hands were soon red with cold.

'Don't leave stuff all over the place!'

'But what about Michael...'

'He's done his already ... and he's out of the bath. Hurry up. I don't want you wasting the immersion... and that Agatha Christie's on in half an hour too. I thought you said you'd watch it with me.'

HERE IN VICKY'S bathroom the air was scented with baby soap, and moist from Tom's recent bath time. A plastic bottle of Matey bubble bath stood on the side of the bath, its lid missing: a sailor without his hat. Around the bath was a smudged blue line and on the towelling mat were traces of damp footprints. I sat on the lid of the toilet and tore off a strip of paper then folded it as small as I could, until I couldn't fold it any more. I don't know why but I was crying fat, hot tears like Tom's when he'd been told he couldn't have any more sweets. The hum of their voices came up through the floor of the bathroom, like listening to the radio. If I lay down and curled up on the bathmat, I wondered how long would it take for them to notice I wasn't there. How long until they came to find me? I could close my eyes and lie down.

It only lasted a couple of minutes. Not long. I flushed the paper away and rummaged in a pile of wet plastic toys to find the lid of the bubble bath, then screwed it on firmly, turning the sailor to face the window.

I went downstairs and said yes.

FOURTEEN

NO TIMETABLES, NO urgency, no change in the weather. I hadn't expected such intense heat, the relentless blue sky or the sameness of every day. Apart from buying food and cooking, or remembering to put on sunscreen during the day and insect-repellent at night, there was nothing I needed to do. For a couple of days I coped with the lack of structure, but then the days started to blur: mornings by the pool, long siestas and beers in the afternoon, wine and spirits late into the night. It was my first holiday without Mum. I needed to have something to do.

At first I hunted for the shade and avoided the pool surrounded by a mist of silvery olive trees and shrubs, glistening like a turquoise jewel. Holly and Tom spent every morning there until Vicky forced them inside in the heat of the day. I soon slipped naturally into the role of helping out. Vicky constantly told me how grateful she was 'So good to have you here, Helen.' But after all the conversations we'd had leading up to the holiday, all the anticipation of being abroad, she wasn't as relaxed as I'd expected but increasingly bad-tempered and jumpy.

At first I put it down to insect bites and her tendency to overreact.

'I must be allergic. They're agony.' Vicky looked across the lunch table and flapped away a scrabble of flies buzzing over a plate of fanned-out salami that was beginning to turn brown and glisten with oil. She scratched at her ankle making a dry, rasping sound with her long fingernails. The couple of red pinpricks above her sandal strap were keeping her awake all night with intolerable itching she claimed. And Sam was making it worse.

'You don't have a husband who snores all night.'

'Have you taken an antihistamine?' I asked. 'I've got some– '

'If she takes anything else she'll explode.' Sam muttered.

'Just wait till you're suffering.' Vicky gave him a Medusa stare.

'Honestly, you'd think she'd been bitten by a snake,' he said.

I tried not to laugh but was unsuccessful and snorted uncontrollably. 'Let me find you some cream, Vicky.' I went up to my room.

The dynamics were changing. Sam and I had fallen easily into a spirit of light banter at Vicky's expense and it was almost like the old days when we spent hours on the school field sparking off each other. The first evening, when Sam opened beers for the three of us, he'd clinked his bottle with mine: 'To my old new best friend.' Vicky had raised an eyebrow. 'Don't listen to him, love. He's such a flirt.'

He was only trying to be amusing. She was married to him but she didn't own him; we could still be friends.

Upstairs I switched on the air conditioning before rummaging in my bag for sting relief. From Tom and Holly's room next door came the muffled sounds of a Disney animation.

As I looked through the gap in the shutters, I could see Vicky and Sam sitting at the table. He leaned over to whisper in her ear and Vicky did something I'd never seen her do – she simpered and looked almost girlish or coquettish, then she put her hand up to ruffle his hair and kissed him on the end of his nose. I drew back instinctively then grasped the tube of cream and ran back down, scuffling my feet noisily on the gravel path to interrupt them.

'Oh, Helen, what a star! Always so calm and looking after us all. I didn't even notice you'd gone!'

Vicky unscrewed the cap from the cream, squeezed out a blob onto the end of her finger and placed her foot on Sam's thigh, then she circled the ointment into her ankle with the tip of her finger, gazing up at him. I didn't want to watch, but seeing him respond was fascinating. He leaned towards her and started to slide his hand along her leg. Perhaps this was what was making her so bad-tempered. I tended not to think about all that physical stuff. I thought about Ed's bitten nails. That smell of fried fish and musty laundry. Some of us had managed to get through life on very slim pickings in that department.

Vicky, so it now seemed to me, was at the other end of the scale.

'So much better and . . .' Vicky glanced at her mobile. 'Three already. Time for our siesta.'

Her precious siesta. From the beginning of the holiday she laid claim to time like an indisputable right. While she disappeared upstairs, Sam kept an eye on the children and came into the shade for a wallow in the past with me. But that afternoon the mood of the day had changed. They scraped back their chairs on the hot stone of the terrace and almost skipped upstairs like a pair of naughty children.

In any friendship there is a tendency for three to split into two plus one. That afternoon it was my turn to be the outsider.

What were their real motives for including me in their holiday? What if Vicky had organised the whole thing to have live-in childcare? I was growing fond of the children, but I didn't want to be dumped with, like an unpaid nanny. I'm sure it wasn't the sort of scheming Sam would indulge in, he was much more straightfor-ward. I didn't want to spend my precious holiday looking after their children so they could go and ... enjoy themselves. I could feel pressure building up, my jaw tensing and my breathing shallow and quick. I cleared the table and washed up, then went outside to find a bench in the sun to read. Trying to calm myself.

AFTER THEIR LONG siesta that day the beers started earlier. Then wine. By the time we'd eaten, and were standing on the terrace enjoying the remaining heat as the sun went down, all of us were slightly drunk.

Vicky hugged me. 'What a marvellous Aunty, you are. Isn't she, kids?'

'And she's not got orange peel skin like you.' Holly giggled.

Vicky tickled her. 'Cheeky girl! All that money I spend on anti-cellulite cream–'

'But Mummy is so cuddly.' Sam grabbed her, catching a handful of her waist. 'Mmm, let's have an early night, my little fleshpot.'

'I think you should,' Vicky said, turning towards me for safety. She hugged me.

Sam winked at me, and I was back there on the school coach again – a captive audience for their adolescent groping. I needed to be on my own.

Vicky mouthed, *It's true what they say about sex and alcohol.* Then yawned and declared, 'Anyway, I'm tired.'

And went to put the children to bed. I turned to go too but Sam stopped me.

'Nightcap, Helen? More of that horrendous lemon thing you seem to like so much.'

'It's like sherbert lemons,' I giggled. 'Or kayli'

'What?' He poured the liqueur into two glasses and dropped in some ice.

'Kayli. We used to buy on our way home from school? Fizzy sugar in a paper bag – you had to lick your finger and dip it in.'

'Sounds disgusting. Must've been you and Vic.'

Vicky used to make me dip my fingers in then she'd suck each one of them until they dripped with her saliva. I refused to do it to her.

WE SAT ON the terrace. The air was cooling and across the valley, lights flickered from other houses and streets on the wooded hillsides. The candles were still burning, and a buzz of hornets droned around them, then disappeared over the wall to their nest. Snatches of talk and laughter came from other villas on the estate, and flurries of Italian from the village further up the hillside. Above us stretched the Milky Way. In the background the constant chitter of crickets grew to fill the night.

'Shooting star!' Sam pointed.

'Missed it.'

'Keep looking. There'll be more.'

'How do you know?'

'It's the Perseids meteor shower. Every August.'

'I've never seen one…oh!' Out of the corner of my eye there was a streak of light. 'Was that one? … And another!'

In my excitement I spilled my drink. 'Michael and I used to make wishes on stars.'

'Have they come true?'

I laughed. 'Can't remember…I don't think so.'

He picked up his guitar and started humming *When you wish upon a star* but soon stopped. We sat without speaking. I looked up at the stars. The air trembled. Cool breezes brought the scent of dried grass from the garden surrounding the terrace. There was stillness, then another burst of laughter from the Italians.

Suddenly everything seemed to come into focus. It was so simple.

'If everyone could look up at all these stars for a while and *think*,' I said, 'we'd all be happier.'

'How?'

'So many people give in to their emotions and end up making the wrong decisions.' It must've been the drink that made me philosophical.

I sensed him smiling in the dark. 'Wise words from the Quiet Water Spy.'

'Well … adapted a little from Jane Austen.'

He laughed. 'Trouble is we're human, not machines. We value logic but we're not great at following it. Don't tell me you've never been led by your emotions?'

'I don't think I have particularly strong feelings about anything.'

'Or maybe you've never had the opportunity to?'

Mum's empty room. Dust in the air. My new life ready to start. 'Perhaps. But mostly I've done what I thought I had to do ...' And that was true. 'Like Fanny Price.'

'Who?'

'You know – *Mansfield Park*. Austen. My favourite.'

'Her! The one who sits and never joins in? Not much of a role model. Too fucking passive. Quietly condemning everyone.'

'Only the ones who let their emotions make them do stupid things!'

'Well, I guess I should read it again – as an English teacher.' He yawned. 'Can't recommend all that emotional stuff anyway. Exhausting. Vic and I came back to Holdersea to escape it.'

'Oh?'

'Water under the bridge.'

'Ah.'

So something had made them come back to Holdersea. It wasn't just the fresh air and fun. Maybe Vicky's tour rules? But here on holiday nothing mattered. I didn't need to know.

We sat watching the sky until I started to shiver.

'Cold?' Sam reached out in the dark and put his arm around me. 'Time for bed. Enough star-gazing for a first session. I was supposed to be having an early night!'

He helped me up and yawning and swaying gently, led the way back across the terrace to the villa. At the entrance he stopped and bent to kiss me 'Good night, little Helen.'

In the harsh light of the house we were both momentarily blinded, well I put it down to that or the loosening effect of alcohol, and he kissed me on the mouth.

'Sorry. But very nice. Night night.'

On the way to my own room I stood outside their door listening to the sounds of water flushing and the creak of floor boards, the murmur of their voices. I didn't want to know, but as I undressed, I held my breath to hear any hints of their 'early night'. It wasn't until I was in bed that the stentorian snoring of a drunk middle-aged man began to echo through the villa. A perfect evening. I'd found, or re-found, someone I could talk to. About real things. About books, the things that mattered. For a little while I had Sam to myself. That was enough. I fell asleep thinking about Fanny Price waiting so long for her cousin Edmund to realise he loved her. Good things come to those who wait: look at Penelope waiting faithfully for twenty years for Odysseus to return.

FIFTEEN

IN YORKSHIRE YOU don't get many chances to sunbathe, so I took advantage of every opportunity to build up a tan. I needed to show Irene in the office what a good holiday I'd had. As I walked out into the garden the next morning, the air was already bursting with heat and heady with lavender. No splashing from the pool so the children were still in bed, and the cicadas were silent; once the temperature rose they would start their racket then no one would have any peace. I found a place to spread out a rug near an olive tree. *Make sure you keep the sun off your head* Mum's voice always reminded me, after that day.

It was the same summer they turned off the lighthouse. I spent a long afternoon on the beach building a sandcastle with a moat, and pieces of carnelian and shells for decoration. There was a sea breeze to keep me cool. Dad had been in the lea of the windbreak reading his paper and doing the crossword with his sun hat on. Michael must have been at home with Mum. It was one of my happiest times. Just Dad and me. Until I went home for my bath when in the shock of the water, my back and shoulders were raw and red and suddenly I felt as sick as a dog.

Outside Michael and his friends were still playing. I could hear the rhythmic bump of a football against a wall, the rise and fall of their voices. But I lay in a darkened room sipping water. Dad, who'd fallen asleep on the beach, offered to read me a story but I couldn't even bear the sound of his voice. Poor Dad – Mum was shouting at him:

'You know sunstroke can be a killer!'

'She can sleep it off and–'

'Just like you did!'

'When she wakes up she'll be as good as new. Don't worry so much, Elizabeth.'

'*If* she wakes up …'

I was hot and suffocating, my heart beating wildly. The room swam in front of me as if I was wading out into the sea. I dreamed Vicky was in the room with me, smelling of juicy fruit chewing gum. In my dream, she lay down on the bed next to me, so close her skin was burning into mine, and slowly her long hair wrapped itself around me like seaweed, pulling me down under the water.

AFTER THAT I was wary of the sun. But now, here on this holiday I challenged it. I didn't have to stay in the shade. I didn't have to be like Mum. I could do what I wanted. I took off my dress and lay down in my newly-bought *tankini*. A bikini was going too far I'd said when the assistant offered me a selection of viciously coloured scraps of fabric that would have left little to the imagination.

'That one's perfect.'

I'd already been awake for a couple of hours, and my head felt as if it was filling with cotton wool. I was falling into a half sleep where you let go completely but are still conscious of all the sounds and smells around you: the hum of the pool's filtering system, bees in the wild mint. Lying on the ground, my head in the shade and my body in full sun, I was like a child, or a small animal. Probably a cat. I was more like a cat with the will for my own pleasure. I was a cat stretching out in the sun and Vicky was rubbing sun cream on my shoulders and stroking her warm hand down my back.

Something woke me. Not a noise or a smell. More a sense that the air had changed. I was lying on my front and there was someone on the blanket next to me.

'Miss Farrish, what are you doing?' His voice was so close I jumped. 'You are going to boil like a lobster.'

It was as if I'd conjured him up.

'Let me put sun cream on your back?'

'I've done it, thanks.'

'I'm sure you could do with more.'

'No thanks, Sam.'

Our evening of stargazing had been perfect; now he was annoying. I preferred the other Sam. But would his hands be smooth or rough. They'd certainly be warm, and the cream would be soothing. No. I wouldn't think about it.

'Sure?' His voice was closer now, gentle. 'You look very relaxed lying there, almost as if you were waiting for something… Or perhaps someone?'

I turned over and propped myself up to look at him, smiling. Oval shadows from the leaves of the olive tree speckled his face and pale blue shirt. There was a smell of dried grass that seemed so essentially English it was out of place. When he smiled, something twisted deep in my belly.

He leant back for his cigarettes.

'Ah well, a fag will have to do. Don't worry, I'll keep away. I won't breathe smoke all over you!'

I stared at him. Don't keep away, I wanted to say.

He stood, then lit a cigarette. Smoke rose up dirty white against the sky.

'Keep the sun off your head, Miss Farrish. It's going to be a scorcher!'

He turned slowly and strolled up to the house.

The heat was oppressive, yet I was cold, almost dizzy, as if I was falling into the smell of parched grass, back to long summer days at high school.

WE SPENT LUNCH hours on the school field laughing and chatting, Ann making daisy chains while I lay on the grass, trying to read, but so sleepy I could feel the earth turning slowly underneath me. The air was heavy with cut grass drying in the sun and gradually changing into hay, and high above us wheeling and singing, a lark was outlined against the sky. There were always skylarks. And often, the smouldering smell as a wisp of grey plumed up across the perfect blue – Sam using my glasses to set light to handfuls of dried grass. He could never sit still for long. The kind of day when I thought – yes, this is what summer is supposed to be; and I wanted it to stay like that, for time to stop.

But once – burning pain on my arm.

I turned over and sat up. 'That really hurts, Sam!'

'Ach so, ve have vays of making you talk. Call yourself ze Quiet Water Spy? Not so quiet now, mein liebling!'

'Give me them back!'

'Fight me for them!'

He was laughing. I wasn't.

'All right!'

He pushed me back onto the grass and pinned me down by the shoulders. It was play fighting. But, for the first time there was something else. A new, different kind of feeling. He stopped and looked down at me. He was going to say something. Or do something.

I never found out what it was.

The smell of smouldering was stronger. Smoke billowing.

'Christ!' Sam jumped up and stamped to put out the fire, then off he went cartwheeling in a lazy circle around us. He did a few handstands, just for the old pleasure of it, then laughed and flopped down next to me. His eyes were so blue in the light.

'Helen you're going to burn. Let me shade you.'

He sat up, blocking the sun.

'Thanks.' I was so drowsy I could hardly speak. 'I'm falling asleep.'

There were grass stains on his palms and fresh sweat wafted towards me. He was giving off heat from the exercise and breathing fast. Over his top lip was a growth of fine hairs I'd not noticed before and his lips were so full and pink they were almost girlish. His eyes reflected the clear blue of the sky. If I'd owned a camera this was the look I'd capture: at rest, eyes half shut, thoughtful. He moved slightly and for a moment sunlight dazzled me.

I followed his gaze.

Vicky was lying on the field, sunbathing. She'd pulled her shirt up so high you could see her bare stomach, golden brown. The tiny hairs must have been nearly silver in this light. I caught his eye and for a second he reddened, bit his lower lip and moved away.

Sam rubbed his eyes hard with the back of his hand. 'Got something in my eye. Can't seem to shift it.' He laughed loudly, as if he wanted to be noticed, then glanced over to where she was lying.

Vicky sat up and yawned then straightened her shirt, stood up and stretched. She strolled towards us, smiled briefly showing how white her teeth were, then she walked on, back down the field to the school building, leaving a heady trail of coconut oil.

Sam was trying not to, but his eyes followed her in the too-short skirt as she walked away, shiny blonde ponytail swinging, and out of sight.

It was only a week later that Ann and I saw them on the beach together.

SIXTEEN

I WOKE EARLY as usual, made myself breakfast and went to sit out on the terrace. Before the family got up, I had time to think and didn't need to be on my guard. In this temperature the polyester dresses I'd brought were torture, clinging to my skin as soon as I moved. So I had to wear my new skirt, the silk one with a tasselled fringe that I'd brought for best. It was like wearing a second skin.

As the working day started the sound of farm machinery drifted up the valley and near where I was sitting the leaves of a fig tree rubbed together with a soothing papery sound. Swallows skimmed across the view that opened out to a plain in the far distance. I took out my bookmark where I'd stopped reading last night.

'Will you take us to the pool?' Tom had crept up on bare feet. His hair was tousled and he had clumps of sleep in the corner of his eyes.

'*Please*. You forgot to say please.' Holly nudged him.

'Please, Aunty Helen.'

I put my book face-down at the open page. 'Let me

finish my coffee. Five minutes.' They stood and watched me, their eyes fixed, willing me to finish my drink. None of us spoke. What had I said about time to think? But it was good to be needed and once the caffeine got to work I began to rally.

'Have you got sunscreen? Towels?'

Holly gestured to the kitchen where a pile of coloured towels lay folded on the table. Vicky had never struck me as a person of habit, but in spite of the heat and alcohol she'd established a pattern of daily laundering. She even ironed underwear, which I'd never do. Her domestic arrangements were impressive. All Sam did was lounge around and play his guitar, or tell long stories. At least Vicky *did* something.

I found the factor fifty and my pool bag then, in imitation of Sam, I whispered, 'Race you to the deep end.'

Running from the shade of the terrace into a blast of heat, I regretted it at once and slowed down to a stumbling walk, letting the children win easily. Holly dived in and came up with her dark hair plastered to her head. Tom, who hadn't learned to dive, ran and jumped in, making a splash that dotted my skirt. The new silk one. It was too late to go back and rinse it out. I just hoped the sun wouldn't rot it. Ten thirty and already you could have cut the air with a knife. Soon the cicadas would be revving up and spoiling what peace was left.

'Don't stay in too long. And no fighting, okay?' I tried

to keep the irritation out of my voice. Here I was looking after Sam and Vicky's children again while they were having a lie in. With all that entailed.

I dragged a lounger under the shade of a cerise parasol and attempted to settle back to my book, looking up intermittently to check on the children. There was an undeniable satisfaction in being useful to another human being, no matter how small; and I was certainly well equipped after twenty years of mothering my own mother. Later, when Sam and Vicky showered me with praise and thanks, it would only be made sweeter by being tinged with their guilt at having used me as a childminder. But my heart was rattling about in my chest. I tried to take some deep breaths to calm down again.

There was a great deal of shouting and splashing; I muffled it by focussing on the book I'd picked up in the house: *Under the Tuscan Sun* – some American woman with more money than sense, renovating a villa in Italy and cooking extravagant meals. I was beginning to wish I'd picked up something more challenging when I heard Holly shouting.

Her voice was shrill and urgent. 'I can't get him out!'

I was on my feet before I had time to think.

'He's too heavy! I can't get him out. He won't open his eyes.'

At the shallow end of the pool, his torso white under his tan, his legs green from the reflection of the tiles under the water where a cloud of rusty red flowered, Tom was slumped in his sister's arms like Michelangelo's Pieta.

'Aunty Helen, there's blood all over. Mum's going to be so cross!'

I waded in.

'It's okay, Holly. Let me ...'

I lifted him up, slippery with sun cream and cold as a little fish. He hung in my arms for a moment, then as I struggled back up the steps, he folded his small body into me, clamped his legs around my waist and started to cry. There was a zigzag gash from his hairline diagonally across his forehead. Blood was dripping down my skirt and legs.

Holly joined in loudly with his crying.

'I think he's just dazed.'

She was trying to hold my arm, but I needed both hands to support him, so I angled my body towards her.

'He's fine. Cuts on the head always bleed a lot.' This came from long experience of working in a school. 'He'll have to stay out of the water today.'

It wasn't until we were nearly back at the villa that Sam came running out, barefooted and buttoning his shirt.

'Christ! What have you kids been up to now? You know you're not supposed– '

'Aunty Helen saved Tom.'

She looked up at me, eyes shining.

Sam hugged us all like a father at the end of a movie.

'Thanks, Helen.' He was warm and there was a faint but not unpleasant smell of sweat, of morning breath. 'Let me take him.'

Tom lunged away from me as if I was a diving board, and into his father's arms.

Suddenly I was shaking. I couldn't speak.

'Let's go and have a coffee. Or maybe something a bit stronger!' Sam reached out and wiped the blood off my cheek. 'Thanks, Helen.'

His hand was so warm against my cold face, for a second I thought I was going to cry too.

'Thank God you were there,' he said. 'She'd never have got him out on her own.'

***

USUALLY I WAS the one standing at the back watching. Sam was the practical one. Such a boy scout, even if he'd never been one, jumping in to save animals or birds. It was one of his most attractive qualities. I often went to his house after school, doing our homework together, watching TV or chatting in the garden. His mum didn't mind. Vicky was probably there too sometimes, but she had so many ballet and drama classes, all I can remember is it being Sam and me.

One day we found a baby bird.

'Here. You hold it,' Sam said.

'I can't. I'll drop it.'

'Have a go. Open your hands. You can do it.'

I cupped my hands and he put his above mine, gradually opening them to allow the tiny ball of feathers to drop into mine.

'Now, close them.'

There was no weight, only a tickle of feathers and the cold scratch of its feet against my palms.

'It's so light I can't feel it.'

'You're okay.'

'But what if I...? It's going to...' The bird was trembling and for the first time I was aware of how fine the border was between life and death and how little I knew about it.

'Okay?'

As I stared down at my interlaced fingers, Sam put his hands lightly on my shoulders.

I opened my hands a little. 'I'm worried it won't be able to breathe.'

'We need to get a box then we can take it to the vet. Don't move.'

While he ran inside, I stood in the garden under the tree. By the time I saw him loping back across the wet grass holding a shoebox, my hands were cold; I'd been standing so still that my knees felt locked.

Inside the box was hay from his pet guinea pig and cotton wool.

'Sorry I took so long,' he said cheerfully. 'Let's go over

there.'

He directed me to a picnic table, where burnt down candles in jam jars from the previous summer had gradually filled with rainwater. On warm evenings Sam and his parents had their meals together here, on their own or with friends, long after it was lights out time for me. 'Right, put it in here.'

'It might fly away.'

He laughed, and I did as I was told. The bird looked like a flattened bundle of feathers on top of the cotton wool.

'Is it still …?' There was no movement, and then a feather was lifted by a current of air. 'Yes. Look, its wing …' I must have been holding my breath.

Sam stroked it slowly with one finger then looked at me and shrugged. 'Too late. We'll have to bury it instead. Are you familiar with the funeral service? I know a brilliant poem we can recite: "The lord's my shepherd…"'

***

THIS TIME I'D acted instinctively.

While I took a shower to clean off the blood, and found a bucket to soak my skirt, Sam attended to Tom's wounds and Holly's tears. 'Okay, everyone? Great. Emergency over.'

We were all settled with drinks and biscuits, he picked up his guitar.

'You're a good father, Sam,' I said. 'Good at looking after people.'

'As long as everyone's happy, I'm happy. *The greatest happiness of the greatest number.*'

It was true. He tried to amuse, to please people. To be sociable. I'd always felt safe with Sam. He started playing and humming quietly.

'Still waters run deep. I'm impressed you didn't panic, Helen.'

Thank God you were there.

'Is Vicky alright?' Where was she? I thought most mothers leaped from their beds at the sound of their crying children?

'She's shattered.' He stopped playing. 'As usual.'

The way he spat out the words put a stop to the conversation. Something had happened between them but it was none of my business. I left it at that and started reading again, letting the sound of the guitar drift around on a warm current of coffee and antiseptic. It was only later, when I couldn't get the tune out of my head that the words came back to me. *The first cut is the deepest.*

VICKY STAYED IN bed for most of the day. Sam took food up but came back down with it untouched, and a message to thank me for my heroics. The children weren't allowed to disturb her. No explanation was given.

She was often 'shattered' and things were 'too much' for her, Sam told me as he prepared the children's early tea. We'd started the first beer of the evening when she appeared, her face pale with dark shadows under her eyes. But she was smiling. Immediately she sat on the bench where Holly was teaching her brother how to play a card game.

'How are you, little Tom-Tom? Hmm. Going to have a scar.' She looked sharply at Sam. 'Don't you think he ought to go to the hospital?'

Sam took a swig from his beer. 'If you want to take him, you can, but he's fine. It's tiny. You don't need to worry.'

'A scar's cool, Mummy. Like Harry Potter.'

'There you are, Vic. All is for the best in the best of all possible worlds.'

Vicky kissed Tom then came over to where I was standing.

'How's my heroine?'

I remembered the tiny claws of the bird in my hand, Tom's cold slippery body. 'It was nothing, Vicky.'

She saw my skirt soaking in a bucket. 'Your lovely skirt!'

I thought about asking her for the price of it but it would have been churlish. After all, I was having a free holiday. 'I've had it for ages. Practically worn out.' I said.

'When we go to Florence I'll buy you another one,'

she said. 'In the market they practically give silk away.'

I WAS USED to swimming in a heat-controlled, indoor pool with no possibility of wildlife falling in. No flies, or mosquitoes or snakes but my unexpected immersion made me curious. Out under the deep blue of the sky, the air was scented with lavender, sage and an occasional waft of sweetness as the fig tree dropped its heavy fruit, each oozing with a bead of juice, onto the tiles surrounding the pool. I slid into the warm embrace of the water.

After a swim, Vicky liked to reach up and eat figs straight from the tree. Cupping one in her hand she'd said, 'Sam, darling they're so warm from the sun. Somehow they remind me of you. Now, why should that be?' and giggled like a schoolgirl. I couldn't remember what he'd said or how he'd looked; I'd been far too embarrassed to notice.

After only a few lengths I was out of breath, so I stopped to enjoy the view – a silvery haze of olive trees undulated down to the deeper green of oak and chestnut. In the far distance the plain was dotted with churches and villages. Now that the noise of strimmers had become part of the background of the holiday, it was peaceful. The only other sound was the occasional buzz of an insect and the bubbling of the pool filter. For the first time I didn't mind that I'd given up my daily rituals and freedoms. I'd hardly thought about Yorkshire or work and even Mum's voice was starting to fade away. If she'd been here she would only have spent the whole time complaining about everything.

I was in Italy. And I was free.

'You look like a mermaid!'

How long had he been there?

Sam walked to the edge, coffee in one hand, and looked down to where I was leaning with my arms on the side of the pool.

'Or Ophelia.'

I pushed my wet hair back out of my eyes. 'So, I'm half fish or half dead…Is that supposed to be a compliment?'

He laughed. 'Enjoy your swim.' Then went back up to the terrace. I heard the scraping of one of the sun loungers. He would be finding himself a spot in the shade to read another of the tourist guides to Tuscany that filled the villa, or to do a crossword. With six full weeks to catch up, you would have thought he'd be reading a contemporary novel or revising the old classics. The tang of his cigarette drifted over and spoiled the scent of the plants growing around the pool.

My status as life saver was already forgotten. How like him to move on to the next thing so quickly.

I felt suddenly very hot, my neck burning and my heart racing. I swam twenty fast lengths to dissipate my mood then walked back to the villa to shower. Sam's eyes were shut, his book open on the ground. But he wasn't asleep. As I passed him he murmured, 'She walks in beauty like the night…'

All these quotations made him sound clever – he was an English teacher after all – but they masked the fact that he had very few of his own ideas.

SEVENTEEN

THERE HAD TO be at least one big day out; it was inevitable. After nearly a week of the pool, ice cream and sunbathing, everyone was fidgety and the children were bickering.

'Go and play, kids' Vicky dropped the book she was reading onto the terrace, and forced herself up onto one elbow. 'Go and explore.'

'We're bored of Italy.' Holly was pulling flowers off the bushes next to the pool. Sharp wafts of scent caught on the warm air, mixing with the chemical smell of chlorine.

'It's too hot,' Tom added, his voice muffled by the towel he'd wrapped himself in, after an hour in the water.

'Can we *go* somewhere?'

'You said we could go up the Leaning Tower.'

Vicky yawned and shut her eyes. 'Ask your father. He's the one who likes driving like a local.'

On the narrow road that snaked up to the villa we'd had a few near misses and I knew there was no way Vicky would spend a whole day getting lost in an overheated car with two squabbling children.

I was only a guest and not party to family negotiations but I was curious to have more time with Sam, even if he irritated me now and then. Perhaps I could please everyone, myself included.

'I don't mind going, if you'd like to stay here, Vic.'

I'd picked up her nickname, although it felt wrong in my mouth. Like *nick* or *slick*. It was short and sharp like a razorblade. It made her sound like an East End gangster.

'That wouldn't be fair.' Vicky turned to me and smiled. 'You're used to your own space. Child-free.'

'But I've never seen the Leaning Tower.'

'It's no big deal and Pisa's a dump.'

'I don't mind.' I sat up. 'I'd like to see more of Italy, now I'm here. And you can have a day to yourself.'

'God, that would be amazing, Helen. But I can't inflict those two on you.'

In spite of the steadily increasing heat, the children had started a game of chase around the pool. I could see the eagerness in Vicky's eyes.

'It would be lovely. I like looking after them. And I can practise my Italian.' The phrase book slipped out of my hand and landed open on the page 'Ordering a meal.'

Vicky turned over heavily on her sun lounger and looked at me, adjusting her top which had ridden up to reveal her slack belly.

'Helen, that's sweet of you, but you came here as our

friend, not a nanny!' She picked up her book and found the page. '*And* you'd have to put up with Mr Grumpy,' she said reaching for her sunglasses. 'I couldn't inflict him on you either.'

I followed her gaze to where Sam was completing the last few of his fifty daily laps of the pool. His skin had lost its pale English luminescence; he was one of those lucky ones who never burned, unlike Vicky, smothered in sun cream as well as insect repellent.

'Samuel, *mio caro*!'

He didn't hear, or chose to ignore her, but after another lap pulled himself out of the water and adopted a body-builder's pose. 'That was great. Just like this superb, sun-bronzed body.'

Vicky didn't hesitate, in spite of her protestations. 'Helen's volunteered to go with you to Pisa. With the kids.'

Sam smiled down at me. 'Terrific. We could do with a day away from this hell hole.'

I tried not to mirror his smile, to keep my voice flat and ordinary but a thrill fluttered through me. A day out on our own, away from Vicky's beady eyes.

WHILE SAM DROVE I navigated, the map open on my lap. After the stillness of the villa we seemed to fly along the autostrade, as if we were running away together. The undulating, olive-covered hillsides glistening with tourists, gave way to the Pisan plain, as we dropped down to the ordinary life of Italy. Each time we caught a glimpse of the Leaning Tower, rather squat and uninspiring, the children called out, 'I can see the Tower!'

After hours looking for a carpark we were all hot and irritable when we finally started to climb the stone steps inside the tower. Sam took my hand to help me; but I could feel Holly's possessiveness.

'Dad! It's slippery!'

He let go of mine and took Holly's hand. 'You go ahead, Helen. I don't want another accident!'

Bereft without his hand, I gripped tight to the rail. For a second my head spun and I moved to allow other tourists to make their way down. It's only Sam. A friend.

From the top I half expected to see the North Sea, and for it to be cold, as if I'd been climbing up the Holdersea lighthouse. But, even with a breeze the air was hot and, beyond the red-tiled roofs, a gold flatness unrolled away from us. Somewhere in the distance the River Arno was a thread of silver that ran into the sea. It was hard to tell where the land finished and the water began.

'*I'm* not going to.' Holly marched away when Tom asked her. 'And Dad isn't either.' In the centre of the stone floor was a glass panel where tourists were daring each other to stand and look down.

'I'm too busy admiring the view.'

'Will you, Aunty Helen?' Tom said.

It looked solid. Others were doing it. Why not?

It was like standing on a sheet of thick warm ice. Perfectly safe.

'Look! Aunty Helen is so brave! I bet Mummy would never…'

'Say cheese, Aunty Helen!' Sam took a photo on his phone.

WE FOUND A restaurant that served pizza, one of the only things the children would eat.

'What a lovely family!' I translated, when the waitress looked admiringly at Holly and Tom quietly eating. My Italian course coming in useful at last.

'So we're married.' Sam laughed. 'You're a quick worker!'

'Vicky doesn't really deserve you,' I joked, and touched his arm.

Was it the weather? Being on holiday? Or confidence from our stargazing evening that made me so bold? It was only flirting but the mood coloured the rest of the day.

'Wonder what Vic's up to …' He looked at me over his glass. We were sharing a bottle of red wine.

I checked my watch. 'Must be siesta time.'

'And she's feeling *shattered*,' we both said, and then

laughed so much I nearly choked and a waiter came to check if I was okay.

'Tutto a posto' I managed to croak. 'Everything's fine.'

ON THE WAY back I woke to find the car stationary, Sam looking at the map, the children sleeping.

'Nope. No idea where we are.'

'Let me see.' I looked too, remembering the hours with Dad planning summer holidays, maps spread out on the kitchen table.

Our heads were almost touching. 'You smell nice.' Sam said. 'Your hair's different. Suits you. I meant to say that earlier.'

'Too hot to straighten it!' I said, and smiled. 'Thanks, Sam.'

'I think it must be this way.' I pointed. As he took the map and examined it, his hand touched mine. Something flipped inside me. The answer to a question I didn't even know I'd been asking myself. When does friendship tip over into attraction? Or is there an element of being drawn to someone in any relationship, any encounter? Is there a continuum? A sliding scale?

'Okay. copilot. I think you're right.'

We'd missed the autostrade so had to wend our way back through the hills. The sinking sun cast long shadows from the cypresses lining the road then, gradually the moon rose up behind us huge and full. Smiling to himself Sam started humming under his breath. 'When the moon hits your eye like a big pizza pie ...', on the steering wheel his hands were relaxed and brown, the dark hair along his arms curling over his wrists.

IN THE LIGHTS of the terrace, we could see Vicky asleep on one of the sun loungers; the towel covering her had slipped off to reveal her lower legs still dotted by angry-looking bites.

'There you are!' She untwisted herself and sat up. 'Good day?'

'Aunty Helen stood on top of the Leaning Tower!'

'And we'd still be on the road if she hadn't been such an expert map reader.' Sam squeezed my shoulder. 'How was it here? Miss us?'

'Too hot. Too many bugs.' Vicky scratched her legs. 'There's food if you want.' She gestured to the table, set with salads and bread. 'Thought you'd be back ages ago. You must've had fun.'

I sat down more out of politeness than genuine hunger. But suddenly I was ravenous.

'Can I pass you something, Vic?' Speaking through a mouthful of bread dripping with olive oil, Sam was obviously hungry too.

'I'm going to bed. The heat's got to me. Can you do

bedtime, Sam?'

Our day away from Vicky's gimlet eyes had been the best day of the holiday so far.

EIGHTEEN

VICKY CLAIMED HER turn a few days later and Sam stayed with the children by the pool while we escaped from the confines of the estate. Vicky drove us to Florence, for some culture, but more importantly, she said, to look at the markets.

'Must find you something pretty to take home, Helen.' She didn't mention my skirt. I think she'd already forgotten. 'Something to wear.'

We'd always shared a love of dressing-up. Looking through the Grattons catalogue on Vicky's kitchen table we giggled over the bras and knickers, laughing at the before and after of a woman with her *lift and separate*. I fell in love with the men and cut pictures out then imagined how glamorous our lives together would be. But when the clothes arrived in their crinkling plastic, they were always less shiny, less silky. Nylon or polyester. Crimplene.

Walking through the street market, the smell of leather was all pervasive and we had to buy straw hats to keep off the sun. I was like Vicky's dark shadow, her maid servant following close behind as she ran her fingers over soft leather purses, silk pashminas and cashmere sweaters. Everywhere we went, men buzzed around her like the hornets that blindly crowded around the candles on our terrace each night. I suppose she was the type Italian men are attracted to – tall, voluptuous. After so much sun, my skin had darkened as if I'd been stained with walnut juice like the heroine in a fairy story; Vicky was like a golden-haired Sophia Loren, her shoulders sprinkled with freckles.

As we pushed through Friday tourists looking for souvenirs, the stall holders' set phrases followed us like a chorus: *Pretty lady! Very beautiful!* It was midday and stifling. I tried to stay in the shade but Vicky kept calling me. As soon as I found something interesting, she dragged me onwards, on her own agenda.

'Helen, this one!' Vicky pointed to a fine purple shawl. 'This is your colour.'

She held the shawl next to my face. In the heat my hair was going its own way – twisting and curling. Out of control. But in the hand mirror the swirling patterns of lilac and pink lifted the sallowness of my skin.

'Beautiful lady. Only forty euros'

Beads of sweat trickled down my back.

'Go on, love. It's perfect.' Vicky fluttered a wink at me. 'It makes you look gorgeous.'

'Maybe.'

'To you, *bella*, only thirty-five euros.'

'Twenty-five and no more.' Vicky had done this before. And I couldn't refuse a bargain.

The silk shawl was warm and slippery; it rustled in the paper as I dropped it into my bag.

***

THE SUMMER WE were old enough to sprout hard lumps behind our nipples, we played dressing up at Vicky's house. Huge roses stencilled on the walls. Pictures of ballerinas in tutus. Her own paintings and drawings professionally framed. When the afternoon sun came through the curtains it made everything gold and warm. Like being inside a flower.

Sometimes Vicky tried to teach me ballet words: plie, arabesque, entrechat in a French accent like her teacher and we laughed so much I needed to go to the toilet. When we were small we used to pretend to be mums, but now our favourite game was dressing up and dancing to music on the radio. One day when we'd danced so much we were hot and out of breath Vicky said, 'Let's pretend we're strippers. Then we can cool down.'

Vicky's games always started that way, with a *let's pretend*. An *us* which suggested *we* were together in a shared game. Only it was always Vicky who started it. The *us* was a myth. It was always and only Vicky.

In the mirror her skin was creamy-white and her hair

a soft gold, rippling down her back. I looked nice too, but not as nice as Vicky.

'When I'm a proper actress I'll have to kiss people so let's practise.'

I wanted to, I really did, but at the same time I felt sick. I moved away.

'You need to practise too, Helen. Or how will you know what to do when you're married.' She grabbed at my hand. 'Come here.'

Her tongue was wet and very warm. She tasted of apples. We watched ourselves in the mirror and kissed until we were out of breath and had to lie on the floor and giggle. Every so often the music stopped and the radio crackled and buzzed; then through the floor we heard the vibration of the sewing machine. Her mum making Vicky another new dress.

The next time I went round we found a couple of old sleeping bags at the bottom of the dressing up box which we zipped together to make a tent.

Sylvia said, 'When you're older you two could travel round the world!' and gave us a thermos of orange squash, a plate of Rich Teas and Vicky's dad's torch. For a while we danced to the radio but that made us so hot we had to take off all our clothes to cool down then we crawled into our tent. First we made ghost faces and scared each other, and shone the light under our hands so they look like skeleton hands in red gloves. Then we looked at our new breasts again.

'Yours are going to be bigger than mine, Helen.'

I was glad she'd noticed. It was important not to be flat-chested and have to cheat with a padded bra, otherwise when it was your wedding night your husband would find out and he might change his mind.

'I've got some hair now. Have you?'

In the torchlight the hair under Vicky's arms glowed almost silver. Mine was dark.

'Have you looked down there?'

'Of course. Ages ago,' I lied.

We took turns sticking our legs up in the air and examining each other.

Vicky put on a deep voice and shone the torch between my legs. 'Now, Mrs. Jones, I just need to . . . No, I know. Let's pretend I'm your husband.'

She switched off the torch and kissed me on the mouth pushing her tongue in until I could hardly breathe. Her fingers brushed my hip.

'Now it's your turn. You have to touch me down there. It's nice.' she said, breathing in my ear.

She was smooth like me with only a few tiny hairs.

'Ooh, that's lovely! Only you taste of baked beans, dear heart!'

I drew away. Vicky was giggling. But inside the sleeping bags it was stuffy, and smelled too much of us. A hot stale smell.

Below, the sewing machine started again, distorting the music on the radio; then it stopped. There was a long silence. I felt around for the torch and switched it on.

'I need to go now. I've got to do my homework.'

'Scaredy cat!' said Vicky, under her breath and grabbed at my hand.

I wriggled my way out of the sleeping bag. The room was nearly dark. The street lamps had come on and an artificial orange light glowed through the curtains, enough light to find my way across the room to the light switch.

'You're very pretty, you know.' Vicky's voice was lower than normal. She was lying on her back, one hand behind her head. The silky green of the sleeping bag outlined her legs and hips. Under the ceiling light her blond hair was silver, spread like seaweed over the pink pillow, like a princess in a fairy story.

'You look like a mermaid,' I said, and she smiled up at me.

I was getting cold as I reached for my underwear. In the mirror my eyes looked huge. My hair was tangled. My mouth, rubbed red.

The sewing machine started again.

'Come on, cowardy custard. It's nice and cosy in here.'

Vicky's reflection smiled at me as she pushed back the top sleeping bag, one hand lying at the top of her thigh.

Downstairs the hum of the sewing machine stopped;

there were footsteps on the stairs. I fumbled on my clothes.

'Helen!' It was Sylvia. 'Time to go home, love.'

'Bye, Vicky,' I whispered and opened the bedroom door, shutting it tightly behind me.

After that day Vicky always made me play our camping game. If I didn't, she would tell my mum what we'd been doing; Her mum didn't mind what we did, she said.

NINETEEN

AGATA, FROM THE village, was cooking for all the holidaymakers staying on the estate when we arrived back. A long table was set up on the terrace, next to our villa. Until now we'd only been on nodding acquaintance with the other families, a honeymoon couple and a family of fair skinned Scots, and I was reluctant to be sociable with so many strangers.

Although the day in Florence had been hotter than ever, back at the villa a breeze came from the sea just over the hills, so after a shower, I put on a long dress and tied the silk shawl loosely around my shoulders; they were burnt and red from standing in the market in the midday sun, but the silk slid over them, cooling.

I watched from my window as everyone gathered. The Scottish family were prompt and even the newlyweds left their bed to join us. Vicky was busy organising the children and Sam sat playing his guitar, until the arrival of a new couple – Peter and Sarah – marked the start of the evening. They'd driven down from London and brought an exciting air of metropolitan sophistication. She was young and pretty in a pale way; he was either rich or clever – or possibly both – because strikingly unattractive. At a distance it was an unlikely marriage of opposites, but when I finally went down, the pressure of Peter's handshake and the two kisses he gave me said it all – he had the assured confidence of the wealthy.

'Helen. An English rose with a Greek name.'

Throughout the meal it was me Peter chose to talk to, predominantly about the history of the area. Sarah clearly used to this, probably even a little bored, turned to flirt with the newlywed husband.

As the sun dropped behind the hills leaving the sky streaked with gold, and voices grew louder, I imagined we looked like a scene from a Fellini film. The air was warm and I rested into the evening like a cushion. This was the moment I'd been waiting for all my life, the culminating moment when I was the main character in my own life. Emma Bovary at the ball.

Leaning back on her chair and fending off the children Vicky looked tired. I pictured Sam's hands resting on the map. His voice in my hair. *You smell nice.*

AGATA HAD SURPASSED herself: home-made ravioli with walnuts, chicken with tender green spinach, then the juiciest peaches, still warm, and a speckled vanilla *gelato*. After the meal Sam raised his glass: 'To the chef. And friends old and new!'

Then the children disappeared to play with the kittens that roamed free on the estate, and we sat drinking glasses of the inevitable limoncello. As I leaned forward to pick up my glass, the shawl slid off and onto the ground. Peter picked it up and replaced it, casually stroking my neck as he did so.

'Silk. How lovely.'

A blush bloomed over my whole body, almost as if he'd said *let's go to bed*. 'Thank you. From Florence. The market.'

'Now I don't suppose you know this, but as part of the local silk production process female workers used to keep silk worms under their clothes to protect them. Help them hatch.'

'How revolting.'

'The smell probably was. And the sound of munching on mulberry leaves.'

'Glad I didn't know that when I bought this shawl!'

'Would it make any difference?' Peter leaned in closer. 'There's a fine line between pleasure and disgust, don't you think?'

He breathed the words into my ear; he was so close the linen of his shirt brushed my arm.

'I'm sure you have a dark side too, Helen.'

Then he laughed.

I was stroking the fat stem of the glass, almost caressing it; and when I realised, I laughed too. For what felt like the first time in years I laughed completely, without holding back. On holiday, at a party the normal rules didn't apply. I caught Sam's eye and he looked away, frowning then left the table and went to play his guitar. It was irrational yet I sensed I'd betrayed the intimacy we'd developed on our Pisa trip. But I was too busy congratulating myself to be concerned for long. I let Peter top up my glass with the chilled lemon liqueur and settled down to enjoy our conversation. Although I cautioned myself not to be naïve, I'd made a conquest.

WHEN SAM CAME back to the table Vicky laid claim to him by kicking off her sandals.

'Let me put my feet on your lap, love.' She was smiling and relaxed for the first time all day, mosquito bites and tiredness forgotten.

'Comfy now?' He shifted in his seat until he was leaning back, hands clasped behind his head, a smile on his lips.

Something warm glanced against my ankle. One of the kittens? Then it rubbed the top of my foot and in between my toes, then up and down my inner calf.

'Enjoying yourself, Helen?' Sam looked at me.

Playing footsie like an adolescent while Vicky's feet were in his lap. But I didn't want him to stop.

'Sam. You're wriggling,' she said, laughing. 'You're making me feel sick!'

His naked foot was cool but persistent against my sunburned knee. His toes played a rhythm as if they were dancing to an internal tune. I'd forgotten how ticklish I was. If he didn't stop I was going to laugh. I put my hand under the table and pinched his foot as hard as I could.

'Ouch! Bloody mosquitoes!' he yelped. 'Watch out, Helen, there's one under the table. Just got me.'

He sounded so put out I laughed anyway.

'The stuff's in the kitchen, love.' Vicky didn't make a move to get up, but she glanced at me.

'I'll find it,' I heard myself saying. Since when had I become a nurse for the whole family?

'Terrific. I'll come with you then you can put the cream on for me, Aunty Helen.'

Vicky lifted her legs so he could move, then put them on his empty chair. 'Watch him, Helen. He's drunk and disorderly. Make sure you keep your distance!' She laughed and turned to answer one of the children.

Everyone was listening to Peter holding forth about something. Vicky was on her second or third glass. We all were. Everything was taking on the gold haze of holiday memory. Things happen and there are no gaps. You glide between moments. One minute at the table. The next in the kitchen looking for insect repellent. Then in their room and Sam has lifted my dress up, sliding his hands over my breasts, between my legs, trying to find a way in. Kissing me.

'Not here…Sam, stop it…no, we need to go back.'

His voice in my ear: 'You're right. I'm sorry, Helen. You're so desirable.'

Outside Vicky put her feet back on his lap.

'Better now? Has Aunty Helen looked after you?'

Not here.

AFTER LUNCH THE next day, none of us could stay awake; even the children climbed into the hammock to play, then fell asleep. Vicky insisted on her siesta, but until then I'd resisted. What was the point of being on holiday if you slept all the time?

Maybe it was being away from home, plucked out of my normal routine, the lack of structure. Or was it the wine, the drowsy sun, the hum of the bees in the lavender? The way the house stretched out in the sun like a cat on warm terracotta tiles. Something made it happen. It wasn't me. It's not what I wanted. He held my glance for too long when I said I was going to have a rest. Sam willed it, not me.

I went up to my room and left my door open to let in some air. I undressed and lay down on the bed, covering myself with the new shawl. I wasn't waiting, in fact I'm sure I fell asleep. Then there was a sound of undressing, the clink of his belt buckle as it dropped onto the floor, the dry heat of him stretched out behind me, a hard insistence, gentle but determined. So different from Ed's fumbling efforts. We didn't speak. But we were both too needy, too vigorous. When he'd gone and I turned over, there was a fine trail of red dotted across the sheet, as if I was a deflowered virgin.

TWENTY

FROM THEN ON we all loved our siestas. It became a new routine; it wasn't a secret. *Tour rules.*

It was a tacit agreement – for the first couple of days always from behind as if neither of us wanted to admit it was happening. Then I was too curious, I wanted to see him, to watch him; we literally faced up to it, frank and unguarded. We became more adventurous. More experimental. We explored each other. There was still silence between us, a kind of intense otherness. Like a spell in a folk tale – if either of us spoke, the spell would be broken and that would be an end of it. Apart from one time when he called my name aloud. I cut it out of the air and stitched it tight across my breasts, like the name on my school PE kit: a white aertex shirt emblazoned in ruby stem stitch. But I never said his name.

On the surface the holiday continued as it had started: the usual teasing between Sam and me, practical conversations about the children with Vicky, and for me, a sense of each day being bathed in a glow of physical satisfaction and anticipation. Every day I swam in the pool letting

Sam enjoy looking at me. Legally as it were. I loved the sensation of being free, anticipating siesta time. The water held me as he did.

I collected every detail to make a new story to tell myself at night when I was back home and on my own again. Like a holiday scrap book.

THE LAST MORNING of the holiday I woke from a dense sleep, my body a heavy weight pressing down into the bed. I'd slept the sweetest sleep for a long time and it wasn't engineered by alcohol but by exercise and sex. The pleasure of physical exercise, like childhood days spent doing handstands until my whole body ached with it.

Above me a large hornet landed on one of the thick wooden beams then buzzed away out of the open window. At some point during the night I must have felt cold because the sheet was pulled over me and the quilt was covering my feet. The air was already hot and clammy, so I threw off the covers and watched the sun on my body as a warm breeze drifted through the room.

The hornet was soon back again, taking off and landing at intervals on the chestnut beam above my head, boring small holes and taking the wood away to add to its nest. The previous day, Sam had taken me down to the cellar to see it. Hanging high in the corner, where a crack above the shuttered window let in the light, was what looked like a distorted paper lantern. It was the length of my arm and coming from it a constant drone, like a machine.

'The buzzing sounds angry.'

'Only your perception, Helen. It's efficient. Buzzing with new life. Making a new colony.'

'As if they're trapped inside–'

'Recycling the old wood–'

'Isn't it dangerous? What about the kids?' I held him back. 'Don't get too close!'

'Stealing from the structure of the house to make their own.'

'Vicky said one sting could kill a horse.'

'What?'

'She said one sting could– '

'I've told her it's no worse than a wasp. She's such a drama queen.'

He laughed and came back to the doorway where I was standing, keeping my distance from the nest.

'I didn't think they'd bother you.' He pulled me into the room and shut the door. 'You'd make a hopeless spy after all, Agent Farrish,' he said, in a mock James Bond accent. 'I think you need someone to show you how it's done properly.'

Then we kissed to a background of insistent buzzing, until Holly shouted that it was time for supper and we had to pull ourselves apart and join the others.

'Later?' I'd suggested.

Sam nodded. But it had been impossible. The heat had floored Vicky and he had to spend all day with the kids, or attending to her demands – she could be a real bully sometimes. He had to do everything. Which lessened any guilty feelings that might have crept up on me. *Tour rules.* No, I wasn't guilty.

THE SOLITARY HORNET continued its work. I ran my hand between my legs to finish what we had started in the cellar. Until Sam and I started this thing, I'd been almost paralysed from the waist down. I looked back at the woman I was before this week, with an almost detached pity. I could hardly imagine that grey shadowy life.

Nearby a cockerel crowed. In the distance car horns sounded as drivers tackled the hairpin bends leading down to the town. Perhaps we'd find time today. Vicky said she'd take the children for a bike ride and ice creams with the other families. With their talk of schools and catchment areas, they were all best friends now, even exchanging email addresses. No one would get up early after another heavy evening of food and wine, although no doubt the children would be first.

When my door opened it was as if I'd summoned him. The sun highlighted each tightly curled hair. A haze of stubble darkened his chin and for the first time I noticed a reddish mark on his inner thigh – a strawberry birthmark, usually hidden by his swimming trunks. I was ready for him and he slid into me as if he belonged there. I tried to be quiet but he was shushing me like a child, calming me, gentling me as you would a wild animal.

When he left, the hornet was still working, carrying wood away from the rotting beam. I fell asleep and dreamt about the house disintegrating and dissolving, as a gigantic hornets' nest inflated in its place, until it burst with a bang like the paper bags Dad used to scare me with when I was a child. I woke to the intense gold light of mid-morning, and the shutter banging open as the children came in to wake me.

'Aunty Helen! Will you take us to the pool?'

It was the last day of the holiday.

TWENTY-ONE

THE MAN NEXT to me fell asleep as soon as we started taxiing on the runway. If I needed to go to the toilet, it would be difficult to get out. But I had the view. Once we'd broken through the layer of white cloud that looked solid enough to keep us up there, there was no apparent movement. We were stuck in a continuous present. Apart from glimpses of the sea, then the Alps, and occasionally whole towns hanging onto mountain sides, there were only clouds. For two hours like the recycled air we were breathing I held on to Sam. I breathed him in.

They were two rows ahead so I couldn't see him, but Vicky's hand would pass sweets or bottles of water to the children to keep them happy. For the second hour they must have dozed off, full of junk food and lulled to sleep by the hum of the engines.

I imagined us as three points of an equilateral triangle. Sam. Vicky. Me. If no one broke it, and as long as everyone's needs were met, it was a stable shape. It could go on and on. I needed to keep Vicky at a distance then Sam and I could still be friends. At least. I didn't want any of it to end, to turn back into nothing.

When the clouds cleared, I could see tiny ships tracking across the sea leaving white trails. Peaceful. Like an illustration from a child's picture book about the seaside. Like a postcard of Holdersea. I wrapped the silk scarf around my shoulders and let myself drift off, picturing the view from the promenade.

***

ON THE RARE days it was warm enough, Ann and I went to the promenade to spy on the boys, desperate to be noticed, not to be left behind. As we sat eating ice creams on the edge with our legs dangling through the metal rail, noise and cigarette smoke drifted up from the beach where people rested their backs against the concrete wall below us. The tide always seemed to be out, the sea a thin blue line blending into the sky. Sometimes it was so far away you could hardly hear it – a faint hiss behind the voices and shouts. Where the sand had flattened, children paddled in the shallow water and, with my glasses on, I could make out the black dots of swimmers.

A few days after he'd watched her sunbathing on the school field I saw them. Even from that far away I knew it was them. Like looking at a silent film through the wrong end of a telescope: the blond flip of her ponytail, his long brown legs with trousers rolled up above his knees.

He was showing off – cartwheeling along the water's

edge. Then a handstand that went on and on.

'I know … have you got any money left?' Ann ran over to a free set of binoculars. I crammed in my coins and there they were, in close up. I wished I could lip read, but I didn't need to – I knew what Vicky wanted. That look. Her voice teasing me: *scaredy cat.*

'My turn!' Ann took the binoculars. 'I can't believe it. He's letting her kiss him!'

'Let me see.'

Against the blue of the sea, Vicky's hand was a white starfish climbing up his brown leg, then it disappeared under the flapping sail of his school shirt. There was an acid burn of chocolate and ice cream in my throat. I watched until the money ran out and it went dark. My hands smelled of ice cream and the metal railings. Like a child. From then on they were inseparable.

AFTER A-LEVELS IT was traditional for the sixth form to spend an afternoon on the beach, whatever the weather. The summer we finished school was no different – there was a sense of expectation, as if something immense was going to happen, all our lives spreading out from that moment, from that small seaside town.

By mid-afternoon when Ann and I walked down to the sea front, a crowd had gathered on the beach, some with large bags and picnic rugs, some attempting to erect their parents' windbreaks, others with just a towel or a bottle. Mum insisted I make enough egg sandwiches and sausage rolls to feed twenty. There was beer and cider and Sam had raided his mother's drinks cabinet, mixing vodka with orange juice and passing it around in paper cups. I could see Julia giggling with the God Squad, continually glancing in Sam's direction.

Right in the centre of the sprawling group, tying her hair on top of her head, allowing a few fine wisps to frame her face, was Vicky. When she saw me she waved and came to talk to us. Her nails were painted a fuchsia pink to match her bikini.

I only had my school black swimming costume. I hadn't thought about putting it on before I set off, so while Ann held a towel around me I struggled to get into it.

Vicky had a teasing way of speaking to everyone; she came right up to us, smiling. 'Let me help.' When she took the towel out of Ann's hands hers were warm against my cold skin. 'Is that all you've got? You could've borrowed one of mine.' She had a drawer full of swim-wear.

I was trying to stop the towel from slipping down as I pulled up the straps of my costume. Vicky was making it worse.

As she bent towards me I could feel heat from her body. Loose strands of her hair blew across my face and into my mouth. I could taste her shampoo. Smell her sweat under her deodorant. The feline smell I remembered from our camping games.

'Are you going in, Helen?' Vicky said, once my swimming costume was on.

'Probably just paddle.'

'You have to! Everyone's going in!' Vicky slipped off her flip flops and ran towards the sea. 'It's the last chance you'll get! Come on!'

Minutes later I turned to see that Sam had joined her.

Ann and I walked further along the beach, away from the group and paddled in the frothy water that ran over the sand at the edge of the sea.

'*Break, break, break on thy cold gray stones, O Sea!*' Ann declaimed.

'*I have heard the mermaids singing each to each!*' I said and we both laughed. It was a favourite game, exchanging quotations. I was heading north to university; Ann was going south.

Life was opening out for all of us and we were superior to the others. We were the intellectuals.

But, above the sound of the waves crashing onto the sand I could hear Vicky squealing and shrieking:

'Come on, Helen! You're such a scaredy cat!'

I could see Sam's hands around her waist, one of hers like a starfish on his shoulders, pulling him towards her, her lips parting. Her pink tongue.

AFTER SWIMMING IN Italy in the open air, the chlorinated pool at the gym was contrived and cramped. So the first warm day back in Holdersea I put on my tankini and waded out into the sea. A starfish was suckered fast to a rock looking as if nothing could shift it, but a wave came in and sent it flailing into the water, sinking down and away. The cold made me gasp. The water was a brownish-grey, and my feet kicked up clouds of sand so I couldn't see the bottom; ribbons of seaweed wrapped around my legs like long hair. The ground shelved away steeply. I was falling. I was going to drown here, with no one to help. With my second stroke I caught a mouthful of salty water that stung my lips, still sensitive and burnt from Italy. I was soon out of my depth. As far as I could see, waves rolled in towards me like long fingers sliding sideways under the water, lifting me. There was nothing else to do: I had to swim. I swam until my toes no longer fumbled over pebbles. Until I was far enough out not to be dragged in by each wave. For the first time in my life I swam in the sea.

Looking back at Holdersea the caravan parks expand-ed along the coast like lichen, and the lighthouse stood out bright against the sky. There were visitors on the viewing platform. One day, I'd go up there myself and look at the view. As I swam further out, the town and even the lighthouse became insignificant against the immense backdrop of sky and farmland. In a hundred years or so, even with sea defences, it would all be washed away, tumbled and smoothed into sand, deposited on the curling spit of Spurn Point. Flattened like a sandcastle.

This life, what I had left of it, was all there was. I needed to come up with a guiding principle, rules, and a way of life to make the most of what I had.

And more than anything, I needed to forget about Sam.

But in bed I was like a child wanting the same stories over and over again, flicking through my metaphorical scrap book – Sam that last morning, his long legs gold-haired as I wrapped myself around him, the taste of cigarettes and limoncello on his lips. The neat strawberry mark on the soft skin of his inner thigh. The hornet's nest growing fat with new life. Each time I told myself it was just a holiday romance. A fling. To stop making myself miserable, or I'd end up like my mother. But the storybook in my mind always fell open again at the same few pages. I found myself spraying sun cream on my hands and on my neck to bring him back. I even found myself doing something I'd not done since assemblies in primary school: I prayed for it to stop. I wanted my quiet life, the life where I had only just acquired the freedom to do whatever I wanted.

In some way I blame Vicky for the whole thing. She wanted to be my friend. She emailed me. She phoned me. She arranged times to be together. Vicky wouldn't let me go.

TWENTY-TWO

'THERE'S SOMETHING WRONG with it, don't you think?' I said.

'What?'

'The sky.'

We were walking along the beach with the kids and their dog. It was warm for late August, but after the heat of Italy it felt cold.

Vicky frowned.

'It's pale, washed out. As if someone's put a grey filter over it.' I took my glasses off and rubbed them on my shirt. 'Or is it my eyesight?'

Vicky grabbed hold of me, linking arms and half skipping.

'Shows how often you've been abroad, Helen! In Tuscany the sky's always bluer – you're so much further south! All those Italian Renaissance painters didn't exaggerate! Next time you won't even notice.'

But now I did. Stripped back to grey northern skies and cold. On my own again. I shivered.

'There will be a next time, won't there? You're glad

you came with us, love?' She hugged me, kissing me on the cheek. Her lips were sticky with spray from the sea and I smelled her perfume. In my heightened state it was the smell of innocence.

'I loved it. I didn't want to come home.'

'We loved having you there. Both of us. And the kids too.'

She let go of my arm and started to run towards the children, calling back, 'I always wanted a sister. Horrible being an only child.' Her voice was whipped away by the wind. '… never anyone to play with.'

I thought about Michael. One minute a snotty little brother hogging the bathroom, and the next, on the other side of the world, as far away as possible. Vicky ran back and her long fingers wrapped around and between mine.

'Och, your hands are so cold, Helen.' A perfect imitation of her mother.

'Cold hands, warm heart.' I said.

My heart, the size of my fist, a creature beating with its own life. I had the urge to pluck it out and stamp on it. To throw myself at her feet and ask for forgiveness, like someone in a gothic melodrama. This must be what guilt felt like.

She squeezed my hand. 'You always felt the cold, even at school. Come on! You need warming up.'

In spite of her size, Vicky could still produce the burst of strength that had given her a place on the school netball team; she dragged me into a run along the flat ribbed sand towards the children and the dog.

'Warmer?'

I was out of breath, my heart was rattling against my ribs.

'Vicky, I need to …'

My voice came out like a sigh and was carried away by the wind. What did I want to say? Did I want to confess? I had no idea. But even if I'd shouted my confession she wouldn't hear it; she wasn't listening. She was running to where the children were crowding round the dog, and poking at the sand with a stick. The dog was barking madly, Holly was shouting and Tom was crying.

'Christ kids, couldn't you stop her?'

Then I could smell it. Alfie had found something washed up by the sea; the smell of rotting fish was overpowering.

'Helen! Can you take the dog while I get rid of …' But, before I got there, Vicky grabbed the dog's lead and kicked the remains back into the sea.

'Let's go – the smell is making me feel sick!' Vicky yanked the lead and the dog whimpered. 'It's disgusting!'

Imagine having to live with a craving so strong you couldn't control it. Each day dragged by the nose with unthinking desire. I took my eyes off the remains floating in the shallow water, threatening to be washed back in at any moment.

Surely it was possible just to be friends. I could settle for friendship. 'Who wants an ice cream?' I said. 'Race you to the steps!'

VICKY LICKED HER cornet to stop it from dripping, and pulled a face. 'Nancy always says you shouldn't eat ice cream in this country. Too sweet. Sickly.'

Nancy always had a lot to say about everything. It made a change for Vicky to listen to someone else's advice.

'No it's not, Mummy. We both like it, don't we, Holly?'

I bit into my ice cream. The cold hit a nerve in a tooth and I winced.

Vicky stroked my bare arm. 'You look better for it, sweetheart – you wouldn't get such a lovely tan here!'

I shifted slightly along the bench away from her.

She carried on eating her ice cream. 'I'm sorry we didn't find you a man. Apart from that creep who was so in love with himself...Peter. What did she see in him?' When she laughed I could see a drip of chocolate on the corner of her mouth like a beauty spot.

'He was interesting,' I said.

'Interesting! You need more than that, love. What you need is a handsome Yorkshireman. Or a rich Italian to give you private Italian lessons.'

I shook my head.

'Helen, you're mad!' Her voice was so low I had to lean in to hear her. Her breath was scented with mint choc chip ice cream. 'Do you really not see how lovely you are? You always were.'

'Vicky, stop being so–'

'Honest?'

I tried to laugh it off. 'I was thinking more… embarrassing.'

'Sam thinks you're great, you know.'

My stomach plunged.

'You must've noticed how he's been looking at you. I admit when I first saw you I hardly recognised you. But a bit of sun, sea and … you know.'

On the horizon a tanker made its slow way south. Above us the air was full of herring gulls, hanging against the grey-blue of the sky, waiting for crumbs of cornet.

As usual Vicky was exaggerating. It was her luvvie act. She didn't know anything. It was all over and done with. A mistake.

The children finished and started to race up and down the promenade. Fag ends, sand and broken coffee cups scuttered at our feet.

'Well, here we are back to reality.' I tried to steer the conversation away from the holiday. 'What are your plans for the rest of the summer?'

The children were at the far end of the promenade,

preparing to race towards us. I could see Holly had given Tom a head start. But she would easily win.

'Can I...?' Vicky pushed a strand of my hair back behind my ear. 'There, that's better...the beach. Days out...' She sat back. 'Now, look at me properly, and smile. Tell me you're glad we're friends again.'

I tried to shut my mind down so that I wouldn't think about any of it, to keep it inside me, to leave it there, like a dead thing. 'Of course I'm glad.'

She put her arms around me. 'Och, you funny wee thing, Helen! You need someone to look after you.'

Her touch made me shiver. I wanted her kindness. I wanted her to hold me as she did Holly or Tom. To say: 'It's all right. It's over. You can cry.'

'Winner!' Holly arrived and bumped into Vicky, panting.

'It's not fair. She cheated.' Tom walked back dragging his feet then slumped down next to his mother. 'She always wins.'

From now on it would be ordinary. We'd all just be friends. I willed this to be true.

TWENTY-THREE

FROM THE ALMOST cobalt blue of Italy the grey of the Yorkshire coast was flat long lines and the lighthouse stood like a dead monument to the past, a useless Victorian phallic symbol. Its shadow passed over the houses like a sundial, marking time that no one cared about or could read. Ships didn't need light; they had sat nav now. They could navigate in the dark. Much as I could. Back to Sam.

I looked up from my garden at night and hunted for shooting stars. *When you wish upon a star.* I made wishes like a child. But I forced myself to keep away – I worked extra hours at school. I didn't answer the phone. I imagined Sam was doing the same. Keeping away.

I made a start on the garden, to lose myself in repetitive activity. Mum made gardening sound like an art to be initiated into, but I used to watch Dad pruning the apple tree – it wasn't difficult at all; and there was something satisfying and calming about tidying and sorting out. Cutting out the weak and broken branches, bagging up dead leaves. People always tell you how therapeutic it is, don't they?

The apple tree was now so diseased it only produced tiny fruit pitted with brown scabs. Michael and I used to collect the windfalls for Mum to make apple jelly, while Dad was sent up the ladder to pick the best apples. We were never allowed to – a mixture of fear that we would fall and his old-fashioned pride in being the man of the house, the provider. As Mum peeled each apple a long spool of skin unwound onto the table. Once I was old enough to roll out the pastry I helped, but it was always Mum who cut the edge of the pie crust with a knife, the pastry shreds stretching and falling down to leave a perfect circle.

I was failing to cut back the tree with a pair of blunt secateurs when Vicky saw me in the front garden. She was driving back from teaching her ceramics class. She rolled the window down and shouted.

'You look like you need a hand!'

I was hot and sweating from the effort, my trousers stained and ripped and my hair full of dead leaves. 'It's okay. Thanks.'

'I'll send Sam round with a saw. Keep him out of my way!'

'I can do it. I don't need any help.'

But as she drove off the engine drowned my voice.

So you see? I didn't ask her to send me her husband. She did it out of the kindness of her heart. And, to some extent, so did he.

BUT I DID try. When he arrived I practised the art of invisibility, turning off my body language, and not meeting his eye. He, in turn was bright and cheery.

'Right, Miss. Where is the offending plant?'

I pointed to the decaying tree whose twisted and browning leaves had already started to fall, although it was only the beginning of September.

'Ah ha. Just leave this to me, young lady.' He took off his gloves and gave them to me. They were still warm and held the shape of his hands. I put them carefully on the kitchen table. His hands.

Exquisitely aware of the space between us, we danced around each other. Like a pair of boxers.

'Got a ladder?'

'In the shed.'

'Okey dokey.'

Almost like a soft porn script, although is any porn ever 'soft'? I tried not to remember the holiday. But how could I not?

A black line divided the garden in two – the shadow of the lighthouse. If I stayed on the right, and Sam stayed on the left, everything would be fine. Nothing would happen.

As I steadied the ladder he climbed up, whistling into

the crown of the tree, then started to saw off branches.

'You can see the sea from here. Did you know?'

'We weren't allowed to climb it. In case we damaged the apples. I think Michael–'

'I spent hours climbing trees…it's amazing living so close to the lighthouse. The view must be great.'

'I've never been. One day I might.'

He worked on, humming to himself, sawing at each branch and letting it drop onto the path behind me. Through the cold aluminium of the ladder, I sensed each time he moved. The backs of his calves were still tanned, like they were at school, and the muscles stretched and retracted as he reached up and cut at the rotting wood. Sawdust fell steadily catching in my hair and in a cobweb suspended between lower branches of the tree. A spider sat in the middle waiting, its striped yellow and brown legs moving restlessly.

'Okay down there?' Sam's breathing was becoming heavier and more laboured. 'Watch out. This is a big one. It might…'

There was a crack and a large branch fell straight down, glanced off the ladder and jabbed into my upper arm. I lost my grip.

'Did I get you?'

'I'm fine. A flesh wound.'

'Fuck! I'm sorry, Helen!'

I clasped the ladder again and tried to ignore the

stinging sensation, but Sam clambered down.

'Your sleeve's torn. I've hurt your arm.'

I looked out of the corner of my eye at the jagged rip, blood tingeing the pale yellow of my shirt.

'It's just a scratch'

'A hit. A very palpable hit.'

'I've got plasters and the shirt's old. I can darn it.'

'I'll cut this wood up then take a look.'

I FOUND ANTISEPTIC and cotton wool, and poured it into a small dish. A sharp smell from childhood – cut knees, nettles, then the reassuring clean smell of the cloudy liquid.

'Let me.' Sam rolled my sleeve up and dabbed the graze.

I flinched.

'Did that hurt? I'll try to be gentle.'

He reduced the pressure but it still stung. His hand supporting my lower arm was warm, and dry with sawdust. I concentrated on the dripping kitchen tap, counted the seconds between each drop. One day I'd get it fixed.

'You've gone pale.'

'It's that smell of metal.'

'Iron in the blood. You're definitely not anaemic. But you're covered in sawdust.' He laughed and dusted down my cheek and I remembered the pool, how grateful he'd been, how he'd wiped Tom's blood off my cheek as I carried him out of the water. The child's bony chest, each rib outlined under taut young skin. How cold my face had been under Sam's hands. Like the tiny feet of a bird. The trembling border between life and death. The feathers of the bird fluttering against my palms.

His hand stayed a second too long. He crossed the line of shadow separating us, and time expanded in all directions.

'You too?' he said.

'Yes.'

'But we–'

'No, you're right.'

He dried my arm then pressed a plaster firmly over the cut.

I thought of Celia Johnson's character in *Brief Encounter*, Mum's favourite film. 'You have something in your eye. Let me help, I'm a doctor.' Wartime heroine resigned to her fate. I could be good and noble. Self-sacrificing.

'I'll put the kettle on,' I said. 'Thanks, Sam.'

'My pleasure.'

The shadow of the lighthouse fell between us again.

WE DRANK OUR tea on opposite sides of the kitchen table.

Conversation drifted along safe ground. We avoided the real subject between us. Neither of us mentioned Vicky. But when his phone bleated there was no need to name her.

'She's going out in a couple of hours. Catching up with Julia. I need to look after the kids.'

At the door we kissed in the conventional way, a peck on each cheek. As I thanked him again, his hand pressed on my lower back.

'Take care of yourself. Look after that injury.'

Then he went, driving off noisily as if underlining the point.

And that was that. I'd been good. I'd done the right thing. I hadn't given in.

BUT DOING ONE'S duty can be a very dry affair, like eating digestive biscuits without a cup of tea. It didn't give me much pleasure.

The warmth of his hand stayed with me like a hand print from a slap. I was uncomfortable, disturbed, aroused. The phrase *heavy with desire* bumped around in my head like a Victorian poet in a graveyard.

I was going to take a long bath to relieve myself, but I was starving. After a snack of sardines on toast and another cup of tea I went into the garden to sweep up the remains of the apple tree. In the fading light, under a pile of twigs and branches something glinted. Sam's pruning saw.

At first I didn't allow myself to touch it. I'd phone Vicky and tell her to pick it up when she's next passing. But what if he needs it?

I texted him.

Hi Sam, you forgot your saw.

Blimey! On my way. Don't want you doing any more damage! xx

By the time the doorbell rang I'd changed into linen trousers and a fine jumper made of silk and wool, ten percent cashmere *and* machine washable. Deliciously soft next to my skin, and it didn't affect the cut on my arm at all. I draped the scarf around my shoulders and ran downstairs. Sam would get his saw back.

I did think briefly of Celia Johnson. But such a poor, wartime diet. All that rationing. That was all in the past. I was very hungry.

And so it seemed was Sam.

TWENTY-FOUR

YES, I PUSHED Celia and her piles of darning onto the track, just as the express was coming. No, even better, I tied her down, and I made sure the knots were tight. Don't be so bloody self-sacrificing I said, and she went without a murmur. I chastised myself for even thinking like that in this day and age. Life's too short.

The second time was *almost* an accident. I still had some lingering reservations – guilt and all that malarkey. I'd gleaned which days Sylvia picked the kids up from school so that Vicky could work late at the studio. Oh yes, I knew what the arrangements were but I needed to test it out.

I texted him from work: *free for a cuppa?*

Or something stronger . . .? he replied.

Ah that lovely ellipsis. Three little stepping-stones into the imagination. And out of the lion's cage.

HE WENT THROUGH the ritual of making me a coffee with his new espresso machine. How he loved his toys and

189

gadgets. Finally he passed me what I knew was Vicky's favourite cup – with an image of a New Look housewife declaring *I always have my cake and eat it*, brushing my fingers with his. It was corny, but it worked. That wringing out of desire. Call it lust if you want. Labels and names don't change anything.

I only went round to see how he was, to say thanks for the gardening and for everything he'd done for me on Saturday. I wasn't going to give in to him. Oh no, I was not. But the warm lip of the cup touched mine as he held my gaze just that few seconds too long and suddenly I was all of a flutter, eyes downcast, looking sideways and blinking like that flirting disingenue, Princess Di.

I wanted this to accelerate into the bright blue. I wanted to be held in that safe place above the clouds, travelling motionless yet almost at the speed of sound. I wanted to find that place and stay there.

Outside a gull squawked like a cicada revving up, and Sam's aftershave was sharp on the cup's handle as I drank the last of my coffee.

'Anyway. Choir tonight. Need to change out of these work clothes.' Damn did I mention clothes? Heat rose to my face.

'If you must, Miss Farrish.' Sam was laughing.

'Lovely to see you.'

I was standing at the door now.

'See you soon.' He gave me a chaste goodbye kiss on

each cheek. 'Mwah. Mwah.'

My hand was on the door. I was going. I nearly went.

A TRAIL OF my clothes, his clothes, up the stairs and into the spare bedroom where the sofa bed sits, still a sofa. Pause.

'Fuck it. We'll have to use my bed. I'm not messing about getting sheets.' He turned to me. 'You don't mind, Helen, do you?'

Mind? I was entering the heart of the rose.

AT ONE POINT he called out, 'Helen, you are *so* light!'

What could I have said without sounding uncharitable?

Then the room settled into focus – pink ceiling and pink wallpaper. Degas' little dancers everywhere. Black and white photos of Holly and Tom. The picture of Vicky en-pointe at age sixteen. If I closed my right eye it all became a pink blur and I was back in Vicky's bedroom in her mum's house, the sound of the sewing machine as we played our favourite dressing up and camping games.

On the side of the bed where I'd ended up, Vicky's, there was a book on Clarice Cliff with a postcard of Florence marking her place. The sheets and pillows were white sprigged with roses. For a mad minute I thought it could have been the ones I'd sent them as a wedding present, but Vicky would have replaced them by now. She liked things to be new. In alcoves on either side of the redundant fireplace were huge mahogany wardrobes for all Vicky's clothes, and against the wall was a long, low chest of drawers on top of which Vicky's jewellery was spread out, sparkling in the light from window. So much of everything. Even a large white sheepskin rug on the floor – to protect her pudgy feet from any cold or discomfort. No, that was going too far. I would have loved something so luxurious. Further along, pushed into a corner was a trouser press – presumably for Sam's work suits.

I took all of this in slowly, as we lay in that delightful post-coital, spooning position. There was a deep but comfortable dip in the bed; I was nestling in the space Vicky normally occupied. I wriggled round to look at Sam and take in the other half of the room. On his side of the bed was a battered copy of *Tess of the D'Urbervilles*, a notepad and pen, his watch – brown leather strap, gold with a cream face, and his pack of cigarettes.

At the large bay window were blinds as well as heavy curtains with swags and tails (for a house that was only rented!)

'I can see your mother-in-law's been busy with the sewing machine.'

'Too much for me. But when did I ever have a say in

these things?' He yawned. 'Only ever come here to sleep. Mostly.'

'Oh, is that how it is?'

'Yes. Unfortunately.'

'Well, I hope I've been of some use.'

I said this evenly. He could take it either way. He stretched his hand out to the bedside table.

'Is that a scar or a birthmark?'

He stopped and looked down at the bumpy red patch on his inner thigh. 'What? Oh yeah. Strawberry mark. Like Anne Boleyn. A mark of the devil!'

'And look what happened to her!'

'Ha!'

'And actually shaped like a strawberry!'

He leaned over for his cigarettes.

'You are such a cliché, Sam Taylor!'

'How?' He was searching for a lighter in the drawer.

'Smoking after sex.'

'Vic makes me go into the garden. But when she's not here…'

'You can do what you want!' I stroked his thigh and reached up to kiss him. This time, as if we had all the time in the world.

TWENTY-FIVE

POOR VICKY. WHAT she needed was a good friend to help keep things together and ease the pressure on their relationship. To keep the triangle strong. There were so many reasons why we should continue. In fact, from that day on, the more often we met, the more convinced I was that I was providing a useful service. Even better, and cheaper, than a marriage counsellor you might say.

FOR A FEW weeks Sam and I were both so hungry we gorged on each other at every opportunity; no matter how short and sweet. I gave him a key so he could let himself in and I'd be waiting, somewhere in the house – a delicious game of hide and seek. Sometimes the intensity of it made me ill and exhausted, and I had to keep away from him for a few days, to bury myself in the ordinariness of work or domestic chores. I took time off work and stayed in bed, to sleep and recover – I had no qualms about it; my sickness record had always been excellent.

This, at last, was the beginning. The real start of my

new adult life. When I closed my right eye and the world juddered out of focus, that was our world – the world of imagination and possibility. The ellipsis.

There was an element of guilt, a tiny sliver, irritating away under the skin. A splinter in a perfect world. But that was easily dealt with. Sam had made the choice. And he'd chosen me. I wasn't the one who was married. I didn't want to be cruel. Not really. I went out of my way to protect Vicky until such time as she would have to know. We were the best of friends. We met for coffee regularly and I sometimes brought the children home for school for her, if I was finishing early. We still had our lovely, happy family Sunday lunches. I made sure Vicky knew absolutely nothing.

I wasn't totally naïve however, I knew it would take weeks or months, possibly even years, but it was only a matter of waiting before we could be together. Look at good old Fanny Price waiting without hope, living off her little leftovers. If she could do it then I could live off all these scraps of Sam until the right moment.

Surprisingly, on such a poor diet, I even started to put on some weight. Not too much of course – I wasn't trying to compete with Vicky in the field of voluptuousness.

At work I had so many compliments: 'Helen have you had your hair done?' 'Have you been to the gym?' 'You look so well.' I smiled to myself and thanked them all.

I WAS BLOOMING, thriving on my rations. So much so that late one afternoon, towards the beginning of October, Sam started to panic. No, it wasn't anything like that. Goodness, I wasn't a complete beginner. I took precautions.

'But aren't you 'on' this week?' He'd quickly tuned in to my monthly cycle. We didn't have sex when I had my period. Far too messy. The first time it happened he didn't mind; I think he even took a perverse satisfaction in it. But he wasn't the one who had to buy biological washing powder to get out the stains.

'Nope.' I stroked his cheek with one hand, then found my way to the buckle of his trousers with the other. 'All clear.'

'You're not . . .?' He pulled away and held me at arm's length.

I laughed, and put both hands on his belt again.

'Helen, be serious. Are you …?'

'Of course not. My cycle's just messed up. Don't worry.'

We were in the hallway; he'd only just arrived.

'This isn't a good idea.' He put his hand on mine to stop me undoing his belt. 'Maybe we should stop.'

'Let's go to bed.' I caught hold of his hand and pulled him towards the stairs. I couldn't understand why he was making such a fuss.

'No, Helen. Not today. I don't think we …' For once

he sounded unsure of himself. And before I could say another word he was out of the door and walking away down the path, with only the slightest backwards glance.

It was the first time I hadn't been able to keep him.

Should I be upset and cry? Is that what you were supposed to do in these circumstances? To be honest I was pretty sure he'd be back. What I had to offer, and what we both had together, was not to be sniffed at. A whole life of pleasure, away from Vicky and her perfectly manicured fingernails; he wasn't going to give that up in a hurry. So I didn't waste time blubbing and making a mess of my face. I took off my silk negligee, then made myself a cup of tea and a toasted crumpet. With butter and jam. And I sat and waited. Well, figuratively speaking.

The next day he was back, secateurs in hand, with an apologetic shrug, which I assumed was for the previous day's nonsense.

'I can't keep helping you in the garden, Helen.'

'But you're doing such a good job.'

He turned over in bed and raised himself onto his elbows. 'Vicky asked me if you were entering Yorkshire in Bloom.'

I laughed. Apart from cutting down the tree that very first time, the garden hadn't changed. I hadn't given him time for that.

'I'm serious.' He sat up, leaning back against the headboard. 'She's very sensitive, you know.'

'And I'm not?' I sat up too.

Was this going to be an argument? We sat there like a proper married couple.

'It's not the same for you. You don't have to …'

'What?'

'She keeps saying when is *our* garden going to get sorted out?'

HE WAS RIGHT. It had been at the back of my mind for a week. I'd bumped into Sylvia at school and she'd asked how the garden was progressing, even threatened to drop in one day to see it. I'd suggested she wait for the spring when the bulbs would be showing. To tell you the truth, I ought to get on with my own gardening and leave him to do his. Gardening wasn't that difficult. If Mum came back, she would have been shocked at the state of it.

As for his own predicament, it would have to be something that required him to get hot and sweaty and need a shower afterwards; and also allowed sufficient time for our liaison.

You see I really wanted Vicky to be happy. Well, until she had to face the reality of where she was placed in the triangle.

I was the one who came up with the idea and, on my advice, Sam joined the local gym and took up running.

To throw her off the scent, a week after this conversation, I steeled myself to sacrifice a session of love making, and arranged to call in to see Vicky at the same time as Sam was 'going to the gym.' Easy peasy.

Vicky was preparing dinner; Sam getting ready to go out.

'But it's only an hour, twice a week.'

He thrust his arms into his coat, fastened the belt with a snap and rammed on his hat as if he'd been called to an emergency. Vicky cut the top and tails off half a dozen carrots, then scrubbed them vigorously under the tap with a small brush. Sylvia was coming for the evening, so she was making a hotpot.

'You're the one who said I was putting on weight.'

'And going for a pint afterwards is going to help?'

She glanced up from chopping onions, to the fridge where a photocopy of *Eat your way to the perfect weight* was pinned, with four cupcake fridge magnets.

Sam's shoulders drooped dramatically. He inhaled and mouthed counting to ten.

'Okay, boss. I'll say no. This time.'

I'd suggested he make some friends at the gym, take up offers of drinks. It would all normalise the situation.

He winked at me, with the flicker of a smile and the slightest shrug, unseen by Vicky, then left, slamming the front door. He was enjoying this, almost as if he was getting his own back. A few minutes later we heard his car reversing down the driveway.

'He's so weird at the moment.' Vicky chopped the carrots into rings 'I only mentioned middle age spread as a joke and suddenly the house is full of diet books and bran. He's even trying to cut down smoking.'

She pared cloudy, white fat off the lamb, until there was a pile of glistening pink meat on a plate and the scraps of fat tangled in a heap.

'The sensitive male ego!' I laughed, as she scooped up the fat and flopped it into the bin with a clang of the lid.

'He's started using moisturiser…says the sea air dehydrates his skin.'

'No!'

'I've no idea what he's playing at.' She sliced the meat quickly. 'Sometimes he disappears for hours on end in his study. God knows what he does up there.'

I imagined him in his clean uncluttered space high above the rest of the house marking his books and planning his lessons. Planning to meet me. Thinking about me. Texting me. The regular ping of text bouncing back and forward. *Ten minutes? Ready.*

Vicky washed her hands then leaned back against the work surface. Her cheeks were flushed and shiny and she was breathing heavily, as if she was the one going to the gym.

'It's mad, but I've even asked myself – what if he's having an affair?'

The word floated up between us like a bad smell – a

fat bubble of rotten eggs. Like a stink bomb.

'That would be mad, Vicky,' I said as calmly as I could.

'Has he said anything to you? Have you noticed anything? I know you two are as thick as thieves!'

'Nothing. He's mentioned names. Colleagues. But nothing like that.' I thought for a moment. 'Vicky, you don't mind us being friends, do you? I mean Sam and me.'

'Of course not. Not you, Helen. We're all old friends.' She picked up a pan. 'But every time I talk to someone back in Manchester. Nancy. Other couples. They ask.'

'Not Sam. He wouldn't do that to you.' My voice bounced round the kitchen like a power ball.

'Why not? What's so good about *him*? What's to say he's not meeting someone at this precise moment? One of those smooth-thighed adolescents flashing their eyes at *Sir*.'

She went back to the cooker and threw meat, onion and carrots into the pan. 'You remember what it was like in a secondary school!' There was a hiss of damp vegetables hitting oil, and blue, smoky steam rose up around her.

'Come on, Vic! You're being melodramatic. Sam's not the type.'

'Yeah? How would *you* know? You got him under surveillance? Are you tracking him?' She laughed suddenly and clamped a lid on the pan. 'Let's have a glass of wine . . . bastard!'

I laughed too.

TWENTY-SIX

BUT SAM WAS right. She was more sensitive than I'd ever given her credit for. We would have to be more careful. New rules were agreed, and a weekly and daily pattern became established. I must never text after nine o'clock when he was putting the children to bed. He must always give me time to be ready for him, not to turn up unannounced. I must *never* tell Vicky. And, on no account must he talk during sex.

I loved to take my clothes off without any dialogue. He liked to watch. I liked him to watch me. And I loved the silence when we were in bed. It made the frisson of words afterwards like drinking a glass of the coldest, clearest water. After years of silence, I was addicted to words. And he had so many of them. Not the dull crossword kind I associated with Dad, dear man he did love his crosswords and meanings, all his maps and newspapers, facts and figures. No, it was words in the poetry sense, leaping off the tongue – I know I complained about his quotations, but really I loved them. I wanted them all the time. I wanted to be his muse.

We were getting so close to the time we'd be together, I began to feel sorry for Vicky, all alone with the children ousted from the double bed. Perhaps it could happen naturally and we could be a ménage a trois, only she would be Fanny Price in her cold, single room without Edmund.

ONE SATURDAY AFTERNOON we lay in bed, sweat cooling on our bodies. One of those autumn days when there was still enough warmth in the sun to give the illusion of summer; but the light would fade early then the temperature would drop, and you couldn't fool yourself any longer – change to colder weather and dark evenings was inevitable.

Apart from the beat of my own heart quietening in my ears, the silence was so complete, I imagined I could hear the waves crashing onto the sand in the distance. A few streets away came the sound of the ice cream van and I wondered who would buy one when it was so cold? But we were warm in my bed, safe on our own island.

'*Alas, my love, you–*' I began to hum.

'*Sweet Helen, make me immortal with a kiss,*' Sam said, as if he'd been waiting for his cue to speak.

'Do you never stop being an English teacher?'

'A quotation for every occasion. No job too small.'

'Even this one?'

'*From here to eternity.*'

'*To infinity and beyond.*' I countered as he kissed me. I sat up and stretched. 'Let's go out and *do* something.'

'Where could we go?'

'Anywhere.'

'No, I meant where could *we* go?'

'Wherever we like.'

Sam frowned and shook his head.

I wound myself around him, putting my thigh over his, and tangled my fingers in the hair curled in the dip of his breast bone. 'A walk. Just us.' I moved my fingers down to the soft skin of his stomach. 'And a walk would be good for you too …'

'Little Helen, look at me.' Sam pulled in his stomach as he smoothed my hair away from my face. 'We can't go for a walk. We're not 'going out'. We're not *going* anywhere.'

'What about Pisa? We spent a whole day together.'

'That was different. We were on holiday and we had the kids with us. It was all in the open.'

He pulled me down and wrapped his arms around me.

'*Come, Helen, come. Give me my soul again*! It's not time for talking. You have such a beautiful mouth, such soft lips. We haven't got long.'

I wanted to push the boundaries, to move on to the next stage, but he stopped me with kisses. I thought of the steps winding up to the top of the tower in Pisa, of how at first he'd held my hand ready to guide me up to the top. No one had minded that. Vicky had been happy for us to go. We were friends, weren't we? Okay, we were more than friends but that didn't stop us doing ordinary friendly things in public. It was going to take time to make Sam understand. I really did have my work cut out. So, I gave in to him, to the mindless pleasure of it all. We could talk about going out somewhere next time. We could make plans for the future, step by step.

AFTER HE'D GONE I lay on the bed dozing, replaying the afternoon's session with my own hand. Of course we were going somewhere. We needed to be together. He was my Edmund. Something so big and important couldn't be contained in one room. We needed to expand our horizons. Daylight faded and the shadow of the lighthouse gradually filled the room.

When Michael and I were children and shared a bedroom, the lighthouse beam used to sweep over us all night. Light then dark. Light then dark. A constant rhythm, a visual heartbeat as we fell asleep. Until the light came back again, we used to hold our breath in the dark then make a wish. Could I wish on a shadow instead?

The lighthouse.

THE STAIRS WOUND up to the top of the lighthouse like the inside of a snail shell. I counted as I climbed to control my excitement. After much persuasion, Sam agreed to meet me there, but he refused to walk together. It was too much in the open. Someone might see us.

'So you want us to rendezvous like secret agents? Do we need to synchronise watches?'

'Ha! I'll meet you at the top at three.'

I decided to go later. I wanted him to be waiting for me, to be fretting. It would add piquancy to the game. It was like playing spies as a child; or possibly the pleasure went further back, to the dark thrill of hide and seek, the excitement of the chase or, even better, waiting to be found, squeezed into the under stairs cupboard with the ironing board jabbing into me, and the smell of Brasso and Pledge.

One hundred and forty four steps to the top was twelve times twelve: a square number, satisfying, and almost magical. I was out of breath, my heart hammering. Of course it was mainly the effort of the climb, but there was also the anticipation. Like going to a forbidden place for the first time. I'd never been up the lighthouse.

Sam was standing on the viewing platform, looking over the rail at the town spread below us on all sides and out towards the sea in the distance. The air was so still that smoke from a bonfire drifted up in a single grey plume. It was the end of the season. The holidaymakers had gone home leaving their caravans like crops of barnacles along the coast.

We kissed for a long time up there – above the town, above our work, our friends, his family. If anyone had glanced up from raking leaves in the garden, shopping on the main street or playing football in the park, they would have seen us like a scene in a Hollywood romance kissing at the top of the lighthouse. In full view. Out in the open at last.

RUNNING EASED HIS conscience and the lighthouse became our place.

There in 10? he would text.

And he'd arrive, in jogging bottoms, a tee shirt stretched over his flattening stomach. Hot and sweating. I didn't mind. *Top of the world, ma.*

But it wasn't enough. I liked being outside with him. We needed other venues. It was a risk, now that the Taylors lived on the same road as her, but I asked Julia to design an arbour for my garden – the garden as an outdoor room was all the fashion she told me one evening after the rehearsal. She said she'd advise me. I didn't tell her why.

Vicky heard about it and came to quiz me.

'You and your secret places, Helen. Always hiding away. Such a hopeless romantic.'

'I want somewhere to sit after work in the summer and read or have a glass of wine.'

'I'll look forward to it, love. Honeysuckle. Roses. Warm scented evenings.'

'If we're lucky,' I said.

'Sitting in your arbour like the lady of Shallot. Or some kind of pre-Raphaelite! … Your hair's growing so long. I remember how it was when you were little – rippling down your back while mine was dead straight. So envious.' She caught up an end of my hair and wrapped it around her finger then let it unravel. 'So gorgeous. I was always jealous of you!'

In my mind I took the picture of Vicky in her pink bedroom, her hair spread like seaweed on the pillow, and before I could remember anything else, clicked the light out. Firmly.

I WENT TO Hull on the bus to buy more clothes – beautiful fabrics: silk, linen and cashmere. Nothing synthetic. Clothes that were simple to slip on. Or off. With easy access. I bought necklaces, earrings and bracelets – I liked to keep my jewellery on like a Baudelairian femme fatale. Jangling, tinkling, sparkling. Shiny. I bought more and more.

I wanted to buy presents for Sam too. 'Why have all this money if I can't spend it? Mum saved a ridiculous amount. I want to spend it on you, Sam.' I was like Madame Bovary. Although I wasn't a damn fool like her. Arsenic poisoning – *les atroces douleurs*! Not bloody likely. I wasn't going to end it all because of a man.

I went to York and searched the second-hand bookshops – I found Sam a Penguin edition of *Lady Chatterley's Lover* and gave it to him one afternoon when we were in bed.

'This would give my A-level students something to think about! But I can't take it home, Helen.'

'Leave it here then. We can act out your favourite chapters next time!'

'You are incorrigible, Miss Farrish.'

'I hope so,' I said, and went to find a bookmark.

SOMETHING WOKE ME with a jolt. I'd been dreaming about the market in Florence, walking with Sam, not Vicky – his weight, the smell of him, his hand on the small of my back so close together we were almost walking as one. The dream stayed with me, as if he'd only just left the room. I sat up in bed and listened. I couldn't exactly describe it, but there was a tingling everywhere, a kind of singing in the room. It was as light as a childhood summer morning when you know the day will stretch ahead effortlessly, and each moment will join to the next without any awkwardness. Smooth and seamless.

I dressed quickly and I did something I'd never done before –I went out and walked down to the beach without having breakfast first. The air was cold but the sun, rising over the sea through the mist, breathed out warmth and cast a sheen on the water. The long, broken lines of groynes held back the sand and stopped the sea from washing it away. I'd always seen them as sad or decrepit with a hopeless task. They'd never be effective. Suddenly they were heroic, picturesque; they had a job to do and were doing it well. They were part of growing up by the sea watching the waves gradually cover the groynes as the tide came in. Looking back to the town, the houses nestled closely, almost snuggling in together like houses in a child's picture. Everything was clear and purposeful. As I walked home feeling hungry and ready to eat a huge breakfast, the houses weren't turned inward, introspective; there were invisible lines of communication linking us all together. Like the cobwebs in my front garden, damp with dew and picked out by the light.

And Sam was here, in Holdersea. In some senses he was Holdersea – I could breathe him in with the light and with the ozone breath of the sea. He was here, holding my hand, touching me. Kissing my lips and breasts, running his fingers down my inner thighs. He was turning cartwheels for me along the line of surf. His long legs running to see me. He was running up the stairs to the top of the lighthouse because he wanted to see me. He'd stopped smoking. He was risking everything for me. And there was nothing I wouldn't do for him. We each invent our own worlds; we choose what we want to see, how we see it. Perhaps it was all in my head – which is the only world I knew or could understand. Perhaps nothing had changed. But to me, the only explanation to account for this shift in perception, was that I'd arrived at a new place. The past had caught up with the present. I was living the life I wanted. I was happy. I was in love with Sam. And I needed to tell him.

TWENTY-SEVEN

'MUMMY'S A WITCH. What are you, Aunty Helen?'

On the doorstep a giant orange face grinned and flickered malevolently and the hallway was draped in fake cobwebs and plastic bats. A warm smell of nutmeg and cumin mingled in the steam of the kitchen where Vicky was stirring a pan of pumpkin soup.

It was a children's party, but any available adults were roped in to help. I was sure she'd only invited me because I was child-free; but I didn't mind. I liked to be useful and more than that I *wanted* to be her friend. In spite of everything, I liked Vicky. She didn't intimidate me anymore.

Sam and I would have to be on our guard not to be too obvious, of course – we'd have to fold everything away and play at being friends, to remember not to touch or kiss. None of that. But it was a chance for us to be together without any sense of guilt, in a public place. And this evening I'd be able to tell him how I felt, how much I loved him. My dear Edmund.

Sylvia, wearing a witch's hat, was laying out party

food: lychees decorated with red food colouring (eyeballs); a pink jelly that had been frozen in a washing up glove (a witches' hand) and hotdogs oozing with ketchup (severed fingers).

'We've been busy all morning' she said. 'Vicky's exhausted. What we mothers do! You don't know how lucky you are, Helen.'

I went into the kitchen to see if I was needed there, just as Sam came in from the garden where he was putting up fairy lights.

'Bubble, Bubble, my trouble and strife. Soup smells good.' He put his arms around Vicky, but she pushed him away and sighed.

'Go and look after our guests. Helen hasn't got a drink yet.'

His fingers stroked mine as he passed me a glass of mulled wine, full of floating shards of fruit. 'Helen. I need to look after you.'

I gave him a warning look but he left the room and went to attend to other guests.

Vicky had made an effort to dress up, but the effect was grotesque. The black cloak emphasised how much weight she'd put on; and her hair stuck out in blond tufts around her face like a mangy lion's mane. Poor Vicky, no wonder Sam turned to me. I'd gone for the more glamorous vampire look, without the teeth. Black and more black. Even my underwear. I felt so light with

happiness every step was like dancing. As if I was drunk –
and I hadn't even tried the wine yet.

One day soon, she would wake up, look in the mirror
and give in gracefully; she just needed time to come to
terms with her lot.

'Smells amazing.' I said, peering into the pan of soup.

'I've been hacking away at that pumpkin for so long
I'm worn out. It's starting to make me feel ill – slimy
stuff. It's for the adults. Unless you'd like to eat eyeballs
and severed fingers!'

'Let me help.'

'Thanks, love.' She wasn't slow to hand me the spoon,
then flopped onto the sofa. 'You look gorgeous, by the
way. Even when you're dead.'

I concentrated on stirring the soup. Roasted garlic and
caramelised onion made my mouth water, but I didn't
want to eat too much. I had other appetites to satisfy.
Tonight, once the party was underway, I would tell Sam
how I felt. We could slip into one of the bedrooms while
the games were going on.

'At this point I always ask myself why I invited so
many people. What made me think a party was a good
idea!' Vicky laughed to herself.

'I'm here to help. Just let me know what to do.'

'Keep an eye on Sam for me. You know what he's
like. Parties are his element. He likes an audience.' She
yawned and added quietly, 'He's still being weird,

Helen – one minute he won't leave me alone, and the next dashing off to the gym. But at least he's not smoking. He's finally quit!'

'He looks better for it.'

His hands, his lips, his tongue.

THE HOUSE WAS beginning to fill up with small witches, monsters and ghosts. A few parents hung around for a while then left saying they'd be back at eight, when the party finished. So, all the work and tidying up was going to be left to Sylvia and me. Not exactly what I'd planned.

'We're missing you at choir, Helen. How are you enjoying the garden?'

It wasn't until she spoke that I realised Julia and her daughter had arrived.

'Lovely to have a secret place, Julia. So sheltered and private. I'm looking forward to the summer when I can use it properly!'

Sam gave her a glass of wine. 'Who knows what she'll get up to?'

'Well, she's too busy for choir I hardly see her any more. I was just saying to Ed I think something's going on!'

'Still waters run deep, don't they, Helen?' Sam nudged me and winked at Julia.

I wanted to run upstairs with him there and then.

'Ooh! Sam Taylor you never stop, do you!' Julia brayed with laughter and knocked back her wine.

'How are the rehearsals going, Julia? How's Ed?' I said.

While we chatted the two girls disappeared upstairs together and came down minutes later, mouths scarlet with lipstick, reeking of *Miss Dior*.

'Holly, I've told you not to …'

'You never use half that make up, Mum!'

'It's the smell, darling – you only need a little. Not the whole lot.' Vicky put her hand to her face as if to stop the smell.

'Overpowering!' I laughed.

'They start so young nowadays.' Julia refilled her glass. 'She won't listen … '

The girls giggled and ran away to the sitting room where Sam was in charge of party entertainment.

'She's started wearing makeup to school. I don't know what to do with her, Vicky. I got called in by her head of year.' Julia downed her second glass of wine. 'I hope she's not a bad influence on Holly.'

'You worry too much, Julia. Look at them. Quite happy to play old fashioned games.'

'As long as she keeps away from boys a bit longer than her mother.' Julia laughed as she made her way to the front door.

Soon the noise was intolerable. Sam was directing the

children in a chaotic game of apple bobbing when the bucket was knocked over. I was the one who went to fetch the mop. Vicky didn't move, although I suspected she knew I'd sort it out as she looked over at me and carried on talking to her mother. I dragged the mop and bucket out of the cupboard and saw Sylvia handing her a cup of tea. Still being waited on hand and foot by her mother. At her age.

Suddenly I couldn't stand the noise, the mess, the frustration. My hopes of time alone with Sam were misplaced. It definitely wasn't going to be that sort of party. All I could do was carry on playing the useful friend, and anticipate the next time we'd be in bed, or perhaps up on the viewing platform of the lighthouse, when I would be able to say openly: I love you, Sam Taylor.

There was a brief lull while Sam took the children trick or treating followed by a house full of overexcited children stuffing their faces with sweets. At last it was eight o'clock and a stream of parents arrived to take them home. Nasty, brutish but thankfully short.

Once they'd gone, the house was blissfully quiet. I helped Sylvia tidy up. Vicky had fallen asleep on the sofa and didn't wake until I banged the lid as I scraped the remains of severed fingers into the bin.

'I'm worn out. Shattered.' She yawned and sat up. 'Never again!'

As if she'd actually been doing anything! She constantly complained about feeling tired, even more now than when we were on holiday. Constantly *shattered*. It was beyond a joke; it was boring. She was leaving all the work to other people, me included.

We looked at one another and she smiled weakly. I had a sudden plunge of anxiety in my stomach. A vision of absence.

There was something wrong.

'You okay, Vee? Always so tired.'

'I know.' She yawned again. 'No energy.'

'Maybe you're anaemic? Have you been to the doctor? You might need some iron or vitamins.'

What if she was really ill?

The air around us was vibrating. Everything was exaggerated – the smell of the soup, the sickly, sugary party food, fumes from the mulled wine. It was too hot in the kitchen. What if she wasn't there anymore? What would happen to our little triangle? Poor Vicky. Poor Sam. Who would look after the children? What would I do? This wasn't in the plan.

'Can I get you another cup of tea or something, Vicky?'

'No thanks. I'm okay. Feeling sick, that's all.'

Then she absently placed her hand flat on her lower abdomen. It was a gesture I recognised from films, from other women. As he came into the room Sam saw it too.

Vicky looked up at him, tears in her eyes.

'Yes,' she said her voice hardly more than a whisper.

I watched the slow dawning on Sam's face, as disbelief changed to a smile.

'Vicky! My little dumpling.'

He put his arms around her and held her so close I had to grip the edge of the table to stop myself from tearing him away from her. I looked out into the dark of the garden, but all I could see was a reflection of Sam's back, his hands stroking Vicky's bare arms.

Stupid fat cow. How could she?

'Congratulations!' I said. 'How long?'

Sam stroked her hair as she leant back and rested her head against his stomach. Under his shirt the long dark line of hair ran down his taut skin, across his belly.

'Four months already. The end of March. A spring baby.'

'Feeling okay? Apart from the tiredness?' I asked.

'Could be better. Not usually feeling sick at this stage.' Vicky turned her head to look up at Sam.

'So you were pregnant on holiday, little peach?' Sam laughed under his breath.

'I started feeling sick in Italy but thought it was just the weather!' She sighed. 'Suspected it, but finally did a test today. Mum already knows, don't you?'

Sylvia who had come in quietly while we were talking, put a pile of plates on the table. 'Another wee one. She was going to tell you tonight, Sam. After the party.'

'Always the last to know.' Sam kissed the top of her head. 'Well done, little Vicky.'

He didn't once look at me.

Tom came running into the room. 'What's the matter? Why is everyone crying and laughing?'

Then Sam found a bottle of Prosecco left over from the holiday and we had to celebrate. Apart from Vicky. 'Just juice for me,' she said virtuously.

After what I thought was a reasonable time, I left them to it.

'I'll see you to the door, Helen.'

Sam didn't touch me. His lips barely touched mine when we kissed goodbye. He kissed my cheek. He didn't wave, and before anyone bothered to shut the door I heard him:

'What do you think, guys? Another brother or sister! What a clever Mummy!'

TWENTY-EIGHT

FROM THE VIEWING platform, the town was a toy village, scattered along the edge of the land. Even the sea looked artificial – like cheap viscose with a scalloped edge of dirty surf. Main roads cut through the town until they reached the heart, where they became narrow streets winding between houses with red roofs, interspersed with the grey of slate, then continued out and into the distance in three directions. Although I'd looked at the view many times now, I still expected to see the smooth red of roads you would have found on an old AA map spooling away from here. It was more like Google Earth – the streets were hidden down between buildings; and then, once the routes reached the edge of town, they barely scratched the sudden green of fields.

Sam and Vicky's house was solid and unremarkable amongst other stone villas. Nothing scrawled on the roof to say *solid as sin.* If I clicked onto StreetView I'd see them through the bay window – the kids watching DVDs and Vicky trying to have her Sunday nap, complaining she was feeling sick and moaning at the noise.

Deep in the shadow of the lighthouse my semi-detached curled into itself like a snail under its slate roof. And there at the far end of my garden was my new arbour, bulbs and plants dormant, waiting for the spring. Bare and exposed.

'Race you to the top'. Voices rang out from the lighthouse garden – a family on a Sunday outing. The wind was keening in the railings around the platform and seagulls wheeled and mewled, diving for scraps.

Sam would be getting ready. Soon he'd be on his way. I was wearing his favourite outfit: tight jeans and a loose-fitting shirt, my hair held back to stop it blowing in the wind. I thought back to standing at the top of the Leaning Tower in Pisa, the shock of the heat. Before all of this had started. Today I felt chilled. After a week of rain it was bright but cold. He would soon be here to warm me up.

Ten minutes?

Of course.

Since Vicky dropped her bombshell, I'd left it up to him to contact me. He needed breathing space – time to get used to another mouth to feed, another call on his time and energy. To tell you the truth I felt sorry for him. All week since the party I'd been waiting for him to text.

In the distance, I could see all the way to the horizon: like an indelible line written in blue crayon in a child's hand. I watched the sea rolling in, eating away at the shore, constantly shifting the coastline. But our relationship was as safe as houses. Nothing between us had to change.

As soon as it was dark there'd be a bonfire on the beach and a firework display. Sam was taking the children. I'd promised Vicky I'd help him while she stayed at home to rest. We would have time together in the evening too. Tom was scared of loud noises, poor lamb – although he pretended he wasn't – I would make sure I held his hand.

Footsteps clanked on the metal of the platform but it was only the family I'd heard down in the lighthouse garden. Sam was late. He was never late. It was a long ten minutes. Probably more like half an hour. The family walked around several times exclaiming in an inane way as people do, then one of the children heard the ice cream van, so they all went down and left me. I was getting cold and seriously thinking he wasn't coming, when there was a tang of cigarette smoke, and single footsteps – the right weight and rhythm – clattered on the stairs of the lighthouse. He was in running gear, out of breath and sweating.

'Ten minutes!' I exclaimed.

'I'm sorry, I had to– '

'More like ten hours!' I ran up to him. 'Never mind, you're here now.'

I put my arms around his neck and lifted my face up,

eyes closed, for him to kiss me.

'I'm sorry, Helen.'

He held himself away stiffly, resisting me, as if he wasn't allowed to touch me.

I opened my eyes. His mouth was a grim line, like the pumpkin lantern.

'Sam?'

He held me at arm's length, then brought me in to his body in a hug that enveloped me; he squeezed me so hard I was scared he'd crush me. The smell of his fresh sweat was delicious.

'I'm sorry.'

His voice in my ear was an octave lower than normal; I had to hold my breath so I could hear him. The wind was stronger now, moaning in the railings. It was growing darker by the minute. We didn't have much more time until the lighthouse would shut for the evening.

'This has to stop, Helen.' He hesitated. 'Vicky …'

'Is she okay?'

I stepped back to see his face more clearly.

'Yes, she's fine. She's well.' He turned away and looked towards the sea. 'But, I can't do this.' His voice was caught up and whisked away by the wind.

I looked too. Grey clouds were beginning to build up in the west. But the horizon was more precise now; like a thin blue line on a pregnancy test.

THE FIRST THING I did was to walk. What else could I have done? Go back to my own house crouching in the shadow of the lighthouse? It would be like going back into a prison cell.

I was shaking with cold and I suppose I was in shock. It had come out of the blue. He was giving me the elbow. Rejecting me in favour of Vicky. How could he?

As it grew dark and all over Holdersea the lights flicked on, I walked the streets, the promenade, and finally along the beach. The waves rose up and tipped their burden of water as if nothing had changed. Over and over again. A mindless repetition. No pathetic fallacy. I wanted to run and keep running, but a sense of self-respect stopped me. I avoided the crowds milling around and waiting for the firework display to start. What if I met someone I knew? What would they say? I couldn't speak to anyone. The words would come out like a roar of disbelief.

I walked along the shoreline until I was both soaked with hot sweat and freezing cold. I walked away from the town as far as I could and looked back. The lighthouse glowed faintly in the orange reflection of the streetlights like a stick of barley sugar being licked away until it finally dissolved into the night and became an absence.

The clouds that had been slowly ganging up to the west had blotted out the horizon. The wind became stronger. When the first drops fell on my cheeks it was almost a relief, as if the pressure had abruptly been lifted, then without warning the skies opened and the rain came in waves, solid sheets of water. There was water everywhere. The sky, the sea. At last I allowed myself to cry, to release the boiling rage at his cowardice.

What on earth would make him choose Vicky over me? What did a snivelling little baby that wasn't even born, have to do with us?

Nothing.

Sam was pushing away the greatest love in his life for some perverse sense of duty. And I knew all about *duty* – its corrosive, acid effect. I'd had twenty years of it. Vicky wasn't going to produce another little monster just to keep him trapped with her and her brood.

Tears burned my cheeks and the rain soaked my jeans and shirt, drenched my hair until it hung down in rats' tails. Like Smelly-Ann at the bus stop. *It'll all end in tears.* The smug phrase made me a child again, crying at rejection and shame. Summoned in by the teacher and told not to show my knickers. Trapped like a fly behind glass. I was part of the whole sodden mess of the day. There was no one nearby and the crash of the waves covered my stupid sobbing. I let myself wail as loud and as long as I could and then, once I had no tears left, I blew my nose into my sopping handkerchief and turned back towards the town. As I walked home, via the back streets, the rain was easing off to a fine drizzle. It wouldn't stop the fireworks or the bonfire; they would go ahead and everyone would be there. But not me.

By the time I was dried out and warm, fireworks had started to perforate the early evening peace. I shut the curtains so there was no hint of a gap, but they weren't thick enough to hide the light. I mentally blocked my eyes and ears to keep them out.

Sam would be getting ready, making sure the children had hats and gloves. I wasn't going to offer to help. If the phone rang, I would ignore it. He would have to go without me. Vicky could lie on her sofa and swell up like a cow, like one of those cows slaughtered because of mad cow disease, belly heavy with gases. I wasn't going to do anything for them.

The walk had made me hungry, so I cooked a pile of toast and scrambled egg, and washed it down with a mug of sweet tea. Then the rest of the evening I cleaned. I scrubbed the kitchen until my hands were aching, then I did the same to the bathroom. I would soon clear every trace of him from the house – well, at least until I'd worked out a scheme to get him back – and tomorrow I would start on a forensic clean of the bedroom.

After that I was so much more like my old self that I found the bottle of sherry I'd been saving for Christmas, the one I'd planned Sam and I would enjoy in bed together, not that I could even allow myself to think about that scenario, and I polished it off. Then I went to bed. It must have only been nine o'clock.

But I couldn't shut out the fireworks. It was like a war zone instead of a quiet seaside resort. All those chemicals and colours. What a waste of money. I put my pillow over my ears and turned away from the window. The room was tilting gently – possibly the effect of the sherry – so it was like stepping into a rowing boat and drifting off to sleep. In the morning I would come up with a plan.

TWENTY-NINE

I SLEPT SOUNDLY and woke refreshed. My anger was quiet like the lion asleep in its cage. As I lay on my back thinking, the mattress held each vertebra, and my limbs and muscles were heavy with a kind of relaxed exhaustion.

I mustn't think about him in a pathetic, lost kind of way. Forget him for a little while and focus. I was a big girl now. I could wait. The supine state is one of the best for coming up with creative ideas. I lay there and let my mind do its work. I'd given it the instructions the night before and all I had to do was to wait. All my Fanny Price training in patience was never more useful. You can't bully ideas into ripeness – all you end up with are thin spindly things like Dad's forced rhubarb. I had to let it happen naturally.

But then the emotion seeped in. Sam had said *no* to me. Sam had put a stop to it. In one fell swoop he'd ended my pleasure. I gasped for air, like the time when a boy at school, whose name I've forgotten, swung his duffel bag into my stomach and I was doubled up with a spasm of sickness, the breath knocked out of me. I could almost cry again with frustration. I wanted to run to Vicky for her to comfort me; she was the only one who could make me feel better. My lovely friend, Vicky. I wanted to get it all back again – my *grande affaire*. I wanted Sam.

So I texted Vicky.

Any chance of a shoulder to cry on?

She had been a good friend to me. And, for a mother of two expecting her third, as well as running a small business, she embodied the cliché 'if you want something done, ask a busy person.' She rarely said no.

Come over. Any time. We're just having a quiet day.

That 'we' rankled, like a whining mosquito, but I didn't let it spoil my mood. I set to work cleaning the bedroom and the rest of the house. Lastly I ran myself a bath and poured in a few drops of bleach. I immersed myself in the cleansing, chlorinated water. I soaked my wounds, so to speak. I washed him off me. He was a cowardly adulterous hypocrite. But I still had a glimmer of dignity. I'd go round there and take my comfort from Vicky.

As I RANG the doorbell, I noticed a rocket stuck in the hedge. There were others on the grass at the front. Burnt out cylinders of cardboard with sad broken sticks.

'Come in, love. I'll put the kettle on.' Vicky answered

the door bringing with her an enticing smell of roast meat and vegetables. Sunday lunchtime. Since Italy they didn't always invite me, but today it felt more like a deliberate omission. Had Sam said something? Had he put a stop to it?

In the hallway his guitar was leaning against the wall, abandoned among shoes and trainers. My fingers itched to stroke the fingerboard where paler areas were worn away by his fingers. Fingers that had …No, I couldn't afford to think like that. Too dangerous.

I could hear them in the garden; he was playing the good father as if he'd had a new lease of life. I sat with my back to the window.

'Won't be long, Helen, then you can tell me all about it.'

What was I going to say? I really wasn't sure. I tried to be rational. My friend Vicky is making me a cup of coffee. Her husband, Sam is playing with their children in the garden. I have come to visit. Everything is fine.

She pressed the hot coffee into my hands with such a kind look on her face, tears started welling up.

'What is it, sweetheart? I hate to see you so upset.'

She sat on the sofa next to me. She smelled of a new, fresher perfume – a smell that reminded me of baking, of paring the rind off lemons to mix into biscuits when I was a child, before Dad died, in the days when Mum was comparatively happy. Michael would be playing with a lump of dough while I rolled out the mixture on a floured board. The whole scene was gold with low autumn sun. The yellow simplicity of fresh lemons – juice and rind. The oven warmed the kitchen and flour dust covered every surface. Each time I cut out the crinkled circles, gently pushed them out of the metal cutters and placed them in rows on the baking sheet, square and slicked with melted butter, a dozen on each, everything was ordered and perfect. Just as I'd done with Holly and Tom.

Vicky pressed herself close to me and stroked my hair. I was surrounded by a kind of citrusy goodness. It was foolish to give way. But I did, and as she let me blub on her shoulder, she stroked my hair with a mother's hand.

From outside there were shouts and yells.

'Daddy, look at me. I can go so high'

'Great, Tom.'

'But I can go higher, Dad. Let me have a go. It's my turn.'

'Is it a man, Helen?' Vicky asked me, out of nowhere. 'You've been different recently.'

I shook my head.

'You've been seeing that idiot, Ed again, haven't you, love?'

'I didn't want to tell you …' I managed to say, between sobs.

Vicky passed me a tissue and, without forethought, without any conscious planning, I told her all about the lover who had let me down so badly. I let her believe her own story.

It wasn't difficult. And, in a sense it was true. Fundamentally it was a creative act. I borrowed a little of Sam to add to the authenticity of the portrait – nothing she would recognise, just a few of his phrases – *I'm sorry, Helen* and *This has to stop*. They were so generic, so uninspired that I would give nothing away by repeating them. They were hardly in Ed's vocabulary anyway. In fact there was a delicious pleasure in saying them; and doubly so in seeing and hearing her reaction.

'Does Julia know?'

'I didn't want her to be hurt too.'

'I didn't think he had it in him. What a bastard!'

At that moment there was a ring on the doorbell.

'Sorry, Helen. It must be Mum. You okay?'

'I'll get it!' Sam called from the hall. There was a gust of cold air as he opened the front door, and Sylvia bustled in.

'I've brought an apple cake. Her favourite.'

'Ah, the Mother-in-law. Here to rescue me at last!'

'I'd like a cuppa first, Sam? How is she? I hope you're looking after her.'

I could hear him singing in the kitchen as he boiled the kettle; and the clatter of crockery as Sylvia found plates.

'We're in here, Mum.' Vicky called.

'She's always loved my apple cake. Even when she was wee. And she needs feeding up. Eating for two now, you know.' Sylvia was saying to Sam as she brought in three slices of cake. She put down the cake then came over to give me the usual embrace. 'Helen! I'll get another plate. Vicky's looking well isn't she?'

'Helen. I didn't know ...' Sam sat down heavily in a chair next to Vicky. His face was a picture. 'How's it going?'

'Could be better.' I smiled, then blew my nose into another of Vicky's tissues.

She whispered something in his ear, presumably explaining my tearful state, my being there at all. He looked at me briefly, blankly, then concentrated on eating his cake. For the first time in his life he couldn't think of anything to say.

'... And when the baby comes I'll look after the children. What a good thing they're back in Holdersea. I can help every day!' Sylvia hadn't stopped talking since she arrived. It was like a restless stream in the background.

'Lovely cake, Sylvia. You must give me the recipe,' I said.

Sam left the room and came back with a bottle of red wine.

'Glass of wine, Sylvia? To celebrate.' He didn't sound as if he had anything to celebrate.

'Tea's fine for me, Sam dear. I'll just fall asleep if I

drink at this time of day.'

He poured himself a large glass then set about cleaning the grate to make a fire. Sylvia was too fretful about Vicky to notice my red-rimmed eyes. I excused myself and went up to the bathroom. Once I'd splashed my face with cold water and patted my skin dry with one of the thick, fluffy towels, I looked closely in the mirror. Not as bad as I'd feared. I searched through the cabinet to find one of Vicky's moisturisers and dabbed some on my face. There was some mascara and blusher in a basket – I was sure she wouldn't mind.

Downstairs, the children had been called in to see their grandmother. She'd brought them sweets so they were sitting quietly in front of the smoking fire, pink cheeked now they'd come indoors.

'You'll have to make sure you're good for your mummy. She'll need lots of help when the baby comes,' Sylvia was saying.

'What about a glass of wine for Helen. I think she needs one too.'

Dear Vicky, what an attentive friend she was. *You okay?* she mouthed at me as I sat down.

'A small one, Sam, thanks. A bit delicate today.'

He handed me a glass, studiously avoiding eye contact; then, as Sylvia doled out pregnancy advice, and Vicky kept giving me little glances and encouraging smiles, he proceeded to finish off the bottle, without offering it again, ostentatiously attending to the fire, which was producing a lot of smoke and no flames or warmth.

It was soon dark and, when I looked at my watch, nearly five o'clock. After a large Sunday roast, they would probably have a late tea; but I'd had no lunch and only a piece of cake; I was suddenly ravenous. I also needed to do my ironing and preparations for the following week at work.

Vicky came to the door with me.

'Now, love. Remember I'm always here. You're better off without that idiot anyway.' She hugged me hard. 'If only I'd known you were seeing him ... He's really not worth it.'

I shrugged and sighed, forcing a watery smile.

'Julia can look after herself, but I think you need someone to guide you when it comes to men, little Helen. We'll have to find you someone else. You're exhausted. Sam will run you home.'

'I need the walk. Thanks, Vicky.'

I knew he was less than pleased; and after a bottle of wine he was hardly safe to drive, was he?

LATER THAT EVENING, when I was running a bath, I heard the ping of a text. I ran down to the kitchen, almost forgetting my dressing gown.

Don't do this. We need space.

It was curt. Rude even. I didn't answer.

I'd give him his precious *space* but he wasn't going to spoil a pleasant afternoon with my friend, Vicky. He still needed me really. Let him wait.

I was making a strategic retreat. *Reculer pour mieux sauter*, as the French say.

THIRTY

IN THE COLD light of a Monday morning as I hurried to work, the previous day seemed less of a success. I'd acted instinctively in 'confessing' to Vicky and she'd been convinced, but I'd not endeared myself to Sam. Looking at it positively, Vicky was still my friend and I would be welcome at their house; I would still be able to see him. On the surface, nothing had changed. Our little triangle was damaged but not completely broken. Sam would soon realise how much he missed me and needed me. In fact we could start again, as friends and work our way up gradually to a full-blown relationship. As Vicky's pregnancy progressed and she became less able to provide him with what he really wanted, he would need a friend. *A friend in need* as they say, *is a friend in deed.*

I knew those first weeks wouldn't be easy; but with careful planning I could survive. I'd put up with worse – twenty years of Mum's declining health had given me a slow-burning endurance. I was a marathon runner, not a sprinter. And good things come to those who wait.

The first major obstacle to my peace of mind was the

gaping hole in my life without Sam. It would have been easy to fill it with a blank sense of loss; I could sit around and weep and wail. But, whatever happened, I must not turn into my own mother, addicted to tranquilisers, that was the bald truth of it, and scared to leave the house. Poor Mum. She never got over Dad's death.

Luckily I had work. And other friends. Julia was happy to go to the cinema.

From brief sightings of him wandering on the beach with his metal detector, I knew Ed's relationship with Julia was very casual, she had exaggerated to Vicky as she always did. He was still living in his grubby flat with his keyboard and headphones. At the party he'd fixed me with such a ridiculous doe-eyed look I knew he still pinned his hopes on me. After all this time. It was embarrassing. I'd progressed to better things. Sam had spoilt me. No. Ed was only required as a man who could fix things of an electrical nature. Not broken hearts.

It would have to be my usual means of solace in troubled times – I would redouble my efforts at the gym, the pool in particular; and I'd do a thorough cleaning of the house. If I swam three times a week for an hour and set aside two hours a day for the Big Clean, I would hardly even think about Sam. Let alone mope.

AFTER WORK, WHEN all I wanted was to go home and

open a bottle of wine, I forced myself to go to the gym; when I imagined slipping my body into the cold pool I always thought: No, I can't face it today. But once I pushed off under the water and came up for air I knew I had to do it: the water held me and let me be myself.

Push, kick, glide, breathe. Push. Kick. Glide. Breathe. It wasn't as free as the sea but you'd have to be mad to swim outdoors in the winter; the repetition hypnotised me into a state where I could let my mind free-fall. After twenty lengths my thoughts would begin to order themselves. I'd buy a nice bottle on the way home and get into my jimjams with a large glass of wine.

After thirty the nagging voice in my head slowed to a murmur and sometimes stopped altogether. Everything merged into a pattern: down, up, down, up, down, up then turn. After forty odd disconnected thoughts popped up – the sting of nettles, Vicky's high ponytail blowing in the breeze, the hornets' nest, Sam's long tanned legs. They were all part of me. I almost became them. I could be anyone. I'd swim, and clean, and become whoever I wanted to be.

I NOTICED A woman tearing up and down the pool at a fast front crawl. When she got out, she was heavily pregnant.

'Surprised you can swim so well. Is it your first?'

'My second. A girl again. She swims when I do!' She towelled herself vigorously. 'My other one's with her gran. How about you? Kids at school?'

'Yes!' I laughed. 'Two of them.'

I always made it a rule to join in a conversation, keep the social oil flowing, keep everyone happy. She wouldn't recognise me – her kids weren't school age. I was practically a mother to Holly and Tom. It was only a white lie.

In the weeks that followed, even though I never saw her again, I found myself imagining her baby kicking and pushing inside her, swimming with her; and inside the unborn daughter's tiny ovaries, the eggs of her grandchildren already forming, like a Russian doll. My own womb was as clean as a whistle, nothing growing in there, thank goodness. Just a heap of potential – tiny unfertilised eggs discarded each month.

After fifty lengths, I slowed to a jogging pace, my arms and legs weary of making the same movements, then climbed out. As my feet touched the wet tiles, I felt the thudding pull of gravity but for an hour, after a shower and coffee, all those endorphins lulled me into a state of bovine pleasure. My heart slowed down and thoughts stopped jumping around. I even felt hungry. For an hour I was tranquilised.

But it never lasted much more than that, then the door of the lion's cage would slide shut.

Only one glass but I'd fill it more than was comfortable to hold, then drink it quickly to make it easier to cup in my hand. White chilled me and made my head ache; but red was like a transfusion, changing my blood into a stream of dark red wine. One glass slid down so seductively that another was inevitable, then another, until TV dramas became incomprehensible, and self-control slipped away; then I was there again: sticky glasses of limoncello, shooting stars, the strawberry mark on his inner thigh. Thoughts rose straight up like helium balloons that burst in the dark and disappeared. Another glass then sleep was easier to find. Until I woke myself coughing, a couple of hours later, with a parched throat. Then I'd be awake for hours – thinking and remembering. And it was no better in the morning, the empty glass on the bedside table.

So I stopped. No, I'm being dishonest – I cut down. It was seeing myself like my poor mother that did it, the glass of wine next to my bed, like reaching for the pack of pills under the mattress. I must never do that. I must be strong.

SO I KEPT moving. If I didn't go to the pool, I walked, with no particular aim. Until, one late afternoon I found myself on the doorstep of Sam and Vicky's house. I must have decided to go and see Vicky. Oh, but it was one of her ceramics evenings so she wouldn't be there. It was what had been one of our 'days'. I couldn't help it. I'd tried to stay away.

'Vic's at the hospital. Antenatal appointment. Just doing some marking while I've got peace and quiet.'

'You'll be ready for a break.' I took a step forward.

'No, not really. Snowed under.'

'Sam! Come on, let's have a cuppa. We're friends, aren't we?'

He mumbled something I didn't catch, and then finally let me in. Really, he was making it difficult. Because it was obvious Sam still wanted me. I could see it in his eyes, in the way his voice softened when he said my name, in a kind of gentle surprise.

Other people would have given up long before. Some would have called me persistent; the more cynical would have said stubborn. But there was no one to tell me what to do. I was playing the long game.

Sam tore at the skin on the side of his thumb. He seemed nervous. Instead of tea, he poured us each a glass of white wine.

'Everything all right, Sam?'

'Fuck it, Helen! What do *you* think?'

It was the first time I'd ever been at the receiving end of his 'teacher' voice. He took me off guard. I'd heard him before, of course, in the middle of some domestic crisis or other. I remember once being surprised at how disproportionately angry he had been when he'd lost his keys.

'They were here – I always put them here. For fuck's sake where are they? I'm going to be late!'

Tom had crunched himself lower over his Lego and looked at me then whispered, 'Aunty Helen why's Daddy shouting so much? It's scary.' He dropped the brick he was holding and his hand slid into mine.

'Vic, where are my car keys? Where did you *put* them?'

Vicky had rushed to calm him down, producing the keys from a bowl in the hall as if by magic.

At the time it had been comical, a cliché, the voice of an irate teacher. Now I understood how Tom felt when he'd shuffled closer to me to take my hand.

Sam had swollen up ridiculously. Like the hornets' nest.

But I wasn't a child. 'Mr. Taylor, are you going to give me a detention?' I fluttered my eyelashes at him.

'Helen, please stop.' That voice again.

'What do you mean?'

He went to the kitchen door and looked out at their garden. It was raining and the light was beginning to go. If he didn't get out there with a rake soon, fallen leaves would start rotting and ruin the grass, and the flowers, turning into a black slimy mess. 'If I were you I'd– '

'It doesn't work like that. We can't suddenly be friends.'

'Why not?' I walked over to where he was standing

with his back to me. 'I'll always be your friend.' I added, and tried to put my arms around his waist; but he pushed me away.

'Come on, Sam. Friends hug. Vicky's always hugging me. We're friends too.'

'Look, I've got work to do. You need to go.'

His face was pink and blotchy. For a moment I thought he might cry.

'But we *are* friends, Sam. Aren't we?'

'OK . . . yes. But we need to have rules.'

Men love their rules and regulations, don't they?

'So?'

'No calling round unexpectedly. And no coming round when Vicky's not here. No physical contact.'

The acidic wine burned my throat and I almost gagged. But I assented. I had no choice.

At the door he held onto my shoulders. I thought for a moment he was going to shake me. Then he kissed me firmly on the lips.

'Now go. Before–'

'Before what?'

'Just go.'

ALL THE WAY home my lips tingled. But as soon as I shut the front door behind me, I ran up to the bathroom and washed my face, then changed into old jeans and the shirt

I used for housework. I wasn't going to let Sam direct my life with his petty rules – and even if he thought they were set in stone, I'd soon chip away and erode them. It was all a matter of time and timing.

I started in earnest on the Big Clean.

THIRTY-ONE

I'D BEEN SLACKING. It was nearly a year since Mum died and there were still old suitcases and bags I'd not opened. Until I began sorting out the box room, I'd forgotten all about the china figurine. But as soon as I saw her it came back to me.

She was wrapped in Dad's green scarf and much smaller than I remembered; now she fitted into my adult hand as she had into Mum's. I ran my fingers over her to remind myself of the smoothness, but around her waist and neck tiny fibres of wool were caught in the cracks, as if she was wearing a hairy necklace and belt over her pink wedding dress. She had been inexpertly glued back together.

Mum collected Royal Doulton figurines and once a month we set them out on the kitchen table and cleaned them with old toothbrushes. My job was to wash off the dirt, then Michael polished them with a glass-cleaning cloth. Always on a Saturday afternoon while Mum prepared dinner. Our cleaning became linked to the smell of raw onions and browning beef. She was probably her happiest then, the two of us scrubbing and polishing and steam condensing on the kitchen window. As the sky darkened the view of the garden was slowly blotted out until all we could see, reflected in the glass, was ourselves bent over the table, Mum chopping and smiling to herself.

One Saturday not long before I was due to go to university, Michael and I were on our own in the kitchen. He was only twelve or thirteen, desperate to get out with his football.

'When can I stop? It's going to be too dark ...'

'Mum will be home soon, then you can.' I had all my packing for university to do too. 'You're not the only one who's got things to do.'

When she came back from visiting Dad at the hospital, her face was drawn, and her eyes were puffed up and swollen. I'd never seen Mum cry.

'I need a cuppa, Helen.'

I searched for her favourite cup, the one with: *A present from Scarborough* in gold around the rim; Dad gave it to her on their honeymoon. She sat holding the tea trying to warm her hands.

'They said your dad could come home ... if that's what we want.' Her voice was distant.

'When?' I was glad – he didn't like it in hospital, and it meant Mum wouldn't be on her own when I went away.

'The ambulance will bring him on Friday ... on Friday morning they said.'

Michael put down the ornament he was polishing. 'Great! We can play football!' He ran out into the garden.

Mum looked at the china figurine, as if she'd never seen it before. Odd considering it was one of her favourites. Then she picked it up and went into the lean-to where I cleaned my shoes. There was a sound of something breaking, then the sweeping of the dustpan and brush.

It happened so quickly; then she came back in and sat down to finish her tea.

'Get me a digestive will you, Helen. There was nothing to eat in that hospital.'

The next day she must have found the pieces and glued them together again.

I held the china ornament and warmed her in my hand. She looked modestly up at me, a small posy in one pink-gloved hand, the other lifting up her veil.

Poor Mum. She couldn't even let us see how angry and upset she was. As far as Michael and I were concerned, Dad was coming home because he was better. It didn't occur to us that he was so gravely ill. I was due to leave home for university in a couple of weeks and Mum, on some level, wanted me to go. She hid the seriousness of his illness from everyone, herself included. But when he died she couldn't hide it any more. All that rage and sadness. She collapsed. I was the one who had to come back to glue her together.

I found an old toothbrush and rubbed away what I could of the green fibres, then sponged the china figurine clean. She could stand on the dresser next to the photo of Mum and Dad's wedding and my first school one. A shrine to my childhood. From a distance no one would notice the cracks. Mum's life ended at forty-two but, in spite of a few setbacks, mine had just begun. I would not be like her and stay in the house; I would go out and do something.

Day One of the Big Clean. I was making progress.

THIRTY-TWO

'YOU COULD PAY extra for 3D or 4D, but we'll see it soon enough.'

I put my glass down. The image was unclear and grainy, like something taken from outer space. It was only black and white, not at all what I'd expected. But definitely a baby.

Vicky was twenty weeks pregnant. Five months already. She'd had her hair cut in a short bob and wisps of it softened the outline of her face. She was plump and glowing like a pink sugar pig. In the terms of her pregnancy books, she was blooming.

But she reminded me of the courgettes Dad used to grow – dinky green tubes the size of his fingers which, overnight would bloat into cumbersome, flavourless marrows that Mum insisted on using. *If you'd lived through the war* you'd be grateful she said, and stuffed them with mince and rice then baked them. The stuffing was perfectly good, but there was always a plateful of wet, fibrous marrow to get through, like chewing sodden toilet roll.

I could see the outline of the baby's skull, and the arch of its backbone. There were limbs too. But the main impression I had was of head. I remembered the school video of childbirth. This creature was going to force its way out of Vicky's body. Grotesque.

'All okay?' I asked.

'Big for five months, so I may have my dates wrong.' She laughed. 'But it's not as if we log it every time we have sex.'

'Speak for yourself,' Sam commented.

Vicky threw a cushion at him.

'Is she sucking her thumb?' I asked, focusing on the photo to blank out the image of them in bed.

'She/he is,' Sam said. '*It's* ruining its teeth already…probably be born looking like Bugs Bunny.'

Vicky looked for another cushion. 'They do all sorts in there. Yawning. Belching… Just like its father!'

Sam reached over for the picture again. 'Bizarre, but life's not validated unless we can show it to someone else. So much time recording and sharing, we forget to live our lives. This one will be born holding an iPad.'

Vicky raised her eyebrows. 'Ouch! I hope not … But it's definitely going to be an active child. Thumping and kicking me. Do you want to feel, Helen?'

I was curious to touch this new life. But there was also something too intimate. I clasped my hands together in my lap.

'It's okay, love,' she said.

'I don't want to hurt the baby. Or you.'

'Tough as old boots. It's what we're designed for.' Vicky took my hand and guided it onto her belly.

'Evolved, darling. Not designed,' Sam picked up the TV remote.

Vicky put her hand over mine and pressed it down gently.

'Feel that?'

Under my palm something rippled, like a muscle contracting, like the fluttering of a tiny bird.

'Was that it? Oh, I felt it again. Quite hard.'

Vicky smiled. 'Strange, isn't it? But you get used to it. Nancy used to love it when she felt them moving. She said it was like learning Braille. Like reading what the baby would look like.

'Exactly the sort of thing your friend Nancy *would* say.' Sam said, and switched on the TV. 'Don't think of *Alien*, Helen.'

It wasn't space creatures bursting out that I thought about, it was the hornets' nest in Italy – swelling and buzzing with new life. While Sam and I were enjoying our siestas, this thing was already growing inside Vicky, cells dividing and multiplying like a cancer. But unlike the hornets' nest there was a silence, a complete blank, like looking through binoculars at two people running on the beach – the blond flip of Vicky's ponytail blowing in the breeze. Sam showing off – cartwheels at the water's edge. His long tanned legs. The flapping sail of his school shirt. Vicky's hand climbing further. Then click and the money's gone.

The baby wobbled under my hand again. Pressing down on mine, Vicky's was hot and slightly clammy. I sat back and she let my hand slip out from under hers, almost as if she was reluctant for me to take it away. It lay there at the top of her thigh.

'Sorry, Helen. A baby's like central heating!'

I picked up the scan photo again. My own hand was cold from where Vicky had withdrawn hers.

The image was flimsy and would easily tear, but it was solid evidence of the past, and of what the future would bring. They'd invited me to share their moment of celebration. And something more. There was always something more with Vicky. I looked at Sam, distracted by the TV, his lovely profile frowning. Were they in this together? Had he been involved in planning this humiliation, to show me she was going to win him back with this trophy? The sand under my feet shifted. I needed to think. I needed to be at home, in my own bed.

I stood up unsteadily. I was wrong; I couldn't do this on my own. I needed to talk to someone who knew Vicky from the old days. Not Julia for obvious reasons. It was time to contact Ann and tell her about Sam. She knew the kind of things Vicky could get up to and would see the world from my perspective.

PREGNANCY HAD CHANGED Vicky; she had mellowed; and she was beginning to tone down her luvvie act. As I put my coat on she held her arms out to me.

'You're always so calm. I love having you around, Helen.' She sighed happily. 'Such a relief.'

'Being pregnant?'

'Oh no, although that too. Sam.'

'How?'

'Bringing me cups of tea in bed. Being nice to me all the time.'

'Or maybe he's guilty about something?' I was sailing close to the wind with that question.

'I was wrong about an affair.' She lowered her voice and curved her hands over her belly. 'All his jogging and joining the gym was to deal with coming back. After Manchester. And the new job. Me being sick all the time … Everything's going to be okay. We're all fine, aren't we?'

I nodded.

'It wasn't planned,' She stroked her swollen abdomen, 'but this baby could keep us together. I'm going to let Sam look after me even if it's against my feminist principles. I'm just so tired.'

'That's great to hear,' I lied. I moved towards the

door. I had to get away.

'When you're not busy come and help me choose some baby clothes. I got rid of all the rest ... And I'm going to buy you something pretty to say thank you for all the times you've looked after these two...' She laughed. 'Do you think you're up to looking after three?'

'Aunty Helen likes looking after us, don't you?'

I landed a kiss on Holly's soft cheek. As I kissed Vicky goodbye, I tried not to breathe in her perfume. It smelt like cheap toilet cleaner.

'Remember I'm going to buy you something really nice!' she called as I walked away.

***

VICKY MADE SUCH a show of giving me presents I sometimes thought she wanted to buy my friendship. One summer she forced me to go down to the seafront after school.

'Shut your eyes!' her own were wide and, in the afternoon light, the darkest blue. She smiled, showing her white teeth and neat pink tongue. My body was tight with anticipation.

'I don't like surprises.' I moved to the other end of the bench.

'It's something nice. A present.' She leaned over, laughing. I could smell Juicy Fruit chewing gum mixed with cherry lip salve. 'Go on, shut your eyes. I'm not going to hurt you.'

I did as I was told, then there was a warmth on my skin as she reached round and fastened something around my neck.

'Open!'

I slowly let out my breath.

'What do you think? It suits you, goes with your eyes. I didn't want you to have to put it on when it was cold … so I've been wearing it all day under my school uniform. Warming it up for you.'

My cheeks were burning. I couldn't look at her. Why did she always have to be like that?

'You always feel the cold, don't you?'

The smell of her chewing gum was too close.

'You need something to keep you warm. Or maybe someone.' She added this so quietly I wasn't sure if she'd really said it or not.

I put my hand up to touch the pendant against my breastbone.

'It's sea glass. I know you collect things like that, you little magpie.'

The glass was a dark brown heart with bubbles of air trapped inside.

'Do you like it?'

'But it's not my birthday …'

'You don't have to wait for birthdays.' She was like a puppy with a string of saliva dripping from the corner of her mouth. 'You like having pretty things, don't you?'

'Of course. Thank you. But I have to go now.'

'I thought you were coming to my house. I thought we were going to play…'

'I need to go home.'

'Oh.' Her voice was suddenly hard and brittle. Then, as if to a cue, she manufactured a brilliant smile. 'Well, see you tomorrow, sweetie!' She stroked my cheek slowly as if she never wanted to let me go. Then she sighed and planted a kiss on the end of my nose. In a flurry of school bags and cherry lip salve she was gone.

All the way home, the chain was heavy around my neck and I found myself tracing each smooth oval where her fingers had already been. I pushed it under my school uniform before I reached home. I didn't want Michael teasing me. In my bedroom I unfastened it and held it in the palm of my hand. It was so warm it was like something alive. I stuffed it in a box under my bed and never wore it again.

I DIDN'T WANT to spend time waiting for Vicky to patronise me with embarrassing presents. I would avoid any shopping expeditions to look for baby clothes.

I emailed Ann.

THIRTY-THREE

I HADN'T GIVEN Christmas much thought and my only plan was to make it as different as possible from the previous twenty years. So there I was on Christmas Eve at Vicky's, drinking dry sherry while the children wrote letters to Father Christmas.

'Leave some for Santa, Aunty Helen.' Tom had dictated his letter to me and was now laboriously copying it onto notepaper.

'One glass is enough for me. I'll leave him the rest.'

Holly, with the efficiency of a seasoned consumer, was flicking through the Argos website for product codes and prices, then adding them to her letter.

'Granny likes sherry too…they'll have to share it,' she said.

Vicky and Sam had gone round to a neighbour for drinks and I'd agreed to mind the children so Sylvia could concentrate on preparing the meal. I could have gone too, I'd been invited, but small talk with people I had no interest in had never made sense to me. I was happy to sit by their fire and keep an eye on the children.

WHEN VICKY INVITED me to spend Christmas with them I'd been torn. I liked being Aunty Helen and, more importantly, it would give me an opportunity to spend time with Sam. But with alcohol available who knew what might happen? On the other hand I'd been saving DVDs of my favourite films – *Brief Encounter, Jane Eyre, Mansfield Park* – for months, and had bought a selection of frozen meals on special offer. Of course I was going to miss her, now Mum wasn't there to insist on her version of Christmas, but I'd so looked forward to doing exactly what I wanted.

But Vicky was insistent.

'You can't be on your own at Christmas.' She massaged her swelling bump. 'You have to spend it with us.'

'Vic, stop being such a bossy cow. Maybe Helen *wants* a quiet Christmas.' I knew what he really meant. Obviously Sam wanted me to be there, but he couldn't risk sounding too enthusiastic, could he?

'But she'd be all on her own.'

'And if she came here, she'd end up having to cook and look after the children.'

'Not when there's you and Mum, darling!'

'Thank God for Sylvia!'

SYLVIA, WHO USUALLY spent Christmas with them in Manchester, was excited at staying in Holdersea.

'Last year I was stuck for two hours in Doncaster *and* the buffet car ran out of sandwiches!' She was making mince pies and listening to the carol concert from Kings College. 'So lovely to sleep in my own bed, Helen.'

The children were quiet, concentrating on their letters. The only sound apart from the hiss of damp wood on the fire and the ethereal sound of carols, was Sylvia's running commentary.

'I'll prepare all the veg for tomorrow, then I'll come and have a wee chat . . . The stuffing's nearly done!'

I'd just picked up my book again and was rereading the same paragraph, when she scuttled in and poured herself a second glass of sherry. 'Finished at last. I'll have this then I'll put the children to bed. Or you can, Helen'

'We've got to post our letters first!' Tom said. 'Show me, Aunty Helen.'

I knelt in front of the fire with him. 'This is what you do. Hold my hand. One, two, three and . . . whoosh.'

I helped him throw his letter into the fire; soon it started to smoulder then, just as a flame licked around the edges, a draft caught it and the letter floated up and out of sight.

'Make a wish!' I whispered. 'Close your eyes.'

He frowned. 'Do you think I'll get what I want?'

'I'm sure you will.' I squeezed his little hand.

'Will you get what you want, Aunty Helen?'

'I hope so.'

'You need to write a letter then.' Sylvia laughed.

I thought, then quickly scribbled a note and threw it on the fire.

'Yours only had three words on it, Aunty Helen. That's not a proper Christmas letter,' said Holly.

'It's different for grownups, Holly. Different rules.' I pictured the scrap of paper floating up the chimney, blackened and singed. *Look at me.*

I helped Holly put her letter on the fire, then took them both up to bed and read a story. By the time I came downstairs, Sylvia had dropped off to sleep too, her face flushed. When I closed the door she woke with a start.

'Don't worry, Vicky. I'll be over as soon as I can. Oh . . .!' she said. 'I thought it was tomorrow.'

'It's okay, Sylvia. Still Christmas Eve.'

'I said I'd be here at nine at the latest to put the turkey in. They take so long, don't they?'

'To be honest, I've never cooked one. Mum said there was no point buying a whole turkey for two.'

'Right enough, dear. It would've been a waste.' She sighed. 'I'm glad you're going to be here. For your first Christmas without her.' She reached towards the sherry bottle. 'They'll be home soon. How about another wee glass? One for the road.'

The fire had begun to die back – a glowing pile of logs falling slowly away to ash.

'I hope I'm not speaking out of turn, Helen, but

you're still young, relatively speaking. Not like I was when my Ian died. We'd had a good life together. I didn't want to marry again. But you ...'

I smiled modestly and shook my head.

'There was young Ed. But he never seemed your type. All those computer games. And looking for bits of metal.'

His stubby chewed down fingernails. The smell of fried fish in my hair, on my clothes. The sad smell of tumble dried, over-heated clothes on him. 'That's all finished, Sylvia. He wasn't my type at all. Julia seems to like him.'

A year from now, perhaps even less, Sam and I would be sitting in front of a log fire like this. Celebrating on our own. He *would* tire of Vicky. He'd see the light soon. All I had to do was be there, to point out the contrast – look, that's what you're stuck with at the moment, but this is what you can have if you want it. Just *look at me*. You know that's what you really want.

'... you're attractive. You'd be a catch for any man. And you could still have children. Lots of women in their forties do nowadays. Look at Vicky.'

I crossed my legs and drank my sherry. Children? No thank you. On the mantelpiece, amongst photos of the summer holiday was the one Sam had taken of me in Pisa, at the top of the Leaning Tower. My smile and look had been only for him, not for general viewing. It brought out the rich auburn of my hair. I'd been surprised Vicky had allowed him to put it there.

'I like being an aunty to those two. That's enough for me at the moment.'

'Early days, love. Not a year since poor Elizabeth passed away. They say it takes at least a year. You need time to come to terms with the loss, then maybe you could think about finding a boyfriend.'

'Perhaps this time next year I'll be sitting by the fire with my new man!' I laughed, then helped Sylvia to one more drink before we heard the key in the front door.

THIRTY-FOUR

CHRISTMAS DAY I basked in a late, solitary breakfast in my own home. Mum would have been up before it was light to put the chicken in the oven; and I would have been expected to start peeling sprouts and chopping onions for the stuffing as soon as I'd put down my cereal spoon.

'Come on, Helen. There's so much to do, if we're going to be ready in time.'

It wasn't as if anyone else was ever expected. Yet she had to keep the rituals going and I had to help her.

Michael's card with a surfing Santa and kangaroos, was on the dresser in its usual place, alongside a few from work and choir, one from Ann of her Oxford college, and one of the lighthouse, with added glitter from Vicky and the family.

I bathed carefully and dressed in the new short, back-less dress I'd ordered on the internet. I would wear the shawl from Florence for warmth but, as Vicky loved her cosy fires and always had the heating blasting out, as if she'd never heard of global warming or gas bills, I could let it slip off my shoulders and expose my back and shoulders, unmarked by child-bearing and over-eating. *Look at me.*

'We all get tarted up for Christmas, even Sam,' she'd told me; but she'd find it hard to look glamorous with a bump the size of the East Riding.

In the long mirror I'd bought for my bedroom, my reflection looked back at me, hostile. Not the impression I was aiming at. I smiled revealing my newly-whitened teeth, then applied a little make-up, not too much; I didn't want to compete with Vicky and her professional slap.

There was something missing. I needed something around my neck to show off the creamy darkness of my skin. Mum always said, 'You don't want to look like an over decorated Christmas tree, do you?' So I knotted the shawl around my shoulders. That would have to do.

But something was still missing. Something that had been so much part of my life, since I was four years old that, once I realized what it was, I felt naked and exposed. I laughed out loud and the sound reverberated in the empty room. My reflection was laughing too. So much had changed since I cleared this room, Mum's old room, and danced round in her ancient green party dress. I leaned in to examine my face closely. I wasn't wearing my glasses.

My Christmas present to myself was contact lenses.

'Who is the fairest of them all?' I declaimed. 'Why you, my dear,' my reflection replied.

My tongue glistened. Pink and wet, like a delicate but muscular sea creature. No wonder they're always cutting it out in stories to stop her talking, to punish her for wanting more than she's already got. The Little Mermaid wants the prince. Oh no you don't, *unless you give me your voice.*

I was more than a little in love with myself. I was a woman in the prime of life about to spend Christmas at the heart of the family who loved her.

IT WAS HOLLY who spotted it first and announced it to the whole family; she was always a very observant child.

'I knew something was different, but I couldn't think what it was. You sly thing ... it was me. I told her to lose the specs, Sam.' Vicky chinked glasses with me.

Sylvia was in charge of the turkey, Sam the vegetables, so all Vicky and I had to do was set the table, then sit around looking alluring. To be honest we shared the task: she did the sitting and I provided the allure; although we both admired each other loudly and repeatedly, especially after the third glass of champagne.

'It's Christmas, Sam. Don't be a party pooper!' Vicky refused to give in when Sam offered her cranberry juice instead. 'The baby loves the bubbles.'

Sam looked at me for support. But honestly she'd read all the baby books. She knew the risks as well as anyone. If she wanted to give birth to a stunted baby, that was her choice.

At last we sat down to eat. It was like a scene from Dickens – I'd never seen anything like it: candles, flowers, crackers, paper napkins and so many different vegetables and sauces, not to mention sausages and stuffing. There was going to be so much waste.

We toasted each other. We toasted the new baby. And finally Sylvia raised her glass. 'To my dear friend, Elizabeth.' She patted my arm. 'And to the future – a baby for Vicky and Sam; a grandchild for me. And a lovely man for little Helen!' She gave me a wink.

I couldn't help giggling and tried to avoid Sam's eye. But, in the general jollity, it didn't matter.

'Almost time for the Queen's Speech,' Sam suggested, to change the subject.

'It's nearly three. I'll go and switch the TV on.' I made a move to get up and nearly upset my wine glass.

Vicky laughed. 'We were joking, love!'

'Mum always …'

'I thought no one watched it nowadays.' Vicky looked at Sam.

'We had to wean Sylvia off it the first time she came to Manchester, didn't we, Sylv?' Sam nudged his mother-in-law, and she hiccupped loudly. 'Pardon me. Too much food!'

'Before the mother-in-law embarrasses herself any further, it's time for presents everyone.'

The children raced to the Christmas tree and found the presents I'd bought them – *Jane Eyre* for Holly and a set of *Thomas the Tank Engine* books for Tom. As an English teacher, Sam would approve of my choice, and it would counteract Sylvia's mountain of expensive plastic rubbish.

Holly gave me a grateful smile and skipped over to hug me. 'It's nice to have a grown-up book to read.' She added it to the pink and fluffy presents stacked in a corner of the room, then put the wrapping paper in the bin.

'Too many words.' Tom looked despondent. 'Come and read it to me, Aunty Helen. When it's bedtime.'

'Mummy and Daddy are always busy,' Holly called over from the floor where she was sorting out her presents. 'They always say *in a minute, we're just…*'

'Talking and drinking wine,' Tom added.

Sam cleared his throat. 'Maybe Aunty Helen will teach you to mind your own business, Thomas.'

He was smiling, but I could tell he was irritated.

'Daddy's only teasing,' I said to Tom. 'Now mine for you, Vicky.'

It had taken me hours to choose a suitable present. I didn't want it to be too personal – to be reminded every time I saw her. I suppose I didn't want it thrown back in my face, once Sam and I announced our plans for the future.

'A spa day!' Vicky tried to stand, but the effect was more like a walrus attempting to roll off a rock. I bent over and let her hug me.

'Perfect. A day of pampering. You're always so thoughtful.'

'They only give you fruit and water in those places. You'll have to smuggle your chocolate supply in, Vic.'

'Och, Sam! Leave her alone.' Sylvia, slapped him playfully. 'She needs to look after–'

'My turn,' Vicky broke in. 'Tom, crawl under the tree. Yes, that's it.'

It was a large, flat box tied and as I pulled the gold ribbon a trace of Vicky's perfume drifted up and mixed with the resinous smell of pine from the Christmas tree.

'Careful, Aunty Helen. It's delicate.' Holly sat next to me on the sofa. 'I helped Mum wrap it up,' she added. 'When *you* were in bed.' She looked sharply at her brother.

'It's beautiful.' Everyone was looking at me.

'Mum made it. Daddy only wrote his name.' Holly sat as close as she could, crumpling the fine silk of my dress. 'Try it on, Aunty Helen.'

It was like a scene in a film – a close up of her small hands fastening the clasp at the back of my neck. Like Vicky on the promenade, all those years ago. Except

Holly's hands were clean and cool. Innocent.

'Your aunty looks gorgeous.' Vicky caught my eye and smiled. 'As usual.'

'Like a princess,' Holly said.

'All you need now is a prince!' Sylvia exclaimed.

'Not many of them in Holdersea,' Sam said, adjusting his paper crown.

'Thank you, Vic. It's really … unusual.'

'You do like it, don't you?' Her breath was warm, as I bent to kiss her. 'You recognise it, don't you?'

Of course I did. She hadn't thrown it away, after all these years.

Vicky had re-used the brown glass heart, the necklace I'd parceled up and posted through her letterbox, the one I thought I'd never see again. She'd repeated the pattern hundreds of times to make an elaborate chain of tiny clinking ceramic hearts, with the glass heart in the centre. It sickened me to think she'd kept it.

'To show you how much you've always meant to me, even if we had our differences! Life's so intense when you're at school, when you're curious about everything and it's so new and exciting. But it was always fun, wasn't it?' Vicky laughed. 'Look under the tissue paper.'

I wasn't a schoolgirl. It was only a necklace. But my heart was racing. It was like a school lucky dip, only I didn't feel lucky. It was more like the booby prize. I almost wished I was at home with Mum, safely watching the Queen's Speech.

Covered in handmade paper, inset with pressed flowers and glowing with painted roses, was a photo album.

'I copied it from the original photos … well Sam did it for me, didn't you love?'

She tousled his hair then pulled him in close for a kiss.

I flicked open the book and there was her perfume again, as if she'd marked her territory like a cat: school photos, a strip from a photo booth of the two of us, blond and brown hair knotted together like a Victorian keepsake, the sixth form beach party with me in the distance chatting to Ann. Then a gap of twenty years: the pool in Italy, the pair of us taken by Tom. Finally – a recent one of me on the promenade eating an ice cream, here in Holdersea. I had no recollection of her taking it. In every photo I was smiling.

'Thank you, Vicky. It's beautiful.' The book was a dead weight in my hand. 'When did you find the time?'

'Always time for you, love,' she said flirtatiously then laughed again. 'I wanted to make you something special now we're all such good friends again.'

I had to stop myself from ripping off the necklace and throwing the album at her.

'Can I see?' Sylvia opened the book. 'Och, what a talented daughter I have!'

Vicky was lying on the sofa, a faint smile on her lips. I think she knew she'd startled me. It was how she always used to be.

I took some deep breaths to calm down. It was my turn. I crossed my legs, letting the silk of my dress rustle slightly as I gave Sam his present: a framed Victorian print of the lighthouse with *'happy memories'* etched in a curling font along the lower edge. When I'd bought it I hoped the irony wouldn't be wasted on him. A private joke between us. Now it felt like a step too far.

'Thanks, Helen. Good to see the lighthouse has always been a part of happy times.' He kissed me with the lightest pressure possible.

'When Ian and I came to Holdersea we loved the lighthouse. So unusual to have it in the town. A shame it's not working anymore, but the museum's very informative, and they do a nice afternoon tea.'

'And the view from the top is spectacular, isn't it Helen?' Sam said with his back to me as he placed the picture on the mantelpiece with all the others. 'At least I think so.' He bent to put more logs on the fire, so he couldn't gauge my reaction; but the blood rushed to my face. I was gripping the photo album so tightly my fingers marked the cover.

'That's it. Present-giving over for another year.'

While I opened their cluster bomb of a present he'd been quiet. I'd hoped he would give me something himself. I had to hide my disappointment.

Holly and Tom went to watch a DVD and Sam

turned to Sylvia, who was bringing round liqueurs and chocolates. 'Thank God eh, Sylv! Next year there'll be complete chaos … '

'Goodness me, Sam. What are you blethering about?' Sylvia picked out a chocolate. 'Look at us sitting here all cosy and warm in front of the fire. And the baby to look forward to. Just wheesht now!'

Within a few minutes she was asleep. I looked through the photo album; Sam reached for his guitar.

'Come and sit next to me, Sammy. You can massage my feet.' Vicky pulled him towards her, kissing the top of his head. 'Thank you for a lovely Christmas,' she whispered, then yawned. 'An early night I think.'

'I should be going.' I put down my drink and started to tidy my presents.

'Let's have another.' Sam reached for the bottle.

'Stay and keep us company, love. He'll only put the TV on and we'll end up watching repeats of *Morecambe and Wise*.'

Sam leant over for the Radio Times.

'Don't let him, Helen. Oh God, he's going to be so boring.'

'Okay then, just a little one,' I said.

'Not for me, Sammy.' Vicky stretched in her most cat-like way, and settled herself more comfortably, pulling a blanket over her legs. 'You two go ahead.'

Within a few minutes, her face relaxed and she was

asleep too. In the warmth from the fire there was a delicious heaviness in the room. I could have happily slept too – anything to escape from the shock of the present.

'I can't believe I'm drinking this after so much to eat,' I said.

Sam downed his and poured another. 'The festive season. What else is there to do?'

'Mum and I used to eat at one, then watch the Queen's speech. Usually a game of Scrabble and the ballet on TV, then cold chicken sandwiches and a pot of tea at six. An old black and white film after that then bed at ten.' It was like someone else's life. As if I'd been asleep all those years.

'Cosy … I guess.' He leant back and put his arms behind his head. 'How about your brother? Never thought of visiting him for Christmas?'

'He'll phone on New Year's Day at some unearthly hour.' I laughed but I didn't want to talk about the past. 'Thank you for inviting me, Sam. It's been a lovely change.'

'Not much choice in the matter.' He tilted his head to where Vicky was sleeping, curled up like a baby.

'Well, I'm glad you agreed. But I should go now, before I fall asleep too!' I tried to make light of his comment. Of course he'd wanted me to be there. He was just covering up in case her majesty was still half awake.

'Yes, time for bed then.'

Sam held my gaze steadily then lifted his eyebrows just the slightest.

'I'll walk you home, Little Helen.'

PUTTING MY SHAWL on in the hallway, the necklace caught and I reached around but couldn't untangle it.

'Hang on. You don't want to tear it.'

His fingers on the back of my neck were efficient, teasing apart the chain and the warm fabric of the shawl. In the mirror his eyes were dark, concentrating; I could see Vicky in background, asleep on the sofa.

There was a pause or was it a hesitation? Then his fingers traced my neck, my shoulder, down my spine to the curve of my buttocks.

He met my eyes in the mirror and abruptly moved away.

'Sorry. Out of order. Too much alcohol. Come on let's get going.'

As we walked back, I chatted about my plans for the next couple of days. I was getting up early for a walk then going to meet our old friend, Ann.

'Smelly-Ann?'

'I wish you wouldn't call her that'

'I'm sure she smells of old libraries and ink!' He paused for a moment. 'Well, think of me starting the day at six with Disney and Coco Pops.'

At my front door he gave me a quick peck on the cheek.

'Look I got this for you, Helen. If you don't like it give it away.' His voice was gruff. Awkward. 'A peace offering. From me to you.'

A slim parcel. Light.

'Open it later. I'd better go.'

I watched him walk, a little unsteadily, down the garden path where he opened the gate then turned and gave me a brief wave and that self-deprecating smile. 'Happy Christmas, Helen.'

As soon as I'd shut the front door I sat at the foot of the stairs and opened the parcel.

There'd been other presents – on my birthday in May they'd given me plants for the garden and spinsterly candles and bubble bath, signed from both of them, but I knew Vicky had bought them herself. This was the first present Sam had ever given me. He had gone into a shop to choose it himself. His fingers wrapping the box. His handwriting on the label. His distinctive looping writing. Two kisses. From him. I fumbled the slippery paper and nearly dropped it.

It was another necklace, a simple chain. The label said: *For Fanny Price, 'a plain gold chain, perfectly simple and neat.'*

He had remembered. After our conversation in the summer. He'd read *Mansfield Park* after all. For me.

He was saying: I understand. I know you're waiting. I laid it on my bedside table. It would be the first thing I saw when I woke up the next day.

IN THE NEW Year I'd go to Hull and give Vicky's necklace to a charity shop.

She was always like that – the most extravagant, the one who had all the awards, the gold stars. The one at prize-giving shaking the head teacher's hand. Before we fell out completely. Before Ann became my friend, I'd spent hours sewing a butterfly to show off all the embroidery stitches I knew. I was pleased with how neat it was. Vicky's of course was perfect.

'Yours is so realistic, Vicky.'

'So pretty. Just like you.'

A group of girls crowded around her chattering.

Vivid swirling colours. I could see it from where I was sitting. Mine was drab and dull, like a dusty moth. The scissors glinted. I should cut the whole thing up and throw it in the bin. Tears pricked my eyes then fell onto the fabric, silvering the wings of my butterfly. At that moment I hated her. I wanted to hurt her.

There was a quiet voice at my ear. 'Helen, what's the matter?'

She put out her hand and touched mine lightly. Her hand was soft and warm. A girl's hand. Smelly-Ann. How could she be so kind? After what we did to her.

'Yours is lovely, Helen. Can you show me how you do that stitch?'

Her comforting homely smell.

'Of course.'

As she sat down next to me, her hair fell forwards and caught the light glancing through the tall school windows. She smoothed it back with both hands and smiled at me.

'Vicky hasn't got you all to herself for once.' She pulled a paper tissue out from her pocket. 'Here. It's clean.'

'Thank you, Ann.' I wiped my eyes then picked up my sewing. 'It's satin stitch. First you have to start at the back …'

I couldn't see Vicky but I could hear her. 'Miss says I have a natural eye for colour. She says I'm very artistic.'

Julia sat down with me. 'Show me too, Helen?'

Soon there was a small breakaway group around my table.

'You're so good at explaining things, Helen. Isn't she?' It was the first time I'd heard Ann speak in a voice above a whisper. 'So patient.'

'You should be a teacher, Helen.'

'And so pretty too.' Another voice.

'Let *me* see her butterfly.' Vicky pushed her way in but all the seats were taken.

She had to stand on the outside. It must have been

the first time. Ann smiled at me. I smiled back at her. From that day I knew she was going to be my best friend and I could get away from Vicky.

THIRTY-FIVE

A COUPLE OF days before New Year I went to meet Ann. It must have been ten years since we'd seen each other. Her academic work took her all over the world, but she was based in London. We'd only met when she came back to Holdersea for flying visits while her parents were still alive, and kept in touch by letters, then by cards with a scribbled note on birthdays and Christmas, and finally by email. The internet was a lifesaver; I used to sit in my room and chat as long as I liked, while Mum was downstairs watching *Antiques Roadshow*. Ann often tried to persuade me to visit her in Oxford but, after my abortive trip to university, I was always wary. The contrast between us would have been too great for me to bear. But this time I said yes. I no longer had Mum as an excuse, and my newfound success with Sam gave me confidence.

SHE WAS ON her way back to London after spending Christmas in Edinburgh, so broke her journey in York. We met for lunch in *Betty's*, famous for its afternoon teas.

I wore Sam's necklace; I'd let her know it was from him.

Ann's hair, once so mousy and stringy, was cut in an uncompromising 1920s bob and coloured dark aubergine, framing her oversized tortoiseshell spectacles and ruby lipstick. On the table were two glasses of prosecco and silver platters heaped with sandwiches. When she saw me she dropped her mobile into her bag and stood up to take both my hands in hers; and launched into the conversation we'd been having by email.

'Helen! Thank God you've come to your senses!'

'Meaning?'

'You've escaped from that daft relationship with Sam Taylor. You look surprised but I know what you're like. Your emails. Everything revolved round fucking Sam. You're transparent.'

Ann still had her broad accent – perhaps moving south had forced her to hold onto it whereas mine had been drilled out of me by weekly elocution lessons. *Oh don't say 'masster' it sounds so common.* She'd also retained her Yorkshire directness.

'We're friends now. And Vicky too.'

Ann was about to say something then stopped herself. 'Fuck! You're still in the middle of it, aren't you?'

'It's fine, Ann. I had Christmas with them and–'

'No, it's not *fine*. He's a charmer and he's clever – well he used to be. One of those boys who always have to *look after* something because he gets off on being needed.

A sucker for a lost cause or an injured kitten. Not that you're either. But I know how you react when things go wrong for you. When your dad died. Your mum. Your emotions go all over the place then you stop eating, stop sleeping.'

'But I'm fine. We're friends … he gave me this necklace.'

'He just wants to *control* you because he can't control Vicky. *Don't* let him take you in.'

'Ann, it's more than that,' I said calmly, fingering the chain. 'He still loves me, but at the moment we can only be friends.'

Ann sighed. 'You're not his friend. You can't be friends with a man you've been having sex with. Or his wife. Well you can but…' She looked out at the crowds drifting around the January sales. 'It takes time. Years of not seeing each other. All he's doing is buying your silence.'

'I know what I'm doing.' Under the table my nails were pressing into my palms.

'It's a cliché, but I've been round the block more than you. So I– '

'What? Round your ivory tower?'

'Touché …' She laughed. 'I've seen how these situations resolve themselves. People get hurt, end up in therapy.'

I snorted. 'That's ridiculous.'

'No, it's not. It's experience.'

'Oh?'

'Yes.' She paused to let me take in the implication of what she'd said. 'And there's Vicky-darling. I can't imagine she's changed for the better.'

'Now she's had children she's softened. Mellowed.'

'Oh Helen!' Ann laughed again, and shook her head, making her hair slice through the air like a curved knife. 'I think you should try living in the real world, for a change. This isn't Mills and Boon. You've had an affair with an idiot; and Vicky-darling is bored so she's decided to keep you to herself again.' She made a sideways sweeping motion with her hands to punctuate her little speech. 'You need to forget the whole lot of them!'

'I know what I'm doing.' I wouldn't let her tell me what to do. I'd had a quarter of a century of being a dutiful daughter. I didn't have to do what anyone told me anymore.

'You always had your head in a book or in your own thoughts. Such a dreamer, playing at spies and fantasy.' She ordered us each another glass of prosecco. 'Do you remember that summer you made me follow Sam and Vicky?'

I smiled. 'I can't remember.'

'We were a right pair of stalkers.' She piled sandwiches on her plate. 'And your mother didn't help. She made you *wash* your shoes, for fuck's sake. Nowadays she'd have social services breathing down her neck… Like my mother.' Ann laughed. 'Only yours didn't drink or forget to feed you!'

Mum was a sick woman I tried to say. I was brought up to keep things clean. It hadn't done me any harm.

I'd taken Michael to play on the beach, keeping him out of Mum's way. I had no memory of telling Ann about it. When we came back she was busy in the kitchen as usual.

'I've just spent an hour cleaning that floor and now you've brought the beach with you!'

I scrubbed our wellies and put them outside to dry on the porch.

'You call that clean!' She gave me a toothbrush and some cold, soapy water in a bucket.

'Now, go back and clean them properly.'

Michael was too small so I did his as well. To tell you the truth, a toothbrush was perfect because I could get every single grain of sand off.

'Talk about care in the community! You're bright – you could've done anything you wanted … and all you did was stay at home and become a school secretary.' Anne said.

'*Administrator.*' I don't think she noticed how stony cold my voice was.

'Oh, Helen, I'm only cross with you because I feel so helpless. I'm used to sorting things out. You need to open your eyes and look at things properly, Helen. Straight on … Contact lenses are great by the way.'

'There's nothing to sort out, Ann.'

'You don't need a man in your life to make it worthwhile. Or kids. It's not too late to *do* something. Move away from Holdersea. There's a whole world to explore.'

A whole world. Italy. Standing on the top of the Leaning Tower with Sam. On top of the lighthouse. There was nowhere else I wanted to go.

We sat in an uncomfortable silence and both drank our prosecco, then she started again.

'Let's not fall out about this. We're adults. In spite of everything we're real friends. Old friends.'

She pushed up the sleeve of her shirt. 'You can hardly see it.'

I'd forgotten how her arm bent unnaturally since the accident, the skin puckered in an ugly white line below her elbow.

'I'm sorry, Ann.' I'd never properly apologised at the time. We never talked about it. Whether it was remembering her arm or having to listen to all her advice, I didn't know; but my head started to spin and bile rose in my throat.

'I never blamed *you* for that stupid game. It was Vicky. Conniving cow. We were just kids. Kids are cruel to each other. But you were kind. The only one in that dump who wanted to be my friend.'

I smiled thinly.

'Oh fuck. I've said too much, haven't I? I can never tell with you, Helen. You have that serene look that never seems to be ruffled. Have I offended you?'

'Of course not. We go back a long way. We've been friends for a long time,' I said evenly.

Ann reached into her bag to check the time on her phone. 'Shit! Sorry, I have to go. My train's in half an hour.'

'Oh no. We still have loads to talk about.'

'Next time I'll make it longer. Meeting Doug tonight. Over from the US. Booked a room at the St Pancras Hotel for a couple of nights … but after your last email I *had* to see you. Before you do something completely daft!' She got up quickly, checked her face in a mirror then, as I bundled the last few sandwiches into a paper napkin and put them in my bag for the journey, she said, 'Let's walk to the station together. We can talk on the way.'

I was only half-listening. She filled me in on her sisters – one in Canada, one in the Japan. They'd all moved as far away as they could – escaped their family. So the girl with the buggy I'd seen the night I visited Sylvia was no relation at all. A ghost of Smelly-Ann's past. Of my past.

'Well, hope to see you soon. I'll email you,' I said.

'Make it less than ten years!' Ann laughed. 'We'll be fifty by then! And remember what I've told you … put your lenses in and *look* properly! Get away from the fucking Taylors. And Holdersea.'

As she climbed onto the train, she was already moving on to her next meeting, fingering the screen of her phone.

AT LEAST I didn't have to cook with my bag full of sandwiches to keep me going. But I wasn't even hungry. All I wanted to do was sleep. Ann was full of herself and her opinions, one of those people who drain you. Sitting in her ivory tower judging me; and she was the one jumping from one boyfriend to the next as if she'd never grown up. She didn't have the staying power I did. I was right all along: no wonder I'd put off meeting her. We used to be friends but now we had nothing in common apart from the past. And the past was dead and gone. An irrelevance.

As the bus drove towards Holdersea, the lighthouse beckoned like a pale orange candle in the glow of the street lamps. Out at sea a tanker drifted across the skin of the sea, its lights a faint gleam. Under the water were the ruins of buildings and streets – old churches that had been washed away. Old rivalries forgotten and reduced to rubble. Along the main street, rows of Christmas lights looked defiant – primary colours standing out against the blackness of night.

On the walk from the bus stop my breath steamed.

There was a frozen slick of ice at the bottom of the boating pond where we used to play.

***

WHEN THEY EMPTIED the water out of the boating pond it always felt like the official end of the summer. Then all winter it looked grey and sad, forgotten.

On our way home from school one day, long before I became her friend, we saw Smelly-Ann on the other side of the road, wearing her thin raincoat. Vicky and I had proper winter coats. Mine was navy blue with a hood. Vicky's was red with a fur collar and a scarf her mum knitted – white and fluffy with pom-poms.

'Let's ask Smelly-Ann if she wants to play the Helen Keller game,' I said to Vicky.

She took off her scarf and gave it to me. 'But it won't be any good because she hasn't played it before. And I don't want her to get my scarf dirty.'

'Do you want to play, Ann? We put a blindfold on then you're Helen Keller and we have to look after you,' I said.

'Then what?'

I tied the scarf around Smelly-Ann's head. I didn't want to touch her hair but I had to. Vicky had let me use her scarf.

'We go around town. Then at the end there's a surprise,' I said airily. 'Something really nice. But you're not allowed to speak. Or you can't play.'

She held onto my coat and first we took her to the amusement arcade to get warm. Older boys hanging around and smoking, pointed and sniggered, but Vicky put her nose in the air and led us away. We bought Coke with my money – there wasn't enough for Smelly-Ann but it didn't matter because we were letting her play with us. She started making a sort of 'ugh, ugh' noise.

'No speaking or you'll spoil the game.' Vicky drank the last of her Coke; then we walked along the promenade as far as the slipway, with Smelly-Ann gripping on to my coat. We pretended we were smoking, our breath clouding in the cold air. We ignored her noises.

By the time we reached the boating pond it was dark.

'Ugh. Ugh.'

'If you talk, we'll not let you play.'

'Ugh. Ugh. Ugh!'

When Vicky whispered in my ear her breath was sugary, and her hair brushed my cheek; she was like a movie star, the way she tossed her hair over her shoulder.

'Right Ann. It's time for the surprise,' she said.

'You have to walk on your own now,' I added. 'But slowly or you'll spoil it.'

'Ugh. Ugh.'

'No talking.'

'Or you'll ruin it.'

'Ten steps … and you've got to count.'

Smelly-Ann let go and put her arms out, then she stepped forwards towards the edge of the boating pond her lips moving, counting under her breath.

Vicky and I had played this hundreds of times – one of us always shouted 'stop' just at the right moment. That was the fun of the game. The exciting part.

I don't know why – we didn't plan it, so it was no one's fault; but this time neither of us said a word.

There was a moment that was almost funny, where we could see her arms flapping about like a cartoon girl trying to fly; and we both rose up on our toes for a second, trying to help her stay up. Then there was a sort of flump and she was gone. And a silence. I wanted to run, but something made us walk to the edge. Smelly-Ann was sprawled at the bottom of the empty pond, pulling the scarf off. Her face was shiny with tears, her coat soaked from puddles of rainwater and there was a spreading pool of something steaming.

'That's what she kept trying to say,' I whispered. 'She needed a wee.'

Smelly-Ann wet her pants.
Fell down . . .

The rhyme went round and round in my head like the tune in my jewellery box.

But there was something dark that wasn't water or

wee and a white thing poking out from the sleeve of her coat. The silence went on and on.

'She's so disgusting!' said Vicky. 'Let's go. She'll be fine. Someone will come.'

But I had to do something. I said 'It's okay, Ann. I'll get help. Don't worry.' I ran like a character in a film running to save the whole town from aliens. I ran faster than I'd ever run before, all the way along the promenade, back to the park where there was a mum with her daughter. I was about to ask for help when I heard a siren and saw a blue flashing light. Vicky caught me up.

'Why did you run away? What's wrong with you? Didn't you see that man with the dog? He phoned 999. They're taking her to hospital.'

I WAS LATE and Mum was about to shout. But when I told her Ann had fallen and broken her arm, she took off her washing up gloves and gave me a hug. 'You did your best, pet.'

Ann didn't come back to school for a fortnight. Vicky and I carried on as normal and didn't even mention her name. But I couldn't eat or sleep. Whenever I closed my eyes I saw Ann's flapping arms then the spreading pool around her and the bone sticking through her sleeve.

Mum brought me cups of tea and toast in bed. She even let me stay off school because I was so tired. I couldn't tell her but I had to do something, even if it was only small.

We always bought three for the price of two, so there were usually a couple at the top of the bathroom cabinet. Mum didn't notice. It was awkward, embarrassing, but the day Ann came back to school, as we were putting our coats on in the cloakroom, I gave her the pink, rose-scented roll-on *Mum* deodorant.

She looked confused, surprised, and then smiled. 'Thank you, Helen.'

I didn't have time to say sorry. Vicky was at my side, pushing between us, turning her back to Ann. She didn't see what I'd done.

'Hurry up, Helen. You're coming to my house. Mum's making shepherd's pie. Then chocolate pudding.'

Now, as an adult, it was obvious. I didn't need to feel guilty about a little childhood accident. Ann and I had nothing in common; I didn't need her friendship and she didn't deserve mine. I should have been stronger. Like Vicky. But I took Ann's advice, probably not in the way she meant.

THIRTY-SIX

ANN TOLD ME to open my eyes and *look at things properly*, so I did and came to the same conclusion: Sam would come round in the end. I wasn't about to abandon my quest. All I had to do was give it time and wait. So, for the next few weeks I stayed away from Vicky and Sam and set about some early spring chores. On a day trip to Hull I'd bought some fabric; Sylvia was happy to run me up new curtains for the living room. When she came to take measurements, then to hang the curtains, I knew I'd find out what was going on at *The Laurels*. Sylvia always enjoyed a gossip.

'Vicky has to rest a lot now. Sam's been an angel – he looks after everyone, then stays up all night marking. Vicky doesn't mind him having his wee dram. Kids are excited – never stop squabbling. But you know how it is, Helen.'

Even without going there I had a good idea of the mood in the house.

THE FIRST DAFFODILS were starting to push their shoots up through the wet soil. I was never one for leaves and damp and mess; but it had to be done, so one mild day I got on my boots and Mum's old blue coat, and started on the garden.

The weight of the secateurs in my hand took me back to when Sam came to help with the apple tree. I still had a tiny mark on my arm. I've always been the kind of person who scars easily. We'd come a long way since that day.

The ground was claggy, and the soles of my boots were soon so built up with mud, that when the phone rang, my feet were skittering and sliding along the path as I ran to answer it. Not to mention mud all over the kitchen floor.

It was his voice. But there was an edge of urgency.

'Helen!'

I wanted to put my arms around him. 'What's wrong?'

'Can you pick Tom and Holly up from school today?'

'Of course.'

'And keep them till I get back from the hospital.'

'Hospital?'

'Vicky's gone into labour. God, Helen I'm panicking. What if something happens?'

'Of course it won't. She's in hospital. She'll be fine.' Something might happen.

'But it's so early. They've tried to stop the labour but

it was too late.'

'Don't worry, Sam. I'll pick them up. Go and look after Vicky. Text me how things are. Give her my love.'

'Thanks, Helen. So good to have a friend when it's like this.'

You see, Ann. We're friends. Sam *is* my friend.

THE BABY WAS born that afternoon. Five pounds one ounce – and six weeks early.

Everything was okay, but it hadn't been easy – a ventouse delivery. Vicky had lost a lot of blood so they had to stay in hospital for at least a week, maybe longer, Sylvia told me when she came to pick up the children. Sam would be busy going backwards and forwards to the hospital so Holly and Tom were staying with their grandma for a few days until everything was sorted out.

'A wee girl. They're going to call her Nancy after Vicky's friend in Manchester. You know, the actress.'

'Vicky's always talking about her.'

'She's like you, Helen. Still single, poor thing. But she always finds work – acting jobs, radio plays, that sort of thing. She and Vicky are very close. Almost like sisters.'

'Aunty Nancy isn't a real aunty, you know.' Tom said and Holly nudged him.

'And Sam?' I asked.

'Exhausted. Such a shock. But when it comes down to

it I can always rely on him.' She finished her wine, and sighed heavily. 'He's everything a son-in-law should be.'

'Oh yes, Vicky's so lucky.'

'And on Valentine's Day too … Sam said why not call her Val, but Vicky had already chosen the name. And you know Vicky likes to do things her way.' Sylvia laughed. 'She probably gets it from me. Ian always said I was stubborn.'

'What does *stubborn* mean, Granny?'

'Like you. Always wanting your own way,' Holly hissed and nudged him even harder.

'Liar!' He was on the verge of tears again as he had been since I brought them back from school.

'It's a shame Ian's not here to see another grandchild,' I said and took hold of Tom's hand. 'Let's get your coat on. It's time to go to Granny's.'

'I want to stay with you, Aunty Hel. I want you to read more stories.'

AFTER THEY HAD gone, I had a long soak in the bath. I'd looked forward to having the place to myself, free from their bickering and the noise of children's TV, but instead the quiet was heavy and deadening. The house very empty without them.

I poured myself some more wine. Sylvia had dropped hints that she'd like a glass, when I'd been quite happy with a cup of tea. But now it was open I might as well have another. And in the bath. Why not? I could do as I pleased.

When the doorbell rang again I'd been lying in the bubbles trying to relax for half an hour. The last person I expected was Sam. Honestly.

'It's you,' I said. My hair was dripping all over my bathrobe.

'Botticceli's Venus!' Sam attempted to smile and walked slowly into the hall.

'Ha! I'll find a towel then I'll be with you,' I said, running upstairs. 'You must be worn out.'

He's here. He's come to see me. My *friend*, Sam. See, Ann!

I dressed quickly and went back down. Sam was sitting at the kitchen table, his head in his hands. He looked up; his face was grey and strained.

'Cup of tea? Something to eat?' For a change, it was my turn to look after him. I wanted to hug him. But I knew I couldn't cross that line.

'Already eaten – hospital egg sandwich. Cup of tea would be great.' He breathed out heavily. 'Fuck, it's an overrated, messy business.'

'What?'

'Giving birth. Definitely loses the argument for design.' He smiled. 'Glad you were in, Helen. Needed to be somewhere normal.'

'Vic okay?'

'Tired. *Shattered* in fact.' He laughed. 'But both doing well, as they say.'

'When can I visit? I've never seen a newborn baby.'

'In a couple of days.'

'But everything's all right?'

'Oh yes, they don't anticipate any complications. They need to monitor them both.'

'So who does she look like?'

'Or what … a sun-dried tomato crossed with frog. She'll look more human in a few days. They usually do.'

I laughed. 'And you're calling her Nancy? It's a pretty n–'

'Not my choice…' He banged his mug down. 'Sorry, Helen. My wife is so fucking determined. I'm calling her Lizzy. *Elizabeth* Nancy.'

'What have you got against Nancy?'

'Where do you want me to start?' He drained his tea and I went to put the kettle on again.

'How about something stronger, Helen? We could wet the baby's head. Although I can see you've already been doing that – literally and metaphorically.'

There were a few inches left in the bottle Sylvia and I had started, and my hair was still dripping. I laughed and picked up the towel to rub my hair.

After the wine had gone, Sam went into the garden for a cigarette while I searched for another bottle – but my small store had inexplicably vanished. The only alcohol I could find was a bottle of limoncello shaped like the Leaning Tower of Pisa, a souvenir from the summer. I put it on the table with some sherry glasses.

'Sorry, don't have anything else . . .'

'Needs must. Here's to–'

'To the new baby. Whatever she's called. And,' I added quickly, 'to friendship.'

Sam drank down his small glass and pulled a face. 'Tastes even worse here.'

'Not bad after a few though.' I poured him another.

After several more, Sam levered himself up to standing using the table and yawned. 'Ought to get going. Do something useful.'

'Why?' my voice said. 'It's late. And I don't think you could walk that far.'

'I'll get a cab.' He combed his fingers through his hair and stretched.

'Stay here. Sleep on the sofa.'

One of us must have made the first move. It happened so quickly. His mouth tasted of cigarettes and lemons. It was so familiar.

V for victory.

THE NEXT DAY was Saturday; he could have stayed; but when I came downstairs for a glass of water, there was a note on the kitchen table.

Sorry.

I scrumpled up the paper and stuffed it in the bin, releasing the acrid smell of his cigarettes. *Sorry.* What did that mean? Sorry he had to get up so quickly? Sorry for spending the night? Sorry for everything?

From what I could remember, we had both enjoyed ourselves. And each other. I was in a cushioned state of relaxation and triumph but I dwelled on that scribbled word. As I cooked breakfast the flashes of memory were so vivid I groaned. That strawberry mark. His legs …His tongue. I couldn't wait much longer, so I sent a text.

Later?

The reply came pinging back within a few seconds.

At hospital. You can visit tomorrow.

I was being far too eager. He couldn't make any promises if he was stuck in the hospital with Vicky and the baby, could he?

Basking in the after effects of that warm cocooned feeling, even though it was February and cold and wet, I finished off the work I'd started in the garden; only yesterday but it felt like months ago. Out in the fresh air to disperse the fug of alcohol, then a quick trip to the corner shop for a bottle of wine. Or maybe two, just in case.

He'd probably call round in the evening – Sylvia would bring the children to visit their mother then take them back to make sure the house was ready for when Vicky came out of hospital. He would be free again tonight.

I checked the hospital website: visiting hours finished at eight. So I could expect him at nine at the latest.

I LOOKED IN the mirror. How did I look? The same as usual. But there was a difference. You couldn't see it. No camera could record it. It was too subtle. Sam was mine. I'd won. All I needed to do was to wait.

When it got to nine-thirty I couldn't sit still anymore. I threw down my book and jumped up. I puffed up the cushions and ran to look out of the window. Another five minutes then he'd be there.

Nothing.

I checked my phone.

Nothing.

I changed out of the dress I'd chosen into another – shorter, closer fitting. I tidied the kitchen and put out two glasses and the wine. I went upstairs and made sure the bedroom was ready: candles, matches, massage oil. I sprayed on more perfume.

Then I checked my phone again. Nothing. I picked up the phone in the hall and checked for messages.

Nothing.

Well I'd better nudge him. Give him an opportunity to respond.

Time for a drink? I texted him.

Sorry. Mistake.

The sleek metal of my mobile was cold greasy fish batter in my hand.

No, I won't give up. I told myself as I sent another message.

Just a quickie.

Five minutes later, as I was polishing the mirror in the hall, I heard the ping of his text.

Stop it. I can't.

My stomach dropped and my heart rate shot up as if I'd run to the top of the lighthouse, to the empty viewing platform. The wind howling around me, the dark emptiness all the way to the horizon.

Shoulders down. Slow breaths in and out. In and out. In. Out. I forced myself to relax.

One more try.

I'm here. Waiting.

I walked around the house, moving cushions, straightening furniture. I lit a candle in the bedroom and laid my shawl across the bed. The scent of jonquil, vanilla and lavender filled the room.

After twenty more minutes. Ping.

No

I was like the pressure cooker shrill with the rising steam, about to hurl hot burning soup everywhere if I didn't calm down. I ran up the stairs, retching and choking. I threw up what little was in my stomach into the toilet then sat panting on the edge of the bath. My whole body was trembling. I wanted to get away from everything. What could I do? Nothing would help. I bent over the washbasin and gulped down water straight from the tap, splashing it onto my face until it hurt. In the mirror, make up smeared off, my face was blotchy and shiny with water and tears. It wasn't my face. It was Mum's.

Her little blue pills were in the bathroom cabinet. I'd never tried one. But I'd seen the effect. I took two and blew out the candle in my bedroom. I got into bed and curled myself into a tight ball. It would be better in the morning. Surely I couldn't stay as angry as this. Moments later it was like heavy blinds rolling down inside my head. My skull was emptied out like a pumpkin lantern. Hollow.

WHEN I WOKE the next day, it was as if a slab of stone had been lowered onto my chest, pressing me down into the bed. I didn't get up until two in the afternoon.

Then the only thing I could do was walk. Through unclosed curtains I caught glimpses of Sunday cosiness –

people playing at happy families. An old man sitting on a bench in the shelter on the promenade, leaning on his stick gazing mournfully out to sea, was joined by another man. They shook hands and smiled. Friends. I walked on the wet sand along the shoreline, a tiny, insignificant insect against the canopy of the sky and sea. When I looked back at the town, the lighthouse stuck up like someone giving me the middle finger.

Then I couldn't stop the snivelling. I was choking on my own tears. I was a useless dead thing kicked back into the sea. I was disintegrating, like the beach. Tumbled with stones and sand and washed away, swept away far down the coast, and dumped on Spurn Point, slowly becoming an island.

He was still going to choose Vicky over me. It was happening again.

THIRTY-SEVEN

THAT HOT SUMMER, the first time we followed them, I was with Ann.

'Do you think they've done it yet?' With all the sun, Ann's skin had improved; she was less pale, less grey under the eyes. 'I reckon Vicky's the kind who won't say no.'

'Sam's not like that!'

'But boys change, Helen. Hormones!' She laughed, showing her newly-capped teeth. Now she had a social worker and her dad was *away*, there had been changes in Ann's life. 'My mum says they're all the same – brains in their trousers!'

My fingers itched to slap her hard or pinch her, like I used to do, but I laughed.

'Let's follow them. Let's find out!' I said. 'And we can tease him all about it ...'

The tide was in and grey clouds rolled in from the sea. It was like the spy games Vicky and I played at primary school. No handbags or mirrors, but still the thrill, the anticipation of something about to happen that we couldn't control. Bubbles of laughter kept rising up and popping out.

Ann spotted them on the promenade, and we followed at a distance; when they sat down on a bench we hid in the shelter where the old people sat and took turns being lookout. They were so close together, their eyes locked tight, on the verge of kissing.

'They're moving. Come on, we can go now,' Ann said.

Arms linked around each other's waist like a three-legged race, they walked to the steps and down onto the sand. To allow them to stay ahead, we sat on the bench where they'd been sitting. It was still warm and there was a lingering smell of Vicky's musky perfume.

We followed them onto the sand; they were walking towards the dunes, so absorbed in each other that they didn't look back. This far along the beach there were fewer people, so we had to be careful but that only increased the excitement. The wind flicked my hair into my eyes, and I shivered in my thin gingham school dress. Ann wandered off to the tide-line, and soon her pockets were bulging with stones and shells. Like a ten year old.

Snatches of laughter and conversation blew back towards me. Not sentences but the occasional word: 'Oh, cheri!' in her ridiculous French accent.

Near the golf course they disappeared into the dunes, and cigarette smoke drifted up.

Ann crunched back over the pebbles. 'Where've they gone?'

'The dunes.'

'Thought so!' She dropped her cache of shells and stones onto the dry sand like an offering, like a cat dropping a dead bird. 'I found some carnelian. It's semi-precious.'

I ignored her. 'Let's go and see what they're doing.'

'But what if they see us!'

'They're too busy. Let's leave our stuff here.'

Where the dunes bunched up along the edge of the golf course, the sand was soft and dry, but cold underfoot, and spiked through with clumps of marram grass.

'Ow!' Ann stifled a shout and hopped around in pain. A piece of beer bottle, buried under the sand. She was biting her hand to stop herself from crying, but under her tan she was pale. I remembered the boating pond. Her silence. Why do some people have victim written all over them?

'We'll have to go back,' I hissed. Just when we were going to find out.

For the first time since we'd become friends, she really irritated me. I took tissues out of my bag and made a wad of them, then she struggled into her greyish white socks. Her hands were icy and she was shaking. It was only a small cut but she leaned her whole weight on me.

'I'm sorry, Helen.'

There was a faint haze of smoke over the dunes where Sam and Vicky had disappeared, the only sound, apart from the distant boom of the sea was Ann sniffing back her tears.

A spot of rain touched my cheek. The clouds were darker than ever, gunmetal grey. Then it started.

Golfers trundled their bags past us, keeping dry under umbrellas. 'Good weather for it!' one shouted. 'Having a nice shower, girls?'

By the time we'd reached the promenade our clothes were soaked and we were both chilled.

***

I WALKED UNTIL my feet ached and there were blisters on my heels. I wanted to feel them burst. I wanted sharp pain – some physical manifestation of how I felt.

But eventually, I don't know how many hours later, the brain chemicals kicked in and did their work; and even though the tranquilisers had worn off completely, there was a new kind of calm. Now I was an adult, not an adolescent. I didn't have to give up.

At home I showered, plucked my eyebrows, shaved my legs. I washed out the bath and polished the tiles until they shone. I ate fruit. I drank water. I made myself clean inside and out. Then, on the third day, I rose from the dead and went to visit Vicky in hospital.

HEAT HIT ME like a fist. The smell of bodily substances mixed with school dinners thinly veiled by disinfectant was overpowering; the noise was constant – visitors arriving and departing, nurses wheeling squeaking trolleys. Any brief bubble of peace was punctured by the squawking of babies. It was like a scene from hell.

The fire door of her private room squeezed itself shut behind me and instantly switched off the noise. Vicky was alone, asleep in a hospital bed with a metal side. A narrow shaft of sunlight fell on her tangled hair. She was sleeping like a princess in a fairy story and for an absurd second I saw myself as both the evil godmother about to bundle away her baby and, unexpectedly, the prince come to save her.

There were hefty bunches of flowers on a side table and on a shelf next to the TV – red roses from Sam with his flair for self-conscious cliché, and the lilies speckled with brick-red spots, their stamens chopped off to avoid pollen stains, must have been from Sylvia. *He's everything a son-in-law should be.*

In the plastic cot next to the bed, wrapped in a yellow hospital blanket, the new baby. Tiny, but at the same time dominated by a head that was grossly large, and much too hairy. I didn't want to think of the whole process of dilation, suction, extraction that had moulded and bruised her head. She looked like no one I'd ever met; there was something repellent, hardly human, but I bent over to have a closer look. Was I allowed to touch her? That would be like reaching inside Vicky to touch some private internal part.

The baby opened her eyes and looked at me; inky blue eyes grew wider as her limbs began a jerking dance and her mouth opened to a pink circle of noise. Vicky moaned slightly and woke.

'Helen, love! You're here.'

'Of course.'

'So good to see you.'

But she was leaning towards the cot. It wasn't really me she wanted to see.

'Pass her to me, will you. They said I've got to try and feed her.'

I had to touch the baby. She was warm, hot even and much heavier than I'd imagined five pounds of human could be. And getting louder all the time. I manhandled her over to Vicky. Perhaps it was a trick of the light but when her eyes met the baby's, Vicky was miraculously transformed, coated in a golden glaze. There was a faint gold haze of hair on her forearms too. Her nightgown was unbuttoned, and as she took the baby from me, her breasts were hot and hard against my arm.

'Babies are heavy!' I said. 'No wonder mothers develop huge muscles. I thought it was all that washing and using the mangle. My dolls were so light and easy to carry around.'

'Helen, you're such a romantic! Get me some water will you. Every time I feed her I feel like I'm going to die of thirst.'

I poured her a tumbler of lukewarm water from the plastic jug on the bedside table. While balancing the baby at her breast she almost snatched it from me, and downed it noisily.

'More, please! God, it's so hot in this place.'

The baby had stopped writhing and bleating and, as if it knew what to do, which I suppose it did, was latching on to Vicky's left breast where the veins stood out like pale blue lines in marble.

'Don't look like that! It's completely natural.' Vicky laughed. 'You're still such a prude, Helen.'

'But it's so weird watching you ... What's it actually feel like?'

'Fucking hard work at first. I'm like an old goat that can't produce anything useful. Got to build up the milk supply.'

'Gives the baby immunity or something.' I'd been reading Vicky's baby books.

'And shrinks your uterus back ... Fuck that hurt! Oxytocin.'

'What?'

'Same hormone as in an orgasm. Breast feeding's sexy, you know.'

'You're joking?'

'No, once we get going and we're a proper little team, I don't even want to talk when I'm feeding. Sometimes I actually climax – not the ideal moment to have a conversation!'

I half believed her. But with Vicky I could never be sure. I'd have to Google it.

'If I'm in the way of you and your new lover …' I said, my face burning.

'Lover! That's the last thing I need at the moment.'

We both laughed. And I saw him leaning into me, the strawberry birthmark, the taste of lemon and cigarettes. I wanted to tell her. I wanted her to know. I even owed it to her to tell her, didn't I? I left a suitable pause then asked, 'Where is Sam anyway? Thought he'd be here giving you a helping hand.'

'Catching up on sleep. We had a busy night…' Her voice tailed off. There was a dreamy expression on her face.

'You're not…?'

'God no! Just tired. Back home we'll do this all day and fall asleep together. Mum's going to look after us.'

'Then you can get strong again.'

'And have visitors. I want you to come and see me every day.'

'Of course. I'll do the school run. Shopping. Whatever you need.'

Vicky yawned and the baby fell away from her breast,

asleep again. A buttery white bubble of milk dripped out of the corner of her tiny mouth and her head lolled back like a drunk.

'Must be good stuff!'

'First two weeks they sleep most of the time. Then they start being awake more.'

She yawned again and this time I took the hint.

I quickly kissed her cheek. 'Give my love to Sam when you see him.'

The words hung in the air for a few seconds, before dissipating. But she was fast asleep. I carefully prised the baby out of her arms and put her back in the cot.

When I got home it took me nearly an hour to wash out the cloying smell of milk. It was in my hair, on my body and on all my clothes.

FOG. ALL NIGHT I dreamed I couldn't see where I was going, as if I had a patch over my good eye and I was running away from the foghorn. The lighthouse flashed and I saw glimpses of Vicky and Sam; Sam and Vicky; Vicky and Sam. Then it went out and I was falling into the dark.

THIRTY-EIGHT

MY FIRST VISIT since Vicky had come home with the baby. In the park the trees were changing quickly. Glossy buds on the horse chestnuts already started to split and poke out their green hands, and floods of daffodils submerged the dying crocuses; I was surprised again by how blue their leaves were against the canary yellow of the flowers.

'They're poisonous, you know,' I'd once told Sam when he suggested planting some under my new arbour.

'Daffodils?'

'The bulbs.' Dad had warned me never to eat the bulbs, always wash my hands after touching them.

'Well I won't eat them then!' he said.

'Surprising how something so innocent and beautiful can come out of something so toxic.' I said.

He'd pulled me towards him. 'Like you?'

'Oh no. I'm the opposite. Deadly – like a drug.'

'And you think I'm addicted?'

'Absolutely.'

'Wondered why I was feeling so sick … must be

withdrawal symptoms.'

BUT NOW, AS soon as I arrived, Sam made himself scarce, muttering about a pile of marking he had to do. After a week of paternity leave, work had probably built up, but soon the sound of his guitar drifted down. He was avoiding me.

The dining table was covered in presents for the baby; and every cupboard top, window sill or mantel piece was decorated by greetings cards and flowers. When we were children, Vicky once had a fairy party and we were told to dress up. I arrived late, proud of my lumpy coat hanger wings, only to find Vicky in a white satin dress with ruffled feathery wings that flew in the air as she danced and spun to music on her new record player. My offering of a packet of Bird's toffees and a homemade card was childish next to the mountain of presents already torn open and laid out on an empty bed for us to admire.

This time I'd not tried to make a card, but the yellow-striped sleep suit which, in the shop looked like a symbol of spring, was dull and practical alongside frilly dresses and tiny lambskin bootees.

I should have been rosy-cheeked after the walk in the cold air, but a glance in the hall mirror showed I was windswept and pale. If Sylvia hadn't been so obsessed with looking after everyone, she would have told me I was sickening for something I was so *peely wally*. Whereas Vicky, lying on the sofa with the baby asleep next to her in some sort of lacy Victorian cradle, was the perfect picture of motherhood. No indication of sleepless nights, nappies or vomit. Everything was tidy and in its place and, after only a week, Vicky's complexion was glowing, her eyes bright, her hair shining.

The baby too looked better; she was less red and shrivelled, and the bruising on her head was beginning to fade. Vicky assured me it would disappear completely over time. 'Dad said I looked like a pug, when I was born – my face was so squashed!'

'Och, Victoria you do exaggerate.' Sylvia flapped her gently over the head with the flat of her hand. 'You were beautiful, even then.'

I tried to picture my own mother contemplating pregnancy and childbirth. She must have dreaded it. And *beautiful* wasn't a word she ever used about anything.

FOR THE NEXT couple of weeks, Sylvia clucked around and made cups of tea, finding any excuse to take the baby out in her pram to be admired. But then she went away for a week to Ibiza – the holiday was planned long before the baby was due and no one had expected little Nancy to be so early.

I had some annual leave to use and nothing better to

do. I was happy to help.

It wasn't exactly arduous – laundry, some cooking and a spot of cursory cleaning. It put me in mind of the last few weeks Mum was alive as Vicky was sometimes so demanding and helpless. Of course I didn't breathe a word of this to her. I didn't want to bring the odour of the sick room into her fluffy little nest. With the children at school, and Sam at work, we could chat and cement our friendship. While Vicky and the baby had an afternoon nap I often went into Sam's study with its view of the sea, and looked through his papers, read his emails, breathed in his familiar smell. I liked holding his pen and examining the books he was marking. Sometimes I wanted to make my own comments about their sad little essays. Trying to please Sir with their adolescent efforts. I always put everything back exactly how I found it, but threw out the cigarette butts and beer cans and got going with the *Mr. Sheen.*

When no one else was there to offer – and Vicky wasn't glued to the sofa breastfeeding her – I even held little Nancy. It wasn't so bad really, as long as she was asleep or quiet. I pictured myself as a new mother, nurturing the next generation. But as soon as she started crying it cut through me like marram grass, and I was quick to pass her back. It affected Sam like that too: he walked up and down with the baby on his shoulder, but as the noise increased, he got faster until, when the wailing reached the level of a house alarm, he remembered lesson planning he had to do for the next day, and practically threw the baby into Vicky's lap.

Those were the moments when I offered cups of tea.

'Or something stronger, Helen?' He said without a double entendre.

New babies cause such chaos. No wonder couples split up.

Vicky was beginning to lose the weight she'd put on over the months. As if the fat was being melted down into milk. Little Nancy was putting on weight like a suckling pig. A pink sugar pig. Vicky took her to the clinic to be weighed every week, just to prove the gold-top quality of her breast milk.

Mind you, Vicky had a long way to go: there is womanly and there's voluptuous; but there's also just plain porky.

'AUNTY HELEN, IS there a baby in your tummy?' I was putting Tom to bed while Vicky had a bath and Sam was at the gym. 'When are you going to have your baby?'

I finished reading him a story and kissed his plump, little cheek.

'You have to be married first, stupid!' Holly jumped into her own bed and pulled the duvet up to her chin. 'Don't you know *anything*? Mum and Dad made the baby. Dad put his seed inside Mum.

'Night, Tom Thumb,' I said.

'Night, night, Aunty Hel.'

'Anyway, Aunty Helen is an aunty. She's got us instead,' Holly went on.

'Maybe Daddy can give her a baby.'

'Then she'd be too busy to read us stories. Would you like a horrible old witch to come and put you to bed?'

Tom looked worried. 'Auntie Hel, tell her … '

'Don't tease him. He's only eight.'

'Well he ought to grow up then. It's boring having a *baby* brother and a baby sister.' Holly switched off her bedside light and turned to face the wall.

'I'm *not* a baby!' Tom began wailing and a second later, from Vicky and Sam's room, came an answering cry. The baby had woken up.

'Not again!' Holly pulled the duvet over her head.

'Can you get her, love?' Vicky yelled from the bathroom. 'I'll be there in a minute.'

I didn't have time to calm Tom down. I ran to see to the baby. The cot was next to their bed, in the pink palace. The bed where Sam and I had … but the noise was so intense I couldn't finish my thought. The only way to stop the sound was to bend down even closer and pick her up.

'Sorry, Helen. Take her downstairs. You'll have to walk around. I'll be as quick as I can!'

The bathroom door was half-open. I caught a glimpse of Vicky in a cloud of steam pulling her towel around her and, one leg glistening and pink, stepping out of the bath.

The best method of reducing the sound was to carry the squalling creature upright, her tiny mouth an O of noise next to my ear. Her body was a tightly coiled spring arching and bucking against me, the mouth rubbing wetly, sucking at my cheek. I put my little finger in her mouth as I'd seen Vicky do, and for a moment it pacified her. Then the noise started again, drilling into the evening.

Mum had prided herself on her controlled crying technique – four hourly feeds, no giving in to a small baby. 'You've got to show them who's boss,' she'd said to me, after Sylvia had been round to tell her when Holly was born. 'Can't go picking them up every time they cry. Never did you any harm. Good exercise for the lungs.'

I was torn between the need to comfort this desperate animal, and a slow ripple of revulsion. If I dropped her on the cold tiles of the kitchen floor that would stop the noise once and for all. Did mothers ever think like that? I was sure they must. Anything to get it to stop.

'I'm so sorry.' Vicky made me jump. 'Let me take the little monster.'

I felt the weight being taken off me. I gave her up like giving up a primed hand grenade. Let her sort it out. She had the advantage of mother's milk. I could never match that.

Vicky sat on the sofa with the baby. 'Come and chat, Helen. Don't worry about the dishes.'

I'd actually gone to make a cup of tea.

'It's so boring, stuck with a newborn. The highlight of my day has been a bath, and even that was interrupted! I'm a milk machine.' She sighed loudly. 'Come and keep me company, love.'

Dirty plates and cups from the children's tea were still not washed. But I filled a glass of water for Vicky and went back.

Vicky was in her bathrobe, her blond hair damp but beginning to fluff up as it dried; she exposed one distended breast and held her nipple up to the baby whose mouth was rooting to take in the hard pink tip.

'Peace at last,' Vicky sighed 'Pass me a cushion, love.'

The house had settled and my ears buzzed with the after-effects of the baby's crying.

'Tom must've gone off to sleep,' I said. 'Holly was winding him up again. I tried to stop her. I hope he didn't cry too long.'

Vicky moved to make herself comfortable, swapping the baby over to the other breast. 'She's a nightmare. The baby's made her worse. But it'll all sort itself out eventually, I suppose …'

Her face took on a dreamy look. 'You really ought to try this, Helen. Beats sex any time.'

I tried to ignore her, and focused instead on the photos on the mantelpiece – me on the Leaning Tower smiling was my favourite. With a bit of luck, Sam would be back from the gym soon. But Vicky moaned to herself under her breath and muttered 'Helen, why don't you watch? It's okay to look. Helen I…oh, Helen.'

My hands were sweating. When she'd told me about the link between breastfeeding and orgasms I hadn't believed her. I stumbled out of the room into the kitchen and washed up. When I heard the key in the front door and Sam came in, I was relieved, if only so I could escape.

'It's so cold out there … Christ, Vic that child's going to eat you to death. You never stop feeding her.'

'We're both having fun.' Vicky's voice was distant and low.

'Not again! Do you have to be so embarrassing?' He turned to me. 'Has she been…?'

'I need to go. I'm not feeling my best at the moment.' I stood up. 'Actually it's a year since Mum died.' It wasn't the exact date, but it was the first thought that came into my mind.

Sam put his hand out to touch my arm. 'I'd no idea.' But only succeeded in jabbing his finger into a hole in my jumper which was awkward to disentangle. 'Sorry.'

'Helen! Why didn't you say?' Vicky pulled an exaggerated sad face.

I made to go.

'What – no kiss for little Nancy and me?'

As I bent over them, and smelled warm milk from the baby, Vicky's hand was damp where she touched my cheek, her inky blue eyes very bright. 'Scaredy cat,' she whispered in my ear.

OUTSIDE THE AIR had turned frosty and it slapped me like a crisp, cleanly washed pillow case straight off the washing line.

Vicky was not a normal person. And Sam knew it too. He as much as said so. She didn't deserve him.

I found myself walking through the lighthouse garden. I wanted to climb up to the viewing platform. I needed to be as far away from the suffocating intimacy and weirdness of her fetid burrow as I could. I wanted to wipe the smile off Vicky's smug face. To push her from the top of the lighthouse, and see her tumbling down in a big pink heap, those monumental breasts splattering like watermelons.

I had to keep calm. Think. Not feel.

What should I do now?

She was a witch. A freak. I needed to get him away from her. What Sam needed was someone stable and normal. Dear, dear, Sam. My dear kind friend. My beloved. I had to protect him from her.

Tonight he knew what was going on as soon as he

came into the room. He knew the effect she had on other people, and he wanted to protect me. He responded to me when I mentioned Mum, whereas all Vicky could think of was to torment me with her disgusting smut.

Yet he stayed with her. *What on earth made you stay?* He had a compulsion to look after people, to nurture them. He was a teacher, wasn't he? He was kind. He nursed sick birds. Vicky needed to be looked after; Sam liked to fix people. She was a needy, manipulative woman; he was kindness incarnate. It made me feel sick to acknowledge it, but in some warped way they were ideally suited. He must love her enough to stay with her.

But it was only *enough*; it was sufficient, tolerable, adequate. While what I had to offer was so much better. I could give him real love. Like Fanny Price – true, devoted love. Pure love.

Standing in the lighthouse garden I felt sorry for him; he was limiting himself to a half-baked, *adequate* life.

The moon cast the shadow of the lighthouse over the lawn and I knew it was up to me. Waiting patiently wasn't enough. I had to rescue him.

THIRTY-NINE

AND MY RESCUE began with flowers.

As soon as she opened the door I could see them – beautiful yellow roses lit up the dark hallway like tiny suns, little fists of hope in the stuffy air.

'Someone's popular,' I said, taking off my coat and hanging it on the banister.

'And it's not *me*,' Vicky said, her voice serious, quiet.

'Oh?'

'They're for Sam.'

'Your wedding anniversary?'

'They're not from me.'

'A secret admirer? How exciting!' I laughed and shook my hair out from where it had been crushed under my hat.

'Helen, I don't know who sent them.'

On a white card in spiky letters was written: *To Sam-mykins from your little sqirrel. J*

'Someone with a crush?' I said. 'Terrible spelling … not one of his A-level students then!'

'Look on the back.'

I flipped the card over; and there it was in all its glory:

P.S. I love eating strawberries!!!

'What's that mean?' I said. 'Is Sam a big fan of strawberries? Can't get nice ones this time of year...'

'No. Well, yes he is. But no, it's not that.' Vicky looked away. She actually blushed, right to the roots of her highlighted hair. 'Sam has a birthmark. On his leg – a strawberry mark.'

She twisted her fingers and rubbed at her face. 'Only someone who's seen him naked...' She sank down on the bottom step, as if her legs had given way, and started to cry silently, her face buried in her arms.

I felt genuinely sorry for her – for a nanosecond. But I resisted, and pulled my hand back before it touched her heaving shoulders.

'I'm sure there's an innocent explanation. A male friend winding him up. Someone from the gym.'

I sat down next to her. This time I did put my hand out and patted the top of her arm. Luckily I'd always had good balance, because she burrowed herself into me, nearly knocking me off the step. Through the fine wool of her jumper I could feel her bones – weeks of constant breastfeeding had reduced her. As little Nancy continued to balloon, Vicky was shrinking, as if all the air was being sucked out. She was fragile. Breakable.

'No,' she said finally, her voice thick with tears. 'He's seeing someone. I can tell.'

I went to find her a tissue.

'Let's not jump to conclusions. It's probably Sam trying to wind *you* up!'

'This isn't a joke.' She wiped her eyes then blew her nose loudly. 'Someone's trying to give me a message. A warning. I don't know… Why are men so difficult?'

'I'll make you a cup of tea.' I absently rearranged one of the roses that had become tangled. 'I'm sure it's nothing sinister. Someone who admires Sam.'

The smell of the roses filled the hallway.

'Lovely flowers.' I bent close to one of the blooms and breathed in the musky scent. 'Yellow roses are for friendship, aren't they?'

Vicky got to her feet unsteadily. 'No, Helen!' Her voice had a note of hysteria. 'Why are you always so *calm* and reasonable?'

She was losing control, and in a very disagreeable way.

'I'm only trying to help.' I reached up and started to put on my coat. 'If you won't listen to a friend…'

'I'm sorry. Don't go.' She put her arms out and held on to me. 'Please stay. I'm so confused. I need someone calm around. That's why I asked you.'

I unpeeled her hands.

'Okay. No harm done.' I looked into her eyes. 'Come on, little Vicky. Deep breath. Scrap the tea. Let's find some wine and we can think how to play this.'

She followed me into the kitchen.

'We'll sort this out.' I searched for a corkscrew. 'Is Sam out for the rest of the afternoon?'

'Park and pizza – his new dad thing. Just me and the baby here.' She tried to smile, 'Helen, don't leave me, will you? I don't want to be on my own.' Mother, standing waiting behind the door when I left her to go shopping, flashed into my mind. The way she depended on me. This felt altogether different.

'Of course I won't.'

Then she smiled through her tears. 'You're wearing the necklace. Oh, you're so sweet!'

I poured the wine.

'And to cheer you up, I'll tell you about my shopping trip to Hull last week. I bought a lovely dress …'

IT WASN'T A complete lie. I'd been in Hull long enough to walk to the railway station and from there I'd taken the train to York. But I *had* been to Hull. That was true.

Perhaps I'd gone too far in seeking authenticity – once I was on the train, I went into the toilet cubicle and put on my raincoat and sunglasses. I'd considered wearing a wig, but I'd found one of Mum's old headscarves. That would do. The accent I borrowed from Sylvia; the one she slipped into when she was overexcited or talking on the phone to her family in Scotland. I sat in the window seat with a coffee, the sun glancing through grey cloud. Perfect rainbow weather.

It would have been easy to order them online, but I wanted a challenge. And a change of air would do me good too. I'd printed out a map of where all the florists were, but, once I'd arrived in York, unfamiliarity as well as a sudden rain shower confused me. I took off my sunglasses and hid under my umbrella as I walked through endless rows of brick terraced houses in the outskirts of the city.

The first shop only delivered to the local area, the second had closed down but the third – exactly like a fairy story – was able to offer delivery by Interflora anywhere in Yorkshire.

As I leafed through the catalogue, the assistant hovered ready to give advice. It was mid-week and probably not a busy time of year for sending flowers. I sensed she wanted to chat but I needed to concentrate. To take my time.

The choice was bewildering: hand-tied, bouquets, sprays. Apart from the wreath for Mum's funeral I'd never ordered flowers. The descriptions were more flowery than the flowers themselves, sitting in cold metal vases throughout the shop.

If you want to let your friends know how much they mean to you, this dazzling bouquet will do just that.

Bursting with scent and colour it's a big cuddle just waiting to happen!

'So many to choose from. Could you give me some advice?'

Whatever the reason, these roses are simply beautiful.

'For someone special?' she asked.

'My boyfriend.'

'Unusual!'

'Och I know, but you see he's just proposed.'

'So he's your fiancé? Congratulations.'

'Thank you.' I slipped off my gloves and the diamonds flashed. 'I'm not used to wearing a ring!' I said, then laughed in a becoming way.

'Gorgeous. Rose gold, isn't it?'

'His mother's. Genuine 1960's.'

I let my hand linger over the pages. The diamonds sent out beams of light like a tiny lighthouse. 'Sadly she passed away last year.'

She pressed my hand sympathetically. 'That makes it even more special.'

After ten minutes, I found what I was looking for – an overstated bouquet of golden yellow roses, described as New English roses. Scent guaranteed.

'Yellow's good. Perfect for a man. What would you like me to put on the card?'

***

NOW THE BABY was asleep, we could talk without interruption; and after a couple of glasses of wine, Vicky was calm enough for me to leave her and slip up to the bathroom.

'I'll check on Nancy while I'm there. You relax.'

In her cot the baby was lying on her back, her little arms thrown up behind her head, almost like an adult. Her eyelids flickered and she sighed, but settled again.

I opened Vicky's jewellery box and replaced the engagement ring. A diamond caught the light and winked at me. There was so much here Vicky hadn't even noticed it had gone.

In Sam's office his guitar was leaning next to the bookcase. I cradled it in my lap and ran my fingers along the keyboard. I could smell him.

One of Vicky's chipped ceramic dishes was almost overflowing with cigarette ends and burnt down matches. On his desk, three mugs had the remains of tea growing a thick skin of mould. This was the room that only a few months ago was so austere and clean, I sat at his desk and flicked through the pile of books he was marking. A few boys, but mostly girls: Layla, Darcey, Josie. Sam so close to all those girls – leaning over them to write in their books with his beautiful looping writing, their hot bodies bursting with hormones. 'Interesting, Josie. You need to consider how Bronte …'

I spent a long time in the bathroom checking the

contents of the cabinet. There was a bottle of sleeping pills I'd never noticed before – someone feeling the stress of a new baby. I held it in my hand and turned it over to read the name. Sam, not Vicky.

When I came down, Vicky was sitting with her feet on the sofa, glass in hand.

'All fine.' I said, taking a drink. 'Do you want me to stay when Sam comes back? Are you going to confront him?'

'I have to, Helen. Could you? I don't want the kids involved in this.'

AFTER AN AFTERNOON in the park, Holly and Tom were exhausted and full of pizza and fizzy drinks. Tom was already yawning as they took off their coats and dropped them on the floor.

'Flowers, Vic?' Sam sounded surprised.

Vicky ignored him and spoke to the children.

'Guess what? Aunty Helen's here. She's going to put you to bed.' Her voice was straining to be light.

'Come on kids, race you to the bathroom!' I said.

Hearing the adult voices through the floorboards, as I helped the children to get ready for bed, reminded me of my own childhood. Those murmurs that gradually escalated into short angry exchanges.

'What about Nancy?' I heard Sam say.

'Well? What *about* her?'

Holly was obstinately self-sufficient, but I had to help Tom into his pyjamas.

'Why's Mummy shouting at Daddy?'

'It's not shouting. I think their voices are just loud.'

I pulled back the covers so he could climb into bed.

'I don't like it when they shout, Aunty Hel. Can you read me another story? And cuddle me in?'

Holly was already reading and drifted off to sleep quickly, or at least she pretended well, but I had to lie on the bed with Tom for a while. I started to read: '*Far out in the wide sea, where the water is blue as the loveliest cornflower and clear ....*'

When I was sure they were both asleep, I finished reading *The Little Mermaid* to myself. Of course I knew how it ended, and I relished how different it was from the syrupy Disney version, but I wanted to enjoy the argument, rumbling up like a TV drama. I must have dozed off too because I woke with a start as the front door banged shut. As I came downstairs, headlights swept into the hall, highlighting the yellow roses smug and defiant in their clear glass vase.

Vicky was curled on the sofa, sobbing quietly.

'Just leave me,' she said, but I went to find a blanket and put it over her.

There was nothing else for me to do. I might as well go home. Then there was a crackle from the baby monitor and the unmistakable cry of a hungry baby. I made up a bottle of formula and sat in Vicky's bedroom with Nancy on my knee. She took the bottle greedily, still half asleep, and as I looked down at her trusting little profile, I thought how contented we'd all be, how much less arguing and falling out, fewer misinterpretations there would be, if people would only look and judge clearly and accept reality. So many people are led by their emotions and make the most ridiculous decisions.

So many stories involve pain and maiming – the Little Mermaid agreeing to have her tongue cut out, Mme Bovary dying in 'les atroces douleurs' of arsenic poisoning, Anna Karenina mowed down by a train. If I was to rescue Sam, my own story might involve some minor discomfort on my part, and a few twinges for others; but as long as the ending was a happy one I knew I could do it.

ONCE SHE'D DRUNK her fill, I changed Nancy's nappy and slotted her back into her cot. I knew the house so well I could find my way around even in the dark. The children were both sleeping soundly and, downstairs on the sofa, Vicky was motionless. I made sure there was a glass of water on the table beside her and pulled the blanket up to cover her shoulders.

Sam was probably in the pub; he'd find his way back no doubt. Vicky often said he had a homing instinct even when he was drunk.

As I put my coat and hat on, the tiny ceramic hearts on the necklace tinkled together like cut glass. The hall was full of the scent of the roses, sweet and almost buttery now. Yellow roses for friendship the florist said, but, and I kept this hugged tightly to myself, for the Victorians – fond as they were of melodrama – yellow roses symbolised jealousy and infidelity. My own little joke.

FORTY

I HAD TO be like the lighthouse – solid, reliable and always there – a tower of strength. Ultimately, I had to make myself indispensable and wedge my way into their dissolving marriage like a keystone, to hold the ramshackle structure together. I had to be there, yes, but I also had to make sure that I was never seen as a threat. I needed Sam to know I cared about him, of course; but also that I cared about Vicky, which in some way I did.

The cracks in their relationship were growing. I would do my utmost to be seen to provide the glue to stick them back together; but like Mum's Royal Doulton figurine, they would always be there catching the dirt – disfigured and damaged. And I knew exactly what would really help their relationship: a romantic weekend away. Just the two of them.

'I'LL HAVE THE children. And Helen will help out, won't you dear?'

You could almost hear the whirr of the rotating blades

as Sylvia hovered above *The Laurels* ready to winch her darling daughter to safety and happiness.

'Of course,' I said. 'I'll feed the cat, take the dog out. I can stay in the house, if you like.'

Why wouldn't I?

Vicky grabbed another tissue from the half empty box and dabbed at her eyes.

'Helen, that's so kind. We just need time on our own to sort this out.'

'Take all the time you need. I've no other plans.'

ONCE THE DECISION had been made, Sam had little choice.

'I'll do as I'm told. As usual,' he said. 'Now you three have conspired against me!' He laughed, but as he searched for his cigarettes then went outside, pulling up his hood against a fine drizzle, he looked strained and old.

I helped Vicky pack. She'd invested in some new underwear from a website I'd recommended.

'Before we had kids I used to be quite an expert, but I didn't realise these things even existed! Mum always said still waters run deep!'

'Well ... remember Ed? He had a bit of a thing for lace and silk.'

'Ed? I thought Holdersea was all Tupperware parties! No wonder Julia looks so happy!'

She sat back on her heels. 'You don't think I'm going too far, do you? I don't want to put Sam off.'

'What do you mean?'

'Mutton dressed as lamb.'

More like a lamb to the slaughter. 'You'll look lovely, Vicky. And you want this to work don't you?'

'But I'm not sure Sam does. He's been walking on eggshells since those fucking flowers arrived. Trying to be nice. Just like a man with a guilty conscience. Denies it completely. Says she's stalking him.'

'How horrible.'

'It's really got to him. Can't stop thinking about it. Neither of us can.'

I made sympathetic noises and concentrated on folding a pair of jeans. 'He should report it to the head teacher. You can't let her get away with it.'

'That's the problem. This sort of stuff happens all the time in secondary schools. Crushes on teachers. Sam wants to ignore it. If they do an investigation he's worried what else might be said.'

'Sounds like he's covering something up.'

'You know what he's like, Helen.'

'You mean there've been other times?'

'There was something in Manchester. Similar story. There was nothing in it. But mud sticks. He doesn't want to put us through it again. I don't know whether to believe him or not. I don't know what to think. But someone sent those flowers. Someone's trying to get at him. Or me.' Vicky sighed and carried on packing. 'I hate to say this, but he suggested it could be you. You might be playing a trick on him. You two are always teasing each other.'

She looked at me. Pointedly.

I met her gaze and didn't look away.

'How mad would that be, Vic? And why?'

'No, love. I told him you wouldn't do anything like that.'

She carried on taking clothes out of the walk-in wardrobe then changing her mind and putting them back. So many clothes. More than I'd had in my whole life.

'I still can't see us coming back from Whitby on Sunday night like a pair of honeymooners, can you?'

I couldn't, and obviously had my own reasons why not.

I shrugged. 'But a happily married couple who've gone through a sticky patch … that's something to aim for, isn't it?'

Vicky reached over the open suitcase and stroked my cheek.

'You're so wise and sensible, Helen. What would I do without you?'

She sighed again and got to her feet. 'I'll have to put Sam's stuff in for him. Why is it some people don't know how to pack?'

While she was searching in their wardrobe, I took the letter out of my pocket (it was nicely creased, as if it had been read over and over again) and tucked it down the side of the suitcase. There was the risk that Sam would find it before her. But knowing Vicky as well as I did, the first thing she'd do when they arrived would be to unpack. And if Sam found it … well, something interesting was bound to happen.

AS I WALKED the children back from school to Sylvia's, everything was bright and full of hope. Now the baby was completely bottle-fed, all three children and the dog were going to stay with her for the weekend. I was on call if she needed me but I knew she wanted to keep the grandchildren to herself. She'd promised to show Holly how to make one of her famous chocolate puddings, and if the weather was good there was always the beach.

I left them settling in to a weekend of baking, and unlimited sweets and fizzy pop; and as the front door closed behind me and I walked down the path, I breathed in deeply, and relaxed. I'd walked up and down this front path so many times recently, it was just part of the background. But that afternoon something stopped me; at the gate I half closed my eyes and breathed in again. There was a smell – high pitched, scented like a tom cat. An old smell, a heady part of early summer when the days started to lengthen, and in the light evenings the streets filled with the clear call of blackbirds. The pungent scent of flowering blackcurrant.

The bush at the gate of Sylvia's house, where Vicky grew up. I picked off one of the long pink and white flowers and rubbed it between my fingers. Here. I remembered the sick excitement of adolescence, the weight of a brown package in my hands, and how I ran back along the path to Ann.

***

THAT DAY THERE'D been another note from Vicky folded in my school coat pocket:

Let's be friends, Helen.
Please. xx

When I showed it to Ann she asked, 'Do you want to be her friend?'

I pictured the swishing sound, and the sting of a cane. Red wheals, purple bruises. The smell of florists' roses. I shook my head. 'No, I don't…I hate her.'

'Right. Let's stop this.' Ann had torn a page out of her exercise book. 'You write. I'll dictate.'

Dear Vicky,
please stop bothering me.
I'm not your friend anymore.

Helen.

Then she helped me wrap everything in brown paper.

'Ready?' Ann looked hard at me. 'Come on then.'

At the house, the feel of her gate, even the colour of her front door, made me want to run away. But Ann pushed me up the path. 'Just do it!'

The TV was on in the living room and I could see the outline of the family on the sofa. I shoved the package through the letterbox and heard it thud softly onto the mat, then the cover of the letterbox clunked shut again. I'd given Vicky all her presents back: the pendant with the heart, a strip of photo booth pictures and the notes. I'd ended it. The smell of those cards and notes stuck to my hands. I wanted to wash myself inside and out. I ran back down the path and we ripped handfuls of the pink and white blackcurrant flowers and put them in each other's hair. We couldn't stop laughing.

When I glanced back, there was a shadow, a silhouette in Vicky's bedroom window.

The following day at school, our coats were dumped on the cloakroom floor, footprints all over them. In the afternoon I found chewing gum in my English book. On the way home someone laughed and a stone hit me on the cheek, with a burning sting. I waited for another blow, but that was it.

'Let's ignore her.' Ann and I carried on chatting until

we parted at my road. The cut blazed on my cheek.

That day Mum had made scones; it was one of her good days. There was tea with sugar, and I didn't have to get changed out of my uniform straightaway. Vicky was annoying us, I told her, but I didn't tell her about the stone. I'd scratched my face on a twig, I said.

'Vicky's a bit spoilt … all that acting and dancing,' she whispered, and hugged me. 'You and Ann are friends now. But remember Sylvia and I have been friends for a long time, so mind you don't do anything mean. It's not Vicky's fault she is how she is.'

***

As I LET myself into *The Laurels* the house was already beginning to smell different – the smell of an empty house that greets you when you come back after a holiday, when nothing can mask your own animal smell.

First I would start on the cleaning. They'd be delighted to be met by the smell of polish, instead of damp dog. Once that was all done, I was planning a surprise meal for Sunday evening, to celebrate the success of their weekend.

Vicky was a slapdash cleaner, allowing dirt to accumulate behind and under furniture. She claimed that having three children was a hindrance to efficient cleaning, but from the amount of dust and sand in the hoover bag, they spent more time on the beach than was good for them.

The bin was overflowing – plastic trays, aluminium

takeaway containers and pizza boxes. Had they never heard of recycling? And scores of beer cans and an empty whisky bottle; someone was drowning their sorrows in a big way. Behind the fridge, the wads of fluff and animal hair were shocking. Amazing the children hadn't been struck down by cholera and the house infested with cockroaches. There were so many crumbs in the toaster I had to slide out the tray and carry it into the garden to scatter for the birds – ashes to ashes, crumbs to crumbs. The deep fat fryer was unbelievable. I lost track of time cleaning it but once I'd finished, it looked as good as new – I could see my reflection: my hair tied back in a ponytail, stray curls and thin spirals framing my face. My skin was glowing, almost dewy; my eyes were bright, shining dark brown.

All evening I worked steadily in the kitchen with a quick break for a cup of tea and a sandwich and by eight o'clock I was exhausted, my arms like lead weights from all the scrubbing. As I caught my breath, sweat slowly evaporated and I began to cool down; everything was clean and burnished, and I was surrounded by a haze of polish and bleach that was the essence of happiness.

I took out my silk pyjamas and laid them on the spare bed then ran a bath in the bathroom next to Vicky and Sam's bedroom. *Make yourself at home, Helen.* I opened a bottle of good wine.

As I lay there, the bubbles popping around me, I gave

a thought to their little holiday spree. Thanks to my support and vigilance, our tight little triangle was strong but soon it would be Sam and me lounging in a warm bath together, before, after and during. The triangle would be broken and smashed.

I dried myself on the thick towel Vicky had laid out then I wandered naked around the house, examining my good work. In the pink palace one of Sam's shirts – pale blue denim – was draped over a chair as if he might walk in any minute and put it on. It smelled of him. On his pillow there were tiny hairs, just long enough to begin to curl. I pressed my face into the cool cotton and breathed in his smell. It was the faintest hint but definitely him. Why waste fresh sheets when this bed was ready and made up? Keeping away from Vicky's side, I slid under the duvet. It was lovely to imagine his long legs stretching down, his back pressing into the soft mattress just here. That first time, when we couldn't wait long enough to make up the spare bed, we'd enjoyed ourselves so much here; there was no reason why I shouldn't enjoy myself a little tonight.

It was still light outside and a blackbird was singing as my hand slipped over my naked breasts, across my belly and down between my legs. I soon came to a prolonged and very satisfying climax, almost surprised to hear my own voice calling his name in the empty room. I was blissfully tired but I quickly did it again then curled up into their space and slept a well-deserved sleep. The darkest kind of sleep you fall into after hard physical work.

At some point in the night I must have woken, disorientated and cold. In the morning I was wearing Sam's shirt.

OVER THE WEEKEND I alternated between cleaning and pleasure; although, if I'm completely honest, I could barely tell one from the other. I washed the windows, changed the children's beds, once I'd tidied their rooms, hoovered, dusted and polished everywhere. I left the pink palace until last – that was to be my Sunday treat. A day of rest.

It would have been indiscreet to impregnate Vicky's clothes with my smell, so before I tried them on I had a shower. Of course, nothing fitted. They were all at least two or three sizes too big for me. Even her newest clothes, the ones she'd bought to show off her salvaged mummy shape, hung on me like dressing-up clothes. In the end I threw them in a heap on the bed – so much pink it was like a pile of sticky candyfloss. And all these crystal animals – like a child's collection, a collection of charms. Vicky's shiny toys.

In her bedside cupboard was the usual mix of pills, half-read books, theatre tickets and condoms. Underneath was a Harrogate toffee tin, full of photos of Vicky with a woman I didn't recognise. On the back of the first one I turned over, in large childish writing – *To my darling Vicky. Happy, Happy memories! N.* It must be Nancy, Vicky's acting friend. Oh those luvvies! It was always darling or sweetie or dear heart. Praising each other in their loud braying voices giving elaborate presents. The false exaggeration of it made me sick.

As I lay back on the bed, exhausted, the ballet picture of Vicky en pointe smiled down at me. All that dancing. All her absurd actressy games. I could have kept away from her and her family. I didn't have to get involved with her again. I could have stayed away from Sam. But this time I was the director. I was in charge.

The house was perfect, and this was going to work.

In that soft place between being awake and falling asleep, I allowed myself to remember the games Vicky made me play.

FORTY-ONE

We were lying on Vicky's bed.

'I'm going to be a famous actress,' Vicky said. 'Then I'll be rich.'

'I'm going to marry a French man and live in Paris, but we'll only get married when I've finished university. You have to get an education first.' I said. 'And no babies for ages. I don't want to be like Smelly-Ann's mum.'

'Imagine waking up every day to that smell.'

'I bet people walk past her house and get knocked out by it.'

'She's so dirty she never washes her hair or anything!'

'Especially down there …' I said.

We laughed so much I thought I was going to be sick. I'd eaten too much chocolate pudding too. But it passed.

Then Vicky said, 'Let's practice our ballet.'

She started the tinkly piano music on her tape recorder and we scrambled into our costumes. The tights she gave me were too small and the leotard pulled them right up at the crotch and squashed down hard on my chest. It was like pulling on her cast-off skin. Vicky wore the tutu because she was the one who went to ballet lessons. We used an old clothes stand for a barre. In the mirror I tried to be Vicky's reflection copying the different moves, but she was very bossy and the French words mixing with the piano music made my head hurt. I took off my glasses and put them on the dressing-table. Now everything was fuzzy.

'No! You 'ave to make your leg go like zis.' Vicky put on a French accent like her ballet teacher. 'You look like a wooden doll, not a dancer, cherie!'

Her teacher kept a long stick for girls who made mistakes. Vicky had a cane from her garden.

Whack. She brought the stick down hard across the back of my calf.

I cried out in surprise.

'No need to make a fuss, ma chère. You'll never learn if you don't try 'arder. Let me show you.'

She stood at the barre and demonstrated again. My head ached, and my calf stung but I tried not to think about it.

'You 'ave to keep your head up as well as your leg.' Vicky put her hand under my leg, at the top of my thigh.

I didn't want her to hit me again so I tried as hard as I could, until my leg was aching.

'Nearly darling. Much better!'

Her hand under my thigh was hot and sticky, clamped to my leg.

'I'm never going to be able to do this ...'

'We'll 'ave to 'elp you …' and she brought the cane down hard across my bottom.

'Ow! That's not fair!' Tears pricked my eyes.

'Goodness, child it's only a leetle stick. You 'ave to learn!'

I couldn't see clearly, but in the mirror I saw her move again. She hit me across the back of the thigh.

'No, Vicky, please. I don't want to play this anymore.'

The chocolate pudding sat like a lumpy toad in my stomach.

'Suit yourself.' Vicky dropped the cane onto the floor and released my leg. 'I know, let's go on holiday instead … It's summer and it's so-o-o hot! Perfect weather for camping.'

It didn't take long to zip the sleeping bags together. Our ballet clothes were tangled in a knot on the floor, like pale pink seaweed.

The light from Vicky's torch glowed yellow then faded and finally went out altogether. At first her room was dark then our eyes got used to it and we could see faint shapes of the furniture in the orange glow of the street light.

'Are you scared of the dark?' she asked.

'Not if you're with me.'

'Me too … it's cosy in here.'

There was a pause, as if we were both holding our breath. Then she said: 'Let's practise again.'

Vicky stroked my neck and shoulder, then my chest and stomach. I closed my eyes, forgot about the stinging on my legs and buttocks. I saw Sam turning over the hymn sheets at school. They flapped like white pillowcases on the washing line then I was lying on the grass and it was summer. Sam was flipping up onto his hands and walking towards me, his legs and arms tanned dark brown, then he was kissing me hard on the mouth, so hard it was like having no lip salve and eating fish and chips with salt and vinegar. His voice was saying: 'You smell of *Moonwind*. And you taste of chocolate. I'd like to eat you all up.' There was a pain deep inside me. A sharp, tearing pain. Vicky was hurting me.

BACK HOME, WHEN I examined myself at bath time, there were small bruises all over my tummy. *Down there* was sore and when I wiped myself the toilet roll was streaked with blood. Purply-red lines covered the backs of my legs. The light in the bathroom hurt my eyes too. As the water gurgled away, there were blond hairs tangled around the plughole; and the fat lump of chocolate pudding sat undigested in my stomach. I clambered out of the bath and the oval of the toilet bowl came up to meet me like an angry mouth. I filled it with a stream of acid-tasting chocolate that burned my throat and stung my chapped lips.

I woke in bed, in my pyjamas, with a hot water bottle at my feet. My mouth was dry and I needed to go to the toilet again and again. My head hurt and my body was hot and sweating. Everything ached. The doctor said I had gastric flu and I had to stay in bed and have no visitors. When Mum asked me about the bruises I cried. When Vicky phoned, Mum said I was too ill to talk to her.

After a week, I started to feel better but I couldn't find my glasses and couldn't read without straining my eyes. When Mum found out, instead of getting cross with me she laughed.

'Perhaps I'll need to get contact lenses if I can't –' I began to say, but there was a knock on the front door. Our knock.

'I think I'm going to be sick.'

Mum ran for the bucket then downstairs to answer the door. Sweat broke out all over my back, my throat was tight and although the room was hot, I was shivering.

'Can I just see her for a few minutes? I brought her these.'

I sat up in bed. Trickles of sweat slid down my back, under the waistband of my pyjama trousers and down onto the sheet like wetting the bed. I grabbed the bucket and ran to the bathroom then flushed the toilet several times, banging the bucket on the floor as if I'd been sick. In the mirror my hair hung down like Smelly-Ann's. I washed my face with soap and water, as hot as I could stand then again with a face-cloth and cold water. I scrubbed my skin until my cheeks were raw and pink, glistening with water. Then I brushed my teeth twice, three times to make sure. There was still a taste in my mouth, an ache in my head.

'Have you been sick again, love?' Mum tapped on the bathroom door. 'That's the first time today, isn't it?'

When I fumbled open the lock, she put an arm around me: 'Let's get you back into bed again. I'll bring you a drink.'

I leaned on her and let her lead me back to my room. She had the disinfectant bottle in the other hand, ready to clean up.

I was sinking down into the warmth of my bed, calming down, when she came back with a clinking tray: a glass of water, some bread and butter and a vase of yellow roses.

'Vicky brought your glasses back, and these. You're lucky to have such a kind friend!'

There was a note tucked in amongst the flowers:

To my dearest friend, Helen. Get well soon sweetheart.

I'm looking forward to playing with you again.

There wasn't much smell from the roses – shop ones were never like the ones Dad grew in the garden – but their damp, florist's shop scent filled the room. In the glass vase, bubbles formed around the dark red stems and occasionally one wobbled up to the surface. The flowers were opening, showing me their hidden stamens. I could smell Vicky's house, her bedroom, Vicky herself breathing into my ear. *Looking forward to playing with you again.* The yellow flowers opened, stretching their petals wide, drawing me in. The smell made my ears ring, my head pound. They were glowing gold like her hair, wrapping itself around me, tangling into my mouth, my tongue, making me gag and retch.

***

SUNNY WEATHER, A lovely hotel, no kids to disturb them; Vicky and Sam had everything on their side: a romantic weekend away together. Oh, but what about the letter, crumpled at the bottom of the suitcase, primed like an incendiary device, ready to burn it all down?

On Sunday evening everything was in its place – table set, wine in the fridge, baby asleep. I'd cooked a roast dinner that would please the whole family and Sylvia, the children and I were waiting in the living room watching repeats of *Poirot* on TV, when they drove up in their Volvo, scattering gravel like a machine gun.

Holly jumped up to hug them both and Tom thrust one of his broken action men into his father's face.

'No Tom, I haven't got time to fix it at the moment.' Sam shook his head. 'It's bed time.'

'But Daddy …'

'No. It's bed time, I said. You heard me the first time.'

Vicky hugged me, then went straight into the kitchen with her mother and banged the door shut.

'Bad journey back? The Bridlington road can be awful, especially this time of night. Well, so I'm told. So many accidents. You have to take–'

'Look, Helen. Thanks for everything.' Sam went to the car for their suitcases and a paper bag. 'Here. Thanks for looking after the house. You didn't need to …'

I looked in the bag – lavender body lotion and soap. The kind of present you'd give a maiden aunt. I was in the clear.

'Did you enjoy yourselves?' I didn't want to know any details, but it was normal to ask.

'Actually no. There was a problem.'

'Nothing serious.'

He gave the bookcase a vicious look. 'A ridiculous letter from a student who's obviously read too much Emily Bronte …There's always one who turns into a fucking stalker. Josie bloody Bickley!'

'What do you mean?'

'I could strangle the stupid, little cow. I've no idea how she planted it on me.' He paced towards the window. 'My marriage and my kids are the most important things in the world. First flowers and now this! … I'd never get involved with anyone else.'

Ouch.

Then he added quietly, turning to me. 'I'm grateful to you for letting me off so easily.'

He sat on the edge of the sofa. I shook out my hair so that it caught the gleams from the lamp. I smiled at him. 'A friend in need . . .'

'This couldn't have come at a worse time …'

There was a slamming of doors from the kitchen, then Sylvia came out looking flustered and tearful. For once she was speechless. She looked at me helplessly.

'Sam's told me,' I said. 'I should be going now.'

As I left, the wail of little Nancy waking up joined the general crying. I heard Sam say, 'I knew this weekend was a waste of time.'

Dearest, darling Mr. Taylor (I still can't call you Sam!) I'm trying not to think of you going on hols with HER, but I can't help it. I know it's all because of your kids but she doesn't need you like me. Think about ME when you have to 'perform your marital duties' (that's what you called it). Don't think about HER. Think about my young skin, not her saggy gross body. Then come back to ME. xxxxx

Come come, I said there would have to be a few casualties on the way. This was the twenty first century; I was Fanny Price with attitude. Edmund would be mine.

FORTY-TWO

I TOOK A handful of leeks and scrubbed them under the running tap until the dark soil fell off and changed to mud then swirled away down the plug hole. It might be June, but soup was what I first thought of: all those winter days when we were still a family and Mum used to make leek and potato soup – with a swirl of cream if it was one of her good days – a spiral of white in the pale green of the steaming soup, with bread Dad brought still hot from the bakers. A warm summer's day and here I was making soup – the only one of the four of us left.

I stripped away the outer leaves to reveal the tender, green and silvery white of clean leaves that had never seen the light, then started cutting and slicing the vegetables. I didn't even think about adding butter or milk, let alone cream. To minimize fat, I'd bought an oil spray.

Next I chopped fruit and put it in plastic containers in the fridge, and some in the freezer for later days. I took out a lean chicken breast for dinner and I washed some salad leaves.

I was a nun making a vow of abstinence. I had begun.

I STEPPED UP my exercise routine – as well as a swim three times a week, I began to run. As I jogged along the beach each morning the lighthouse gave me a thumbs up: 'Well done, Helen! Keep going. Nearly there!' Instead of the chemical atmosphere of the pool I had a sense of freedom, of space and fresh air, of running into a new life. I should have done this before. And it was cheaper than the gym.

The weight fell away, like the old apple tree shedding its load of fruit. Each time I looked in the mirror my cheek bones and jaw bone became more prominent, pushing up and out as my fat stores changed to energy and were depleted. Soon I was getting so skinny I couldn't risk going to the pool – in my swimsuit my weight loss would attract attention. Running and jogging became my new exercise of choice.

At first I allowed myself a small daily treat – one biscuit, or half a glass of white wine; but after a few days it wasn't necessary. I didn't need rewards or crutches. I was fighting on my own and the end itself would be my reward. I was going to rescue Sam, to carry him safely away from Queen Victoria and her glorious Empire. Then he would open his eyes and really see me; he would remember at last that I was the one he loved.

Some suffering I could easily bear – after all it was only physical discomfort – but I had to keep up appearances, go to work, shop, speak to neighbours and friends. And I had to meet Vicky.

A SATURDAY. A blue and white day with *diggers* hard at work on the beach creating their little castles and moats, searching for shells and pebbles. Although it was warm, I was now constantly cold; I wore a vest under my shirt, tights under my jeans, and a thick jumper to bulk me up and hide how thin I was becoming. I had to mask how pale I was with so much make up I could have outdone Vicky. Getting ready took me a long time.

Only ten o'clock in the morning and the smell of fried fat and candy floss induced not appetite, but nausea. I leant on the railings of the promenade and watched. A scatter of families was spreading out towels and picnic boxes, laying claim to their area of the beach. Down near the steps, a girl was struggling into her swimming costume while her mother held up a beach towel for her.

'Hello, stranger!' Vicky bounced up to me and enveloped me in a hug that took my breath away. 'Where've you been hiding?'

She stood next to me, her hair blowing in the breeze, and followed my gaze. Unselfconsciously, the younger brother dropped his shorts to reveal his pale white bottom, before wriggling into his trunks then sprinting off towards the sea.

'Easy when you're young!' Vicky said. 'No inhibitions.'

I remembered Mum's shrill voice: *Helen, keep covered up! Everyone can see you!* I would be trying to undress discreetly, while Michael ran around me laughing and pulling at my towel; he was always first in the sea while I was still trying to get into my swimsuit. *Everyone can* see *you, Helen!*

'Look at those two!' Vicky pointed out a couple of school kids linked by every possible surface, every inch of skin, kissing as if their lives depended on it. 'I can't believe I was ever like that …'

I thought about the hours Ann and I spent here on the promenade playing our spy game: watching everyone pair off until we were the only ones left, clinging on to our cornets and sitting on a bench like pensioners. And I remembered the blue of the sea, the blond flip of Vicky's ponytail, Sam cartwheeling along the water's edge, Vicky's hand climbing up his leg, then disappearing under his school shirt. How the ice cream suddenly burned in my throat. How the money ran out, and it went dark.

VICKY LINKED ARMS with me like old friends. 'Come on, let's go for a walk.'

The boating pond was full of model yachts with bright sails and surrounded by families eating ice cream; a few standing back smoking. A man helped his daughter lift her capsized boat out and set it off again; no matter how many times it rolled over, he rescued it and gave the dripping boat back to her to try again.

'And how's the love of your life?' I asked Vicky.

'The same.' She shrugged and sighed. 'But I don't want to think about him.' She pushed her hair out of her eyes. 'What happens when you're forty? Why does it all go wrong? We had a good childhood here, didn't we? I thought everything would be better when we came back. Everything would be fixed.' She dropped my arm and wandered back to the railing.

'You and Sam?' I asked, but she was talking as if I wasn't there.

'I've tried so hard with him, but this schoolgirl thing…' She kicked the railing with her shiny sandal. 'Why would he try to spoil everything? I feel as if I've been cast up on the beach like…'

'Like a whale?' I smiled.

'Hmm. More like a stranded ship.'

And she's clinging by her fingertips to the wreckage.

She looked at me steadily for a moment, then headed off towards the café. 'Come on, love. I'm starving! This calls for comfort eating.'

BACK IN THE Driftwood Café, the two of us at a table in the bay window. Déjà vu. We were starting again, looping back to last year when they'd first come back and we met for coffee. So much had changed. As I took sips of my black tea I watched Vicky gulping down her hot chocolate and Danish pastry. Poor Vicky – I felt a twinge of pity for her – she was on the cusp of losing so much. But joy bubbled up and bounced inside my shrinking belly: she would be okay – she would still have her children, her mother. Everything was going to work out for the best for all of us. I pressed my hands around the teacup and allowed pleasure to warm and fill me, as the hot tea dripped and slid down into my empty stomach.

'Not hungry, darling?' Vicky stirred the remains of the cream into her hot chocolate. 'Everything all right?'

'Yes. And no.' I sighed. 'Trouble sleeping, lost my appetite.' I shifted in my seat and leaned forward. 'My GP says I need some time off work. So I've planned a holiday.'

'Wish I could go away. Children are so stressful, not to mention husbands! But you are okay, aren't you?'

I smiled. 'Ann's invited me. She has a friend with a villa in France. Near Nice.' I sat back.

Vicky's face fell. 'I didn't realise you were still so friendly. I know you met after Christmas but I thought that was a one off. How long will you be away?'

'We've been planning to have some time together for ages. Only a fortnight.'

Outside the sun was bright on the sea with seagulls skimming over the tops of white foamy waves. I had such a sense of freedom, of my new life about to start.

'I can give you a lift through to the station. It's not a

problem.'

I turned back and saw the concern in her face. 'Very kind of you, Vicky. But I've already booked a minicab. You don't need to worry about me too. You've got enough on your plate!' Literally.

IN FACT, I'D heard nothing from Ann for a few weeks. Well, that wasn't strictly true – since our meeting in York she'd bombarded me with daily emails. But I'd had enough of her crowing about her lovers and doling out advice about how I should run my life. *If I were you... Why don't you...* Now all her emails went straight into my Spam folder. I didn't even have to see her name.

Ann couldn't persevere as I could. She lacked the curiosity, the creativity and imagination, to be successful. Ann would never secure the man of her dreams; it was no wonder she was still stuck with a series of one-night stands. A social climber from a sink estate. Mum had warned me not to play with children like her. So much for friendship.

When we'd spied on Sam and Vicky she'd been useless, she'd lacked my staying power; she soon got bored. But I knew where they'd be. Once Vicky found something she liked she didn't give up easily either.

***

THE SECOND TIME I'd gone on my own.

It had been late afternoon, a Saturday, long shadows
from the dunes falling across the beach. At that time of
day it was mainly dog walkers and a few couples. One
child was making a moat for her castle, carefully digging a
long channel down to the pools left by the sea. Further
along the beach her mother glanced up from her newspaper every few minutes. The girl kept her head down,
concentrating on her task.

My heart was thumping. I slowed down and forced
myself to breathe. Mum's blue coat was too big for me
and the arms were too long. I'd wrapped her scarf round
twice so I could pull it up to cover my face if I had to, and
I'd borrowed one of her old woolly hats.

I heard them before I could see them. Vicky's clear
laugh rang out in the cooling air, then it went quiet. As
long as I kept myself low to the ground, they wouldn't see
me; it took a few minutes to worm my way up to the top
of the dune, avoiding the sharp tufts of grass. Dry sand
blew into my face but my glasses acted as a barrier;
sometimes they came in useful.

There they were below me, on the sunny side of the
bank of sand. Entwined. Like our discarded ballet clothes.
Both were wearing jeans so it was hard to tell who was
who. He was pulling hers down. Or was she pulling his?
Both. Her hand explored the curve of his buttocks. He
leaned up to admire her: kissed the tight skin of her belly

with its neat pursed button, the hard buds of her breasts like two tips of carnelian. Then he moved his hand between her legs and started rubbing, as if he was trying to clean a stain off; her eyes were shut but she was smiling like the Mona Lisa.

Then he moved on top of her, his pale buttocks started moving rhythmically. I badly wanted to watch, but I had to turn my head away, to shut out the picture. Someone groaned and I saw Sam look in my direction. I stuffed my hand in my mouth to stop the sound, then slithered back down the dune, back to the beach.

The child digging the moat was decorating her castle with seaweed and shells. If her mum hadn't been looking, I would have kicked over her castle and pushed her face into the pool of water by the groynes.

'Look what I've made, Mummy!'

'Well done, pet. It's beautiful.' The woman dropped her paper and walked down to hug her daughter. 'What a clever girl.' She kissed the top of her head. The girl wrapped her chubby arms around her neck.

I stumbled home to find them all watching TV in the dreariness of early Saturday evening; their faces blue in the flickering of the screen.

'Your fish and chips are in the oven ... we've had ours,' Mum said. None of them took their eyes off the screen.

The batter was greasy, and stuck to the baking tray,

the chips were hard. I left it all on the worktop.

In the bath I examined my body. My dark pubic hair curled like a hairbrush when you don't clean it out. My breasts were better than hers: nipples like underripe raspberries, the surrounding area dark like milky coffee. I let my fingers float into the hair between my legs and rubbed myself like Sam was doing to Vicky. I rubbed hard, until there was a sneezy feeling that made me shudder and gasp. Then I lay in the water until it was too cold to stay in any longer.

Wrapped in a towel, I studied my eyebrows – dark and far too thick. Mum's tweezers were in the bathroom cabinet so I plucked until there was only a fine arch of hair over each eye. Then I cut my nails, and even some of the hair down there. I cut my finger nails so short they hurt. I washed the bath out with scouring powder to make sure there were no hairs or nail clippings and made everything clean; and, when I went downstairs, I wolfed down the cold fish and chips.

What I wanted was that look on Vicky's face. I wanted to be Vicky.

I never told Ann I'd gone back.

FORTY-THREE

THE FREEZER WAS full. I cancelled the milk and shut the curtains at the front of the house, and prepared to spend the next two weeks perfecting my rescue plan. I didn't pick up the phone. I didn't answer the door. I was going nowhere.

Like the caterpillar in Tom's old picture book, I was spinning my chrysalis, only I wouldn't emerge as a beautiful butterfly: I was reversing the process.

Was it extreme? Perhaps. But I knew what I was doing. I was in control.

FOOLISHLY, I'D IMAGINED spending my 'holiday' exercising and gardening; I'd even bought an exercise bike, but it stayed in the front room untouched. I hadn't reckoned with the numbing exhaustion and cold that comes with not eating.

From the first week I established a pattern. Early in the morning after my breakfast I had a little strength, and went into the garden to tend to my summer bedding –

brilliant red geraniums, pink petunias and orange busy-lizzies. Then I rested and tried to get warm until it was time to eat again: a bowl of fruit with a teaspoon of low-fat yoghurt and a multivitamin. I went to bed with a hot water bottle. Early to bed and early to rise ...

At the end of the first week I began the second stage: after every meal of fruit or vegetables, with lean chicken or fish in the evening, I took a laxative. By now, yes there was some pain as well as discomfort, but everything would be all right as long as there was no blood. I knew there was a fine balance between achieving what I wanted, and tipping over the other side, slipping into a place from where I could never return, into deep water where my feet would struggle and thrash to reach the bottom, and I would drown. I had to take it slowly. I thought of others who had suffered, other hunger strikers compromising their health, risking their lives – suffragettes, Maze prisoners. I was one with them, giving up everything for my cause.

Ten days drifted by in mounting discomfort and pain, hiding at the back of the house much as any sick person does, as Mum had done, under blankets and rugs, clutching my hot water bottle. At the beginning I read books from the library, but it didn't take long for me to be so light-headed that I couldn't concentrate; so I watched junk television, or tried to warm myself in the sun, until cramping stomach aches sent me crawling to the toilet. I sipped water to relieve me of the spasms of hunger, and hid the vile taste in my mouth by chewing gum. I'd found one that contained *sorbitol* which also acted as a laxative. I was purging and purifying myself. Flushing everything out. I was making myself clean again and getting ready for victory.

Soon the pain was constant. I was so dizzy I could hardly drag myself out of bed or off the sofa. I craved food. Pain kept me awake. When I managed to sleep, I dreamed of food – plates of pasta smothered in tomato sauce – '*puttanesca,* whore's pasta, my wife's favourite'; the perfect apple pie, pastry falling endlessly onto the floured board as the knife cut round and round, and the branch of the apple tree fell down. I was Ann falling into the boating pond – the snap of my arm; looking down, falling from the Leaning Tower of Pisa with the taste of lemons; the view from the lighthouse spinning like a top; leaves in the garden eddying; drinking sherry and stepping into a sinking boat. Into the fog, the dark. My left eye. My bad eye.

I took Mum's sleeping pills but the dreams were still there, day and night.

Towards the end of the fortnight when I couldn't face the stairs anymore, I decided to sleep on the sofa; I surfaced from dreams one morning to find myself crouched in the larder, trying to prize the lid off the biscuit barrel full of the chocolate biscuits I kept for visitors. My own weakness had saved me: soft and fragile through lack of vitamins, my finger nails were broken and chipped. I didn't have the strength to unclip the lid.

AT LAST THE two weeks was up. It was time to emerge from my chrysalis. I crawled to the front room and dragged open the curtains. The morning light streamed in and dazzled me, and particles of fluff and hair writhed like the motes of dust in a beam of light. I didn't have enough energy to lift a duster, and, for the first time in my life, I didn't care. It didn't matter anymore. Waves of nausea forced me to lie on the sofa, before I finally made my way up to the bathroom on my hands and knees. I don't know how long it took. It could have been all day. I heard time beating forwards and backwards. I watched the trapeziums of sun on the carpet gradually move like the hands of a clock; and I sat in the middle watching Vicky screaming on the edge of the roundabout as time flowed around me.

Squatting in the shower tray I washed as best I could, looking at handfuls of my hair swirling around then blocking the plughole. Every drop of water was a drumbeat on my body; but I had to make myself clean outside as well as in. I crawled out onto the bath mat and dried myself, the towel rasping like sandpaper against my skin. My knees and elbows stuck out ludicrously. On my arm the veins showed blueish through the skin; and fine downy hairs, which I'd never seen before had started to grow. I lay on the bathroom floor and lifted a hand mirror up to my face; the light caught the side of my cheek; there was more of this strange growth, like the downy fuzz I'd seen on baby Nancy, lying in her crib in the hospital. On my head, where my hair had always grown so luxuriantly, my scalp shone through like Mum's, as she lay, shrunk and flattened in her hospital bed.

Another cramping pain made me crawl, slide to the toilet. I'd always hated throwing up. I thought of Emma Bovary poisoning herself with arsenic: '*Ah les atroces douleurs*'. For the first time I was scared. Perhaps I'd gone too far. Was this the point where the balance would tip?

Now everything was an effort. Pain in every movement. But I had to dress, at least drag on my dressing gown. I had to get downstairs, even if it took the rest of the day. My mind wandered. My body slowly dissolving into foam. Headless coats laughing. The lion in the cage splitting into two, into four, its claws in my back between my ribs, its foul breath. Kneeling on the cold tarmac of the playground. The photographer's flash and yellow after-images and a glassy orange sweet that tore my tongue.

It was time to phone. And, at this stage, it didn't matter which one of them answered.

'Hello.'

'Sam, I …'

The phone slipped out of my hand. I didn't have the energy to speak, and as I drifted down to the floor his voice was distant.

'Helen, you okay? How was your holiday?'

I'VE NO IDEA how long I waited; there was simply a dark hole and I was falling, then I came round on the sofa to the sickening smell of toast and someone screaming, which turned out to be the whistle of the kettle.

Sam put a mug of tea and a plate of toast on the coffee table next to me. Even if I'd tried I couldn't eat. I couldn't even lift the cup. Through the dizziness and nausea I was aware of his eyes on me. He spoke in a soft voice.

'Christ, Helen! How long have you been like this?' He looked away, at the chaos of the room.

I tried to smile. I must have looked like a skull with skin, as my dry lips slid over my teeth. I couldn't speak.

'I want to hold you, but I'm scared I'll break you.'

He knelt next to me. There were tears in his eyes.

'Vicky said you were going away for a rest. She's always telling me how fragile you are; but you're so calm, so in control of your life I never believed her.' He touched my hand gently. 'Fuck, I didn't expect this… You haven't even been away, have you?'

I motioned no with my eyes. My head wouldn't move.

'I think I should phone your GP.

I tried to speak, but no sound came out apart from a moan.

'I need to call your GP. Or an ambulance … Right. Where's your mobile? His number must be in there.'

I moved my head again to say no. 'Julia.' I managed to say.

He bent his head close to my ear. 'What did you say?'

'Julia.'

'Okay. Your phone must be somewhere near. You phoned me.'

It had slipped out of my hand. I remembered that.

Something rustling. Sam was on his hands and knees rifling through papers and books on the floor next to me. Then I sank away again to that dark place. I was falling into nowhere. A blank.

His voice somewhere in the room. A shadow fell over me. He was near the window. 'Julia, it's me. Can you come over please? … It's Helen … I don't know. No I haven't. Not yet.'

Then time jumped forward. They were both in the room, talking in whispers.

'Yes. After her mother died,' Julia was saying. 'She wouldn't eat. Couldn't sleep.'

'What did the doctor say?'

I drifted again. I was swimming far out in the sea, floating, looking back at the lighthouse. The water holding me. There were sharp stones somewhere. Vicky with her cane in the mirror, slapping me. The toilet bowl coming up to meet me like her dirty mouth.

'Sometimes Sylvia. We took turns.'

Julia's voice became a hissing, that turned into a scream. The kettle boiling again.

Then it was only Sam.

He held a cup up to my mouth. I tried to sip – but could only wet my lips. I struggled to swallow.

'Come on, you have to drink. I've put sugar in. You've got to let me help you. I'm going to help you get better.'

Eventually I managed a few small sips; then I opened my eyes.

My mouth felt raw, as if my tongue had been cut out. My voice was hardly more than a murmur. 'Thanks, Sam.'

Part of me had feared his disgust; that I had gone too far and he would turn away, that I had tipped the balance. I remembered his hands over mine as he dropped the bird into my cupped fingers, how light it had felt, how it had fluttered then been still, its heart racing.

'Good girl, well done.' He stroked my arm with one finger.

I closed my eyes and fell back into that black hole.

SAM WAS SO dedicated you could almost see the Boy Scout in him pulling up his socks and polishing his badge. I was his task and he wasn't going to fail. It was the Sam I loved. The same kindness Edmund always showed his cousin, Fanny Price.

When I'd refused, Julia must have gone ahead and contacted my GP. He prescribed a white, fatty powder to be added to my food to build me up. During the day, while Sam was at work, Julia came. But after a few days I said I could cope on my own.

'I'm so much stronger. You don't have to stay.'

Julia was insistent. 'The doctor said you have to rest, and you have to eat properly.'

She was kind; she cared more than I ever gave her credit for; more than I deserved. I gave in.

It might have been a dream – the next few weeks were spent light-headed or asleep; and there were so many levels of consciousness, I only came up to the surface for air. So it might have been a dream. But in dreams do you notice smells? I don't think so. And there was no doubting the lingering smell of her cloyingly sweet perfume. Before they were washed away or dissolved, I caught at words and phrases Oh *Helen, what have you done to yourself?* It could have been someone else, I'm not sure; everything disappeared in a mist of pain and confusion. But the image was so strong, and I couldn't place it anywhere else, any other time: Vicky's face so close to mine I could see the curl of her eyelashes, the pink bloom on her cheeks, the curve of her lips. Then it dissolved into water as if warm rain was falling on me. *He can look after you. You don't need me. Sleep.* And a goodnight kiss was warm on my forehead then fluttered on my swollen, cracked lips. *My lovely Helen.*

WHEN SAM CAME after work that day I was determined. I stood up slowly and tried to take a step, but it was like walking on the edge of knives. I was so dizzy I stumbled. He caught me.

'Helen, you're in no state to get up.' He was gentle but firm. 'Lie down.' And he carried me back to the sofa. 'So light. Just skin and bone. You have to rest.'

He put a pillow under my head and tucked a duvet around me.

'Are you in pain?'

'A little … tired.'

'Then you have to sleep. Here's your mobile so you can call me.'

As he went out, he called back, 'I'm going to look after you until you're properly better, whether you like it or not!'

I had no choice. I gave in to him. I did what I was told.

ABOUT A WEEK later Vicky finally phoned.

'How are you, love? Sam says you can talk now.'

'I'm okay, Vicky.'

'Hang on a minute, Helen.' There was the sound of raised voices and crying. 'Holly can you take … Sorry, Helen. I'll have to speak another time. I know it's not infectious, but to be on the safe side. You don't mind, do you? Mum's going to bring some flowers. And you don't want this lot tearing around the house and bothering you … No, Tom, you've had enough biscuits.'

That was something I hadn't anticipated – Vicky treating me as if I had the plague and the family could be tainted by my illness. I wondered what Sam had told her. When it came down to it, he was a poor second to her children; in fact, conveniently for me, he was almost expendable. She was happy for him to look after me.

Some hours later, when I woke, Sam was offering scrambled eggs on thin toast and a cup of tea. Endless cups of tea. On the sideboard were pink roses with fluffy white gypsophila (baby's breath).

Darling Helen, let Sam look after you. Get better soon xx

FORTY-FOUR

MY HAIR SLOWLY started to grow back and my bones were gradually hidden in an insulating layer of fat; the pain steadily withdrew like the tide, leaving me cast up safely on the shore. I was a new creature – I was Botticelli's Venus.

There were visits. People were kind. Julia made sure I had everything I needed during the day; Sylvia brought homemade cakes, soups and news of the family; work colleagues sent flowers and cards. But it was Sam who came to see me morning and night; before and after work. Sam who looked after me.

After a few weeks he tried to bring the children – it would do me good he said – but it was a long time before I could bear the sound of their high little voices: they grated on me, especially the younger two, and they had so much energy; they couldn't sit still and talk quietly which was all I could bear.

Holly was older, more sensitive to the needs of an invalid. She came to sit with me. Often she sat quietly and read to herself or did her homework; she was peaceful to have around. Undemanding and comforting. One day when I was able to sit up, and perhaps aware of my increasing strength, she put down her book and took in a deep breath.

'Aunty Hel, when will you be better?'

'Soon I hope. The doctor says I need to rest.' I'd used my voice so little it sounded rusty.

She put out her hand to touch mine.

'Your hands are so thin …'

'Don't worry, Holly. I'm getting better. How's your mum?'

Vicky sent presents via Sam or Holly: scarves, chocolates and flowers. But she kept her distance.

Holly frowned. 'Busy. With the baby. Always on the phone. Chatting and laughing with Aunty Nancy… I can read to you, if you like.' She skipped over to the bookshelf and came back with a book open in her hands: *Mansfield Park*. 'This is the same author who wrote the book you gave me for Christmas. Dad's been reading it to me. He said it's one of your favourites.' She took the bookmark out. 'Is this where you're up to, Aunty Helen? You've nearly finished!'

I shut my eyes and let myself doze as her soft young girl's voice drifted around me reading the familiar words about the moment when Edmund at last falls in love with Fanny. *'Loving, guiding, protecting her, as he had been doing ever since her being ten years old … he should learn to prefer soft light eyes to sparkling dark ones.'*

Holly finished the last chapter then closed the book and put it down.

I opened my eyes, and put my hand out towards hers. 'That was lovely.'

She frowned. 'Dad says she's just shy but I think Fanny Price is boring. Always hiding away and not saying anything.' She looked at me as if waiting for my disapproval, then picked up the book again and flicked through the pages. 'It's a bad idea to wait around and be so scared of everything. And wait for a man to fall in love with you.'

My eyes were dazzled by the light pouring in. My voice wouldn't come out.

'It would be silly if people really did that.'

I didn't have the strength to answer her.

'Don't cry Aunty Helen. It's only a story... Oh, here's Dad to take me home.' She jumped up. 'He'll make you a cup of tea! Then you'll feel better.'

BY EARLY JULY I was able to take a proper walk, leaning heavily on Sam's arm. The first time, we went to the lighthouse garden. It was a warm day so he wasn't wearing a jacket and his arms were already beginning to tan. By contrast my poor arms, although much stronger than they had been, were white, the blue veins still shining through.

I suppose it was a warm day, but I shivered and he put his arm around my shoulders, still scrupulously careful not to overstep his self-imposed boundaries.

'I shouldn't have brought you out here. It's too soon.'

'But I love it. Oh, look at them all!'

Hundreds of seagulls swung through the air; the light reflecting off their bellies and flashing white. An old man fed them chips from a paper bag.

'It's so good to be outside and feel the sun!'

'You're much more like your old self.'

I looked up at him, smiling. 'What do you mean?'

'Growing lovelier by the day.' He squeezed my arm. 'Do you think you could cope with the beach?'

The air was still. It was late afternoon, mid-week and few people were on the beach. It was the kind of day that invited something. For a while we walked near the shore line, where the sand was flat and hard so that it was easier to walk. I remembered that day, so long ago, watching him and Vicky through binoculars.

'Funny how things change. You used to love doing handstands and cartwheels, Sam. I remember how you–'

'Here, sit on this rock.' He helped me to sit down and wrapped my scarf around me. 'Okay?'

And off he went. cartwheeling along the firm sand in a wide arc, then back again. He was breathing heavily and laughing when he sat down next to me, his shoulders heaving. Then he hugged me gently.

We sat together, not speaking as he caught his breath. I could feel the warmth of his arms against mine. He breathed in slowly then let it out with a sigh.

'When I saw you that day ...' He turned away and looked out to where a group of children were splashing and paddling. 'I'm so glad you're...'

Their voices grew louder – laughter and shrieks carried to us against the boom of the surf on the sand. An image of my shrunken body lay like a piece of driftwood on the tide line then, as the waves frothed in over the pebbles, it was washed away and out to sea.

Sam stood and brushed the sand off his hand on his trousers, then reached down to pull me up. 'Time to take you home. Enough for one day.'

He held my hand all the way back to the steps, then up and onto the promenade.

A FEW DAYS later, it must have been a Saturday, he drove me down to Spurn Point. It was the first time I'd left Holdersea for months. I watched the reflection of the lighthouse in the wing mirror – shrinking away, until it disappeared, like an insignificant symbol of the past.

'Vicky's generous, letting you spend all this time looking after me.'

'She can spare me. Her mother's practically taken over. Ever since that infatuated sixth former ...' He snorted.

'Did you speak to her?'

'The girl? Josie. God, no! Made sure I was never on my own with her. Saw her a couple of weeks ago with a boyfriend. All over each other. She's moved on to someone her own age, thank God.' He put his foot down hard on the accelerator.

I let him drive without saying anything.

'How people can be so fucking obsessed I can't understand.' He banged the steering wheel then had to brake hard as we came to corner, to avoid a truck.

'You're smiling, Helen. But it was one of the worst experiences of my life, finding that letter. Like a scene from Thomas Hardy!'

'But everything's okay now?'

He pulled up and parked the car. Then got out and helped me out.

'To be honest, I've no idea. I'm just doing my best. Can't do more than that, can we?'

He looked out towards the long spit of land curling away from us. No one would ever stand in quite the same place again: under our feet the sand moving and shifting, the waves teasing it out and relentlessly changing the landscape. The wind sawed in the grasses on the dunes. A flock of birds rose up and flew away.

FORTY-FIVE

AT THE BACK of my mind I was worried about Vicky. Not about her health: either mental or physical. More about what she was thinking, what she was planning. Presents arrived with meticulous regularity and she phoned every day. After a month there was no reason why any illness could possibly be contagious. But she still didn't visit. Something had changed.

It was nearly the end of the summer term, almost the long summer holiday. My doctor said I needed more rest and signed me off for another six weeks. I was stronger – almost my normal self – but I took his advice and I didn't go back to the school, not even for a day. I would have the whole summer holiday to recover.

Then a letter arrived from Ann. I'd not answered her emails for months; she knew something was wrong with me. The same tired old advice: keep away from the Taylors, you don't need a man, you can do something with your life. I skimmed over it once then ripped it into the smallest pieces I could.

Then one day in the middle of July, there was a knock

at the door. Vicky at last. But only to offer practical help.

'Julia's busy so I said I'd do your shopping for you.'

'I'm sure I can manage to–'

'But you can't even walk very far! And you don't drive.'

'I can order online…'

'I'm going to do it this time.' She put her arms around me. 'And Sam has to do all sorts of things now he's Head of department. Did he tell you? And an end of year production!' She looked down sideways and blushed. 'I wish I could tell you about everything. It's all so exciting! But I'm going to make sure you don't starve again!'

She was the picture of health – content, calm, radiant. Her healthiness was contagious, like laughter. I didn't want her to go. I think for the first time, I really was glad to see her. But she didn't stay. And later, when she drove up in the Volvo with bags of groceries, and an air of efficiency I'd never noticed before, she bustled in, put things away in cupboards and filled the fridge. She was smiling but could hardly meet my eye, almost as if she didn't want to be too close to me. As if there was something unsaid, something she was keeping from me. I realised it was happening at last. Vicky was finally retreating. I'd set this in motion and I wanted it to happen. Of course I did. But where was the feeling of victory I'd expected? Why did I want to hold onto her and keep her with me?

SAM CAME EVERY day, knocked on the door then let himself in. He made cups of tea, cooked meals and put out the rubbish. Regular as clockwork. One afternoon he even mowed the lawn without asking if I wanted him to. It had grown so long and lush it was like a meadow. When he'd finished, the short stumpy grass was damp and yellowing, sickly. He assured me it would grow back. Then off he went: to change nappies, have dinner with Vicky and the family, read bedtime stories.

Sylvia brought cakes and casseroles, then rushed off to help with the grandchildren; but Vicky was generous with Sam's time. It was almost too good to be true.

And seriously unnerving. I was growing stronger, I was so close to winning, so nearly there; but at night when I switched off my bedside lamp, something gnawed at me. Perhaps it was an after-effect of fasting, some aberration of my thought processes and memories; but a repeating loop of images flashed in front of me, like someone drowning: Vicky in bed, one hand resting on her thigh; Vicky in hospital after Nancy was born, her hair spread out on the pillow; the picture of Vicky en pointe as Sam and I made love in their bed; Vicky's soft white hands fastening jewellery around my neck. I did my best to quash them, to stamp them out, but they revolved slowly and repeatedly inside my head like the beam of the lighthouse. I was scared of losing her; Vicky had always been so much part of my life. What would it be like without her?

I found myself thinking about how the children would react when they realised I was taking their father away from them. Baby Nancy was too young and wouldn't remember me, but Tom was sensitive; he would be unhappy and angry. I would get the blame. More to the point I felt close to Holly; she was like my younger self. Holly would be disappointed in me; in fact she might really hate me.

Here you are on the eve of victory, hair blowing wildly on top of the barricades, about to storm the Bastille and let out the prisoner. After waiting so long it's natural to have doubts. Who wouldn't? You're like any bride before her wedding day. And Holly would learn to cope.

Sometimes, if Vicky had eaten with the children, Sam and I shared meals, as if we were already married. While the warmth of the long summer days lasted, and until we were forced inside by the cold air rising from the sea, we sat under the arbour, surrounded by the sweet smell of nicotiana and jasmine. Everything was going so well; this was what I'd wanted. But for the first time I had a creeping shivering feeling, like the beginning of a cold, when you know something is going on just under the level of consciousness; that you're about to come down with something. But I couldn't quite put my finger on it.

THEN VICKY'S FRIEND Nancy came to stay, and Sam and I had a whole week of what should have been beautiful, quasi-romantic evenings.

'You don't mind, Helen? They start all this luvvie stuff and talk about people I've never heard of. She's a complete cow. Abrasive. She says teachers are control freaks, keeping children in prison. I've never been her favourite person.'

'*Shades of the prison house*,' I said, and laughed, but he didn't recognise the quote. 'If anything, you're the opposite, Sam ... Maybe she had a bad experience at school?'

'More likely a bad experience with men.'

'Unlucky in love?'

'That kind of thing.' He jabbed at his steak.

'You really don't like her!'

Sam didn't smile. 'She's Vicky's friend. Not mine. She brings out the worst in Vicky.'

'How about the children?'

'Aunty Nancy's *very* popular. She lets Tom go wild on the beach and encourages the drama queen in Holly. Winds them up till they're exhausted, then I'm the one who has to put them to bed. Not like you at all. They're so much calmer when you're around. I think she does it to annoy me.'

'So you *are* a control freak! Regular bedtimes, *please* and *thank you –*'

'Let's change the subject.' He went into the house for his jacket.

'You don't mind do you?' He waved his unlit cigarette at me.

'As long as you don't do it anywhere near me.'

'Yeah, I know. Filthy habit. Everyone tells me. Especially Nancy.' He pulled his lighter out of his pocket. '*And* she's vegetarian.'

'Ah, that's why we're having a steak!'

He sat on the seat near the lilac. Soon all I could see was the bright orange tip of his cigarette, and the curl of smoke as he exhaled, quickly blown away by the freshening breeze. He looked vulnerable, not a man but a boy, nursing his petty arguments and little comforts. Not the boy he once was, cartwheeling over the school field or on the sand, swinging across the river on a Tarzan rope, building dens and rescuing stray cats. He looked defeated.

I imagined looking down at us from the viewing platform, together yet separate, confined in the small rectangle of my back garden. But there was no one to watch our drama unfold apart from the silent lighthouse, brooding above us. Sam coughed a thick, phlegmy cough which left him looking even more tired. In a 19th century novel this would have been a sign of a life about to be cut short. If he was really ill, the children orphaned and Vicky a widow, I always thought I'd be the distraught one who leaped into the grave. But suddenly I saw myself putting my arms around her, and comforting Vicky. It was something I'd never imagined. Almost something I wanted.

I broke the spell and went inside; and was soon so absorbed in washing up that when Sam came in I jumped, and the pan I'd been drying slipped onto the floor with a clang. When I picked it up the mirror surface was pushed in, elongating my face into a mask. The dent would never come out.

'Sorry, Helen. Sometimes I have to take myself off to think things over. I'm sorry to be so gloomy. *I grow old, I grow old . . .*'

I slid the damaged pan onto its hook. The handle had pressed a red weal into my hand.

'Anyway, I've *delighted you long enough*, as Miss Austen would say. Time to go home to read bedtime stories... Can't wait till Friday ... if I haven't rammed a bloody nut roast down her throat before then!'

At the gate he turned with the old rueful expression and a shrug. 'Vic will be moping after Nancy goes. She'd like to see you. Why don't you go round, if you're up to it. I've been telling her you're too fragile but she'd love to see you.'

'Of course I'll go. And Sam, you don't have to look

after me anymore.'

He waved and blew me a kiss. 'But I like looking after you.'

FORTY-SIX

IN THE SHOWER that morning I examined myself for the first time in weeks. Although I'd kept out of the sun, my skin had lost its waxy sheen. My breasts were fuller, my belly taut but no longer hollow, and my pubic hair luxuriantly dark. I prepared thoroughly to make sure I looked my best. As if I was getting ready for a date. I searched for the necklace she'd made me, in the bag ready for Oxfam, and put it on. The tiny ceramic hearts rattled and rubbed against each other as I moved. I thought of that first time I'd gone for lunch with them. But this time was so different. I was finally myself again. No, even more than myself; I was going to claim my prize.

How could I be her friend, now that I was on the verge of acquiring her husband? It would be heartless, wouldn't it? Hypocritical. But Sam had suggested it. It was like a force pulling me against my will. As soon as I knew she would be on her own, without her friend, Nancy the Actor, I went.

VICKY WAS STILL wearing her pyjamas and hadn't brushed her hair. Her eyes were red but she smiled through her tears. I'd not let her know I was coming. I wanted to have the upper hand. There was a lingering smell of burnt toast after Nancy's early morning exit; the washing machine was rumbling in the background as usual.

'Oh, Helen! You're here at last! You look so much better, love.' She fell on me and kissed me then stepped back and wiped her face with the back of her hand. 'How's Sam?' she said quietly.

'Shouldn't I be asking you that?'

She took a deep breath. 'Come and sit in the garden. Is it warm enough for you? I'll make coffee. We can talk.'

'Oh dear! That sounds ominous.' I tried for a light tone. But she ushered me through into the garden. 'Here, you might need to dry the chairs.'

During the night it had rained and everything looked washed clean. Dew on the grass reflected tiny rainbows like the Swarovski crystal animals Vicky collected. In the quickly growing heat, mist rose from the children's trampoline and from sheets already hung on the washing line. I wiped the seats with the towel she'd given me and sat down. There was scarcely a breath of air. In a sheltered corner of the garden the baby was asleep in her pram.

When Vicky came out to join me, carrying a tray, she'd washed her face and brushed her hair; and thrown on a white sundress, slipping with professional ease into her workaday self. But I'd seen it when she answered the door – the girl panicking with an unwanted bouquet of yellow roses, the girl in a state after she found the letter, the victim face we'd enjoyed when we bullied Smelly-Ann. Her vulnerability, that's what I really wanted to see, the face looking up at us from the damp floor of the boating pond. I was tight with excitement.

'I guess Sam must have told you . . .' she started.

'Well . . .' I had no idea what she meant, but she took my uncertainty for something else entirely.

'Helen, stop playing games with me. It's not fair.'

It's not fair! It's not fair! The old playground refrain. Life isn't fair, I could have said as something shivered inside me and turned over. A nettle sting or the smack of a cane. Desire or fear – I don't know which. Perhaps it was the feeling that comes when you know you're going to win.

'I don't know what you're talking about. Sam hasn't told me anything.' I laughed.

'Hang on. Stay there. I won't be a minute.' She jumped up and ran into the house. When she came back, she was holding a photo.

'Look.' Her hands were shaking. Or maybe it was mine. I steadied myself by pressing one hand on the table as I took it from her. It was the one Sam had taken of me in Pisa posing on the glass floor at the top of the Leaning Tower. In the photo my face was transparently in love. Or lust. Call it what you will.

'Well?' I said. In the mid-morning quiet, my voice was loud, forceful even. Nearby a lawnmower stuttered into action so I had to lean in to hear what she was saying.

'. . . so I knew how you felt about him.'

'Don't be silly. I look happy. That's all.'

'Helen, I know what you've been doing.'

'I don't know what you're talking about,' I said again.

'I'm very good at observing people and copying them. I've done it for years. It's what actors do.' She smiled. 'I've seen the way you look at him.'

At that moment Vicky had the same frank, open gaze as I had in the photo of me in Pisa – pupils dilated, lips parted in a smile. This wasn't how it was supposed to be. I was supposed to feel sorry for her.

'What do you mean?'

'Poor Sam. I guess I used to look at him like that. Once. I must've done. A long time ago.' Her smile widened. 'But now, love!'

The lawnmower stopped and we were plunged into quiet. Everything shimmered in the heat haze. Then her face loomed close to me and clicked into brilliant focus, as if I suddenly had the vision of a bird of prey. Vicky reached out her hand and rested it on mine.

'I'm not . . . I don't know what you mean.' Sweat prickled down my sides. Something inside me doubled over and responded to her. 'Vicky I …' I put the photo on the table.

She smiled. 'No, love. Not you.' She sounded wistful.

The lawnmower started again so she pulled her chair next to mine. I remembered her gleaming patent leather shoes, the swish of her ponytail. Sitting there so close to me she was glowing and I wanted to stroke the tiny gold hairs on her skin. To feel the smoothness of her skin.

'No, not you, love. My friend, Nancy. In Manchester. We had an affair...I came back to Holdersea to start again.'

'Does Sam...?'

'Fuck – no! He knows I had an affair, but I let him think it was another actor, not Nancy.' She sighed. 'He's far too straight to cope with that kind of attack on his male ego! I'd never tell him.' She shook her head. 'And when you were still here and free I thought...maybe we could...' She laughed out loud. A brittle sound ringing out in the warm air. 'Then you and Sam. I never thought he'd try to get his own back!'

'But, if you knew...' How was I to say it? 'Why didn't you...?'

'Oh, Helen.' Vicky looked away. 'It was mad. *I* was fucking mad. You won't believe this, but I thought we could share you!'

No. I shook my head violently. No. Vicky had been trying to create her own little triangle.

In the background the lawnmower stopped. Vicky

laughed then smoothed her hand over her dress, letting it lie for a moment at the top of her creamy thigh. 'Every time he came back you were on his skin, your smell fresh on his fingers. I could taste you on his body. I thought everything was going to work out. But then the baby. What could I do?'

'Vicky, I'm sorry.'

Her lips were dull pink, like a rose bud. I thought about our camping games; playing spies; tracking her into the dunes. I remembered her voice in my ear in a haze of pain. Her perfume slipping over me like silk over my naked breasts. Her tongue between her lips was moist and so pink. Her hand grazed my cheek with an electric shock of contact and I wanted to pull her in to me as close as I could and never let go. Then that feeling shivered deep inside my belly again; was it a twist of desire or disgust? Or both?

I didn't know.

But she pulled her hand away. 'No, my little strawberry thief. Don't pretend to be sorry.'

She stood and patted down her dress which had risen up and over her knees to show the soft white skin of her inner thighs. She laughed almost to herself. 'Do you remember all those games we played – how we stung each other with nettles? I hated it. But you. You still love playing games.'

'I'm really sorry,' I said again. But what was I saying

sorry for? The yellow roses, the stupid letter, stealing Sam. Or something else?

'I'm the one who's sorry you had to half starve yourself before I realised how much you love my foolish husband. And how much he loves you. It's just how it is.' She sighed happily. 'Och it's a *sair fecht* as Mum would say. Life's hard. But it made me realise what I had to do.'

We both picked up our coffees. Next door there was the sound of metal on soft wood – the neighbour pruning roses or trimming back a hedge. The sheets on the washing line blew in a sudden warm breeze. Everything was so clear it looked as if it had been outlined in black ink.

Vicky tipped her head back as she finished her coffee showing the pale smooth skin of her neck, then she picked up a biscuit and nibbled it, frowning.

'Sam's always saying he likes to make the best of a situation. And he's good at it. But I want more than just making do, putting up with.'

My coffee was cold. I'd scarcely touched it and a skin was forming. I wanted to run away and not hear this. But I wanted to hear the end of the story. I'd been so wrong.

Her face glowed as she talked. 'What really irritates me is, he always wants to look after me. He has to have a *cause*. And you know how he likes to have his own way. It's a constant battle. I can't bear it anymore. I can't breathe here.'

She started to clear the table, putting cups and plates on the tray and brushing crumbs onto the flagstones of the patio. Almost as if I wasn't there.

'Nancy challenges me, she makes me *feel*.' Vicky put the tray down again. 'We'll fight like cat and dog. We always did. But ...' She broke my gaze for a second then leaned closer. 'Helen, I want her so much.'

The sun blazed down on us in their garden; I could feel it burning my shoulders.

'Sam does love you, you know. When he came back that day, when he found you so ill, he cried. I've never seen him cry like that.'

Overhead a seagull wheeled and mewed. It should have felt like victory.

FORTY-SEVEN

WHAT I REMEMBER most clearly is how, as we walked through the market, the smell of leather assaulted us on every side. *Pretty lady, only twenty Euros.* And how he held my arm or my hand. We were so close you couldn't have passed a thread between us. Sometimes his other arm moved from my shoulder, down my back to my waist, where it would rest lightly, a reminder that he was there. *Bella, only ten Euros.* We were together at last. I would never be on my own again.

I don't know what made us return to Florence – something about going back to where it had all started, retracing our footsteps. I can't even remember who suggested it.

AFTER I LEFT Vicky that day everything happened so quickly it was like turning to find the sea had crept in around me and I was clinging on to one of the groynes as the tide poured in.

It had all been discussed while Nancy was staying with

them. Vicky told Sam she was leaving; she'd already given notice on the house, so would be going first to Sylvia's for the summer, while she sorted out schools for the kids, then back to Manchester, to the family home, and to Nancy.

He appeared on my doorstep with a small bag, his face lined and anxious. What else could I do? He had nowhere to go. I offered him the sofa, took down pillows, blankets and a fresh towel; but in the middle of the night there was a knock on my door.

'Helen, can I come in? Can we talk, please?'

I could hardly say no, could I? For the next hour he droned on about what a mess they'd made of their lives, how he'd let everyone down, how he missed his kids, how Holly wouldn't speak to him and Sylvia had sworn. That they'd come back to Holdersea because Vicky had an affair with someone in the theatre. They'd come back to make it better and now look.

'Yes, Vicky told me. I'd no idea.' I put my arm around him. I didn't have the heart to tell him.

'I blame Nancy. She put all that nonsense about freedom in her head. I've never stopped her doing what she wanted!'

Then he broke down and cried and I had to make him cups of tea, and after another hour, when he said he hadn't eaten all day, slices of toast. By the time he finally stopped talking it was beginning to get light. He curled himself round me and started snoring, sobbing and sniffling in his sleep.

I on the other hand, was wide awake. I slid out and left him stretched across my bed. As I tidied away the teabags and bread, the sun was edging over the wall and lighting up the truncated stump of the old apple tree. After Sam's pruning, it had put out new side shoots and flowered well; now tiny apples were setting and growing. In the autumn, I would make apple pies – I would hold the dish up and slice off long strips of pastry so that they'd fall in a soft heap on the table, leaving the pie lid round and perfect just like Mum did. Everything was going to be alright. In my life nothing very much would change – I'd still work at the school; I didn't need to sell the house. Vicky and the children would leave, and Sam would stay with me. It was all simple – like the inevitable solution of a crossword. Or remembering the word that's been on the tip of your tongue. A relief. The moment I'd been waiting for, the happiest moment of my life. The dénouement.

SO, DURING THE long six week summer holiday, while Vicky and the children were still in Holdersea getting ready for the move back to Manchester, Sam and I rented a villa outside Florence for a month.

The first week was like a honeymoon – gold, circular, heavy – just as it should be, and the sky was as blue as I remembered. Our room was large and airy with a wide oak bed, white lace curtains at the shuttered windows, and a view over rolling hillsides where regimented rows of vines were interspersed with olive trees. We spent nights and days together. It was good. I can't deny that. We were inseparable.

ABOUT HALFWAY THROUGH the second week, I woke early so thought I'd wander down to the village to sit in a café and have a coffee. As I passed the side of the bed where Sam was sleeping, his hand came out and grabbed my ankle. I nearly fell.

'Little squirrel, where are you scurrying off to so early?'

'A walk to the village.' I put my hand on top of his. 'Sleep. I'll be back soon. I'll bring you some bread, or a pastry.'

'I'll come with you. Don't want you getting lost.'

'I'll be fine.' I pulled my leg away from him, but he didn't let go.

'I need to look after you.'

I laughed and tried again.

'You might get lonely without me.'

'I won't be long. Promise.'

'But I thought you wanted to be with me?'

'I do—'

His grip on my leg tightened and he pulled me back down into bed. 'Let's *make wanton the night*, shall we? Strawberries?'

He stopped my mouth with a kiss. And there it was, that feeling – the flicking on of a switch. I had to. And that was the end of that. Later, afterwards, we went out and had our coffee and cakes, together. It wasn't really what I'd meant. But, at the time, I let it go.

BACK IN HOLDERSEA he was true to his word; he would always look after me he said, so when I started work again he took over the cooking as well as the shopping.

'Vic never used to let me cook and I want to make you nourishing food. To build you up.'

'I'm okay.'

'Helen, you know you're not. It takes months to recover from these things.'

'I don't want to get fat and lazy! I like cooking!'

'Nope, I insist. I won't let you lift a finger. And you need to save your energy for …'

And he looked at me in that way. You know what I mean. I couldn't resist him. I suppose I never could.

ONE DAY I came home to find the hallway stacked with boxes and carrier bags. He'd promised he'd move the rest of his things in, and tidy the house. I opened one of the boxes, and there, dumped with all the rest, looking up at me from under her veil was the Royal Doulton figurine.

'You can't throw all these out.'

I picked her up and ran my fingers over her familiar shape. In spite of my efforts there were still fibres of Dad's green scarf caught in the cracks.

'These are *mine*.' I could hear the whine in my voice.

'It's all tacky and tasteless, Helen.'

'This was Mum's.'

'Sentimental. And it's damaged.'

His voice had a sharp edge to it, dismissive.

Through the living room door, I could see gaps on my bookshelves like lost teeth.

'Well I'm keeping it.'

I ran upstairs and put the figurine into my dressing table drawer and locked it; then I shut myself in the bathroom and ran a bath. I didn't go down until I could smell onions cooking.

There was a bottle of wine open on the table, half empty; he'd cooked pasta.

'I'm sorry, sweetie,' he said. 'Here we are. *Puttanesca* – whore's pasta for my little water spy.'

As he placed the dish of spaghetti in front of me, he ran his hand from the nape of my neck, across my shoulder and down my back, and I knew whatever happened, there was something about the way he touched me – the right pressure in the right places – that would always fell me. It was just going to take time, I thought. Other people are unpredictable. It's only when you share a house that you find out all their little habits.

BUT THAT WAS only the beginning. Soon furniture started disappearing: Mum's favourite armchair, the new double bed I'd chosen after she died; and all sorts of smaller things I've forgotten now. Why didn't I protest more? I don't know. This was what I'd waited all my life for; this was what I'd chosen. I half-expected to go back to normal, as if we were still having an affair, but everything was different and unfamiliar. Living with Sam wasn't going to be as straightforward as I'd imagined.

BY THE END of the first week in September they were gone – Holly, Tom, baby Nancy and Vicky. Sylvia was going too, once she'd sold her house.

'She'll never speak to you again.' Julia laughed. 'You should have heard what she called you! I didn't think Sylvia even *knew* words like that.'

Once I gave in to him and handed in my notice, Sam wouldn't let me do anything, apart from dusting and hoovering while he was at work; I had to rest. When he came home in the evenings he took over:

'Helen, you're in my way. I need to sort out dinner. Why don't you go and watch TV. Or read.'

He was fond of quoting the Red Queen: '*All the ways about here belong to me.*' He's always had a quotation for every occasion.

But then he told everybody we were trying for a baby. I remembered the face of the woman in the childbirth film we'd seen at school. And breastfeeding. And the house full of noise and mess when Holly and Tom stayed. And how everything's changed for the worse. They both hate me; and the baby's a brat. So I made sure I took my pill.

He misses his kids. Sometimes when he comes off the phone he cries, and spends hours in his study smoking, or I find the recycling bin full of beer bottles.

When he Skypes them you can hear their squeaky voices in the next room. I keep out of the way. I see enough of them when they come for the weekend.

Last night I heard Vicky's voice; I edged into the doorway so the webcam wouldn't pick me up. She was talking to someone out of shot; I could hear the murmur of another woman's voice. Nancy I suppose. Even with the quality of the picture and the screen freezing, the look on Vicky's face was clear – she was happy. She had exactly what she wanted.

SO I WENT out. As I walked down to the promenade, the lighthouse was glowing pale orange in the streetlights and I could hear the sea breaking on the beach, slowly washing it away. I thought again of that hot summer, when the lighthouse was switched off for the last time. Everyone knew there'd been a change, like a death in the town. Some girls even cried. But after a few weeks we all forgot. We adapted. As I looked out to sea that's what I told myself – you'll get used to it, no need to hurry. It's a transition. Sometimes, even if we think we want something with all our hearts and minds, and particularly if we think we'll never get it, when we finally do, there's a long, slow period of adjustment. Fanny Price probably had a few misgivings about Edmund, although Jane Austen has little to say on the subject of happily ever after. Mind you she never married – so she's hardly an expert.

I stood on the sand and looked at the water, stretching out before me like an invitation. If I walked in, then started swimming, where would I get to, presuming I didn't just drown? Could I reach the dark blue line of the horizon? It was a boundary, a finishing line. I'd never thought there would be anything beyond. Those maps Dad and I pored over: Ordnance Survey maps of the Lake District and Yorkshire, with all their comfortable symbols showing churches and pubs and places of interest were so British. The only foreign map I'd seen was the one Sam and I had on our day out to Pisa, the one I had to use to guide us back.

I was good at map-reading. Yet here I was, living my life in this cut-off stretch of the Yorkshire coast; by choosing Sam, I was choosing tighter lines to circumscribe my life, almost as narrow as the boundaries Mum had set herself.

I had to make sure. I needed to find out what was over there, over the blue line of the horizon. So this morning, in spite of the rain, I caught the bus and then the train from York. It wasn't difficult, and now we're nearly there. You've been very kind listening to me. I'm supposed to be looking for a wedding dress, but you know, I think I'm going to stay for a few days. Or maybe longer.

As Jane Austen says: *if one scheme of happiness fails, human nature turns to another; if the first calculation is wrong, we make a second better; we find comfort somewhere.*

I've got Ann's address in my phone. Dear Ann. She's always been my best friend, you know.

Thank you for reading *One Scheme of Happiness*, we hope you enjoyed it.

Please support the author and independent publishing by leaving a review on Amazon, Goodreads, your blog, or any other book sharing site you may use. They really make a difference for books and authors!

Do let us know your answers to the Book Club questions included in the following pages.

You can let us know what you think on our social media pages using the following hashtags:

#OneSchemeOfHappiness
#RetreatWestBooks

And find us online at:
retreatwestbooks.com
twitter.com/RetreatWest
facebook.com/RetreatWest

Where we chat about all things reading and writing fiction.

To get advance notice of new titles coming from Retreat West Books, as well as exclusive author insights, you can sign up for our newsletter at: eepurl.com/gPzNmz

Acknowledgements

Thanks to my family and friends who have supported and encouraged me in writing this novel.

My poetry friends for their advice, friendship and long walks over many years – Joanna Clark, Jan Kofi-Tsekpo, Fiona Moore, Jeri Onitskansky and Selina Rodrigues, as well as Lucy Hamilton and Hannah Lowe; not forgetting our tutor, Mimi Khalvati, for her humour, gimlet eye and bullshit-detector.

My writing friends from City University's Novel Studio course for their openness, unwavering encouragement and rose wine – Justine, Matt, Paddy and Rachel as well as Tom, Claire, Rod and Andrea; and to our tutors Emily Midorikawa and Emma Claire Sweeney for insightful criticism.

Friends from Scotland, Shropshire and London for reading early drafts of this novel and offering calm and wisdom, in particular Meredith Vivian and Sara Collins for sharing the journey to publication; Julie and Laura for their kindness and emotional intelligence.

Emily Sweet, my agent, for seeing potential in a story set in the north, for encouraging me to push the novel to its limits and for her constructive and rigorously critical insights.

All the team at Retreat West but especially Amanda Saint, who really lives up to her name and who had faith in Helen's story. She has worked unbelievably hard in editing my novel so that it *sings*.

Ken Thurm, my late father, who fostered my love of words and storytelling, and who really did have a quotation for every occasion. My mum for always encouraging me in everything I've done. John for saying yes until he had to say no. My sister and brother for listening. My three incredible children for their love and continued enthusiasm. What would I do without you all?

For all of us with mental health issues who sometimes get lost in dark places – seek help, keep talking and take the pills if they work.

Book Club Questions

Did *One Scheme of Happiness* play out as you thought it would, or were there any parts that surprised / shocked you?

How did the characters change throughout the story? Did any of their actions change your opinion of them?

If Helen had been in a relationship with Sam since school, how do you think everyone's lives would have been different? Would they have been any happier?

How reliable is Helen as the narrator of the story? Do you think her story reflected the truth of the other characters?

Do you feel Helen has learned anything from her experience? How did you feel at the end when she made the comment that Anne had always been her best friend?

How much do you think Helen's decisions were influenced by her upbringing and how much by her own mental health condition?

Coming back to the title, are any of the characters happy at the end of the book? Did the scheme work out? Do you think the relationship between Helen and Sam will last?

If you could meet one of the characters in real life, who would you choose and why?

If there was a movie of the book, which actors would you cast as Helen, Vicky and Sam?

Why do you think the author wrote this novel? What themes was she exploring through this story?

If you could ask the author just one question about this novel, what would it be?

Unprotected
Sophie Jonas-Hill

She's fighting to save everyone else but will she have anything left to save herself? Witty, sharp and sarcastic tattoo artist Lydia's life is imploding. Her long-term relationship has broken down after several miscarriages and she's hiding from her hurt and loss in rage. After a big night out she wakes beside a much younger man who brings complications she could really do without. As her grief about her lost babies and failed relationships spirals out of control, she obsesses about rescuing a wayward teenage girl she watches from her window and gets more involved than she should with her charming but unstable young lover. Unprotected is a raw and punchy story of love, family and accepting yourself for who you really are.

"A raw, viscerally-beautiful gut-punch of a novel about love and loss and heartbreak and hope, and the pain we inflict on each other – and ourselves. Sophie Jonas-Hill is a powerful new voice."

—Tammy Cohen, author of Stop At Nothing

"Unprotected is an absorbing, thought-provoking story of betrayal and bravery. Sophie Jonas-Hill probes the darkest corners of modern society with boldness and sensitivity. I loved it!"

—Ruby Speechley, author of Someone Else's Baby

Remember Tomorrow

Amanda Saint

Evie is a herbalist, living in a future that's more like the past, and she's fighting for her life. She did everything she could to try and save the planet and keep her family safe, but the UK has been cut off from the rest of the world and ravaged by environmental disasters. The young people of this post-apocalyptic world have cobbled together a new religion, based on medieval superstitions, and they are convinced she's a witch. Their leader? Evie's own grandson.

> *"A dystopian future that echoes the present times. A reflection of society in a stark, unforgiving mirror. Unsettling, honest and unputdownable."*
>
> —Susmita Bhattacharya, author of
> The Normal State of Mind

> *"A chilling descent into the chaos that lies in the hearts of men. A searing portrait of a dystopian future where civilisation's thin veneer has been ripped away, and it is women who suffer most as a result. Excellent."*
>
> —Paul E. Hardisty, author of Turbulent Wake

> *"I enjoyed every page of Remember Tomorrow. The writing is beautifully emotive and the characters are wonderfully created. It's a world that we hope won't happen, but it's also a world that may not be too far away. Compelling, gripping and at times, deeply unsettling. Remember Tomorrow is a must read and is highly recommended by me."*
>
> —Anne Cater, book blogger, and book reviewer for
> The Daily Express

As If I Were A River

Amanda Saint

LONGLISTED: Not the Booker Prize 2016
NetGalley Top 10 Book of the Month: May 2016
Book Magnet Blog Top 20 Book of 2016

Do we live the lives we want to or the ones that just happen to us?

Kate's life is falling apart. Her husband has vanished without a trace – just like her mother did.

Laura's going to do something that's going to change her family's life forever – but she can't stop herself.

Una's keeping secrets – but for how much longer?

As If I Were A River tells the interconnected stories of these three women – the lies they tell, the secrets they keep, the love they feel. It is a story of buried secrets, and of finding the courage to question the life you lead.

Are we forever shaped by our past, or can we find redemption in making our own future?

> *"An emotionally powerful story of the impact of secrets and lies on the lives of three generations of women – a deeply satisfying and moving book, and a wonderful debut."*
>
> —Sophie Duffy, author of Bright Stars

> *"Amanda Saint's intricately plotted debut novel is a juicy Pandora's box of mysteries and revelations."*
>
> —Alison Moore, author of The Lighthouse